THE OUTLAWS

First English edition published in 1931 by Jonathan Cape Ltd.

Third English edition published in 2013 by Arktos Media Ltd.

Published in the United Kingdom.

ISBN 978-1-907166-49-5

BIC classification:
Historical fiction (FV)
Classic fiction (FC)
Germany (1DFG)

Cover Design: Andreas Nilsson

ARKTOS MEDIA LTD
www.arktos.com

THE OUTLAWS

by

ERNST von SALOMON

Translated from the German by

IAN F. D. MORROW

ARKTOS
London
2013

CONTENTS

PART I
EXILES

PART II
CONSPIRATORS

CONTENTS

PART III
CRIMINALS

INTRODUCTION

THIS book is of peculiar interest at the present time as showing the confused state of Germany directly after the War, out of which many movements have developed that are to-day troubling the surface of German politics. Probably few people in England then and since have realised how difficult internal political and social conditions in Germany were in those years. The situation at the end of the War was incredible – as the author says, anything was possible and nothing certain. Idealists as well as the more materially ambitious came to the fore and did their best to introduce their own particular form of the millennium. And when they saw that events were not moving as quickly as they wished some of them stopped short of nothing – not even the murder of a great man – in their ruthless determination to get their own way.

The confusion of thought and action that was so typical of the post-War Germany has rarely found better expression than in the following pages written by one who was himself caught up in the mad whirlpool and only narrowly escaped complete destruction. The wild adventures of this boy of sixteen in Courland and elsewhere, his subsequent deeds in the Rhineland, Upper Silesia, and other disaffected areas, and his rôle in the murder of Rathenau give his pages an absorbing interest. It has been thought well to preserve in English as much as possible of the highly individualist style of the German original that conveys so perfectly the author's reactions to events.

THE TRANSLATOR

PART I

EXILES

'Instinct must be wedded to Reason.
Then Spirit is born.'

Franz Schauwecker

CHAPTER I

CHAOS

THE evening sky showed redder than usual over the town. The November mist reflected the light of the few isolated street lamps, which seemed to make the sodden air and the heavy clouds look even gloomier. Scarcely a creature was to be seen in the streets. The wailing note of a bugle sounded from afar off and the roll of drums echoed menacingly from the house-fronts and was lost in dark courts.

Some twenty policemen were gathered in front of the police-station. Their faces were chalky pale and their white-gloved hands hung heavy at their sides. The holsters of their unwieldly revolvers dangled awkwardly from their belts. They were evidently waiting for something to happen, and as my footsteps sounded on the pavement they followed me with their eyes, making no other movement.

One of them wore the ribbon of the Iron Cross in the button-hole of his blue tunic. He was standing a few steps away from the others and seemed to be listening anxiously for the call of the bugle. In a hoarse voice I asked him: 'Has it begun?' and the words stuck in my throat. The policeman stood like a block – I had to lower my head to look at him. His tired eyes were caught by the buttons glittering on my uniform and he looked at me in astonishment. Suddenly he laid a heavy hand on my shoulder: 'Better go home and take off that uniform,' he said. And to me, accustomed as I was to obeying orders, his words sounded like an order. Startled, I stood to attention as if before an officer. 'No, no . . .',

THE OUTLAWS

I said; and after a pause that seemed an eternity again 'No.'
And then I went, running blindly, stumbling through the
deserted streets, across wide squares where shadows lurked,
through parks where my feet rustled among the dead leaves.
At last I huddled shivering in my room, while the bugle shrilled
weirdly through the streets.

I could not bear the silence. I had piled up on my table the
things which might help me to pull myself together: my
father's photograph taken in uniform at the outbreak of the
war, the pictures of friends and relations who had fallen in
the war, my brother's scarf, his sword, his shoulder-straps,
a French tin hat he had sent home, his pocket-book with the
bullet hole through it – the blood on it was dark and patchy
now – my grandfather's epaulettes with their heavy tarnished
silver tassels, a bundle of letters written from the front on
musty paper – but all that had lost its meaning for me. It
could not affect me now. It was connected with the days when
flags hung from every window for our victories. Now there
were no more victories and the flags had lost their glamour.
Now everything seemed to be falling in ruins around me and
the road which I should have followed was blocked. I was
bewildered by the events which were crowding on me, whose
meaning I could not interpret. All I could realise was that
the world I had known, of which I was a part, to which my
youth had been pledged, had vanished never to return.

I leant out of my attic-window and listened to the rain
dripping in the gutters. On the shining pavement far below
me I saw menacing black shadows from the houses and the
bedraggled trees. A clinging mist rose from the street, climbed
up the walls and spread into every nook and cranny. My
candle went out, and I threw all the things which were on the
table pell-mell into a drawer. All night long I lay awake.
I was delivered over to the terrifying silence, knowing only that

CHAOS

I must at all costs be strong to face whatever the future might bring.

When, next morning, I came down into the kitchen, I found my mother cutting the white shoulder-straps off my great coat. I dared not meet her glance, and sitting hunched up with downcast eyes I drank the wretched thin coffee and helped myself to a couple of slices of damp black bread. Then I took my coat up to my room and sewed the shoulder-straps on again. And carefully lifting my feet in their heavy nailed trench boots I crept quietly down-stairs to the hall. I buckled my belt over my tunic in defiance of the regulation which forbade this to cadets. My sword, long and slender in its fine leather scabbard, was shining and pointed but not sharpened. I pulled it out and looked at it dubiously.

At last I went out into the street. Women were standing in front of the shops in long queues as usual, talking animatedly. Their arms folded, carrying purses and baskets, they gazed beyond me, red-rimmed eyes looking out of pale faces. A good many shopkeepers had not yet opened their premises. A little man with a sad face was standing on a ladder carefully scraping off the sign 'Purveyor to the Royal Family.'

I suddenly heard sounds of a disturbance in one of the main streets, and resolved to find out what was happening. I felt very nervous, but I set my teeth and said 'Buck up!' to myself, and again 'Buck up!' as I heard scraps of shrill singing and shouts from many throats, sensed confusion and tumult. A gigantic flag was being carried in front of a vast procession – a red flag. Limp and damp it hung from its pole – then floated like a patch of blood over the crowd which had rapidly collected. I stood and watched. Tired multitudes plodded after the flag; women were in front in voluminous skirts, their grey skins hanging slackly over sharp cheek bones. Hunger seemed to have hollowed them out. From under their dirty ragged head-

13

kerchiefs they sang in trembling voices a song whose martial rhythm was ill-matched with their weary tread. The men, old and young, soldiers, workmen, small shopkeepers, walked with dull, tired faces, in which there was yet a hint of sullen resolution; from time to time they fell into step and then immediately did their best to break step again as though detected in some fault. Many of them carried their food with them; and behind the wet red flag, on which the rain made dark stains, umbrellas billowed over the crowd.

So marched the army of the Revolution. The wild dreams of reform, of blood and barricades, were to be realised by this grey rabble!

I was determined not to give way to them. I stiffened and thought 'canaille'–'mob'–'rabble'–'riff-raff.' I half shut my eyes and watched the vague smudged figures. Like rats, I thought, with the filth of the gutters on them, grey, furtive, with little red-rimmed eyes. Suddenly some sailors appeared. Sailors, wearing immense red sashes, carrying rifles in their hands, with laughing faces under beribboned caps and loose, easy clothes on supple figures. 'Our boys in blue!' shot through my mind, and then I thought disgust would choke me; but it was not disgust, it was fear. These were the leaders of the revolution, these young fellows with their determined faces, these wild lads arm-in-arm with girls, singing, laughing, joking, boasting. A motor car came along, with sailors on the running board, sitting on the radiator, waving a red rag like a pennon. Some of them were looking round for mischief to do, shouting hoarsely; the women yelled to them and pointed. What were they pointing at? At me? Were they pointing at me? Here was the danger! Instantly the thought rose in my mind that whatever happened I must not flinch. I felt for my sword and remembered that it had not been sharpened. However, I kept my hand on the pommel and squared my shoulders.

14

CHAOS

A soldier walked past me, a young fellow, with no belt, wearing brown gaiters and eye-glasses, carrying a despatch case, and with the shoulder-straps still on his greatcoat. They went for him – one of them, an artilleryman, broad and thick-set, with heavy riding boots and a red cockade in his cap: – 'Here's another of 'em!' he yelled as he landed the young soldier one in the eye with his fist. Then he tore off his shoulder straps, so violently that the boy stumbled and nearly fell, went ashy pale and stammered 'But why, in God's name, why?'

The swine, I thought – the cads. At that instant the gunner's eyes fell upon me too. He had little sly eyes, an unshaven chin and bristly hair. He put up his fists, big, red, hairy fists. I looked round quickly. The crowd had formed a circle round me – there were women amongst them – and a man in a bowler hat waved an umbrella at me – somebody laughed – several people laughed – but I only thought of my shoulder-straps. Everything depended on those shoulder-straps – my honour – how absurd, what did they matter – yes, they were all-important! I drew my sword. Then the fist was planted in the middle of my face.

For a moment I almost lost consciousness and blood flowed over my chin. Hit him, I thought, there's only one thing to be done – hit him! I did; but the artilleryman laughed and spat in my face; and a woman screamed at me: 'You jackanapes, you fancy-boy, you ninny.' A stick struck the back of my neck and I fell. Someone kicked me, then the whole crowd seemed to be kicking and beating me. I lay and hit out as best I could in all directions, though I knew it was useless. They all laughed and jeered and hit me. Blood ran from my eyes and nose. Suddenly the tumult ceased.

Someone came out of the Carlton Hotel – with my swollen eyes I could just see that it was an officer. He was tall and slim and wore the blue uniform of a hussar. His cap was tilted jauntily and he had on patent leather boots with silver lacing. On his tunic was the Iron Cross, first class, and in his eye a monocle. He tapped his boots with his riding-whip. He tapped his boots and came straight towards the mob. The women were silent, the crowd parted, the man with the bowler hat vanished, the gunner cleared off. The tall elegant blue figure bent over me and gripped me by the arm. I stumbled to my feet and stood to attention.

'Stand at ease, boy,' he said. 'I've been a cadet too. Come along to my hotel.' I went with him, wiping the blood off my face and saying, 'Anyhow they didn't get my shoulder-straps!'

CHAPTER II

HOPE

AT that time I was just sixteen years old and was in the top form of the Royal Prussian Cadet School. During the first week after the outbreak of the revolution I made a plan to raid the headquarters of the sailors. Some eighty seamen had started the revolution in the town. They formed a 'People's Naval Division,' whose officers were at the police station. I thought that, with a handful of determined companions, I might manage to draw their teeth. But it would have to be done quickly, for the town was still full of unrest and nobody knew just how things would turn out. We should have to get control of the buildings of the newspaper, the police station, the post office and the railway station. Then we should have the upper hand in the town. A hundred armed men could surely manage this. The only question was how to collect them.

There were other cadets in the town besides myself, and I looked them up in turn. They had all changed into the most extraordinary civilian clothing. They were wearing short breeches, left over from the days of their boyhood, or their old uniforms, but with blue shirts and open collars. In doffing their uniforms they seemed to have lost all their assurance. Pale mothers feared lest I should lead their sons into some rash undertaking and the sons stood awkwardly by. One wept. Another said he was glad the revolution had come so that he need not go back into the cadet corps. A third, who stood silent while his mother was talking, ran downstairs after me as

I was going and whispered to me hastily that I was to be sure and let him know if anything came of my plans, but that his mother must be told nothing.

Day after day I wandered round the police station. I even ventured inside; they certainly could not have imagined that anything was to be feared from the shy cadet, in spite of the fact that the unsharpened sword still hung from my belt. Then I looked up Major Behring, a friend of my father's, a red-faced, mustachioed gentleman, who was unfortunately unfit for active service owing to lumbago. I initiated him into my plans, and he was thrilled at the idea, saying that it would give him back all his confidence if the youth of Germany were to stand firm for the old glorious empire and its ideals. Then he gave me his blessing, but pointed out that he himself had a wife and family and he was sure I would understand, but this confounded lumbago which alas, alas, had prevented him from serving his king and country. . . . In any case he hoped I would succeed. As I went on my way, I saw the notices put up by the Workers' and Soldiers' Council. I stood and read them over and over again, without taking in a single word. All I realised was that they meant mischief. I took the leaflets which were being handed out by a man with a red brassard and which proved to be a manifesto of the Socialist Party. So I took a whole packet, but only to push them down the nearest drain. I wandered round the streets, considering and rejecting hundreds of people to whom I might have appealed. The town was quiet, except that every now and then small demonstrations were held at the railway station. At one of these a young officer, in uniform, but wearing an enormous red sash, who proved to be the station commandant, was making a speech and declared that he was completely convinced of the right, the sacred right, of the revolution. I saluted him as I passed, as stiffly as possible. I went close by him and looked at him as was prescribed by regulations. He saw me and stopped in the middle of a word. He half raised his hand, hesitated and dropped it again, and went scarlet in the face.

I only found one person who was ready to help me. 'We'll soon clear out these Red swine,' he said, and showed me his revolver. I think I was especially touched by his readiness to help and the way it was demonstrated, because it was my younger brother, who was also a cadet, in the upper fifth form. No one else would join me. Not the headmaster, who lived on the third floor and who formerly had quivered with rage at the very mention of the word socialist. Now he murmured that all the unrest had made him positively ill. Nor the artist living next door, who had been decorated for his services in the war and was an honorary member of the Naval Union. He was painting a picture of still life, strawberries on a cabbage leaf, and said that he must devote himself to his art. Nor the accountant, a retired paymaster, who continued going to his office every day and simply had no time. Nor the father of my consumptive friend, a textile manufacturer, who was nervous about his business and feared the rage of his workpeople. . . . And they were perfectly right, they were all damnably right from their own point of view. The old order had changed and old ties were loosened. Each man played his own hand and could only be judged on his own merits.

Finding myself unable to collect the men, I collected arms, which was easy enough. At least one rifle was to be found in pretty well every house, and my friends were thankful to me for removing them. After nightfall I transported one rifle after another, carefully packed and tied up with string, and was tremendously proud as the stack in my attic increased. Though I had no idea what to do with this collection, its possession gave me immense pleasure; and it was certainly the knowledge of the danger which I incurred by harbouring it that kept alive my self-respect during my enforced humiliating inactivity.

The terms of the armistice were proclaimed. One among a large crowd, I stood in front of the newspaper buildings, trying to see the big posters with their sensational headlines. The man in front of me was reading in an undertone and stumbling over the words; others were pushing to get a nearer view. At first I could not see anything, but somebody laughed nervously and said that it was all nonsense; that it could not happen and that Wilson would see to it. . . . But someone else said: 'Oh, Wilson . . .' and the first man was silenced. Somebody said that the French had been hoping for this since the beginning of the war, and a woman screamed hoarsely: 'Are the French really coming here?' Then I got in front and began reading. My first feeling was one of anger against the newspaper, because these appalling terms were stated so smugly. Then I felt as if hunger, to which I thought I had grown accustomed, were dragging at my vitals. My gorge rose and a feeling of sickening emptiness filled my mouth. My eyes swam so that I could not see the crowd round me, so that I could see nothing but the big black letters, hammering one horror after another into my brain with hideous callousness. At first I could grasp nothing, had to force myself to understand. At last I realised one thing: The French were coming into the town as victors.

I turned to the man next to me and caught him by the arm. I noticed that he was wearing a red band, but I spoke to him all the same, my voice breaking: 'The French are coming!' I said. He simply looked at the news sheet and his eyes were glassy. Someone said 'We've got to hand over the fleet.' And then everyone began talking at once. I ran home; and was astonished to see that nothing was altered, though it seemed to me that the whole town and every street in it must begin screaming. I still saw isolated groups of people at the corners; street orators holding forth with mighty gesture, and I overheard 'If officers and men had had the same pay and the same food. . . .' One old gentleman was saying that he thought this was not the time to enquire into guilt or innocence. The people should unite, for the French were coming into the town. However, nobody listened to him, and finally he passed on, discouraged and shaking his head. But one man said, looking round nervously: 'I'd almost sooner have the French in the country than the Reds!' And then he disappeared hastily.

Motor cars still race through the town full of armed Reds, and I looked at them carefully, seeing strong resolute figures intoxicated with the speed, and wondered whether the intoxication of resistance to the victorious French might also be expected of them. I read the placards, the red placards with the announcements of the Workers' and Soldiers' Council, and suspected that behind the bombast of their expression there was real energy and a fierce will to succeed. When I saw how it had subsided into a sullen resignation, I even wished for a return of the feverish excitement which had distinguished the town during the first days of the revolution. I was almost terrified by the satisfaction I felt when I heard that the prisons had been stormed and that a fat customer at the Café Astoria had been beaten nearly to death because he dared laugh at a demonstration of men wounded in the war. However, as time passed, instead of ill-disciplined bands of sailors, more and more older men in business dress appeared. These pale office-soldiers came, the red bands looking curiously out of place on their sleeves, carrying rifles instead of despatch cases, the muzzles trailing in the mud as was now the custom. The sailors withdrew sulkily. They were no longer the heroes of the revolution. They felt that they had been slighted and they wandered past the police-patrols with sullen faces and past the special constables, who stood about importantly, following the vagrants with cold eyes.

One night during this disturbed time I dreamt of the entry of the French. I dreamt of it, though I had never seen a Frenchman apart from the prisoners of war. I may say here that as I dreamt of them so I saw them when, seventeen months later, they really did take possession of the town. This is what I saw: They suddenly appeared in the town, where all was deadly silent. Lithe figures they were, blue-grey like the twilight which lay between the houses. They came at a quick-march with fixed bayonets and all their accoutrements shining. Like a shout rose the brilliant colours of their standards; like a shout the sound of the bugles above their short crisp steps. Whence had I that vision of the march past of the Sambre and Meuse regiments? It was like wild fierce music; and before it went panic and the nameless fear of the inescapable.

At intervals came companies of small alert figures, slim, supple, brown, like cats: Tunisians, with feline tread and shining teeth. They marched in a sinuous line, darting lightning glances in every direction, calling up visions of the desert, of unrest under a burning sun, of flickering white sand. Then came the Spahis, in fluttering shining cloaks, on tough little horses, lissom, clever, thrilling. Then the negroes, black as hell, long-limbed, with muscular, sinewy bodies, shining faces, cavernous, greedy nostrils. We were broken by their irresistible force, we were trampled in the dust, we had no rights, we were conquered, shamed, abandoned, for ever fallen. . . . by all that was sacred, it should not be!

'After this revolution a dictator will arise,' I read in a newspaper; and, sure of its subject, the journal pointed to the example of the French Revolution and Napoleon. I still had a picture of the Corsican put away in a drawer, though since the outbreak of war it had not hung over my desk. I looked for the picture and was horrified at the face. It was pale and un-healthy, but the eyes were piercing and full of dangerous secrets under the mass of untidy hair. Of a truth, Napoleon originated in revolution. These stormy eyes – had they not seen chaos, and had they not brought order out of that chaos? Were not France and the whole world tamed by their glance? Thrilled, I read the stories of that naked, burning, Gallic heroism, which drove ragged, hungry, marauding hordes against invading armies, scratching saltpetre from the walls of cellars to make gunpowder, dragging generals to the guillo-tine because, in spite of orders, they had failed to conquer.

Levée en masse – who said that? Yes indeed, it was our duty to rise in a body against the foe. We must make our revolution live; whatever flag we chose must be followed single heartedly, even if it meant learning to love the revolution. Had not Kerenski gone on fighting, had not Lenin declared war on the whole world? We must all carry arms, and we would carry them passionately, determined on the victory which meant more to us than our existence. Who then could resist our revolt? It was a venture worth the daring!

I made up my mind to learn to sympathise with the revolu-tion; perhaps its potentialities had hardly yet been realised. Maybe the sailors were waiting impatiently for a signal, perhaps the workers and the soldiers were already secretly drilling, and the most energetic elements in the nation had already chosen their weapons.

I ran through the town: the town was quiet. I pushed my way into meetings: heated speakers inveighed against landlords, clergy and wealthy merchants and the accursed régime of the Hohenzollerns. I read the proclamations fervently: I saw orders for demobilisation and for the carrying out of the conditions of the armistice. I tore through the streets: people were going to work, hardly stopping to read the bright red placards. They were tired, listless and hungry; they wore old, shabby clothes. If they talked at all, it was in undertones, and the women stood at the corners as usual in long queues, waiting patiently. I importuned the police, but they looked at me suspiciously and answered me as I had been answered hundreds of times before. I saw dense crowds with waving flags and magnificent banners: but all their cry was 'No more war,' 'Give us bread,' while they stood and discussed a general strike and the elections. I appealed to my acquaintances, officers, civil servants, shopkeepers, but they said our first need was organisation; and then they spoke of the disgraceful state of things which our soldiers coming back from the front would find.

Finally, I bethought me of the sailors – the sailors who had led the revolution. They passed boldly through the city, and were the instigators and the promoters of every disturbance. For the second time I went into the police station, went up the dirty, worn steps, and entered a room with rough wooden tables and benches, on which lay a wild confusion of cooking utensils, rucksacks, beer mugs, cakes of soap, combs, tobacco pouches, pots of grease, bits of bacon, all mixed up with cartridges, rifles, swords and harness, while a broken machine gun stood in a corner beside a box of hand-grenades. There lay and squatted and stood the sailors, smoking, gambling, drinking, eating, talking. Over them hung a heavy blue cloud, compounded of sweat and dust and smoke, full of strange, overpowering smells, giving the impression that here were explosives, only waiting for the spark to detonate them

I swallowed my pride. I let them curse me and make fun of me. I refused to be squashed, offered them bad tobacco, hoarsely mixed in their rough talk, laughed at dirty jokes, told one myself, was familiar with them, sought out two or three who were sitting alone, brought out newspapers. One of them,

HOPE

a young fellow with a mean face, catechised me. I lied to him, abused the Kaiser, let him boast about their deeds of heroism, of how they had thrashed their officers, of how many girls they had assaulted. I flattered him, till he allowed me to run down the police, as lazy dogs who would betray the revolution for fear of the bourgeoisie and of the French. I asked him whether he knew that the French were coming; whether they would fight, whether they would resist the French?

Then the fellow laughed and said 'We shan't! – Who cares?' and spat into the corner.

CHAPTER III

HOMECOMING

In the middle of December the troops returned from the front. Only one division, from the neighbourhood of Verdun, was expected in the town.

The crowd was gathered on the footpaths. A few houses timidly displayed red, white and black bunting. There were a great many women and girls, some of them carrying baskets of flowers or little parcels. The main streets were crowded with people who, after some pushing, consented to stay quietly on the pavements, waiting for the troops. We felt as if the depression which had hung over the town for weeks past had suddenly been lifted a little; as if the spell that had kept people apart had all at once been broken. It almost felt like the old days, when a big victory had been announced. We were ready to give rein to our enthusiasm; we were inclined to credit everybody with being moved by the same sensations as ourselves. We had all suffered; and the troops would bring the solution to our difficulties. We stood, craning our necks to see if they were not in sight yet, and all our hopes centred on this one idea: that everything would be changed. We stood and waited for the 'best of the nation.' Their sacrifice could not have been worthless. The dead had not died in vain – that could not be, that was impossible. It seemed significant to me that we were all standing and waiting, each one formulating his own wishes. How various these wishes must be! Yet they must be at one in recognising that each wished for the best. Our troops were coming, our brave army, which had done its duty to the uttermost, which had given us glorious victories; victories that seemed almost unbearably splendid now that we had lost the war. The army had not been conquered. Our men had stood firm to the last. They were coming home and they would knit up all the old bonds.

The multiplicity of the wishes which swayed the crowd sought for expression. There were murmurs, groups were formed, little knots of people surrounded gesticulating speakers. They were saying that the men had come on foot all the way from the front; that they had refused to form Councils; that the French were following at their heels. These troops were not staying in the town. They were departing on the following day. However, the town felt that it was its duty and its pleasure to give them the joyful reception which was their due. Our unconquered heroes were coming, though a jealous fate had denied them the rewards of their bravery. And in spite of sorrow, in spite of the changes at home, it was no more than bare justice to forget small dissensions and to receive them with joy and in unity.

The day was cold and damp and grey. I was wedged hotly and uncomfortably among the crowd. The buzz of excitement re-echoed from the houses, as we waited, listening and chattering, shivering with the cold and damp.

All at once the soldiers appeared. We scarcely heard them, but there was a sudden movement among the crowd. A few shouts were heard, which no one took up and which soon died down again. A woman wept, her shoulders heaving, sobbing quietly, her hands clenched.

The police spread out their arms and tried to keep back the crowd. They were swallowed up as the wall of people pressed forward.

There they were! There they were: grey figures, a forest of rifles over the round flat helmets.

'Why is there no music?' somebody whispered hoarsely, breathlessly. 'Why hasn't the mayor arranged any music?' Indignant whispers; then a deathly silence. Then a voice shouted 'Hurrah. . . .' from somewhere at the back. Then again silence.

The soldiers marched quickly, in close formation. They had stony, expressionless faces. They looked neither to right nor left, but straight ahead, fixedly, as though magnetised by some terrible goal, as though they were gazing from dug-outs and trenches over a wounded world. Not a word was spoken by those haggard-faced men. Just once, when someone sprang forward and almost imploringly offered a little box to the soldiers, the lieutenant waved him aside impatiently, saying: 'For goodness' sake don't do that. A whole division is following on.'

One platoon passed, the ranks close, a second, a third. Then a space. More space. Could this be a whole company? Three platoons? God! how terrible these men looked! – gaunt, immobile faces under shrapnel helmets, wasted limbs, ragged, dusty uniforms. . . . Did they still carry terrible visions of battle in their minds, as they carried the dust of the mangled earth on their garments? The strain was almost unbearable. They marched as though they were envoys of the deadliest, loneliest, iciest cold. Yet they had come home; here was warmth and happiness; why were they so silent? Why did they not shout and cheer; why did they not laugh?

The next company advanced. The crowd thronged forward again. But the soldiers trudged on rapidly, doggedly, blindly, untouched by the thousand wishes, hopes, greetings which hovered round them. And the crowd was silent.

Very few of the soldiers were wearing flowers. The little bunches which hung on their gun-barrels were faded. Most of the girls in the crowd were carrying flowers, but they stood trembling, uncertain, diffident, their faces pale and twitching, as they looked at the soldiers with anxious eyes. The march went on. An officer was carrying a laurel wreath negligently, dangling it in his hand, hunching his shoulders.

The crowd pulled itself together. A few hoarse shouts were heard, as though from rusty throats. Here and there a handkerchief was waved. One man murmured, convulsed: 'Our heroes, our heroes!' They passed on, unmoved, shoulders thrust forward, their steel helmets almost hidden by bulky packs, dragging their feet, company after company, little knots of men with wide spaces between. Sweat ran from their helmets down their worn grey cheeks, their noses stood out sharply from their faces.

Not a flag, not a sign of victory. The baggage waggons were already coming in sight. So this was a whole regiment!

As I beheld these fiercely determined faces, set as though carved in wood, these eyes which looked frigidly past the crowd, coldly, malevolently, inimically – yes inimically – I knew, I realised, I felt numbly – that everything was absolutely and completely different from what I and all of us here had imagined. It must have been different all through these past years. Then what *did* we know? What did we know of these men, of the front line, of our soldiers? Nothing, nothing, nothing. God! This was terrible. Was *nothing* true that we had been told? We had been cheated: these were not our boys, our heroes, our defenders – these were men who had no part or lot among those who were gathered here in the streets. They were of another race, they obeyed other laws. Suddenly everything for which I had hoped, by which I had been inspired, seemed to me shallow and empty.

An officer appeared mounted on a wretched, dirty, horse. He was a major and he passed close by me. I stood to attention, but he did not so much as look at me. He turned his horse so that it stood in front of us and its hind legs pushed aside the crowd. He faced the troops and raised his hand in salute. An officer sprang out from amongst the troops and called out a command. The soldiers came to life: with one movement they turned their heads, their legs seemed to be jerked in their sockets, and their boots rang on the paving-stones.

The major stooped in his saddle. His regiment marched past, their tired, worn-out feet resounding on the asphalt. The crowd stood motionless. The whole affair seemed senseless. What was the meaning of this parade, with no music, no flags, nothing to account for it, no pageantry? Or perhaps after all there was some reason in it; some deeper, more obscure reason than we could probe. Was this a show for us or was it not? In truth it seemed to me that it was a challenge, it was mockery, defiance, contempt; a demonstration of the power of the army: the absurd goose-step, the ridiculous stiffness and the way they threw about their legs! To them it did not seem absurd, they knew that we were ashamed of ourselves; that we could not make fun of them, neither Reds, nor townspeople, though we had been ready to admit in our peace and security and respectability that this goose-step was ridiculous.

The regiment passed on. Even the policeman did not dare to smile. The major put his horse to a heavy jogtrot and followed. Now came more baggage waggons. The drivers sat motionless, and if anyone threw them things they gave no thanks nor even acknowledged them. There were a few tiny flags stuck in the waggons; cheap cloth hanging limply on little sticks. Camouflaged machine-gun carriages rolled past, the men with the girths over their shoulders, eight men to a trailer. Then came big guns, with the gunners sitting on them their steel helmets tilted over their faces by the jolting. A few of the bolder spirits gave them flowers. One man took no notice at all; another accepted the bunch without thanks and laid it down beside him; another looked up dazedly, never smiling, took the flowers and held them awkwardly in his hands.

All this time the woman was weeping with dull, strangled sobs that seemed to come from deep down in her breast.

Then came more infantry, and they took no notice of us either. Was it because they were still so filled with the horror of what they had lived through? This battalion came straight from the front line. These eyes fixed and staring under their helmets had seen things of which we had no conception, in a world which meant nothing to us, of which we had only vague ideas gleaned from sketchy accounts and faulty pictures. Dumbly, drearily they continued their march, as though they were still in the shadow of death. People, Country, Home, Duty – we spoke all those words, and we believed in them. But what about the troops – what were their feelings?

Company after company passed. Pathetic little groups of men, surrounded by a terrifying atmosphere of blood, of steel, of explosives, of fierce contests. Did they hate the revolution? Would they fight against it? Would they come back amongst us as workmen, farmers or students, and take part in our sorrows, our desires, our battles?

Suddenly I realised that these were no workmen, farmers, students, they were not labourers, clerks, shopkeepers or officials. They were soldiers: they were men who had heard the call. Here were no mummers, no conscripts. They had a vocation, they came of their own free will, and their home was in the war-zone. Home – Country – People – Nation – they were imposing words when we said them, but they were shams. That was why these men would have nothing to do with us.

They were the Nation. What we had blazoned about the world they understood in a deeper sense – it was that which had urged them to do what we smugly called their duty. Their faith was not in words, it was in themselves, and they never talked about it. War had taken hold of them and would never let them go. They would never really belong to us and to their homes again. This attempted fusion of them with the peaceful, ordered life of ordinary citizens was a ridiculous adulteration which could never succeed. The war was over, but the armies were still in being. The mob was fermenting, unwieldly, with thousands of little hopes and desires, size its only might, but the soldiers would work for revolution – a different revolution – whether they wanted to or not, urged on by powers which we could not realise. War had provided no solution; soldiers were still needed.

Now came the last battalion in the division. I watched perplexed, anguished, trembling, rebellious. The last platoons swung past. The ground still echoed to their tread and the crowd began moving. I listened to the last steps of the soldiers. What did I care for the revolution now. . . . ?

*   *   *   *

Appeals hung at the street corners. Volunteers were asked for. Companies were to be raised for defence on the eastern frontier.

I enlisted the day after the the troops had entered the town.

CHAPTER IV

BERLIN

'HALT! Or I fire!' He went on all the same. I wondered whether to shoot, but it seemed absurd, he looked so harmless. Still, orders are orders – though nowadays we didn't look on these things quite as they used to in the old times, as Lance-corporal Hoffmann used to say. It was a horrid idea just to shoot the fellow in the back while he was crossing the square, in his shabby clothes, without an overcoat. . . . However, other people began crossing the square too.

'Halt! Halt! Stop! Can't you read? Get back there! Nobody's allowed across here! Why? Because there's going to be firing here directly!'

It was December 24th. We were on duty at the Palace, beside the bridge, and the sailors were quartered in the royal stables.

There was a crack. From the wall above my head flew dust and splinters of stone. A man came headlong round the corner, flattened himself against the wall and laughed. I laughed too. Some women peeped out of the porches and people passed to and fro unconcernedly. I shouted: 'Halt!' A knot of people collected rapidly. A shot was fired from the Palace.

'You can't pass here,' I said and pulled my coat collar up over my chin. A hand-grenade dangled from my belt.

The N.C.O. appeared. We both hurried to get behind the advertising column. There was a large crowd in front of the Palace. 'The General is trying to come to terms with them,' said the N.C.O. Then the rest of my squad appeared, running with their rifles held in front of them.

'We're to go as reinforcements.'

'Why, what's up?'

'Orders are that no one else is to pass.'

A line of sentries surrounded the Palace square.

'What's up? We'd already locked up "the comrades," and the General wanted to arrange matters with them. But then the sailors all came out and some others as well, and now they're all amongst us.– Get back there!'

We fell in. Suddenly we were in the middle of things, and, as suddenly, I found myself alone, hardly within sight of the N.C.O.'s tin hat.

A woman planted herself directly in my way and laughed in my face. She was fat and grey and was wearing a coarse grey overall. There were gaps in her teeth and she had a wart at the side of her nose. I wondered what she was laughing at with her arms folded over a mighty paunch, and decided that it was at me. Devil take the woman – the hag; I felt like ramming the barrel of my rifle in her face – but I turned my head away. If only I didn't look so young! Other people came too. They stood close round me, and presently some sailors joined them, carrying rifles and wearing red sashes. They looked at me and one of them said: 'What are you fighting against us for, lad? Send your officers to the devil! You don't want to follow those slave-drivers!'

I did not know what to do. However, to my relief, I saw the N.C.O. returning. He pushed his way through, looked at the sailors and said: 'Come off it! Mind your own damned business.'

There was a stir in the square. 'Get back!' the N.C.O. shouted suddenly and put his rifle to his shoulder. A space was cleared instantly; there was a horrible noise and women screamed. The sailors ran under the archway. We advanced slowly. At the window I saw a young fellow with red hair, a sailor, who leant out and took a good look at us. Then he quietly removed the pin from a hand-grenade.

A bang – we flopped down – the devil! – it crashed into the pavement. I leapt up and tore back. There were bangs and whistles.

Three men were already lying behind the pillar, and in the square here and there were bundles, queer, dark, grey, long-drawn-out shadows –

The N.C.O. was at my side. 'Where the devil is the machine-gun, damn it?'

At that moment it began firing from behind the other pillar.

'This way!' shouted the N.C.O. Then came the second machine-gun. We moved closer together. 'Now go ahead! Yes you! Let's see what you can do. That's it – stop – not yet – bring her round this way first. Shoot off that chap's head on the bridge! Yes, yes, Lehmann's statue there on the bridge.– That's it – that was fine – now, round with her! On to the lower windows – bring her up a bit! That's it, that's right!'

The wide girths cut my shoulder. The rattling muzzle leapt forward, kicked back. I got the range of the row of windows where the young sailor had stood – he was there again and turned a gun on to us and fired in our direction, I aimed – fired. The window was empty.

We lay there for a long time. Bullets hailed round us – we fired back. 'Good lads!' said the N.C.O.

'Get back!' someone shouted.

'Why? What for? Oh I see, guns!'

We crawled back hastily. At the corner a big gun on its slender wheels stood in position. We had hardly got back before somebody touched it off; there was a roar, the shell

35

screamed over our heads and burst, tearing a hole in the façade, scattering stones. Out of the window was hurled half the body of a man, which was caught and remained hanging in the arches. Slowly the night drew on.

*   *   *   *

Opposite the Admiralty House Sergeant Poessel fell, shot through the head. He was a man who had fought all through the war from the very first day, and he had come through with a few very slight wounds and the Iron Cross, first class. There he lay, by a wooden fence, and his brains were splashed all over it. Above him was a big yellow notice about a ball for some charity for war widows, and behind the fence were the booths and tents of an amusement park, where every evening there were merry-go-rounds and scenic railways and girls enjoying themselves. We carried him through narrow streets crowded with people, past places of amusement, whence hot red lights shone through the opening doors. As we went by, panting for breath, we heard nigger music from bars and dancing saloons, we saw profiteers and prostitutes, noisy and drunk, saw the townspeople and their wives sitting in private boxes, at tables bright with glasses and bottles. They danced their feverish, erotic dances on glassy floors, while the last stray shots of our companions were still sounding in the distance.

*   *   *   *

We exchanged shots with snipers. We tore round corners, hugging the walls, our rifles at full cock, looking for openings; we crouched behind hastily piled-up barricades; we lay behind advertising columns and lamp standards; we forced doors and stormed up dark staircases; we shot at anyone carrying arms who did not belong to our company; and every now and then men would fall who had not been carrying arms; and sometimes

36

women and even children; and the bullets whistled over their bodies.

Behind our line prostitutes were strolling about. They sauntered up and down the Friedrichstrasse while shooting went on in the Unter den Linden. They approached anyone who stood to rest for a moment, giving us, who were still in the grip of this confused battle, who were still sighting the enemy over our rifles, a curious feeling of nausea. It was not the whispered solicitation that seemed so intolerable, it was the calm matter of fact way in which they snatched at our bodies – those bodies which a moment before had been exposed to rivers of bullets pouring from the machine-guns. We forced our way through the disorder in the streets, all our nerves strung up to their highest pitch. We pushed past hordes of beggars, of wounded soldiers, of blind men, and from time to time people spoke to us – one offering cocaine, another a diamond ring, a third Kiesewetter's latest political verses.

*   *   *   *

January 6th, 1919:

'Squad, halt!' Eight of us with a sergeant stood at a street corner. As yet there were not many people about. The sergeant went on a few steps and scanned the main street up and down. He came back shrugging his shoulders: 'Nothing to be seen yet.' A few people stood and watched us; one old gentleman who was passing came to a standstill and beamed on us saying: 'At least we've still got soldiers!' Then he turned to the sergeant and said: 'Well, I suppose you'll soon be clearing up this filthy state of affairs!' The N.C.O. looked at the old gentleman calmly and said: 'I'm a Socialist.' He looked startled, got very red in the face and walked away quickly.

There was a movement of surprise among the eight of us: Sergeant Kleinschroth a Socialist! This quiet, dark, serious man? I eyed him surreptitiously. Lance-corporal Hoffmann looked at me cheerfully and smiled: 'I'll bet you're surprised! I'm a Socialist too. Joined in 1913!'

I was taken aback and said nothing. Hoffmann went on eagerly in a low tone: 'Man, we want to control the State!' And after a moment: 'I've been a workman too, a turner.'– '*Been* a workman,' I thought, '*been*, he says, why *been?*' Hoffmann stared fixedly before him: 'If we want to nationalise things, we're not going to have everything smashed up beforehand . . .' and he stopped.

Suddenly there was a noise. It came from above, apparently from the fog which hung over us teeming and heavy. Yet no – it did not come from above – it rushed in from the left, swelling and swelling, and swallowing up all the sounds in the street. The sergeant ran forward a few steps and then came back rapidly. 'They're coming!' he said and directed us into a dark passage, which, since there was a bend in the road, opened slantways on to the main street. We stood there in the shadow, unseen, but seeing everything. 'Silence in the ranks!' The sergeant looked in front of him, then turned and took three steps towards me, and said threateningly: 'Man, if your rifle goes off before I give the word . . .!' I said: 'No, sergeant!'

Suddenly there were hundreds of people in the empty street. Women ran out of the houses, children collected, drivers stopped their cars. More and more people arrived. The street corners were black with them. The noise grew louder. Accompanied by snatches of the *Internationale*, a carrier's cart appeared, groaning and squeaking, with an enormous red flag rising from it. We stood breathlessly in our entry and stared into the square. Our belts with the handgrenades cut into our bodies; our rifles seemed a dead weight against our legs. We were standing shoulder to shoulder, getting stiff and stiffer.

BERLIN

The whole road was black. It seemed as if the houses were bending over to watch the immense tangled ribbon, unrolling slowly, endlessly: people, people, people.

The red flags made a great splash of colour over the throng, white banners floated among them. A shrill voice cried: 'Long live the Revolution!' The multitude roared: 'Hurrah!' It resounded from thousands of throats, swept aside the fog, rattled the windows. 'Hurrah! Hurrah!' The very ground echoed as the sound rolled on. Again came flags; and amongst the armed men, the sailors, the shining rifles, swayed banners with the legends: 'DOWN WITH THE BETRAYERS OF THE WORKERS, DOWN WITH EBERT AND SCHEIDEMANN!' 'LONG LIVE LIEBKNECHT.' 'HUNGER.' 'PEACE, FREEDOM, PLENTY.'

A pale, enthusiastic young fellow came towards our hiding place. He threw up his hands with excitement and stammered agitatedly: 'It's beginning! Last night they occupied the whole of the newspaper quarter. Liebknecht is speaking at the Brandenburg Gate. You'll be killed! You can't fool with the people in Berlin. . . .' The sergeant said: 'Get out! You've got no business here.' The roar outside stopped abruptly. A little dark pale fellow with eyeglasses, a beard and an umbrella was standing on a cart addressing the crowd. He spoke in short clear sentences. Some of his words reached us faintly. 'The international proletariat . . . our comrades in the whole world . . . our brethren in France, England and Italy . . . Germany's fault. . . .'

By this time the whole square was full. A solid wall of human backs confronted us. Among the crowd were certain men wearing rough white fur coats bulging over tightly drawn belts. Their rifles hung reversed. All at once one of these men saw us.

He started, he shouted, he pointed. My blood ran cold. Thousands of eyes looked at us malevolently, balefully. There was a roar –'Now they're coming,' I thought – they rushed forward. 'Kill the murderers!'– They hissed their hate as water hisses on a hot stove. I saw a confusion of heads, hands, bodies, as the mob rolled towards us.

The sergeant shouted – and the sound gave our cramped bodies relief –'Load!' Our rifles shot up, the muzzles pointing straight at the crowd. Our clammy hands went to the breech, loaded, snapped back – there was silence for several seconds.

Here were eight menacing rifles, and the space before us grew larger. Two lines of men in front of the crowd stemmed the forward rush. The tension grew unbearable, it pulled and tore like a thin red-hot wire. . . .

The little man with the umbrella gesticulated wildly: 'Back! Don't shoot!' Then he placed himself between the opposing forces. 'Go away!' He roared and they obeyed. They moved hesitatingly; he drove them before him; and then he turned to us and said: 'You ought to be ashamed of yourselves!'

We drew our guns to our sides. A little drop of sweat ran down my forehead into my eye. Everything seemed to be going round me in a red mist – I turned feebly and leant against the wall. Above my head was a white poster, with a red border. A few big black words shouted at us from among the welter of small print:

'SO THIS IS SOCIALISM!'

These were the words under which we had been standing.

The square was empty. The street was empty. The cold grey sky was damp, heavy, gloomy.

We fell in. The sergeant ordered us to unload. 'And that's that!' he said, and we marched off.

Lance-corporal Hoffmann said: 'Bloody fools. They miss every opportunity.'

* * * *

BERLIN

(A year later *The Red Flag* described the day's events as follows:

'What happened in Berlin on Monday was perhaps the greatest united effort on the part of the proletariat that the world has yet seen. We doubt whether even in Russia mass-demonstrations have taken place on such a scale. From the statue of Roland to that of Queen Victoria the street was a solid mass of people. They were armed and red flags were flying. They were ready to dare all, to give all, even their lives. Ludendorff himself never saw such an army – an army 200,000 strong.

'But what followed was disgraceful. In spite of the cold, in spite of the fog, the multitudes took up their position and waited from nine o'clock in the morning, while somewhere their leaders sat and conferred. The fog lifted and the multitudes continued their vigil. But the leaders sat and conferred. Dinner time came and with it cold and hunger. And the leaders sat and conferred. The multitudes were in a fever of excitement: they wanted some deed, even just a word, to calm their agitation. But none knew what to say. For the leaders sat and conferred. The fog came down again, bringing the twilight. The multitudes went sadly home: they had been prepared for great deeds and nothing had happened. For the leaders sat and conferred. They conferred in the royal stables, then they went on to the Prefecture of Police and conferred again. Outside stood the proletariat in the empty Alexander Square, armed with rifles, with light and heavy machine-guns – while inside their leaders sat and conferred. Inside the Prefecture weighty arguments were expounded; sailors stood at every bend in the corridors; in the anterooms was a crowd of soldiers, sailors, workers. And inside the leaders sat and conferred. They sat the whole evening, and all night too, conferring. Next morning when dawn broke some were still sitting conferring and some had started all over again. Once more the multitudes went to the Siegesallee, and still the leaders sat and conferred. They conferred and conferred and conferred.

'Truly these multitudes were not yet ripe for power; otherwise they would of their own initiative have elected a leader, and the first revolutionary act would have been to make the leaders in the Prefecture of Police stop conferring!')

*   *   *   *

We stood drawn up in a long grey column. A motor car arrived and a man rose from the cushions and took stock of us. He was tall and thickset with square, rather high shoulders and an absurd little pair of spectacles under his soft felt hat. Our officers saluted him with pronounced coolness and turned their backs on him with their lips twitching. One of them said that it was the new commander-in-chief, Noske.

*   *   *   *

We marched through the suburbs. Greetings and flowers were showered on us; a great many people stood in the streets and waved; and a few houses were decorated with flags. We realised that life flowed in other channels here and was on a different level of refinement – a refinement that matched ill with our rough boots and dirty hands. We knew that our desires did not extend to the things that were treasured in these places – things that were the result of hundreds of years of culture – good breeding, personal freedom, pride in one's work, open-mindedness – all these were exposed to the on-slaught of a greedy mob; and we were willing to defend them because we knew that their loss would be irreparable.

We entered the town – troops were marching in by all the main roads. There was a feeling of fierce excitement in the streets, as though people had awakened after a terrible, paralysing dream; they were hurrying about with an air of cautious aloofness. The choking, quivering, atmosphere threatened to explode into frenzy and death.

We were quartered in schools and offices. We camped in empty, whitewashed rooms, in whose every corner we felt the fustiness of accumulated papers and dry calculations. We lay on bare boards, surrounded with helmets and knapsacks, rifles and cooking pots, tarpaulins and boxes of ammunition. We took turns at sentry-go. We walked up and down, counted the paving-stones, turned to watch every form as it vanished in the darkness and fog, listened to the reports of distant shots. When the pale grey of the dawn crept into the streets, the ground began to heave with the wearisome tramp of countless steps, with the passage of heavy, reverberating waggons, all dismally alike. We were impelled to go out to the street corners, where we stood, carrying our rifles, in the shadow of the houses, as though we had been thrown out by the town and yet were under its spell. We searched the passers-by for arms, our hands running over reluctant bodies. The impertinence of the act embarrassed us, and still more that our only justification for this impertinence lay in the fact that it was an order.

We arrested a Red agitator. He was a thin, dark, elderly man, very well-known among the revolutionaries. We fetched him out of his house – it was a wretchedly poor lodging, in some back-premises, it was not even really a room, only a closet. He came with us quite quietly and seemed to be smiling inwardly. We carried rifles and surrounded him closely on all sides, according to our instructions. Of course everybody in the streets turned to look, but that seemed to disturb this man far less than it did us. We fortified ourselves with a trifle of carelessness and a modicum of weighty significance, while he seemed to notice nothing that went on round him. At the same time, we had no idea what his crime was; but he seemed to know all about us, for he said just once: 'Yes, yes. I suppose it's your duty.' And we were unable to answer him. We never discovered what happened to this agitator afterwards.

What happened to Karl Liebknecht and Rosa Luxemburg, however, we did find out. We heard about it on January 16th. On January 19th, a general election was held by the free and sovereign people of Germany.

*　　*　　*　　*

The house which we had to search was a tenement house in the north of the town, with four courtyards and hundreds of inhabitants. It was a tall grey house, with the plaster peeling off the walls and with innumerable grimy windows. The road had been blocked with two squads of men at each end, under cover of night, and there was also a flying squad, on whom we could call for reinforcements in case of necessity.

The sergeant said at the entrance: 'Keep together all the time. One man is never to go into a room alone. Search all cupboards and beds. Tap the walls. Two men are always to stay on the staircase. Break open locked doors, if the people won't open them. No provocation! In case of danger, fire one shot out of the window.'

We divided. Kleinschroth's squad was sent into the farthest court. We stumbled over the cracked asphalt and hardly noticed when we came out into the courtyard from the archway, for the dark, high walls did not admit the light of the morning sun. The house was still very quiet and we halted at a small narrow door. Kleinschroth knocked at a window, which made it rattle. A woman looked out and recoiled as she saw our steel helmets. 'Open the door!' said Kleinschroth. All at once the whole house was alive.

For the first few moments it was alive like a disturbed bee-

44

hive. There was a threatening hum, at first quite low, then suddenly swelling to a shrill, dangerous, hysterical treble buzz that seemed viciously alert. Then the sergeant kicked in the door. It seemed as if the whole house groaned. Windows rattled, doors were banged, suddenly a gramophone began yowling, and somewhere high up a woman shrieked. She shrieked piercingly, so that the air seemed to quiver, damp and stale as it was and full of stuffy mixed smells. It caught our lungs and made our blood run cold with a kind of panic. We pulled the helmets down over our foreheads and ran into the dark cavern which loomed before us.

'The Noskes are coming! The Noskes are coming!' the woman screamed now and a window shivered and a piece of crockery crashed down.

We had got into the house, at any rate. The staircase was so dark that I fell over a pail. Hoffmann threw open a door, dashed into the room and I heard him say: 'Don't be a fool, man. Hand over that gun.' Inside sat a man who had just got out of his bed and held a rifle in his hand. He fumbled undecidedly for a moment and looked at us. He was sitting on the edge of a rickety bedstead, straw straggled into sight from under the checked counterpane and pieces of it were still sticking in his hair. The room was small; the tiny window hardly admitted any light. There was a stove in the room round which hung damp laundry and in the corner stood a young woman in a long ragged chemise: she seemed rooted where she stood and said nothing at all. Over the bed hung a framed picture such as the reservists used to take home: a coloured print of a soldier, whose head was a real photograph stuck on. The man hesitatingly handed over the rifle, then he suddenly jumped up, seized the picture and threw it down at our feet, so that the frame broke and the glass shivered. Then he raised his naked foot thoughtfully as though to grind the remains with his heel, but checked himself and only said: 'Now get out!' We went.

We were back on the staircase and hardly knew which way to go. The whole house was in an uproar and fiercely hostile to us; it seemed to be charged with hatred, with poverty, with a hundred unknown, lurking dangers. In this building dwellings were huddled close together, like cells in a honeycomb. Life seemed to be a continuous stream, only broken up here and there by walls. The rooms and cupboards threatened to burst with the terrible mixture of smells diffused by the closely herded bodies.

We searched the house dwelling by dwelling. There were dark landings on which stood pails and broken brooms; sooty lamps hung so low that more than one swung against our helmets; the boards groaned and splintered under our tread; our feet kicked against mortar and balks of wood; the ceilings – and how low those ceilings were – showed bare laths and crumbling plaster. Each door was close beside the next one. If one was opened to us, the others flew open too and in a moment the passage was full of people – men, women, and a great many children. Children of all sizes, mostly half naked and unspeakably dirty, their arms and legs so thin that they looked as if they would break if they were touched. They stood on the threshold of their miserable, gloomy rooms and hundreds of eyes seemed to be looking at us. While the others went inside, I stood outside the door and faced them alone; hatred diffused itself about me like a cloud and a confused babel of jeers re-echoed round me. Women pushed by me and laughed and then spat on the floor; and the men, with shirts open so that I could see the rough hair on their chests, shouted to one another: 'Let's kill these swine!' and 'Take the b——r's gun away!' But they did me no harm; they only raised their fists and shook them in my face and imitated the squashing of a bug between their fingers. This went on till the others came out and went on to the next dwelling.

I passed in with them and examined the place. It was a room not more than twelve feet square and crammed full of beds. Seven people were sleeping in this space – men, women and children. Two women were still in bed and each had a child with her. As we entered, one of them laughed shrilly and breathlessly, and the people outside crowded on to the doorstep. The N.C.O. approached, and the woman suddenly kicked off the bedclothes and pulled up her nightgown and burst out laughing. We recoiled, and the crowd outside yelled, they shrieked with laughter and slapped their thighs, they could not stop laughing, even the children laughed.

'Bloodhounds!' they screeched: 'Bloodhounds!' The children shouted it as well as the women, and suddenly the whole place was filled with a howling mob, so that we withdrew step by step until we stood in the passage again.

The gramophone was still blaring behind a tiny door at the very end of the passage. We pushed our way in; a man was standing there in the act of putting on a fresh record, and it bleated at us: 'Splendidly we'll conquer France. . . .' The throng yelled with delight, the N.C.O. stepped back, took a deep breath and roared: 'Get back all of you! Back to your rooms. If the passage isn't cleared at once we'll shoot!' For a moment there was silence. Then there was a buzz and a woman began to scream so that it echoed on all the walls and staircases, a long-drawn out scream, like someone in a death agony. The children were suddenly frightened by it and crept away. It had more effect in clearing the passages than the rattling of our guns. But the hum went on inside the rooms. We heard obscure sounds through the rickety doors, furniture was moved about, there was a clatter of metal, and the woman went on screaming as if she were half strangled.

47

Downstairs they began singing the *Internationale*. One after another they took it up throughout the whole house. Then they stamped their feet in time to the music so that the whole place shook and we stood in the dark passage as if we were in an earthquake.

We continued our search. In one room we came to, an old man was sitting at the table and an old woman stood at the window. The old man rose slowly and moved towards us with trembling.knees. He stood right in front of us, raised his hand slowly and whispered hoarsely. 'Get out!' and again 'Get out!' He crept nearer and nearer, little red veins swelling in his eyes, raised his dirty furrowed old hand and opened his withered lips as if it were his last effort, gasping huskily: 'Get out.' The N.C.O. was trying to pacify the man, when he suddenly swayed, staggered, and fell with the upper part of his body on the table. The woman simply took the N.C.O. by the arm as if he had been a disobedient child, and silently led him out.

The N.C.O. was very pale when he came with us to the next door. We knocked but nobody opened. We knocked again and more loudly, we knocked with nervous, increasing vehemence. Then Hoffmann sprang forward and kicked in the door. In this room were only a woman and a slight, pale girl, with untidy black hair. She confronted us, then retreated a few steps and rested her hands on the table. In the sudden silence she asked in a very low but apprehensive voice: 'How dare you do this? Haven't you murdered enough people yet?' Her voice grew chill. She said: 'You push your way into the house like hangmen. Are you quite shameless? Don't you realise that we are human too?' And again: 'Do you hear what they are singing? Where do you hail from? Who sent you?' People were standing at the door again, but now they were listening silently. The girl went on: 'You are protecting the very class who brought this misery upon us. They exploit

48

and despise you as much as they do us. And now you think a lot of yourselves because you've got guns. Put them away – or, rather, give them to these people who will know how to use them for a right purpose!' Sergeant Kleinschroth said from under his helmet: 'We know all about that, Miss, we've heard it all before. It is just guns that we are after. We don't want anything else. You'd better see to it that these people don't do anything silly.' Then we turned about and went; and we felt better, although it seemed to us that the sergeant might have said something more. However, he only stared before him with curiously unseeing eyes as we made our way through the people, and he did not speak another word as long as we were in that house.

It was impossible to search everything as thoroughly as we had been ordered to do, nor did we want to. When we went into a room we were oppressed by the sickening, stale smell of many people herded together in suffocating closeness, and it induced in us a bitter ferocity. It seemed impossible to defend ourselves against this feeling of oppression, except by demonstrating a firmness that we did not experience and by acting in as assured a manner as possible. Though hate was spat at us from screaming, sneering mouths, we felt in a way as if we were called upon to make a choice – for our sympathies could as easily have lain with those whose rooms we searched as with those whose orders we obeyed. But we stuck to our orders, we stumped through the rooms with set faces, we calmly probed the straw mattresses, raked about under the beds, opened the cupboards, ran our hands through the miserable articles of clothing – and yet felt like thieves. Exposed to the battery of staring eyes, which seemed to burn us in the back, we banged on walls, knocked at doors, pulled bedclothes apart and searched. And we found nothing – nothing in the whole of that immense house, except the one rifle.

Inside the rooms they went on singing and the monotonous repetition was almost soothing.

Then we collected in the entrance. Through the various courtyards other squads came to join us. As we were preparing to move off, the sergeant-major observed that two men were missing. The flying squad went to look for them. The rest of us marched away. The two men were never found. In the barracks the wildest rumours were afloat. Lance-corporal Hoffmann said: 'My God, I've got the hell of a hump!' And after a while: 'I know where those two are. They've simply deserted.'

CHAPTER V

WEIMAR

On January 20th, 1919, the day after the elections for the National Assembly which drafted the new constitution, the commanders of the troops stationed in Berlin came to see Noske. They pointed out that they could not guarantee the loyalty of the troops. So much propaganda was being conducted among the soldiers by the malcontents and the Spartacists, that it would be bad for their morale to remain in the town. Consideration should be given as to whether it would not be wiser to withdraw these divisions to barracks in the suburbs and villages.

*   *   *   *

The government elected by the representatives of the people decided that the National Assembly should meet in Weimar.

Maercker's *Landesjäger* volunteer corps had the reputation for being the best disciplined troop, and it was no doubt intended as a compliment that General Maercker and his men were told off to guard the National Assembly in Weimar. However, the Workers' and Soldiers' Council of Thuringia was not disposed to look favourably upon this distinction and sent an offended telegram to Noske, saying that the Thuringian garrisons alone were able to guarantee the safety of the National Assembly and that the presence of other troops would be most unwelcome.

*   *   *   *

THE OUTLAWS

The difficulties of those days chiefly arose out of the battle for existence that was being waged by the revolution. The Independents and the Spartacists saw a threat to the achievements of the revolution in the meeting of the National Assembly. The slogan of the revolutionaries therefore was 'More power to the Workers' and Soldiers' Councils!' and this slogan was circulated by innumerable posters and found its echo in countless decisions at revolutionary councils and meetings. In the country itself, the authority of the councillors had been practically undisputed. Only in Berlin had there been any breakdown. But now troops were marching on Bremen; and officers and soldiers in Wilhelmshafen were creating a new organization under the leadership of Commander Ehrhardt.

After the first days of the revolution there had been no further mention of Farmers' Councils.

The Soldiers' Councils seemed to carry most weight. They used threatening language in their communications, controlled almost the whole of the government and appeared everywhere as the real wielders of power. They were, however, Soldiers' Councils without soldiers. The returning army was disbanded. The regiments, indeed, diminished in numbers on the way to their depôts. A great many of the men simply fell out as they came near their homes, and the officers made no attempt to stop them. In the depôts were only the oldest soldiers and the youngest – *Landsturm*, recruits and those who were liable for garrison duty. It was they who had elected the councils during the first exuberance of the revolution. Each of the soldiers returning from the front was allowed as much leave as he wanted and the rest took French leave. The Soldiers' Councils had undisputed possession of the empty barracks. They sat at ease in the large rooms, making resolutions, receiving pay and bonuses and allowances, and helping themselves to provisions and other stores. The clerks of the auditing service, out-of-work young soldiers, who came to fetch their pay, deserters and a few professional soldiers furnished the guards. These guards, however, were ready for everything except work or fighting. The Independents had organised police corps, recruited from workmen and demobilised soldiers or deserters; the sailors lived like foxes in their holes in their old quarters which they had turned into fortresses bristling with arms. They had formed themselves into little groups called People's Naval Divisions, and were always ready to shoot, but refused to obey any authority. Besides these, were only the starving masses.

The volunteer corps, which had been raised for the defence of the eastern frontiers, were in the pay of the government and went where Noske ordered. They consisted of a few men back from the front, volunteer students, schoolboys, cadets, officers, workmen, farmers, manual labourers and professional soldiers.

✻　　✻　　✻　　✻　　✻

When the advance guard of the *Landesjäger* came to Weimar, the Weimar Soldiers' Council commanded them to disarm. But the advance guard hastened to the headquarters of the Council. The chairman, standing between two machine-guns, declared that he would yield only to force. So the *Landesjäger* overturned the machine-guns and burst into the building. The chairman of the Weimar Soldiers' Council yielded. This was the only warlike episode which occurred in Weimar.

We heard this story as we entered the sleeping town. At the railway station we fixed bayonets. Our billets were in Ehringsdorf and we marched through the dark streets shivering and worn out by the long night-journey. We halted at the National Theatre. We stacked our rifles and waited, looking curiously at the memorial. Lieutenant Kay climbed on to the pedestal and sat down between the feet of the two bronze

53

figures. The theatre looked white and peaceful in the night, like a quiet temple. Lieutenant Kay said: 'Daylight is really too absurd. Confused, distracting laws and unpleasant events have dominion over the world,' and he patted Goethe's leg companionably. After a little while we marched on.

Weimar was occupied by the *Landesjäger* corps. A few companies only were billeted in the town itself, in the palace and near the theatre. We drilled in Ehringsdorf and in Oberweimar; we mounted guard in Umpferstedt and Süssenborn, we camped in Tiefurt and Hopfgarten. When our official duty was over we were not always inclined to go into Weimar; for the placid town did not gain in interest through the presence of dense crowds of representatives and their numerous speeches – and we were hankering after Berlin.

We had been pulled too suddenly out of the whirl of the mad weeks which lay behind us. Our march from Berlin seemed to us like flight and desertion; and in the intervals between drill and sentry-go, between drinking and cheap dancing saloons, we found oblivion in seditious talk. At first we attended the meetings in the town, at which delegates from all parties spoke, but the spiritual weapons which were offered to soldiers at these meetings made us see the more clearly the value of 15-inch guns. Our life had been passed very far from what seemed to the people's representatives to be the kernel and the essence of things. And Lieutenant Kay used to say: 'Let it all cook nicely, and every now and then stir it up a little, and from time to time light a little fire underneath!'

'What do you mean about lighting a little fire underneath?' I asked the Lieutenant, who was the leader of my patrol, over a glass of wine to which he had invited me. At that the Lieutenant turned round and three tables away sat a little stoutish man in a black coat, wearing horn-rimmed spectacles and carrying a despatch case. 'That's Erzberger,' whispered the Lieutenant and looked at me. 'A most efficient individual' – and he leant over the table. 'What do you think, would there be much cackling in the farmyard if he were thoroughly thrashed one day? – Are you on?'

I said: 'Yes, sir!'

But Erzberger escaped by the window in his shirt when we appeared, and Noske was very much annoyed with us. Apparently we were beginning to worry him. When he was Commander-in-Chief he always took off his hat when it occurred to one of the soldiers to salute him. Since he had become *Reichswehr* minister, an order was issued that the *Reichswehr* minister was to be saluted in due form, yet he himself did not trouble to do more than lift two fingers just short of the wide brim of his hat. And we did take such a lot of trouble! When we were at the barrier at Umpferstedt and saw his car coming, we were delighted. We held up the car and asked for the passes and officiously requested the gentleman to alight, as the car had to be searched for arms.

'Minister's car,' the chauffeur had the temerity to observe.

'Anybody can say that,' we pointed out brusquely, saying: 'Passes, please!' But when we saw the pass, we were suddenly brought up short! Our rifles crashed to our shoulders so that our helmets slipped to one side, and we shot out the right foot and clicked it against the left and looked at the gentleman woodenly. And the *Reichswehr* minister suspiciously lifted two fingers and we did not stir before the friendly hope was growled from the depths of the car that the barrier might at long last be raised!

The minister liked to walk along the line at a review and to ask friendly questions. Thus, one day he asked each man, excepting Lance-Corporal Hoffman: 'What is your trade?' – 'Basket maker, your Excellency!' came the answer promptly. But the captain found occasion later to shake his head and to

remark that we seemed to have our heads full of nonsense and
he supposed we needed a little more exercise.

So we had more drill. Also we drank more. Lieutenant
Kay had invented a mixture which we called 'the soul of
Weimar.' This mixture was very weak and you had to drink
a lot before getting comfortably tight. But we wanted to drink
a lot, and we wanted to dance a lot, and above all, we did not
want to hear anything about what was being discussed in the
National Assembly.

*   *   *   *   *

The inoffensive little town began to put on airs. When
Councillor Ebert was elected President of the Republic, the
whole place buzzed with the fact that he had reviewed the
guard of honour in a soft grey felt instead of a top hat. The
sixty Berlin policemen were dignified representatives of the
metropolis. Frau Zietz's every word was excitedly commented
on at the local tea parties. When Professor Traub lectured,
several houses flew the old monarchist flags. The shops were
literally besieged when it was known that the first consignment
of Italian oranges had arrived. On Sundays the band of the
Landesjäger used to play. The girls of the town refused to be
seen with anyone but officers in public places, or at the very
least with sergeant-majors. The councillors took their wine at
the Elephant or the Swan in the evenings and bewailed the
future of Germany.

In March came the report of the rising in Berlin. At the
same time things began to get lively in central Germany. One
division of the *Landesjäger* was moved to Gotha, others prepared
to go to Halle. In the industrial districts in central Germany
there were threats of strikes. Starving crowds held mass-
demonstrations in the towns. Kurt Eisner had been shot in
Munich on February 21st. After that, the members of the

Bavarian Parliament tried, not without effect, to exterminate each other. Anarchy ruled in the Ruhr district. The necessaries of life were distributed very irregularly from the seaports. In the east, a sort of guerilla warfare was being carried on between our frontier guards and bands of marauding Poles.

Gradually the terms of the Peace were made known.

We soldiers wandered about the streets restlessly. There was no doubt in our minds that these gentlemen in Weimar would accept the terms.

Lieutenant Kay collogued privately with some of us. He talked to Kleinschroth's squad; he collected the cadets; in the billets he sat and talked with the sergeants, in the canteens with people from other battalions, in the Weimar cafés with officers of all ranks.

Gradually he collected some twenty men. They recognized each other by a look or a word and knew that they were all of one mind. They were centres of unrest in their companies. They had not yet got over the war. War had moulded them; it had given a meaning to their lives and a reason for their existence. They were unruly and untamed, beings apart, who gathered themselves into little companies animated by a desire to fight. There were plenty of standards round which they might rally. There were still plenty of strongholds to be attacked; plenty of enemies were still encamped round about them. They had realised that this peace was a delusion – they would have no part in it. An unfailing instinct had kept them in the army. They fought anywhere and everywhere, because they liked fighting. They wandered about the country because they always saw the chance of fresh excitement, because new adventures beckoned to them. Yet each one of them had a different idea of what he wanted. The master word had not been given them. They vaguely divined what this word was – they even uttered it and then felt abashed. They tried it and tested it with secret tremblings. They slurred it over in conversation and yet it obsessed them. The word was weather-worn yet enticing, potent but unsubstantial, idealised in the subconsciousness but unspoken. The word was " Germany."

Where was Germany? In Weimar, in Berlin? Once it had been at the front, but the front had crumbled. Then it was supposed to be at home, but home had failed them. Was it where the German people were? But they were screaming for food and thinking of their stomachs. Was it the State? But the State was fussing about its constitutional form. Germany survived in venturesome minds. Germany was there where swords were unsheathed for her; she was there where armed bands were threatening her existence; she shone resplendent where those who were informed by her spirit wagered all they possessed for her sake. Germany was at her frontiers.

We had been enlisted for service on the frontier. Orders kept us in Weimar. We were guarding a crowd of quill-drivers while our frontiers were threatened. We were living in fusty billets, while French troops marched into the Rhineland. We exchanged shots with undisciplined sailors, while the Poles were burning and pillaging in the east. We drilled and formed guards of honour for umbrellas and soft felt hats; but in the Baltic States German battalions were on the move.

On April 1st, 1919, Bismarck's birthday – the Right Wing eschewed patriotic festivities – twenty-eight of us, led by Lieutenant Kay, deserting Weimar and our division, left for the Baltic States.

CHAPTER VI

ADVANCE!

LOOKING through our field-glasses we could see the outlines
of a farmyard. With my gun beside me, I lay close to the
railway embankment, on a mound covered with undergrowth.
Next to me lay Lieutenant Kay, his short rifle in front of him.
On various parts of his person were disposed a light-pistol,
bags of hand-grenades, a cartridge belt, field-glasses and a map
case. Round about us in the velvety darkness crouched the
Hamburgers with light machine-guns. The trench mortars
stood in a pit with their muzzles pointing threateningly up-
wards. The Eckau rippled in the darkness in front of us,
and occasional stars were reflected waveringly in the narrow,
black, sluggish water. In the shadow of the wood stood the
armoured train steaming gently. The big guns were somewhere on the railway embankment, in charge of the Pioneers.
Everything was brought as near the enemy as we could bring it.
The whole atmosphere of the night was ominous and lowering.
Flexed bodies waited ready to leap forward in one line from the
Bay of Riga to Bauske.

Behind us over Tetelmünde the sky was dyed a dull red. No
challenges were heard from the sentries, no shots disturbed the
night. I felt to make sure that my gun was all right; the belt
had been inserted and the first cartridge was in position for
firing. It stood stiffly on its spidery legs, its lever raised,
its jacket filled. I laid my head on my arms. We were waiting
for the signal, and the Bolsheviks in front guessed nothing of
what was happening.

THE OUTLAWS

With every breath a curious acrid smell filled my lungs. Its fragrance permeated my whole body almost painfully. The scent of this Courland earth made me feel dimly how much this land had to offer us. I dug my fingers into the rich earth which seemed to be sucking my strength. We had conquered this ground: now it demanded some requital from us.

It was certainly not on account of the Bolsheviks that we lay here in ambush, parched with thirst and furiously longing for something, we hardly knew what. The whole front was under the spell of a kind of fierce driving power, a raging determination, a godlike frenzy, which clamped with an iron band the medley of soldiers and peasants; which gave aim to the waverers, hammered cowards into heroes, turned serfs into conquerors and drove a whole people to defend its frontiers. But we were like children with no one to guide our steps. We had sallied forth to protect our boundaries, but they seemed to have melted away. We ourselves had become the boundary, for we kept the paths open.

The Baltic troops, who were massed on the road behind the corner of the forest awaiting the signal for the attack, did not trouble to wonder why they were taking part in this struggle. For them this war was sacred. They were furiously intent on reconquering Riga; for it was their own town and in its citadel lay their hostages, who were threatened with a similar fate to that of the Mitau hostages. I had accompanied Lieutenant Kay when he went to visit some Baltic families who told us stories of the Bolshevik régime in Mitau. There was not a single family from which at least one member had not been carried off or tortured or killed. Often whole families had been exterminated together with their servants; in other cases none but a few of the women were left alive and of these only the older ones. Things had come to such a pass that anyone who spoke German in the streets was liable to be slaughtered out of hand; the word 'German' was regarded as an abominable insult, and the Germans themselves as the most loathsome spawn of the earth. The Baltic girls were reft from their homes; their strong, quiet virtue was insulted; their stern chastity outraged; till, after being tortured by whole gangs, they lay naked and torn in the filth of the streets or in the prison-yard, while their menfolk were shot shot down over their dead bodies. When the Baltic *Landeswehr*, maddened with rage, dared, without orders, to make a final attempt on Mitau and attacked the town from the Tuckum side, the hostages were driven into the courtyards of their prisons and bunches of hand-grenades were thrown in among the closely-herded men. Shot after shot was fired into the massed bodies, so that they were tossed and torn until finally nothing remained of them but a uniform, bloody, shapeless pulp. Other hostages were taken by Red horsemen, tied to their horses and dragged from Mitau to Riga, being beaten all the while with knouts. All along the road to the Eckau the *Landeswehr* was continually finding the corpses of its own people. The vault of the Dukes of Courland had been broken open and the bodies propped up against the walls with German steel helmets on their heads and riddled with shots fired in senseless malice. The perpetrators were Red regiments of Letts revenging themselves on their former lords in Mitau.

The reason which had caused us to be here fighting instead of staying quietly at Weimar, seemed to us to have been explained very inadequately when we enlisted. In the days of the Revolution, the German 8th Army Corps in the Baltic Provinces had simply deserted and had made for home, plundering and undisciplined. Meanwhile, the Red army, in which the elements of a new national and social pride mingled strangely with an Asiatic arbitrariness, pushed its way into the unguarded land. Riga fell, then Mitau; and the ragged horde, confident of victory, swept on as far as Windau,

There the Baltic troops collected and offered the first resistance, and the weak German frontier corps joined them. Ulmanis' Lettish Government, which had fled from Riga to Libau, promised the German volunteers land to settle on, eighty acres of land with important credits and higher rates of pay, if they could reconquer the country. The German troops were commissioned to guard East Prussia and at the same time the eastern frontiers of Germany. The German commander, General Count Rüdiger von der Goltz, thought that the order could only be carried out by taking the offensive. The campaign began in snow and ice, while the first gales of spring howled through the woods. Mitau was delivered. The new front line was established on the banks of the Eckau. Riga, the Baltic town, lay beyond the dark woods, the object of fierce desire. Only the most confused rumours reached the German front from there, gasped from the exhausted lungs of Baltic fugitives, intercepted from the Soviet wireless, forcibly extracted from Red prisoners. But the German Government, fearing the threat of the *Entente*, forbade the German troops to liberate the town.

The appearance of these troops in the Baltic States recalled the days when the Teutonic knights had brought a new faith and a new race into the land. Each company carried its own standard and fought its own battles. The standard of the Hamburg corps was the flag of the German Hansa-towns. But above the flag flew a black streamer, and when I asked one of the Hamburgers whether it was a sign of mourning – and I was really rather embarrassed by my own question – he whistled the first few bars of a pirate song. So it was not mourning; Klaus Störtebecker had long since sailed under a black pennant in his ship the *Speckled Cow*, and at one time it flew over the craft of the great Victualling Guilds. So the Hamburgers' flag had a special meaning in the Baltic States, and it fluttered from every baggage waggon belonging to the company as well as from the field kitchen; in some of the battles, even, it was carried before them – that was possible in the Baltic States, where everything was possible – and it shone blood-red with its narrow white towers and the dark line across. So it often happened – and no doubt this was intentional on the part of the Hamburgers – that the Bolsheviks hesitated to shoot, thinking that it might herald Red troops; and it also sometimes happened that the Baltic companies shot at the Hamburgers – for the Baltic troops could not see anything Red without shooting at it – but then the Hamburgers only had to shout 'Hummel, Hummel!' and the fusillade stopped; for the Hamburgers and their war-cry were well known all over Courland.

They were so well known that the Jews and shopkeepers carefully closed their premises when the Hamburgers entered Mitau for a short rest. The soldiers from other companies came out into the streets and had a good look at the Hamburgers, usually pretty dubiously, for they certainly did not march in the regulation manner: they proceeded in one long line on each side of the street, carried their rifles as they pleased and clubs in their hands. They had allowed hair and beard to grow long; and they only saluted officers whom they knew and liked. It was a great honour for an officer to be saluted by the Hamburgers; for this remarkable corps obeyed none of the ordinary military laws; it was voluntary in its formation and refused to recognise any rules but those of its own choosing. The commander's will was their sole law; and this will was the natural resultant of the dynamic forces which animated the whole company. It was dangerous to tread on the toes of any one of them, for the man who was careless enough to do so instantly had the whole pack at his throat. And whenever Hamburgers and Bolsheviks encountered each other – which occurred pretty frequently, since, if orders kept the rest of the front quiet, the Hamburgers made war on their own – they met with a mutual deadly-polite respect. It occasionally happened that one of the crowd sinned against the rigid laws of the clan. In such a case the company held a short court-martial, and after the mutineer had been buried, the Hamburgers went on, singing their pirate song, completely ignoring all forms of red-tape.

The Hamburg corps had originally been a battalion. But in the very first skirmishes during their advance on Mitau the battalion was so decimated, that Lieutenant Wuth, their commanding officer, was thankful to be able to form even a company with the small remnant that was left.

The Hamburg corps was mainly composed of men from Lower Saxony, who had formerly been in the Hansa regiments, and whom Lieutenant Wuth had gathered round him during the return from the Western front and in the confusion of the march through Germany to the East Prussian frontiers.

Lieutenant Wuth was a big, dark, angular man. One tooth protruded over his lip like a boar's tusk, and he had a habit of whetting it on the bristles of his moustache. He used to change his cap before every fight for a velvet tam o'shanter such as is worn by the various German leagues of youth. Even in pre-war days this lanky man had found that the only possible life for him was among those who could not breathe the stuffy air of conventionality, who dreamt of revolt and of the storm which was to sweep through the fusty rooms. And if there was anything like discipline among the Hamburgers in these days, it was to be attributed to their respect for his character and for his unfailing luck.

Thus the Hamburgers, whose ranks I joined, represented a special type among the armies in the Baltic States.

Among these troops there were plenty of regular units with reliable officers; crowds of restless adventurers, on the lookout for a fight and with it the chances of loot and the relaxation of ordinary rules of conduct; patriots who could not bear the idea of the break-down of law and order at home and who wished to guard the frontiers from the incursion of the Red flood; there was the Baltic *Landeswehr*, recruited from the local gentry, who were determined at all costs to save their seven-hundred-year-old traditions, their noble and vigorous yet fastidious culture, the eastern bulwark of German civilisation; and there were German battalions, consisting of men who wanted to settle in the country, who were hungering for land. Of troops desirous of fighting for the existing Government there were none.

The like-minded ones were soon dissociated from the general mass which was swept eastwards by the crash on the western front. We seemed suddenly to have collected as if at a secret signal. We found ourselves apart from the crowd, knowing neither what reward we sought nor what goal. The blood suddenly ran hotly through our veins and called us to adventure and hazard, drove us to wandering and danger, and herded together those of us who realised our profound kinship with one another. We were a band of warriors, extravagant in our demands, triumphantly definite in our decisions.

What we wanted we did not know; but what we knew we did not want. To force a way through the prisoning wall of the world, to march over burning fields, to stamp over ruins and scattered ashes, to dash recklessly through wild forests, over blasted heaths, to push, conquer, eat our way through towards the East, to the white, hot, dark, cold land that stretched between ourselves and Asia – was that what we wanted? I do not know whether that was our desire, but that was what we did. And the search for reasons why was lost in the tumult of continuous fighting.

The sky still glowed over Tetelmünde, silhouetting the

maze of branches. Did the Bolsheviks really know nothing of our plans? All the last few days there had been unrest along the German front. The troops were on the point of taking matters into their own hands and attempting the attack on Riga, just as the German Government had craftily informed the Chief-of-Staff in answer to his representations, that it could not prevent the Baltic *Landeswehr* from storming Riga, and that then the German troops could make their own lines secure.

In the evening when the order to advance was read, a sudden jolt seemed to wake the troops. And while the men dispersed to pack up and to prepare, the deserted houses burst into flames on all sides. The officers ran up and down swearing, but red tongues of fire shot through one roof after another, illuminating the gloomy edge of the forest, lighting up the dark sky in every direction with a weird glow. The whole of Tetelmünde was on fire, as though it were one magnificent torch, lighted on the impulse of a lunatic, in whom suddenly man's lust for destruction, the most primitive lust of all, had arisen and clamoured for an outlet.

● ● ● ●

The dial of my wrist watch was luminous and told me that it was just on half-past one. I looked at Lieutenant Wuth, who was standing behind a tree not far off, with his eyes glued to his field-glasses. He moved, stooped a little and put a light-cartridge into his pistol. He pushed it home with a little click.

In the distant farmyard a cock crowed. The whole front seemed to be holding its breath. A sort of whisper went through the woods. Innumerable bodies came to attention. In the east a pale glimmer appeared in the sky. Suddenly Lieutenant Wuth raised his arm and fired high into the air.

The whole line became one continuous roar. I spun round and pushed the lever. I could not hear the rattling of my gun any more. The armoured train had arrived and was vomiting long spurts of flame. Every barrel was spitting fire, and we lay man by man, gun by gun, machine-gun by machine-gun. Everything was lost in the furious uproar. The mist drifted heavily through the undergrowth and hung in long streamers in the branches. The farmyard was hidden in a cloud of dust. Trembling, I hung on to the lever of my gun. My eyes strained over the sight to the uncertain target.

I saw Hoffmann hanging half over his gun. He pressed the trigger with his hand and grunted his satisfaction, looking most ferocious. Along the edge of the forest was now one long string of berserk men. We fired whatever would fly out of the barrels. The fields in front of us were razed bare, and it seemed as though all the confusion, all the long-pent-up fury in us were bursting from our finger tips and turning to metal and flame. Out with them! Out with fire, steel, smoke and noise!

In the pale grey light of the dawn the Pioneers threw planks over the water and the armoured train advanced puffing and blowing. The edge of the forest suddenly came alive, and men swarmed out of the bushes. The Eckau splashed indignantly into rings, as the Hamburgers jumped into the shallow water, waded through with rifles held high above their heads, and quickly climbed out on the farther bank.

Hardly had we crossed the narrow stream than bullets hissed round our legs from the distant earthworks. We pushed on, in our ears the screaming of the shells, in our lungs the damp fumes of explosives. At first clumsily, then more and more quickly, we staggered and leapt over craters filled with water, we stumbled over furrows, and came into the zone of fire. With every movement our rage increased and made us feel that any opposition was impudent defiance which must be crushed.

The Hamburgers had already got there. I saw hand-grenades

flying into the trench, and figures rising from the ground and running back. I seized my gun and emptied a whole belt. Spikes of barbed wire tore at my legs. Furiously I felt that it was an act of personal revenge that gunner No. 3 fell at that moment, shot through the head, and with the gun on top of him. 'Leave him,' I shouted to gunner No. 2, who immediately let go the gun-carriage, so that it rushed rattling down the slope. We leapt into the trench. A shapeless brown body lay across the parapet; I stepped on a hand, I fell into a hole which was covered with planks; I heard groans; dim, discoloured faces with tousled hair were embedded in the mud; a man crouched beneath the dead bodies and held a bleeding arm towards me. I had to go on. Behind the breastwork I heard the dull explosions of hand-grenades. I ran as if I were mad or drunk. The trench widened. Three or four Hamburgers slipped out of a smoking dug-out. We climbed over several *chevaux de frise* which barred our way; emerged from the trench and reached the sparse undergrowth which grew among the birches. A machine-gun began firing at us from somewhere in the woods. The Hamburgers broke through the bushes. A clearing appeared, and suddenly, unexpectedly, ten or twelve dirty, ragged figures stood before us, threw down their rifles with a clatter, put up their hands and came uncertainly towards us. But the Hamburgers, hardly stopping, went ahead, and shot straight at these miserable wretches. The men stood still, then a few of them sank to their knees and fell; and one doubled up with a shrill long-drawn-out scream. Murawski, who was gunner No. 2, leapt forward, swinging the butt-end of his automatic, so finally I too fired. I sped past the last few men who were left standing, crashed through the undergrowth, towards the sound of the machine-gun.

In the middle of the forest, beside a narrow clearing, was a small farmhouse. The firing was coming from there. We raced through the wood, feeling nothing but a desire to still the raging of our blood by making a lightning attack on the house. Hoffman panted along beside me with his gun. The wheel of the trench mortar ground on a footpath. Murawski ran back to fetch our gun. We collected such Hamburgers as were in the neighbourhood by shouting the war-cry. At the edge of the clearing we threw ourselves down. One group made a flank attack. The machine-gun spat furiously at them from the farm. While they were getting ready for a second attempt and the belt was rattling through Hoffman's gun, the first shell was fired from the trench mortar. Before the planks and spars fell back to the ground, the earth was thrown up in three or four places round the house, and a deafening crash resounded through the woods. We left our gun to look after itself and ran for dear life.

It was now full daylight. We had already come to the first fences, when a man ran out of the farmyard. 'We've got some prisoners!' he shouted. And then: 'They say Kleinschroth's somewhere in those bushes.'

Kleinschroth had gone off two days before on patrol duty and had not returned. I ran towards the spot indicated and found Hoffman crashing through the bushes too. There lay Klein-schroth.

But was that Kleinschroth? That mess of rags and blood! Could that ever have been human? On the brown soil lay a mixture of clods of earth, blood, bones, entrails, scraps of clothing. The head lay apart, cut off, so that the wound gaped at the skies; there was a thin, dry trickle of blood from the mouth to the chin; the eyes were open, showing only the whites. The ground all around the body had been stamped on, trampled on, kicked up – and among the blood and confusion were little white heaps, almost dispersed by the wind – my God, what was it? – It was salt.

'Prisoners, did you say?' I asked the man. 'Prisoners?' Hoffman had already gone. I raced furiously towards the house. There were the prisoners, and one of them was wearing a blue German hussar uniform with a red sash. 'What, Germans?' he snarled and leapt at him and crashed his fist in the man's face. He recoiled, stumbled and stood up again. 'Now he'll hit back!' I thought, as he pulled himself together, the muscles of his back stiffened and he grew pale, paler than I had ever seen anyone in my life. Two people caught Hoffmann and held him, while he tried, raging, to get at the man, hissing: 'What, *Germans?*' –

'Yes,' said the prisoner suddenly, and spat the words through his teeth, 'I am a German,' and there was boundless hatred in his tone. 'There are a great many of us over there,' and suddenly he roared: 'We shall never rest till the damned country has been wiped off the map . . .'

There were in all eight prisoners: three Letts, two Czechs, one Pole, one Russian from the Volga district, one Ukrainian and then the German. This German had been a prisoner of war in Siberia, had joined the Red troops and now belonged to the Liebknecht regiment, which was chiefly made up of German and Hungarian prisoners of war. He had originally come from Saxony and had been an electrical fitter. During the short interrogation he said that he had no relations in Germany and that he was a Communist. He had been in command of the men who were in the hut in the woods. Kleinschroth had fallen into his hands wounded and he had ordered him to be put to death. He added that he did not care what happened to him now.

Hoffman was already digging furiously at Kleinschroth's grave. The prisoners were taken to the wall of the barn. They went quietly; the Letts and the Czechs took up their positions almost as if they were in a hurry, staring sullenly into the

70

muzzles of the rifles. The Russian and the Ukrainian, both of them peasants with tangled fair beards and very ragged uniforms, took off their caps and seemed as though they were going to cross themselves, but in the end desisted. The Pole trembled and began to cry softly. The German slouched along carelessly.

Lieutenant Kay who had arrived during the storming of the farm, suddenly turned and went away. I looked at Hoffmann digging Kleinschroth's grave and wondered whether to go and help him. A volley rang out.

Then we marched on. We went through the wide dense belt of forest and came to a road, where we assembled. The main body of troops was already there, and the wide street was crowded with men and waggons, all of them pressing forward. We squeezed in amongst them. Just before we got to Thorensberg we heard that Riga had fallen.

The von Medem section of the Baltic *Landeswehr*, with the Baltic shock-troops under Lieutenant Baron Hans von Manteuffel, and the German storm-battery under Lieutenant Albert Leo Schlageter, had broken through the enemy on this road at the first attack. The section had gone ahead at a mad pace; it took no notice of the straggling groups of Bolsheviks on each side of the road; hurtled past occupied and fortified places, raced across barricades and made straight for Riga. Behind this section the battle began again, but the German battalions which were following soon found the weak places and smashed the already breaking Red front. The Baltic troops meanwhile pushed through the enemy, who were taken by surprise, and, unswerving, dashed through the outskirts of the suburb Thorensberg, pressed on through the town, gasping for breath their faces encrusted with dirt, sweat and blood, gained the bridge, broke down such slight resistance as there was, occupied the bridge head, repulsed a furious counter-attack, sent a column over the sluggish Dwina into Riga itself, and kept guard over the single bridge which gave access to the town.

These shock-troops, raging furiously, suppressed the opposition they encountered in Riga, shot down any who stood in their way through the frenzied town, till they reached the citadel and arrived raving and yelling and almost at the end of their strength, just in time to free the hostages who had already been driven down to the place of execution. At four o'clock in the afternoon of May 22nd, 1919, Riga was in the hands of the Germans. Lieutenant von Manteuffel, the Baltic national hero, fell at the bridge, shot through the head, at the moment of his greatest triumph.

All this we heard on the road. This and more. For while we were shouting confused congratulations to them rumours reached us of fierce fighting in the south-east near Bauske. Captain von Brandis had been ordered to advance with his corps, which represented the right exposed flank of the German front. But it was just at that point that the Bolsheviks had decided to take the offensive. The Red army had planned to break through near Bauske as far as the Mitau-Schaulen railway, which was the main artery for the German front. The Red regiments began to advance in that direction and came right up against the Germans. Brandis and his men lay before Bauske in an exposed place, and wave after wave of the Red army dashed through their weak defence.

When we reached the first houses at Thorensberg, we got our orders. We were to leave this part of the line and proceed south-east. Our battalion was to go to Friedrichstadt via Bad Baldon and Neuguth, to deliver a flank attack on the Bolsheviks, so as to give Brandis a breathing space.

* * * *

Lieutenant Wuth woke me very early. An advance party was to be sent to Neuguth, consisting of some Hamburgers and my gun. The rest of the company was to follow immediately on country carts which had been requisitioned during the night. It was three o'clock in the morning and broad daylight when we came into the courtyard and got on to the carts which stood waiting for us. The Hamburgers went ahead. I had to load the ammunition on to my cart and then we ambled along behind. From the observation tower at Bad Baldon a man shouted to me that we should probably find that Neuguth had already been evacuated; the village with its wrecked church could be seen clearly from the top of the tower.

We squatted on our carts slackly and drowsily, with our belts loose. The horse trotted along contentedly in front under its high collar. The little wooded hills round Bad Baldon looked fresh and charming in the awakening day. After all, it was very pleasant to be riding along in the sunlight, through this wonderful peaceful landscape. The tension of the last few days had mercifully relaxed and everything seemed very much a matter of course. Behind me, on the back of the cart, Gohlke and Bestmann, two gunners belonging to my crew, were chatting in low tones and rather sleepily about the war. Both were old soldiers and had fought on the western front through all the four years. Famous names lapped gently against drowsy ears. One of them mentioned Douaumont – spoke of Captain von Brandis, of whom it was said that he was never seen unless fighting or drunk – he had become famous during the attack on Douaumont. I closed my eyes and my mind was soothed by the monotony of their voices. Those names, falling like stones splashing into a still lake – Flanders, Verdun, the Somme, Chemin des Dames – hardly seemed real in this sunlit, gently shimmering landscape, and gave one an even deeper feeling of peace. And yet these terrible words, recalling blood and the clash of arms, and events which I could only faintly imagine, had once been the only reality for these men who now referred to them so casually. Bestmann and Gohlke were gossiping to rest their minds; but they grew more and more monosyllabic until finally Gohlke said with a little sign: 'After all, this isn't a real war.' They were silent for a space. A lark rose from a field. Over the top of a gentle slope we could just see the cupola of the Neuguth church tower.

'If this isn't a war, what are you here for?' I said lazily over my shoulder.

'What you don't understand is this,' said Bestmann with all the superiority of an old soldier, 'We're only marking time. The war isn't over yet, not by a long chalk. The war'll never be over. Anyhow we shan't live to see the end.'

'You're right there,' replied Gohlke weightily. 'But what's the use of our going back to Germany? We don't fit in any more. They think the war's over. Yes, my boy, mark this: So long as we haven't won the war, it isn't over!'

'Here's hoping!' said Bestmann. 'And now I'm going to have a spot more sleep.' And he leant his head against a box of ammunition and shut his eyes. The wheels grated lazily in the dust of the road.

The other two carts jolted along quietly ahead of us. After what seemed a long time the front ones halted. Sergeant Ebelt of the Hamburgers came to me and said he supposed we'd better get off the carts now and stalk Neuguth. 'Oh rot,' I grumbled. 'there's nothing doing there. We'll see soon enough if anything is up.'

Ebelt laughed. 'Oh, all right then, we'll drive.'

So we did, but a little more carefully than before. There was no sign of anything in Neuguth.

The first houses appeared. We clattered cheerfully up to them. A few chickens flapped over the fence. 'Oi, farmer!' shouted Ebelt and cracked his whip. An unshaven peasant came to the door of the first house and disappeared again as

soon as he saw us. Ebelt laughed and we drove on. We arrived
in the village itself. Nobody was to be seen, except a girl
standing at the window of one of the houses overlooking the
market place. Ebelt spoke to her and she came out at once.
She was a pretty little person, dressed quite fashionably,
obviously not a peasant. We all stared at her. And the girl
talked German! And with such a charming voice. She told us
that the Bolsheviks had cleared off the evening before, thank
goodness. There might be a few left over there near the farm.
She herself was a fugitive and was living at the chemist's. She
was a Russian, but the chemist was a Balt. The Reds had done
a lot of damage in the place. 'But now you're here!' she said
and smiled. Ebelt grunted contentedly. We said that we'd just
go and have a look at that farm. Then we'd come back. 'So
long then . . .' She nodded and waved to us as we went on.

We saw very few people. They either could not or would not
understand us. 'Bolshevik nix,' they said. We believed them
and went on to the farm. There were no Bolsheviks there
either. Ebelt decided not to come back the same way. He
wanted to go along the chestnut avenue as far as the church
and rake round after Reds in that direction. There was sure
to be a road from there back to the market place. He had
noticed a narrow passage leading off beside the chemist's shop.
I replied that I supposed he'd better go to the church first,
but that I'd go back to the chemist's and wait for him there.
Ebelt seemed to hesitate. Then he grinned, nodded and went
off. I turned my cart and drove back. Lord, how good the
world seemed!

I sat in front right on the edge of the cart. The others sat
well inside, dangling their legs comfortably. The chemist's
shop was already in sight. We clattered over the cobbles towards the house.

Suddenly we were startled by a crack. It came from close

beside us, just by our heads. The horse reared, then gave one bound and raced down the street. I flew off the cart, over-balanced, fell into the mud and was surrounded by filthy, leaping figures, who swung their rifles and continued to pepper the rapidly vanishing cart with shots. Three or four hurled themselves at me, beat me till I got up and dragged me away with them. I was a prisoner.

I hardly realised what had happened. One of them hit me right across my face with a whip or a stick and asked me something. I couldn't understand him. In fact I couldn't under-stand anything; my mind kept on repeating: 'I'm a prisoner; it's impossible; I'm a prisoner!' They yelled at me; I was dragged this way and that, and suddenly I was standing against a wall. It was white and dazzling in the sun. 'What am I standing here for?' I wondered. I couldn't realise why I stood up against that wall. I turned round and looked into the muzzles of their rifles. Then I understood what I was there for.

The muzzles were straight in front of me – little round black holes. Nothing existed in the world except those muzzles. Nonsense – there was nothing in the world except myself. But the black holes grew larger and larger; then they began to rotate and turned into round black discs. The discs changed to red, to yellow, and white and blue and green. Suddenly they divided and everything began to revolve gently. The whole world seemed to rise up to one side and there was nothing underneath, and then it just swung right over with a single large quiet movement. I felt terribly lonely. All around me was so cold. I was really quite alone. Nothing had ever existed except myself – I should surely have noticed if anything else had ever existed. I thought I would open my eyes, and then I discovered that I had never shut them. Now I found that my stomach was a glass ball. If it was joggled, the end of the world would come, for then it would burst like a soap bubble – and that must not be. I could not believe that I had ever been alive. No doubt I had simply imagined that I was alive. Life was all nonsense. So of course there was no death. If only it were not so blazing hot inside and so terribly cold outside. Somewhere about me there must be water – or perhaps ice. I did not know – and any way it did not matter. On the whole, it was rather good to know that one was all alone in the world and that really there was no world. And now I knew what colour everything was. Lilac. Just lilac. It was rather stupid that one could not move one's limbs, I thought – oh, of course, I had no limbs. So that was the end of it – the end of what? . . . What? . . .

What? . . .

Shots, shots, shots . . . a rushing wind.

Suddenly the blood flowed through my veins again, caught me, shook me, opened all my pores.

The Hamburgers were there – there was the flag! A dark bundle lay in front of me – a dead Bolshevik. And Ebelt ran past me and said: 'Lucky as usual!'

I lay down quite quietly. A little golden brown beetle climbed busily over absurd bits of plaster and vanished in a crack in the wall. And there was a little blue berry – all shiny – reflecting the whole world in its tiny orb.

CHAPTER VII

THE TURNING POINT

FOR four solid weeks we wandered about aimlessly. Under the burning June sun we marched through deep forests, over scented heaths and in the steamy marshes of this curious country. We bathed in the Aa, in the Eckau, in the Dwina. We explored from Friedrichstadt far into Latvia and from Bauske into Lithuania. We rumbled round the whole of that country on our little peasant-carts, visited dreary Lithuanian villages, lonely Courland farms, simple, clean Baltic country houses, asked questions, gave news, searched, examined – but the few stragglers at Neuguth who had nearly done for me were the last Bolsheviks we saw. We never discovered what had happened to the Red army; nor could we find out what was going on in Germany during this time.

We did not get to Riga. When we first heard about the unfortunate affair at Wend, the Hamburgers were rather pleased that the stuck-up Balts should have got it in the neck, and took with the pride of old soldiers the order that the battalion was to go to the new front-line at the Jâgelsee towards the end of June, 1919.

This was what had happened: The German advance towards Riga had obliged Moscow to recall even that part of the Red army which was fighting the White army under Yudenitsch at Lake Peipus. Thereby the Esthonian army which was fighting alongside of Yudenitsch, was relieved. Moreover, Yudenitsch and the Esthonians were supported by the English

Government which had also supported the former Lettish Minister-President, Ulmanis, who had been deposed on April 16th, 1919, by a *coup d'état* on the part of Baron Manteuffel in Libau. The Germans and the Balts and Pastor Needra, the Germanophil Lettish president, did not enjoy England's friendship. Far from it – for England had interests in the Baltic States. And where England has interests she is particular about the maintenance of the balance of Power among non-English states. This balance had been disturbed by the German successes. And Ulmanis made an alliance with the Esthonians against the Needra government, which latter was backed up by Baltic troops. Ulmanis was seconded by Colonel Semitan who commanded the Lettish troops in Northern Livonia. The responsibility for the border troubles, which had occurred during the advance of the Balts on Wend, was laid on Needra's Lettish government by the Esthonians; and small companies of Esthonians and of Semitan's Letts were disarmed in Wend. The *Landeswehr* hastened to the assistance of their countrymen, and some German battalions joined them. Ulmanis mobilised an Esthonian-Lettish army, with English equipment, English arms, English officers and English money. English men-o'-war suddenly began cruising about the Gulf of Riga; and English commissions sat around in the town itself. Civil war had begun.

The *Landeswehr* and a large part of the Iron Division, the Baden storm battalion and the Michael division advanced on Wend. They captured Wend but the enemy eluded them. The enemy was continually eluding them and nobody knew how strong were his forces nor where he was. But suddenly Wend was surrounded. Suddenly there were guns right and left, in front and behind. Suddenly shells fell on peacefully moving German columns. Suddenly the Baden storm battalion was hemmed in, surprised and set upon by troops who wore German steel helmets, spoke German and came from Germany, but yet were not Germans, nor yet Letts, Esthonians nor Englishmen. They were Lieutenant Goldfeld and his men, who had mutinied in the Baltic States and had then deserted to the Letts. The *Landeswehr* was attacked, was subjected to a terrible cross-fire in an exposed position, lost its formation, only just avoided a panic and was obliged to retreat. The new German front was formed along the Livonian Aa, near the lakes in front of the gates of Riga, and all available troops were rushed there.

Lieutenant Wuth whetted his tooth and said: 'Attention, gentlemen: We've been told to go to the Jägelsee. There's a bit of a mess-up there. The Esthonians have attacked. Why, I can't tell you. Why does anything happen? I expect England's at the bottom of it. Anyway, the German Government has forbidden. . . . Shut up, you at the back! . . . has forbidden German troops to enter Riga. Therefore we are now Lettish subjects . . . Ebelt, oblige me by not whispering. If you have anything to say, go and say it in Berlin. . . . Very good. Instructions have come from a higher authority that we are now Lettish subjects. Nobody's likely to enquire in any case. An excellent impression must be left by our march through Riga. There is to be no larking. I expect perfect discipline to be maintained. And no dirty songs.– By the right, quick march.'

The discipline of the Hamburgers was irreproachable. But it was peculiar. Nothing happened on the march through this highly respectable town except that they sang a beautiful song about a sailor. I only hoped that the Baltic damsels who waved to us in their light frocks all along the Alexander Boulevard did not understand the words!

At the bridge over the Aa between the lakes we occupied a hastily prepared position. Troops who were surging back shouted to us that the Esthonians were following close behind. We dug ourselves in, occupied the edge of the wood and the bank of the river and fortified a much-bombarded sugar factory as best we could in the darkness.

Next morning early the Esthonians appeared. There was a slight drizzle of rain. I lay in a hollow and had covered myself with a tarpaulin. Bestmann was on sentry duty. A terrific din wakened me. I jumped out and looked from my shelter. Instantly a machine-gun fired in our direction. We lay down flat in the hollow and Bestmann calmly began to dig himself in deeper. Four vicious shots which crashed into the damp meadows by the Aa thirty yards in front of us covered us with clods of earth and flying splinters. There was no preliminary whine from the shell.

'What on earth is it?' I asked.

'Whizz-bangs,' said Bestmann laconically.

I carefully raised my head to look over the parapet, but I soon dropped down again. There were four bangs behind us. We heard the discharge and the explosion practically simultaneously.

'They'll get us at the next effort!' said Bestmann and flattened himself against the parapet. This was getting really cheerful, I thought! – And was suddenly horribly frightened. 'The next effort . . .' I thought, and lay as close as I could to the ground. There . . . 'Too far,' said Gohlke, but something whistled and flicked uncomfortably close by my head and thudded into the ground; and then I felt as if a gigantic hand had hurled a ball of compressed air straight at my solar plexus. This was the first time I had been under shell-fire. So that was what it was like! There, again . . . my God! . . . 'I expect they're just inside the wood,' said Bestmann and peered carefully in that direction. 'It's only one battery.'

This comforted me to some extent, but I had a vague idea

that I ought somehow to demonstrate special courage before these two old soldiers. So I raised my head and said: 'But they can't . . .'

'Put your head down, man,' roared Bestmann. 'You b——y little fool. D'you think we all want to be killed?'

And those were the last words he spoke. For at that moment the earth opened before us, with a fearful concussion which hurled me to one side. There was a sheet of flame; a deafening explosion; everything seemed to fly into the air; all my veins felt as if they were bursting; it was like a thunderbolt from a raging heaven; there was a sickening stench, stones, steel, heat, noise. My head hit the ground and everything turned black and red.

Somebody shook me. All my joints felt as if they had been dislocated. I raised my head heavily and wondered if any part of me remained undamaged. The ground in front of me was covered with a curious greenish mist, the machine-gun was overturned and covered with mud, the whole surrounding earth was ploughed up. One man was moving, the other lay on his back. I crept over to them. Gohlke was crouching over the recumbent man. There lay Bestmann. A red stream flowed from his breast and he feebly lifted his hand. His begrimed face was greeny pale and a red foam bubbled from his lips which had turned thin and blue. His hand fell back again. I weakly laid my head on the ground, but was ashamed of myself directly. There was Gohlke, quietly trying to set up the gun again and it was up to me to help him with it.

Now came a series of dull explosions from somewhere behind us. Something spat and gurgled over our heads, there was a sort of moan, and then it hit the road just by the edge of the wood. With a muffled roar, six clouds arose from the ground and gradually mingled to form one gigantic one, which drifted slowly and heavily in our direction. Gohlke yelled to the Red-

Cross orderly. Our machine-guns began spitting on either side and our artillery sent shell after shell into the wood opposite.

So Bestmann was dead? I looked at him fearfully. The rain had gradually soaked through to my skin and my clothes hung on me like wet rags. The skin itself felt disgustingly soft and crinkled and it was certainly nothing but the cold and damp which made my teeth chatter. Gohlke laid a tarpaulin over the dead man and I lay down behind the gun. I ducked my head quickly when the firing began again, but the Esthonians were trying for our battery now and the shells whizzed over our heads.

All day long we lay there. From time to time their artillery fired and every now and then a machine-gun peppered us uncomfortably close. We saw hardly anything of the Esthonians; just once I spotted some flat steel helmets through my field-glasses, on a narrow path near the forest. Towards evening the bombardment grew more intense on both sides. The sugar-factory went up in flames and illuminated the whole country-side. We worked busily making our machine-gun emplacements. The A.S.C. men crept from dug-out to dug-out and told us that the Esthonians had taken the Riga waterworks and had cut off the town water supply.

It began raining again. Sergeant Schmitz who was a miner from the Ruhr came over and talked to me. After a time Lieutenant Kay came too. He told us that seven of the company had been killed up to the present, that there was fear of rioting in Riga; that we were situated at the most exposed point on the front, between the two lakes, by the bridge which would make access to the town easiest for the Esthonians. He also told us that there were no reserves behind us, only guns. We crouched in our dug-out, covered with mud and soaked to the skin, staring into the darkness.

Lieutenant Kay went on: 'Here we are, herded together

in this damned hole. We're the last miserable remnant of the German front line, which was once long enough to surround the whole of Central Europe and a bit over; which began at the Canal in Flanders and reached as far as Switzerland; which stretched from Switzerland over the Alps into northern Italy; from there over the Carso to Greece, and again from there to the Black Sea and the Crimea, to the Caucasus and right across Russia to Reval, not counting the various garrisons scattered about other parts of the world. And now there remain ourselves!' He stopped and no one said anything. He continued: 'Riga lies just over there. It is a German town after all, founded and built and inhabited by Germans. It's a pity you haven't seen the Schwarzhäupterhaus and the Peterskirche. The bridge over the Dwina is called the Lübeck-bridge and was built by the Pioneers of the 8th Army. It never belonged to Germany, though. Does it belong to Germany now? No, it's the capital of Latvia and we are Lettish subjects, if you please. That is to say, really we are German soldiers and belong to the German republic. Although, actually, there is no German Republic yet; they haven't finished talking in Weimar, and the peace-treaty isn't ready either. Of course, in reality it must be ready. In its essentials it must have been ready in 1914. Only we have no say in the matter. And the German Republic will be so constituted that everybody will notice how little say we've had. At any rate, here we are – the last remnant of the German front line, who wanted to have the fun of seeing the world – if it is fun to see it. We are German soliers who theoretically are not German soldiers, and we are defending a German town which theoretically is not a German town. And out there are the Letts and the Esthonians and the English and the Bolsheviks – and by the way, I like the Bolsheviks the best of all that crew – and farther south are the Poles and the Czechs, and then – well, you know it all as well as I do. In Weimar they are discussing

84

a match-duty and whether the flag shall be red, black and gold or whether they should keep the old glorious colours, as someone said to me, I forget exactly what it was – anyhow it doesn't matter. And so we hold the fort! I don't suppose we shall be able to hold it for long, all the same. Have you got a cigarette for me, youngster? Thanks.' Lieutenant Kay polished his monocle which was filmed with the rain. Schmitz went on smoking imperturbably and said: 'They won't get through here.'

All at once Gohlke fired off a star shell. We stared over the edge of the parapet. The trench was lit up in a weird fitful glow, in which everything looked completely different. Apparently the battery behind us had taken the light as a signal, for a few moments later six shots were fired. The shells whizzed over our heads and landed in the wood opposite. Immediately there was a spatter of machine-gun fire. Hoffmann's gun answered. After that the trench mortars began from behind the ruins of the sugar factory. The firing from the other side grew more intense and our battery retorted. The whizz-bangs joined in too; but from a fresh place. The whole front got lively and star shells were being discharged all over the place. Suddenly an ear-splitting crash drowned the barking of the smaller guns, then something went up into the air behind us droning and howling, and rushed over our heads with an infernal scream, so that we involuntarily ducked as though before some devilish power. Then it hit the ground so that the earth shook and trembled and groaned as though in agony. The forest over by the Esthonians crashed, splintered and quivered; for several seconds it seemed to totter and the mighty roar echoed from tree to tree into the far distance. Then there was absolute silence. It was as though our 21-cm. gun had taken umbrage at having its night's rest disturbed and had firmly and decisively put an end to the pyrotechnics.

THE OUTLAWS

Schmitz sucked at his pipe and said: 'They're not going to get through here. And I tell you this, sir, even if we have to give way here, which I don't expect we shall, or if we have to retreat from the town, which I don't expect either, we're still in existence. After all, it doesn't matter a damn where we are. It's even possible that we may have to get out of Courland – I don't think so, but it's possible – and it may even happen that the Hamburgers will be disbanded. But all the same, we're still alive. They can discuss things as much as they like in Paris, and what they're jabbering about in Weimar is even less important. Anyhow we're still alive and so long as we are, we shan't give anyone any peace. We shall simply go on fighting somewhere else. It doesn't look as if they could do without us for the next few years. And I tell you this much, sir, that *if* we don't make good here or we get back to Germany and don't get what we want there, and things go on just the same, and the gentlemen who got fat at our expense before the war, and who got fat during the war at the expense of our lives, and after the war are just as fat as ever,– do you remember that lot at Weimar, sir? – well, *if* the bourgeois and all these fine gentlemen think they can go on doing good business in our lives – and they don't care a damn about Germany, no, that they don't – then I know for one what I'm going to do. And I bet you, sir, and the ensign here, know it too.'

'Schmitz, you're a Spartacist,' said Lieutenant Kay.

'Just as you like, sir,' said Schmitz placidly.

I looked round, rather scared, but the others were lying asleep in their dug-outs. Gohlke was on sentry-duty, and sure enough he turned round and said to Kay: 'Anything for a quiet life!' and he grinned and went back to his place.

Kay said gloomily: 'Yes, I know. But it doesn't really help us. You were a miner, Schmitz, and I was once upon a time a student. Why on earth am I here? I might be considering my career too, and my future and my pocket. Then why the devil am I here? – Because I don't care a damn about all that, because I've got to get away from it; because, after all, I feel that this is more important than hair-splitting arguments and preparing divorce-cases and threatening people who can't pay their dentists' bills.– Hell and damnation, it's because I know that the war isn't really over yet; and because I know that I daren't behave any worse than the four thousand men from my old regiment who died and because I know – God! I don't really know anything except that we've got to carry on and it's our job and I'm ready to go through with it.'–

'Oh yes, we'll carry on, right enough,' said Schmitz and then we relapsed into silence.

We occupied that position on the Jägelsee for four days. During that time we were subjected to a bombardment that increased in severity every day. The wood in front of us seemed to be packed to the very edge with troops, and we gradually located twelve batteries. We had built ourselves a splendid machine-gun emplacement, but we had to be continually repairing the damage done by the enemy fire. The A.S.C. only came along at night; and the company had twelve casualties in those four days. The bank of the river was studded with craters and in the mornings it was covered with curious mounds due to the unceasing bombardment. However, the forest on the far side of the declivity was gradually laid bare too. Every now and then curiously hollow barking sounds were mixed with the explosions. Then somebody usually shouted 'Gas!'– but it was quite unnecessary, because everyone could see that it was gas and we had no gas masks, anyway; we used to dip our handkerchiefs in our water bottles and tie them over our mouths.

On the evening of the fourth day we were relieved by a company formed from the remains of the Michael division.

THE OUTLAWS

Our rest camp was in some woods only a few hundred yards behind the position we had just vacated. We could hear just as clearly as up in the front line how the bombardment grew fiercer and fiercer till it reached an intensity such as we had not experienced for a very long time. We stood to arms all night lest we should be called upon to go into action.

Meanwhile Lieutenant Wuth told us what had happened in Riga. Two days previously the Letts had suddenly taken up arms in the suburbs. Companies of Ballod-Letts – so-called after their leader, Colonel Ballod – who were loyal to the Government, patrolled the streets in the disturbed areas. During the afternoon, a shot was fired in Gertrud Street by a Lettish sentry, which killed a German soldier from one of the police companies. This shot acted as the signal for revolution. Immediately, the whole town, which had practically no German troops in it, was in an uproar. There was shooting at every street corner; the Ballod-Letts made common cause with the mob from the suburbs; shops were looted, Balts killed, the German patrols were fired on. The old cries: 'Clear the streets!' and 'Shut the windows!' made the whole affair seem important, as it used to in the old days of the German revolution; and the rapidly assembled German troops cleaned up the insurgent districts with the ease of long custom.

While armoured cars raced through the streets and fireballs set light to the Lettish guard-rooms, the Ballod-Letts explained suavely that the whole thing had been a misunderstanding. Finally the trouble was ended by the very conclusive arguments of the German guns. Nevertheless two days later the much-afflicted town was again under heavy gun fire. The Esthonians systematically poured shell after shell from their long-distance batteries into Riga. Our 21-cm. guns could, indeed, overpower the enemy artillery at times, but the town was in a state of unrest, which rose to a panic when eventually even the

Dwina bridge came under fire. Then we discovered that the shots came from off the sea. We found that it was the English men-o'-war that were firing on Riga. Had Needra's government declared war on England, we wondered? Had the German Government recommenced hostilities? Had German or Lettish or Baltic fishing smacks tried to scupper the English fleet? Nothing of the kind. It was just that England had interests and knew how to look after them. Fires broke out in many parts of the exposed city and, as the waterworks were in the hands of the Esthonians, there was no means of extinguishing them.

The shelling of the town continued throughout the night. Firing in the front-line usually died down to some extent at nightfall. We heard the thunder of the explosions in Riga quite clearly and saw the red glare of the burning buildings. In front of us we had the Esthonians, at our backs a bombarded and seditious city; the Dwina bridge, our only alley of retreat, was under English fire. 'By the way,' said Lieutenant Wuth, 'before I forget, the German Government has ordered all troops in the Baltic States to return to Germany immediately. Otherwise – goodness knows – loss of nationality, I think, and suspension of pay and leave, and I believe imprisonment, for anyone agitating on behalf of the Balts by word of mouth or in writing. Does anybody want to go back to Germany, by any chance?'–'Has it got to be at once?' asked a voice from the darkness.

At dawn the front grew very disturbed. We were continuously under fire, and the shells landed in the wood uncomfortably near our camp. We lay under the trees shivering and weary with watching, listening to the noise forward. Lieutenant Wuth put on his tam-o'-shanter. The firing grew more intense. We lay as flat as we could, when the shells hit the ground near us, splintering and uprooting whole trees.

THE OUTLAWS

I was on the right flank of the company with my gun. Lieutenant Kay with some of the Hamburgers was next to me.

After two and a half hours' bombardment there was a sudden lull. Lieutenant Kay said aloud: 'They're only beginners. They don't seem to have heard of creeping barrages or box barrages or any little jokes like that yet.' Some of the men laughed. We knew that the attack was beginning in front now. Our artillery-fire had ceased too. But all at once shots cracked through the woods. 'Lie down!' shouted Wuth.

On the road to the left of us there was a confused noise. 'They're coming, they're coming. . . .'– 'Quiet! keep still–!' Wuth suddenly stood by me. 'As soon as we advance, Ensign, you will rush your gun as far as the edge of the forest by the stream to the right and cover the bridge. Understand? The boys have got to get back by the bridge!'

A few fugitives came tearing back. 'The line's broken,' one of them shouted, 'Everyone's running.' Lieutenant Wuth stalked along towards the road with his long legs. The Hamburgers rose, thoughtfully murmured 'Hummel, Hummel,' and vanished into the bushes. I seized the gun, and four of us staggered through the wood with it, to the place indicated. To the left a terrific row was going on and the cracking of many rifles. We pushed on, gasping for breath. The forest thinned and we saw our position. We crawled to the edge on all fours, reached it without being seen and concealed ourselves in the bushes. The bridge now lay directly to the left of us and we commanded its whole length. I settled the gun into position, made it ready for firing, brought up ammunition, and then we waited.

On the bridge and on the small stretch of road that lay within our range there was not a soul to be seen.

We listened to the uproar on the road and in the wood. We were not feeling altogether happy. Suppose the Hamburgers failed to drive back the Esthonians! Gohlke seemed to have had the same idea, for he said: 'Take off your helmet and say your prayers.'–

'Is this still not a real war?' I enquired.

'Not quite,' he said, 'but it may turn into one.'

'Thanks,' said a third. 'We didn't often get as much attention as we've had to-day even when we were in Russia!'

We heard 'Hummel, Hummel' and other cries. They came to us faintly through the woods and seemed to be laden with a sullen dangerous fury. 'Isn't it coming nearer, Gohlke? – Damn it – yes, it is!' There they were – there. First singly then more and more of them; the woods were soon swarming with men and crowds came along the road. Now the machine-guns began in the wood, the whole road was one struggling mass, we could see confused bands of men fighting, throwing themselves on the ground, jumping up again, running back. I crouched by my gun with trembling clammy hands. We were posssesed by the excitement of the chase – ha! we had them in the line of fire at last! Gently, gently! Wait! There weren't quite enough of them yet – still not quite enough – just a moment – patience – now they were at the bridge. And the whole street was swarming. Now there were enough! I pressed the trigger.

The gun trembled between my knees like a living creature. The men on the bridge dropped, they fell, they splashed into the water. Dense groups of them dispersed, collapsed, were pressed from behind. They were obliged to pass that way, they all had to; the gun was going for all she was worth and the water was boiling in the jacket. I could almost feel in the trembling metal body of the gun how the shots hit the warm living human bodies. A devil's pleasure, but was I not one with my gun? Was I not a machine myself – cold metal? Shoot! Shoot! Into the midst of that wild tumult. Whenever did a gun have such a target? Now the cartridge belt had come to an end and we had to put in a fresh one; and now Gohlke was firing while I lay on the ground shivering and exhausted and never even looked up again.–

Later we went back to the camp. The Hamburgers did not return immediately, they were first gathering spoils in the forest. Fifteen prisoners were brought in; four of them were Englishmen and three Letts. The Hamburgers had lost two men – how many of the Letts were dead no one troubled to count. At the bridge alone there were so many that we could hardly see the surface of the road. All day long not a single shot was fired from the Esthonian front. Indeed the whole front seemed to be paralysed and we wondered why everybody had stopped shooting. We wondered no longer when Lieutenant Kay came and told us that an armistice had been declared. Our company was the only one which had stayed up the line.

The terms of the armistice were as follows: The Germans were to go back to the position at Olai; the Esthonians were to go back as far as the frontier of Esthonia and Latvia; The Ulmanis-Letts occupied the town of Riga; Pastor Needra was accused of high treason; and England had achieved all that she set out to achieve.

We retired. We marched through the town, the last German company to leave, and the Hamburgers sang their pirate-song.

CHAPTER VIII

MUTINY

IN pre-war days Olai had probably been a collection of rather scattered farms, and some centuries back possibly a frontier station. For the spot on the map which is marked Olai lies on the Misse, a little stream which is almost dried up in the summer and which meanders gently between the royal forest of Mitau on the one side and the swamp of Tirul on the other; moreover a sturdy obelisk with the arms of the duchies of Courland and Livonia stands on the bridge over the road which runs dead straight from Mitau to Riga. At any rate, this spot Olai was of no importance whatever until the time when it came to be decorated with little flags on the Russian and German staff maps. For it was at this point that the German military frontier touched the road, exactly half way between the capitals of the two Baltic provinces. Thus Olai had once more become a frontier town, until the German advance began in 1917, though indeed there was not a great deal left of the place itself. And now, two years later, German soldiers were again occupying the deserted post and were keeping a watchful eye on Riga, which lay fourteen miles away, beyond the mists which hung everlastingly over the Tirul marsh. Once again the boundary was here, and on the bridge stood sentries demanding the papers of every wayfarer. Three and a half miles nearer Riga, just outside the village of Katherinenhof, was the Lettish station, which up to 1917 had been on the Russian line. In between stretched the marsh, a wide, lonely expanse, harbour-

93

ing a few ragged bushes, a great many ditches and swarms of the most vicious mosquitoes. Parallel with the road, and at times cutting across it on to the other side, ran the railway embankment.

The hutments were still in good condition, solidly built with quite decent-sized, lofty rooms. They were not altogether bomb-proof, however, and the trenches seemed to have been dug rather with the loving care bestowed by a good citizen on the construction of a comfortable home in somewhat primitive surroundings. This position on the front cannot have been breathlessly exciting up to the year 1917. There were just a very few trenches along the edge of the forest most pleasingly embellished with now leafless birch trees. In the hutments, among rank grass, some bent iron bedsteads were still visible and came in most useful. Through the tremendously dense and overgrown wood with its swampy bottom ran roads paved with wooden blocks; at times one trod on rusty tins and forgotten pieces of equipment; sometimes even we found the remains of Bolsheviks who had been killed in the previous May.

The Hamburgers lived here for the three months, July, August and September in the year 1919. They mounted guard, they lay in the huts, they hunted fleas and made enormous bonfires every evening in the hope of keeping off the midges, and in order to be able to sit round the fire gambling, singing and drinking. They very seldom had leave to go to Mitau because they very seldom asked for it. They wandered through the woods, visited neighbouring garrisons, and every now and then made strictly prohibited excursions into the territory between the two frontiers and created all manner of curious noises in order to prevent the Lettish sentries from getting bored. If the Letts fired on them, this flagrant breach of the armistice was promptly reported at Mitau, and could only signify that preparations were going on for an iniquitous, malicious and treacherous attack.

Lieutenant Wuth had taken up his quarters in a tiny block-house, in which I imagine one of the staff officers of the Rhine *Jäger*-battalion must have lived. He was evidently of an extremely patriotic turn of mind, for over the entrance to this hut hung a wooden, now somewhat weather-beaten, sign on which was inscribed the earnest entreaty: 'Buy War Bonds!'

*   *   *   *

From the very beginning we felt the urgency of the influence which had driven us into this country, to this distant spot, over whose now deserted battlefields only occasional shots were fired. We felt its potency, even at the time when we still subscribed to accepted rules; when we still clung to those things which led our feet along the traditional ways; when we still had faith and in the consciousness of that faith thought ourselves sure of happiness. We recognized no problems. The world was ours to use. Our fathers had laboured at it and moulded it and had been proudly satisfied. We were meant to enter on a rich inheritance, to carry on faithfully the order of things as they had been handed down to us.

We had been taught what was our duty and what were the privileges we were to cherish. We shunned no trial; and the generation which went to war in the passionate days of 1914 believed that the coming storms would clear the air, and that all was predestined to give us a fuller realisation of our capacities and of the unchanging soul of Germany. No secret was made of our victories – everyone was intoxicated with glory and valour, the whole nation formed one long triumphal procession.

All at once our illusions were rudely dispelled. Suddenly grim, mysterious apparitions attacked the walls of our glorious realm, and found many weak spots: in some places the delusive

95

plaster fell off, and in others the decayed stones crumbled away. The army was paralysed, it was engulfed in filth, in mud, in fire; a ghostly finger traced the boundaries of our land in blood. We had expected to dominate war and it had dominated us.

*   *   *   *

The men who left the trenches in 1918 realised that in order to gain our individuality we must lose the war. They had discovered the great change in themselves. They saw that nothing was certain but that anything was possible. They came – still believing in their country – and found that it was as it were an open festering wound, at whose edges rough hands were pressing. They stood among the ruins and listened with incredulous astonishment to the catchwords and theories which were hawked about as the treasures of the future and as the wisdom and truth of the present. And since they had learnt under the shadow of death to distinguish truth from falsehood, they were not easily duped. They quietly began to do what was needed. A good many of them turned aside rather disdainfully, pinning their faith to nothing but themselves. They returned to their offices, their professions; but they were full of anxiety, they were very lonely, and terribly disillusioned.

There were others whom war still held as in a vice. They saw failure everywhere and felt that they were called upon to be the saviours of their country. There were many who thought that some message must come; but what this message was none knew, though all awaited the summons.

Feeling had not yet been wedded to Reason. We were ready to answer the call of our blood; and what was of real importance was not so much that what we did should be the right thing, but that we should take some action to save us from the lethargy of the times.

*   *   *   *

MUTINY

We kept things lively with 'Shut the windows!' – 'Clear the streets!' and so on! – the most efficient part of the German army went on because it could not help itself; went through the towns fully accoutred, each man charged with a suppressed, aimless energy, knowing that he must fight, fight at all costs, whatever his political aims.

But we who were still fighting under the old colours, had saved our country from chaos – God forgive us, we sinned against the spirit. We thought we were saving the country – and we only saved the bourgeosie.

An embryo thrives better in a state of chaos than in one of order. Lethargy is the enemy of all progress. Since we had saved our country from chaos, we had shut the door to development and had given free passage to lethargy.

        *   *   *   *

Those who recognised this fact hoped that affairs would take a fresh turn. Refusing to resign themselves to matters as they were after the collapse, they had vague hopes of salvation from the East. They felt intuitively that the upshot of the struggle must be to weaken every tie which bound us to the West. To re-establish these ties would mean surrender; would mean submission to the deadly uniformity which gives the West its prodigious power on this globe.

The war had left the way open for us towards the east. Among the multitudes of soldiers in post-war Germany only a small number came to the frontiers, and of these again only a very few went on into the Baltic States. The ultimate reason for our fighting in Courland was the terror of Bolshevism which possessed the West. We made no movement which was not sanctioned by the men whom Germany acknowledged as her leaders. The Government did not issue a single order which was not seen and approved by the Allied Cabinets. Until the

Red army crumbled under our fierce onslaught, we were the hirelings of England, the bulwarks of the West against the mysterious force of a nation which was fighting, even as we were, for its freedom. This was our second sin against the spirit.

*   *   *   *

The *Entente* ordered the evacuation of the Baltic States. We heard of it and laughed. Then our Government ordered certain companies of troops to return to Germany. We were of the opinion that this was some trick of Noske's to deceive the Allies, or to try to draw the teeth of quarrelsome Independents in the National Assembly. Then we heard that parts of the reserve division of Guards and the Pfeffer Volunteer Corps had been withdrawn and sent home from the eastern front, by order of the Government; nominally because these troops were wanted for frontier defence and were more necessary there than in the neighbourhood of Riga. We had no doubt that this measure was only provisional and that the troops would very soon return to the Baltic States. Then we heard that these troops were not being used for the frontiers after all – that the Guards' Division, for instance, had been disbanded because the *Entente* was demanding the reduction of the whole German army, first to 150,000, then to 100,000 men. We were convinced that there was some mistake; for if demobilisation was beginning, surely the least efficient garrisons would be the first to go. Then we heard that the Government was categorically demanding our return to Germany and was threatening to stop our pay in case of disobedience. We were certain that this could not be true, for we knew that the Government had recognised and approved of our claim on Lithuania and our wish to settle there. Finally, the news came that Germany was obliged to agree to the demands of the *Entente* whatever

these might be. Yet every rumour that came to us from home
stated definitely that in no circumstances would Germany sign
the peace treaty.

*   *   *   *

In those sultry summer days in Olai – days which stood
midway between two periods and two regimes – we suddenly
ceased to feel that we were only on the edge of things; we were
entangled in the meshes of a network of unavoidable contro-
versies.

One day soon after the conclusion of the armistice we were
sitting in Lieutenant Wuth's blockhouse. Schlageter had come
to pay us a visit and we were discussing the possibility of
settling in this country. Wuth wanted to buy a house and a
saw-mill near Bad Baldon – the Letts were still in possession.
Then Lieutenant Kay came into the room and said abruptly
into the tobacco smoke: 'Germany has signed the peace treaty!'

For a moment nobody said anything. It was so still that we
almost heard the floor creak when Schlageter stood up. He
put his hand on the door handle and murmured: 'Well, well –
so Germany has signed . . . ,' he stopped, stared straight in
front of him and then his voice grew suddenly vicious as he
said: 'After all – need that really concern . . . us?' And as he
went out he banged the door so that the whole house shook.

We were horrified. We heard the news and were horrified
to discover how little it really affected us. We were horrified
with the icy clarity of vision which comes from the mind and
not the heart. The message seemed to have come from a
distant foreign land; from a country which was tired and grey
and condemned to exist in the eternal gloom of cold, damp
November fogs. It was like a country which was an empty
space on a map – a country which had no real existence –
After all, how did this place concern us?

THE OUTLAWS

We looked at one another and shivered. We suddenly felt icy cold and terribly lonely. We had imagined that our country would never desert us, that we were bound to it with an indissoluble bond, that it sympathised with our innermost desires and that it justified our actions. The signing of the peace treaty had cut us off.

*　　*　　*　　*

Some of the men of the 1st Courland Infantry Regiment were sulkily standing about the railway station at Mitau. It was on August 24th, 1919. Reluctantly obeying orders, the first transport was going back to Germany. The officers walked up and down morosely giving short answers to their men's insistent questions. Entrainment continued slowly. There was still time. Everyone waited, as for a miracle, for the word which should release them.

Suddenly there was a stir at the barrier. A tall sunburnt officer stepped on to the platform. At his neck shone the *Pour le mérite*. He was the C.O. of the Iron Division, Major Bischoff. He looked at the train – the soldiers crowded round him filled with vague hopes. Officers joined them. The major raised his hand.

'I absolutely forbid the withdrawal of the Iron Division!'

*　　*　　*　　*

That was mutiny. In the evening we gave him a torchlight procession.

In those days the soldiers in the Baltic States had a marching song which began with the words: 'We are the last Germans who remained to face the foe.' We felt indeed that we were the last survivors of the German race. We were almost grateful to the Government for shutting us out of the country. For since the connection had been officially severed, our actions need not be

influenced by troubles at home. We should in any case have
acted as we did. We could not feel that we owed any duty to
our country, because we felt that we could no longer respect it.
We were no longer tied to it for orders, nor for pay or food or
any sentimental considerations. A dimly guessed impulse
drove us. We had a fresh source of strength, of hope, and we
were freed from the burden of piteous claims which had
accompanied us day by day and step for step. Outcasts,
exiles, homeless and beggars – we held our torches high.

* * * *

Each one of us was asked whether he preferred to stay or to
obey the order of the Government. The first to leave us were
the loyal corps – to their officers, trained in the old Prussian
tradition, mutiny was mutiny. Then followed the freebooters,
an armed rabble collected from God knows where, on the lookout for loot up to the last minute, but afraid that they would be
dragged into the war which was to come. The A.S.C. vanished,
so did the military police. Nearly all the paymasters cleared off
with the money.

Then the Baltic *Landeswehr* bade us farewell. They came
under the command of an English officer and were transferred
to the newly-formed Lettish frontier against the Bolsheviks.
The Balts were concerned chiefly with this latter question.
They had only one desire – to keep their independence and
not to have to share the lot of the Russian emigrants. A great
many of us went to speed the Balts on their way. All that
were left of the men of this race capable of carrying arms were
drawn up in line. There stood boys, with their school belts
round their narrow hips and almost collapsing under the weight
of their packs, and side by side with them were old men,
provincial marshals, noblemen – with childlike eyes under the
German steel helmets, and tired, haggard faces. They stood

silent and with unbroken pride though they had to face the wretched prospect of a life under the rule of their former servants.

*　　*　　*　　*

A Russian colonel, Prince Awaloff-Bermondt, somewhere about this time began mobilising Russian soldiers, mostly released prisoners of war, to form a White army to lead against the Bolsheviks. He came into the Baltic States, and the English were not particularly pleased to see him. All kinds of fantastic plans were simmering under his Circassian fur cap; and he was inclined to seek the help of the Balts. England wanted to place this restless individual under the command of her friend General Yudenitch; and Bermondt, who disputed his authority, felt safe only under the protection of the Baltic guns. We were ready to make an ally of the devil himself, so long as we could annoy the English and stay in Courland. Negotiations went back and forth and finally a West Russian government was formed with its headquarters in Courland, and with a West Russian army, of which the Balts were the cadre. The German chief-of-staff, General Count von der Goltz, obeyed the call of the German Government, but resigned his command and went back to his division as a private soldier. Bermondt was now the nominal commander-in-chief. A petition was sent to Lithuania at least to remain neutral in case of a West Russian attack on the common enemy – Bolshevism. Bermondt's idea was to push on into Russia via Dwinaburg, as far as Moscow, if you please! Nothing less than that! But Lithuania demanded the withdrawal of the German troops. So Bermondt decided to begin his crusade by occupying Riga, a step with which we all agreed.

We fastened Russian cockades to our caps, though we cunningly allowed the German ones to show over the top of them. We cheerfully took the paper money which Bermondt caused to be printed – its backing being the army supplies which we intended to secure as booty –; we rather sulkily drank vodka and learnt to swear in Russian. So, since we had been discarded by Germany, we became Russians.

The cry 'Down with Bolshevism' was not taken very seriously. We had had enough experience to know who was going to get the benefit of that! We won the first battle for England. In the second we proposed to do the English out of what they had achieved by the first.

*   *   *   *

We were discussing our various possible courses of future action, crouched round the fire which the Hamburgers had built up at the edge of the forest. Our imaginations reached more fantastic heights even than did the flames, now that there was fighting in prospect. Lieutenant Kay had already learnt a Russian song and warbled: 'Whither wilt thou roll, little apple?' – whither indeed!

'To Riga!' shouted one of the Hamburgers.

'To Moscow!' roared Lieutenant Wuth and laughed.

'To Berlin!' Kay's piercing voice was drowned in the delighted yells of the Hamburgers.

'To Warsaw?' enquired Schlageter; and although he spoke low, everyone heard him and there was a sudden silence.

Then Lieutenant Wuth threw up a coin and cried: 'Heads or tails – duty or adventure?' –

Tails turned up.

*   *   *   *

In the first days of October we learnt that the Letts were preparing for an offensive. They could not take us by surprise, for we were also preparing. Our attack was fixed for October 8th, so as to anticipate that of the enemy.

103

CHAPTER IX

STORM

ONCE again I smelt the curious acrid smell that had haunted me since I first came to this country in May. At that time the reek of burning timbers and the disgusting smell of the corpses of Bolsheviks decaying under the hot sun had distinctly taken the freshness from the air. Now mists lay on the dewy ground and the sun shone redly over the forest. I remembered exactly how that smell had seemed to typify everything that Courland meant to me. What I found attractive was the unexpectedness of this country. The knowledge that this idyllic countryside was really a bog seemed to influence even the character of the war. Perhaps it was responsible for the unrest that drove the Teutonic knights in their day from their safe castles continually to seek fresh adventure. I had come here to fight; and yet that very fact had possibly given me a stronger feeling of being rooted there than the inhabitants themselves felt. The wide plain, on to which we were entering by a narrow muddy track, breathed a different atmosphere from any we had known. The landscape was spread out before us in its gentle, deceitful loveliness, and yet we could guess that behind many a bush lurked danger. Far away on the horizon lay the dark line of the enemy's position, which was our objective for the day. And from there came fitful rumblings, so that one's eye involuntarily searched the sky for the thunderstorm.

Lieutenant Kay, beside whose horse I was marching, scanned the horizon with his field-glasses. Then he pointed to a greyish-white line that was coming out of the wood and moving towards the enemy. Kay thought that it must be the first battalion, which was to attack from the road; but I noticed that they had a gigantic flag and knew that the Russians always carried theirs with them. They were proud of their Tsarist banner and the flapping cloth and the bright colours kept them cheerful. I thought there must have been some hitch in the attack, for the Russians formed the reserve and we should have been in front of them. We were some little distance ahead of the company, so the lieutenant sent me back to hurry up the men. The Pioneers were just coming on to the road. Their enormously tall sergeant-major was in front and on the end of a long pole carried the three-cornered streamer with a boot on it, which was the company's badge. Behind him, a Pioneer waved a concertina, playing the Prussian military march, as we had done on every one of the long, tiring marches which we had undertaken in this country. Then, right and left along the road in long columns, came the company, the men carrying their guns as they found most comfortable, clubs in their hands and short pipes in their mouths. Between the files clattered the country carts, laden with machine-guns and ammunition. The line of march was certainly not a magnificent sight from a military point of view. Uniforms were pretty ragged by now and faces unshaven. Even the machine-gunners laid little stress on externals, though the guns themselves were well oiled and carefully packed away in the carts. I went along to look at my gun and discovered that I was attached to the Pioneers for this battle. The lieutenant of the Pioneers came along too, tapped a decayed horsewhip against his badly-rolled puttees and said, without removing the heavy pipe from between his teeth, that to-day the machine-gunners had a chance to show that they could do other things besides looting and thieving. I was annoyed and said nothing; but Sergeant Schmitz, who was marching beside the cart, calmly shoved a box of ammunition into place, and said that, if he remembered rightly, it was the Pioneers who had arrived late for the attack at Baldon, because they had got into a wine-cellar. The lieutenant growled something and then went forward to join his company.

It had gradually become very cold. We stamped our feet on the road to warm them and listened almost in silence to the thunder of the guns ahead.

The sounds of battle grew louder as we hurried on. We marched past the Russians, who were resting in the ditches at the side of the road, and who looked at us, smiling rather shyly. Patronisingly we threw them the few scraps of Russian that we had learnt during the war, and the obscenities were taken in excellent part in spite of our condescending manner. At the railway-crossing stood an armoured car. Its steel sides showed the marks of various hits. The crew was working at the car. Some of them had splashes of blood on their leather coats, and stood round a tarpaulin under which could be seen the outlines of a body. We marched past without asking any questions. The two companies of infantry turned off to the left on to a narrow path across the marsh. Gradually the road grew more populous. The yellow cover of a partly inflated captive balloon hovered in a field on our right. Behind the signal box a battery of heavies was firing. The crack of a solitary rifle rang out by the railway line.

We halted and unloaded our guns from the carts. Since the enemy seemed a long way off, I took mine apart and slung the carriage across my back. The padding had been torn off and the two water-boxes which I hung on in front, pressed the sharp iron edges painfully into my shoulders. We swarmed across the road to the left, climbed over the ditch and splashed into the bog.

It was about noon and we had eaten nothing since breakfast.

STORM

The ground quaked at every step. A thin glassy film of ice
had formed and our feet crashed through it, so that the water
squelched into our boots. The whole swamp was covered with
tufts of coarse grass. Greyish-white wisps of cloud chased
across the sky; the wind cut through our wretched clothes, for
none of us had a great coat. I panted under my load and
shrugged it from one shoulder to the other.

The enemy first sighted us when we had got about 500 yards
off the road. They fired a volley at us, which dropped just
ahead and sent little fountains splashing up all over the place
like a shower of rain. We threw ourselves down. I stumbled
and fell, the water-boxes crashed down, the gun-carriage
sank into the bog and its edge ran into my chest. My elbows
and knees subsided into the slush and the icy water soaked
through my clothes. Beside me the infantry were firing.
Schmitz's gun was also in action. Before I could begin to
mount mine, the order to advance was given. Our wet clothes
stuck to our bodies and icicles formed in the folds. Hand-
grenades were dangling at my belt and impeded my movements. The enemy accompanied our progress with fitful
firing. It began to rain and the cold drops lashed our faces.
Over the enemy lines hung dark heavy clouds. In three or
four places on the horizon arose conflagrations. We kept on
having to lie down, for Lettish snipers were hidden all over
the marsh. Overhead our own shells hissed and screamed,
landing with dull thuds. At last we halted. Between ourselves and the enemy line was an open field, a soft green
meadow sloping gently towards us and partly under water.

It was now four o'clock in the afternoon. We lay behind a
little fold in the ground, which gave us a certain amount of
shelter. We were ankle deep in mud. The enemy's position
was plainly visible; at various points we could see what appeared
to be strongly fortified posts. The Letts were firing with guns

of every calibre. The shells dropped into the field and conjured up all sorts of strange shapes out of the mud and turf. Above the dull roar of the battle we could hear every now and then the sharp rattle of quick-firing guns. We had no support on our right, the rest of the troops were close up to the road. The Letts had at last got our range. Shells fell close in front of us and covered us with mud. Apparently some of the Letts still occupied the space between us and their base, for machine-guns continued to fire fitfully at us. I had set up the carriage of my gun in front of me and was trying to get a little sleep in its shelter. There was a sudden shout of 'Stretcher-bearers!' from our firing-line – we all looked up. One of the Pioneers was crawling painfully out of the line. Someone said that he had been hit in the leg. More shells came over and a second man screamed. We lay in enforced idleness and waited. Time and again we looked up, hoping that the lieutenant would at long last give the order to advance. Our part of the line now came in for a furious bombardment. We were still a good two thousand yards off the enemy position and had to watch the fight without firing a single shot. The whole day was spent in waiting. We felt as if we had been lying in that swamp for long ages and as if we should never get out of it again. The monotonous drone of the guns was not in the least stimulating, and the emptiness of our stomachs and the wet clothes and boots which were rubbing us sore were far more irritating than the gun-fire. The day seemed to be made up of innumerable little mosaic stones which united to form a ghastly wearisome picture. We had been used to fighting of a very different kind in Courland. And the fact that the war recommenced in this way, after the long armistice, seemed to us a depressing omen.

Every house within the range of our vision was on fire and the wind blew burning flakes of wood and soot in our direction. Slowly the day wore on to darkness. Every now and then the rain turned to sleet. The enemy line faded away slowly till we could only distinguish it by the flashes of gun-fire. The shelling from both sides grew more and more intense. At last the lieutenant fired off a red rocket. A few moments later, our own gunners laid down a barrage directly in front of us which rolled slowly forward.

A line of infantry advanced from behind us, the men bent almost double, in open formation, their rifles across their heavy packs. Their badges told us that they were Berthold's battalion of Bavarians. As soon as they had reached our line, the lieutenant who carried the whip pointed forward and sprang to his feet. We dragged ourselves painfully up and plodded along with the Bavarians.

My gun-carriage dug into me at every step. I called to gunner No. 2 who was carrying the gun, and suggested that we should mount it at the very first opportunity. But the line advanced steadily, though not particularly quickly. Our feet splashed into water. The Bavarian next to me crumpled up as though his pack had crushed him. The lieutenant, who suddenly ran across in front of me, changed the whip into his right hand. On his left was a trickle of blood. We advanced more quickly. A Pioneer collapsed, yelping like a dog. Schmitz ran forward to the right with his gun. I looked at the quaking ground beneath my feet and panted in my efforts to keep up with the line. One of the Bavarians dropped his pack and ran on without even looking back. Another suddenly stood still and looked sadly at the ground. Then he sank gently to his knees.

I heard nothing more of the tumult that raged about us. The ground got higher and firmer. The day had waned but the burning houses threw a fitful light over the scene. The men next to me looked like black shadows moving confusedly. Suddenly we came to a barbed wire entanglement. Our feet kicked furiously at it as it wound itself round our ankles like a coil of serpents. I screamed with horror as if I had been set upon with vermin. One man fell against my shoulder so that I staggered. A bank rose steeply before us. I had long since lost the water-boxes. Hindered abominably by the gun-carriage, I dragged myself up by the tufts of grass which grew out of the gritty soil. My foot slipped. Somebody caught hold of the gun-carriage and pulled. I lay panting on the slope. To the left was a barricade, along which the men were hurrying towards a gap which opened directly in front of me. Suddenly Schmitz appeared beside me with his gun. I threw down my gun-carriage and crawled over towards him. He had already mounted his gun when the gunner beside him put his hand to his head and rolled gently down the slope. I threw myself behind the gun and pressed the trigger. I fired – and the stupor which had hung over me all that day vanished. The gun leapt and wriggled like a fish. I held it gently but firmly, and gripped its throbbing flanks between my knees as I pushed one belt after another through it. I could see nothing, but finally Schmitz, shouting and yelling, pushed me aside and took my place.

I seized a hand-grenade and ran forward. We jumped into a trench. I stepped on soft, curiously non-resisting bodies, past dark holes masked with rags. Guns lying in confused heaps barred the narrow way. We heard shouts and the dull explosions of hand-grenades sounded from behind the earthen parapets. Suddenly Schmitz appeared above me, threw his gun across the trench to form a bridge and ran over. I pushed the gun after him and climbed up the wall of the trench. The gap in the barricade was straight in front of me. We stumbled over dead bodies: I trod on the head of one. Behind the entanglement lay the second line of defence, rather higher and built of concrete.

Shots came from a group of houses which cast heavy, dark shadows across the road. I threw myself against a door hung

a hand-grenade on the handle and ran away. The crash shook
the walls. A Pioneer fired a rocket in through the dark opening.
Almost at the same instant the house burst into flames. A
young fellow ran screaming out of the passage holding his
bleeding hands above his head and fell full length. We felt
the hot breath of the flames as they licked after him. Another
man stumbled out of the house, followed by smoke and sparks.
We seized the first Lett and threw him back full-length into
the blaze; he screamed once, and the flames closed over him.
The second fell on to his knees, but as we approached him,
he sprang up, threw his arms over his head and himself leapt
into the fire.

The lieutenant raced past me, his face reflecting thousands
of little red splashes of light. The burning houses made all
around as light as day. One of them collapsed with a dull roar.
From among the ruins came sounds of crackling, and splinters
of wood flew across the road. The lieutenant cracked the
whip above his head and shouted to his company. I tore back
to look for my machine-gun. Some fellows crept out of the
shelters, one of them swinging a shining cooking-pot. I broke
into one of the shelters and pushed aside a Pioneer. A pile of
wonderful English water-proof sheets lay in front of me. I took
one, and inspected it by the light of the fire. It was quite new,
so could be used as a wrap. The Pioneer was leisurely taking
the boots off a dead man. 'Fall in on the road!' shouted someone. I ran on. Everywhere groups of people were looting.
One man was pushing bottles of vodka into his pack. Another
was poking his bloodstained hands into a pot of some yellow
jam and licking it off his fingers, smearing it all over his face.

Gradually we got back to the street. Wild confusion reigned
there. Every path was blocked by columns of men – the field-
kitchens were being stormed – artillery was slowly edging
forward. We pushed through the crowds. Company com-

manders were shouting to their men. The lieutenant stood on a smouldering heap of ruins by the side of the road and watched. My gun was there. The roll was called, and the sergeants made the report. The lieutenant counted the losses in an undertone. He had bound a handkerchief round his left hand, and the pipe was no longer in his mouth. A quarter of his company was missing. Two men were missing from Schmitz's gun-team.

While the Berthold battalion marched into the darkness of the night, the lieutenant said to us that the performance of the machine-gunners had been excellent; that in all his campaigns he had never known the heavy machine-guns not only not to stay behind in such difficult conditions, but actually to get to the enemy lines ahead of the infantry. Schmitz muttered something about preferring a packet of tobacco.

Then we fell in, pushed slowly past the columns, and the forest swallowed us up. The night was dark. Two files marched one along each side of the road, while down the middle went the machine-guns. The lieutenant and one of the company commanders were swearing at one another. I marched beside an enormous horse which breathed heavily down my neck. My gun was mounted and was being carried by the team. For some reason I had elected to bring some S.M.K.* ammunition when we started off from that village. A light-pistol was also hanging at my belt. The boxes were heavy and I had no carrier. So I laid one box on to the shaft of the cart beside me. I almost fell asleep as I walked, and could scarcely lift my aching feet. I had a disgusting taste in my mouth, my clothes were sticking to me, the heavy boxes nearly pulled my arms from their sockets. We slogged along blindly, hardly speaking a word. The only sounds were the crunching of

* S.M.K. ammunition contained a specially powerful explosive, and was used against tanks and armoured cars.

the wheels and the dull tramp of many feet, which were rather soothing.

All at once we encountered a black mass which opened its jaws and spat fire at us. The horse beside me reared, the box fell off, the shaft cracked and broke, I was hurled to one side, rolled into the ditch – what could it be? – what was up? – Was it an ambush. The horses thundered back snorting, and everybody shouted. Men were rolling on the ground, a glowing twitching snake shot forward – through the darkness came a whole row of them – aha! I thought, liquid fire. Two, three, four of them flew over our heads. A long-drawn-out wail came from near me: 'I'm wou-u-nded,' and I fell over something soft.

There was my gun and I was still carrying the box of ammunition. Somebody gave me a hand, we hoisted up the gun and pushed it on to the top of the ditch. There stood the infernal brute, a Cimmerian monster, snapping and spitting fire. We were at the dead angle, I was delighted to remember that we had the S.M.K. ammunition – I inserted a belt, pressed the trigger – fired – our target was the thing in front of us – already we had silenced the beast; then Schmitz came over beside me and pushed me aside. I realised instantly what he was after – he wanted to shield me with the gun. The monster began firing again. I crawled a little way to the right and hit a fellow over the head who very nearly got me first. Schmitz fired, we jumped up and moved a few steps forward. I pulled out my light-pistol, took a rocket from my trouser pocket, slipped it into the breach, raised my arm – fired – there was a hissing sound – I ran back – a metallic crack – a dazzling sheet of flame – snow white clouds of smoke rose from the earth, a white hot wall seemed to shoot up before our eyes, a wave of intense heat choked us – the armoured car was on fire. There came a delirious, gurgling scream and two reeling figures fell into the ditch, with their clothes afire and throwing their arms about wildly. There was dead silence. The glowing wall shone with an unearthly glare.

I lay at the edge of the ditch and hid my face in the ground. I felt as if I wanted absolutely nothing more – I just wanted to sleep. But Schmitz bent over me and asked whether I could spare a smoke for the two Englishmen who had escaped from the armoured car. They stared stupidly before them with glassy, red-rimmed eyes, ragged, bloody and scorched. Men began coming along the road. We went back leading the Englishmen between us. I only missed my water-proof sheet when we got back to the village.

I did not want to be done out of the only prize I had actually won that day – my one bit of loot. The thing must be lying near the armoured car. The company was to stand to arms in the churchyard. I rested my gun among the gravestones. The men dropped among the churned up graves, absolutely exhausted. I caught Schmitz, who was already snoring, by the arm and told him what I was going to do. Then I tramped up the dark road towards the glow.

The ground-sheet occupied my whole thoughts. A whole world of well-being and comfort seemed to be contained in it. Its velvety-soft underside, which I had felt on my bare neck had made me excited and happy. I remembered how supple it was, and thought that to be wrapped in it must be like being caressed by a tender woman. The knowledge that it came from England, called up a vision of the peach-bloom complexion of an English actress whom I had once seen in Germany when I was a child. No doubt the wrap had belonged to an officer. The dug-out in which it lay had been very roomy. Perhaps English officers, of whom the Letts had a good many, had lived in it. How dazedly the Tommy who came out of the armoured car had looked at me! It must have been damned unpleasant to be in that close steel chamber when the whole affair got white hot. The monster was in front of me again and its walls were still glowing faintly. What a hope! Did they really expect to hold up the German night advance all alone and unaided?

I approached the clumsy square machine. A horrible smell of burnt paint and charred flesh came from it. I picked a rifle out of the ditch, and gingerly poked the hot wall with the barrel. Then I walked all round the car. On the other side the door was open, hanging on bent hinges. I looked inside carefully. There was a mess of twisted bars and scrap iron. On the floor was a dingy charred heap. I supposed that it had once been human. Filled with curiosity, I stirred it with the gun barrel. Something hissed, the outer skin burst, the gun sank deep in – the heap seemed to be moving. For a moment I felt sick. I recoiled before the disgusting stench and fumes, and turned away reeling.

I began looking for my ground-sheet. Steps approached from the darkness. A few stray Bavarians came to a standstill beside me. They were looking for their battalion, which was somewhere ahead. One of them said that they had been told to carry on as far as the signalman's box and they would find some of their people. Had I any idea where that might be? Nobody could find anything in this God-damned darkness. I knew the lie of the land pretty well from having taken part in the advance on Riga in May. I tried to describe where the place was that they were looking for. The Bavarians stood about undecidedly. They wanted to know whether it was far and whether I could not guide them to it. I cast about in my mind. It could not be very far. The Bavarians would certainly miss the way in this abominable darkness and might end by falling into the hands of the Letts. But perhaps it would do if I took them as far as the railway and then let them walk along the permanent way. I could always get my ground-sheet on the way back or very early the next morning. One of the Bavarians offered me a drink. The burning liquid trickled gratefully down my gullet. In a moment I felt fresh again, and said I would accompany them.

The wood seemed to be full of mysteries. We felt horribly lonely and it was almost a relief when we suddenly heard shots from the direction of the road or the railway embankment, about where I thought the Bavarian battalion must be encamped. Without hesitation we all of us instantly turned sharp to the left and ran towards the noise, as though drawn by a magnet. Twice I hit my head against trees; I stumbled over roots and undergrowth; the others seemed to be crashing through like myself. Soon there were sounds of rifle fire from five or six different places. Stray shots whizzed past us and were embedded in the tree trunks. Evidently the battalion was heavily engaged. The German fire was easily distinguishable from that of the enemy, and it seemed to us that our men were fighting against greatly superior numbers. We raced towards them. Somehow we must have turned to the right again, for all at once the low slope of the railway embankment appeared beside us. Three or four men as well as myself climbed up and ran on between the lines, while the rest continued alongside the embankment. A hideous noise came from in front and we heard a few long-drawn-out cries. I could even see the flashes from the rifles. We found a path across the embankment, saw the signalman's hut and ran towards it. Bullets whistled round our ears. We were called sharply to halt as we fell noisily into the little yard. A small collection of Bavarians lay there, firing from behind a pile of sleepers. They also had a light machine-gun. Three wounded men lay by the wall of the house. One of them told us a confused and halting story of a sudden attack and heavy losses. A man came round the corner, wounded and gasping, and shouted to us to go on farther down the embankment – that there must be another house some three hundred yards down the line, which we had better occupy and attack the Letts on the flank, so as to give the battalion on the road a breathing space. I ran straight ahead and my few Bavarians, after a hasty consultation, followed. Soon the railway line curved gently to the left; I knew that it crossed the road a little farther on, just where this nocturnal combat seemed to be fiercest. I stood for a moment in indecision while the wood resounded with shots. Then one man saw a light just ahead to the right. That must be the house; we crept towards it across a clearing, through a thin clump of trees, across an open field. Spurts of blue flame showed where the enemy was to be found. The edge of the forest was probably partly occupied by our own men. We advanced stealthily towards the dark mass, in which a solitary forlorn little window gleamed with a faint red light. When we got to the road we opened out from a short line and then made a dash, ran into a wall and found a door. I thundered on the wood with my heels. During a breathless pause which lasted for several seconds, we heard footsteps hurriedly departing, and a faint voice cried out. We roared: 'Open the door!' But not another sound was to be heard, except the voice which moaned: 'Help!' So one man threw himself at the door with all his might, another bashed the unwieldy lock with his trenching tool, so that the wood splintered. Carrying our rifles in front of us we made our way into the yard.

In the faint light which shone from the window we saw a soldier lying on a dungheap, his tunic open and soaked with blood. He babbled and moaned and moved his hand feebly. The whole house seemed to be full of obscure twittering sounds. I was suddenly dead tired and knew with an icy certainty that something ghastly had happened in this place. I sensed again the paralysing, stupefying atmosphere which had seemed at the beginning of the day to typify this country and this war. But now it was mixed with the sickly-sweet smell of blood. I leant on my gun and felt as if I should never be able to move again. I heard one of the Bavarians scream as he sped past me towards the house, his voice rising to a shrill yell. 'Swine!' he gasped, 'Swine; oh, the swine!' and he threw his weight against the door which gave way immediately. His wild, long-drawn-out, half-strangled screams rang through the house to an accompaniment of bangs and crashes. Finally another scream which rose hideously from a low growl to a high treble note, roused those of us who were outside from our stupor. I felt as if a vein had burst in my temple and my blood were suddenly at boiling point. We broke in at the door. Unpleasant fumes met us and seemed to be wrapping our lungs in a damp rag. I felt as if somebody had pushed a fist down my throat and were pulling out my inside. In the entrance lay a corpse. I stumbled over a pair of boots and fell on top of the body. My hand, which I had put out to save myself, sank into a mess of damp, sticky, slippery entrails. I recoiled horror-struck. But the smell of the blood which drenched my hand maddened me and all hesitation left me. I raced towards a sudden light. I saw what I had expected to see.– There they lay, on stinking, blood-stained straw; with crushed skulls from which stared glassy, squinting eyes; with ragged clothing stained blackish-red; with stomachs slit; limbs twisted and wrenched off. Here lay a head apart from the rest, from whose single round wound ran a black stream which had turned into a pitted spongy mass; there a brain covered with a network of fine red veins stuck to the walls in thick grey splashes. From a gaping wound blood dripped on to the floor and made the only sound in the silence – in the deadly silence in which we stood, paralysed. We stood there numbly – we looked with glassy, spell-bound eyes at the dead bodies, in each of which was a ghastly wound – there, among the loathsome confusion of torn clothes – in the middle of each body, between hips and thighs.

All this, this and much more, united to form a single impression which in one second was hammered into my brain for all eternity. Then we all went mad. I saw, as through a red mist, one man seize a sledge-hammer, which lay in the corner covered with blood, and make for the entrance bellowing. We turned to follow, we crowded through the door and tore down to the yard. The noise of battle still resounded in the darkness without. But we paid no heed. We placed no sentries, we took no cover, we forgot orders and instructions. We ran through the yard, poked into every corner, searched every room in the house, combed through the stable and the barn, ready to kill anything that fell alive into our hands, to smash everything that we could find. Somebody dragged out a man from under a broken cart, a tall old peasant who wailed for mercy. Before he was able even to stagger to his feet, the sledge-hammer came down on his head so that he crumpled up like a rag. The cow in the stable was shot; the butt end of a gun caught the little bristly dog and smashed him to pulp. Pictures crashed from the walls, a mirror fell, the doors of the cupboards were burst open, the chairs and tables splintered. It was only when the noise of the battle began to be heard above our own tumult that we manned the wall, hot, feverish, with pulses racing, and shot wildly into the night, just to relieve the terrible tension.

It was not until the early hours of the morning that I returned with what remained of the shattered Berthold battalion, to our position in the churchyard. I had forgotten all about my water-proof sheet. I lay down on a grave and slept until I was awakened by the noise of the counter attack.

CHAPTER X

THE LAST FIGHT

SOME five hundred yards from the churchyard, in a line with the village, a long narrow lake extended as far as the point where stood the remains of the armoured car. About three thousand yards off the road on either side were sundry farms in which we supposed the Letts to be hidden. On the right of the road, between the railway embankment and the farms, lay a patch of wooded country. On the left were fields covered with low bushes, looking like a frayed carpet. Lieutenant Kay was ordered to occupy the little piece of rising country between the lake and the armoured car with a platoon of Hamburgers and two guns. We got under way. The thick brushwood was most awkward to negotiate with the guns, and we proceeded very slowly. It therefore occurred to me to climb up on to the road, which was strictly against orders. So I signed to my gun team and we moved to the right. At the ditch beside the highroad I turned to help the men who were carrying the gun and saw Gohlke standing with his mouth wide open staring into the ditch. I whirled round and went icy cold: thirty yards ahead of us, the undergrowth was swarming with Letts and crowds of them were coming along the ditch. I yelled; Gohlke threw down the gun; like a flash we inserted a cartridge belt, and I just had time to jump away from the muzzle before Gohlke began firing. Kay threw a hand-grenade, and in a moment both sides were at it hammer and tongs. We had stumbled on the counter-attack. The next few seconds showed, in spite of the confusion, that the Letts had already got well past the point which we were to have occupied, and that they were probably massed in the bushes all along the narrow ridge. The bullets flew through the undergrowth with an unpleasant nerve-shattering ping; twigs and leaves flipped round our ears and the sand spurted up right and left and all about us. Gohlke pushed one belt after another into the gun; luckily we had brought plenty of ammunition. Then things began to get lively on the mound behind us. We heard dull explosions from the row of trench mortars, and our heavies sent over a barrage of shells exactly thirty yards in front of us. The machine-guns in the churchyard joined in too, but they fired short and we were most uncomfortably placed between the two fires. I yelled and gesticulated at them like a lunatic, but it only got worse. The men in the churchyard apparently thought it was a Lett making signs to them; so they shot at us the more fiercely; the Letts saw us waving and thereby got our exact position and the air seemed to be cut into tiny snippets which rained down on us.

Our guns laid down a box-barrage and then the enemy got it hot and strong from every kind of gun. In the bushes we could see shells dropping close beside each other. We heard shrieks mingled with the crashes. The line in front of us wavered. Yet the Letts did not retreat; they pressed onwards. At last the people in the churchyard realised our position and increased their range.

I had no firearms with me. Nothing is more demoralising than to be able to do nothing in such a situation. Murawski was next to me, but the blighter was not shooting; his rifle lay beside him and he had hidden his face on the ground. I nudged him and he looked up. 'Why aren't you firing?' I shouted. He looked pale but yelled back – I had some difficulty in making out what he said – 'I must have eaten something that's disagreed with me!' and looked at me reproachfully. I could not help laughing, and that calmed me to some extent, so I got him to give me his rifle and cartridges. Now that I had something to do the tension relaxed; but when I looked at Murawski a few minutes later, he was dead.

Gradually the enemy's fire seemed to waver. It was high time, for our ammunition was running out. Kay, who was lying close to the lake a few yards ahead of me – I just had a glimpse of his greatcoat – suddenly rose to his feet and ran forward swinging a hand-grenade. A few of the Hamburgers followed him. I heard the detonations above the gradually weakening fire of trench mortars and artillery. We left our gun in the ditch and ran after Lieutenant Kay. Reinforcements came from the rear. We fired off rockets, and shells fell in front of us. A few steps farther on we stumbled over the first corpse. And a very little way beyond that it was difficult to move quickly for fear of stepping on bodies that were still warm. In the narrow space between the lake and the armoured car I counted more than twenty dead Letts. We heard the groans of the wounded all around. On the north side of the slope we met with machine-gun fire, and Kay's section retreated, leaving the reinforcements to deliver the next blow.

We had four dead, and on Kay's greatcoat were seven bullet marks. Schmitz's gun was smashed to atoms, Schmitz himself had scalded his hand in the water which boiled and bubbled out of the jacket of his own gun. Only one of the Hamburgers was quite untouched. The dead Letts and those whom we had taken prisoners were all wearing completely new uniforms and had English guns and Sam Browns. Among the prisoners was an officer, a former Lettish schoolmaster. He was wounded and suffering from shock. When he was questioned he was ready to give some information, but a Lettish private, with a bleeding stump in place of his arm, shouted something at him threateningly and he flinched and said no more.

The Lettish counter attack had collapsed utterly. We wandered about the battlefield all the afternoon without firing a single shot. We could not understand why we should not push straight on to Riga. But in the south-east heavy fighting was still in progress; we heard the noise of the guns. Then news came from the north.

The Russians had reached the coast after some desultory fighting among the sand dunes near the Dwina. At Bolderaa they observed the English fleet lying in the Gulf of Riga with the decks cleared for action; and they saw four Lettish steamers plying rapidly back and forth on the Dwina, transporting what was left of the defeated Lettish divisions. The Russians immediately fired on these steamers. At once the Union Jack was lowered from the masts of the ships and the Lettish flag was run up. Then the Russians were covered with steel, fire and sand, by salvoes from the English men-o'-war. England was protecting her faithful and devoted servants.

During the following night the German legion came up from the south, stormed Thorensberg, one of the suburbs of Riga, and occupied the bridges. Our battalion was told off to clear the whole district around the Dwina from Baldon to Uxküll and to occupy it.

*　　*　　*　　*

Below Hill is the last peak in the ridge at Baldon, so-called after General von Below, who managed to ford the Dwina not far from this height in the attack on Riga. On the hill-sides amongst firs and beeches is a series of war-cemeteries. The road to Baldon winds round the wooded slope in a defile on the sides of which stand farmhouses. These farms as well as the sides of the hill were occupied by a battalion of Letts, when the Liebermann division, coming from Baldon, marched along that road towards the bend of the Dwina, at about three o'clock one morning.

The night was very dark, but there was no wind and the air was mild. It was the kind of night that made one feel at peace. And that was just how the Hamburgers who were marching in the van of the column were feeling. They were singing, or rather humming, in time to their march. The first few men stepping on to the bridge over a narrow little stream were amused by the hollow, rhythmic sound their feet made on the boards, so they marked time energetically to the tune of the 'Maiden of Courland.' Then they marched quietly into the defile. They saw the shadows of the buildings on the slopes above them, but the countryside was bathed in peace.

I was marching next to Lieutenant Wuth, who was riding and chatting to me in an undertone. The waggons of the trench mortar company clattered just ahead of us, and behind them Sergeant Schmitz jogged along, more than half asleep, and tied to one of the mortars by a rope.

Suddenly hell was let loose. The first thing I saw was Lieutenant Wuth crashing from his horse into the ditch. The horse lashed out and then lay down. I leapt into the ditch after Wuth and inquired if he were wounded. But he was sitting up by the slope, carefully exchanging his uniform cap for his velvet tam-o'-shanter, and explained that he supposed there was going to be a scrap. The second thing I saw was Sergeant Schmitz pulling his bayonet from its scabbard and with one mighty blow severing the rope that bound the trench mortar to the cart. Then he heaved a box of shells off the cart and I rushed over and handed him one; he dropped it into the gun and fired into the night. The third thing I saw was that the whole column was panic stricken and rushing about wildly. Lieutenant Wuth ran along the road, cursing and laying about

him with his riding whip, and shouting: 'Lie down! Shoot!'
When the first shell exploded, there was complete silence
for a moment and I had the feeling that each man was thinking:
'Hullo! Our trench mortars . . . things can't be so bad after
all.' Schmitz was firing shell after shell, and then Hoffman's
machine-gun joined in. The Hamburgers lay in the ditch,
shooting from behind the carts and dead horses, and the panic
was rapidly quelled by the noise of our own gun-fire. My gun
was nicely packed up in one of the carts, but all I could get
hold of was a box of hand-grenades which lay on top. I hung a
number of them round my belt, and then had a look round to
see where I could make the best use of them.

The heaviest firing came from the direction of the steep
slope in front of the houses: we were trapped between two lines
of fire and were catching it from all around except from the
road itself. It was impossible to retreat, for the bridge must have
given way under the furious bombardment, if we could judge
by the shouts which came from there. Schmitz systematically
rained shells on to the houses and slopes from his trench mortar
– the other two mortars had meanwhile also come into action.
I gave a few hand-grenades to Sergeant Ebelt, who was
crouching behind a cart with some of the Hamburgers and
shooting, and he and his squad followed me at once as I ran
down the road. Soon we met Kay and Wuth who were taking
turns at one of the Hamburgers' light machine-guns. Wuth
looked up in surprise as we ran past and shouted to him:
'We're making war on our own!'

We ran along a stretch of the road, then we climbed up the
incline and immediately saw the Lettish front line on the left
flank of which we were standing. None of them had suspected
or seen our coming. So we simply smashed them up with
hand-grenades. I could not see much and I could not hear
much; I realised vaguely that my body was bending back and

forth, that a bomb flew out of my hand and the impetus carried me a few steps forward, just as many as were necessary for the next throw. That was all done automatically, exactly according to rule, as it had often been practised. I felt a sort of ecstasy in the elasticity of my body, and even when something hit my shin, I still had no doubt that I could be neither wounded nor killed. As one of the houses went up in flames the last few Letts vanished into the bushes.

Hardly were the scattered companies reassembled than we were again furiously bombarded. This time the firing came from a patch of wood behind the hill.

I happened to be standing behind the field-kitchen with Ebelt and was cutting the bloody puttee off my right leg, to attend to my wound, when this second attack began. Ebelt suddenly said: 'I've stopped one!' looked at me as though bewildered, turned round, dropped his gun, sank slowly on to his knees, propped himself up with his hands and looked mournfully at the ground. Then he lay down.

The Hamburgers advanced and the firing ceased at once. Only three Letts were found dead in the wood. When I got back I found our battalion doctor kneeling by Ebelt, and he said he had been shot straight through the heart. I said it was impossible and told him what had happened. The doctor shrugged his shoulders and evidently thought I had imagined it. He investigated the wound on my tibia, and found that it was only a splinter from one of the bombs. Probably I had run over one of my own.

The Hamburgers had four dead, and these were added to the 1917 war cemeteries. A fresh row of graves was begun with Ebelt. Three times in the next few weeks we had to begin new rows.

* * * *

THE LAST FIGHT

We cleaned up that reach of the Dwina. We had to take one farm at a time and to search the whole stretch of country, bush by bush. And when we got as far as the river we had to turn round and capture the farms all over again. The battalion had a front of seven and a half miles to hold and the Letts could get through everywhere. We lay in demolished houses and ruined barns. Day by day we went on patrols, night after night we mounted guard. Our very weak lines of communication on each side and with the rear were cut. We got neither stores nor pay nor ammunition, and our despatch riders had to be accompanied by a strong guard as far as Baldon. In four weeks we were attacked seventeen times.

We lay by the Dwina and watched the smoke of trains on the other bank, plying continuously between Friedrichstadt and Riga, filled with troops. We saw more and more troops going into the enemy's country, we could see the Lettish quarters and could count their batteries of guns; and knew that they had five of everything to one of ours. We carted our trench mortars about and fired a few shells first from one place, then from another, sent up masses of rockets, made a great deal of noise with our rifles, and altogether tried to make them believe that we were tremendously strong. But for every shell we fired, the Letts fired twenty; and they also sent over patrols, each one as big as a company; they used to send them out in the evening and in the morning we threw them back again.

We were armed to the teeth. There was a machine-gun to every three men and a trench mortar to every twenty All the same, the battalion consisted of only a hundred and sixty men. And the cooks and the clerks, the drivers, the stretcher-bearers and the staff-officers all went into the firing line and took their turn at sentry-go and patrol duty. This did not alter the fact that the fighting force was a bare hundred and sixty men. We were hung about with rifles, revolvers, bombs and

127

light-pistols. On the other hand, very few of us had greatcoats – and anyone who had one had taken it off a Lett. The stretch of land that we were defending very soon could not provide us with so much as a fowl, let alone any other sort of meat, and nothing was coming through from the rear.

The first November days brought biting cold weather and snowstorms. We wrapped old rags round our bodies and enveloped our necks and legs in tattered mufflers and got more lice than ever. We plodded through snow-swept valleys and crept through white, deep, still woods. We ranged up and down the Dwina and hid in crumbling holes in the ground. We had nothing to cook; the occasional frozen potatoes were only edible when they were roasted. Our wounded men got gangrene and died. We had indeed a doctor, but he had to take his turn in the firing line, and we had no bandages nor medicines. The enemy was well provided with everything.

At night we lay like hedgehogs round the farms. Each company had a separate position and they were nearly two miles apart. If a company was attacked, half of each of the others came to their assistance, but generally two were attacked and very often all three. We never had a whole night's rest. The horses pined away, for we could get no food for them; the A.S.C. horses were the first to go, then the ones for the ammunition waggons. Only the horses we had got with the peasant carts bore up. The Lettish peasants froze and starved as we did, though most of the farmhouses were deserted.

Nevertheless we should have killed anybody for a traitor who suggested our obeying the Government's order to go back to Germany.

Towards the middle of November the Dwina began to freeze over. Now the Letts crossed the river unhindered; and we began to get news occasionally, but it was bad news. The Letts crossed at Bolderaa, under cover of the guns of the

English men-o'-war, and drove back the Russians. The German legion was attacked near Friedrichstadt, held its own with difficulty in an all-day battle, and then retreated step by step. A Lettish assault from Riga on Thorensberg failed, but this did not prevent their making others.

We held our bend of the Dwina. Our limbs were numbed and the cutting east wind seemed to penetrate to our very bones. We on our side began to make raids over the Dwina, surprised the Lettish sentries and advanced as far as the railway line which we blew up. Next day the trains were running as usual, and on the day following the Letts came over to our side and wreaked their vengeance. We slunk away like whipped dogs, muffled up, ragged, starving, frozen and lousy. We crept from sentry to sentry; we listened to the heavy rumbling from north and south; at night we saw the red glow in the sky, beyond the ridge; we stood on the bank of the river and stared towards Riga with smarting eyes.

*　　*　　*　　*

The order came for us to retire. On the previous evening the Hamburgers had been surrounded and attacked, and the Letts had had heavy losses. However, in the morning came the order, and we marched off to the Eckau. We wondered what had happened. Our officers could not tell us. The despatch riders could not tell us. It was the Letts whom the Hamburgers had taken prisoner on the evening before, who told us. The Letts had broken through north and south of Thorensberg and had surrounded the town, in which the weak army of occupation was fighting for its life. The Letts had pushed back the German line at Bolderaa, and had advanced a considerable distance at Friedrichstadt. The Esthonians had sent reinforcements to the Letts. The Bolsheviks had agreed to a short armistice. The Lithuanians had declared war on the West Russian government, and therefore on us, and had made a

surprise attack on the weak outposts guarding the railway,
which was our only line of retreat. And the Letts, the Esthonians and the Lithuanians were bolstered up by English money.

Then Rossbach arrived. Our appeal reached him at the
frontier station on the Vistula. He notified the Government
that he would no longer obey their orders and started off for
the Baltic States with his volunteer corps. A division of
Reichswehrjäger intercepted him by Noske's orders. But the
Jäger joined Rossbach. The Rossbachers marched through
East Prussia and reached the frontier. They walked over the
frontier guards and marched into Lithuania. Lithuanian corps
barred their way; they cleared them away in a series of rapid
fights. They reached the railway and put it in going order.
They travelled as far as Mitau and heard of the reverse at
Thorensberg. They detrained and hurried on by forced
marches. They collected the retreating columns and attacked
the Letts just outside the town, after an incredible march.
They got into formation for the attack and for the first time
bugles sounded the advance in the Baltic States. Rossbach
charged. Rossbach attacked the Letts who were drunk with
victory, raced into the town, set fire to the houses, destroyed
guns, collected the despairing Germans and led them out. But
we never managed to recapture Thorensberg.

Then the German Government got worried and sent a general
to bring us back to its motherly bosom. Bombs flew round his
saloon car.

The Letts pursued us at once. Hardly had we left a wood
before the snow-covered branches of the trees were tossed and
bullets fell round our legs. We struck out in every direction;
we ambushed in every corner, in every wood, at every brook.
At the Eckau we crept into fire-blackened ruins and turned
every gun on to the pursuers. And it snowed and snowed and
snowed.

THE LAST FIGHT

We made our last push. We roused ourselves once more and charged. To the last man we left our cover and dashed into the wood. We ran across the snowfields and broke into the forest. We took them unawares and raged and shot and killed. We hunted the Letts across the fields like hares, set fire to every house, smashed every bridge to smithereens and broke every telegraph pole. We dropped the corpses into the wells and threw bombs after them. We killed anything that fell into our hands, we set fire to everything that would burn. We saw red; we lost every feeling of humanity. Where we had ravaged, the earth groaned under the destruction. Where we had charged, dust, ashes and charred balks lay in place of houses like festering wounds in the open country. A great banner of smoke marked our passage. We had kindled a fire and in it was burning all that was left of our hopes and longings and ideals.

We retired swaggering and intoxicated with success and laden with booty. The Letts had not held their ground at any point. But next morning they reappeared. The Russians in the north were weak and gave way. In the south, the German legion, which had an enormous area to cover, left gaps through which the Letts were able to advance. Mitau was caught in jaws of steel. The order came for us to retire.

There was not enough room on the carts. The horses had died. We had to choose between taking our baggage or the trench mortar ammunition. We piled up the whole of our baggage, packs, papers, equipment and loot. Then we set fire to the heap, packed the ammunition on to the carts and went off.

*   *   *   *

When we got to the Aa the various companies formed into what remained of each. I was given command of a farmyard at the bend of a little frozen river. There were ten of us, with three carts, two machine-guns and a trench mortar. The wood lay in front of us, open country all around, and, to the north-west, Mitau like a large, smudged, faded spot of ink on a piece of white blotting paper.

The picket to the right of us was attacked during the night. We fired at the enemy's flank and he was obliged to retire. We slept crowded round a miserable little fire which covered our faces with smuts and smoke and forced the tears to our red-rimmed eyes. The noise of bullets striking on the thin walls of the house awakened us. The Letts were in the wood in front. We lay behind mounds of snow and fired. We were attacked on three sides. We could no longer communicate with the other pickets. We could see the shells dropping on Mitau; we saw as it were a light veil hanging over the town, which presently turned to heavy smoke; we saw a red glow forming in the smoke – then a whole series of red glows; and finally we saw all these red points merging into one vast sea of red. We lay in the snow all day, shooting.

Our first casualty was Gohlke. He was lying behind his gun, when a bullet got him and carried away the whole top of his head. One of the Hamburgers was the next to go; a whizz-bang slit his abdomen. As the evening drew on, a third was badly wounded in the leg, and bled to death slowly, with terrible groans, for no one could do anything for him. It was a very long time since we had had any field dressings and, besides, every man was needed in the firing line.

Meanwhile Mitau was burning. The Letts continued firing on us, but they stopped bombarding Mitau. So we knew that Mitau had fallen. We lay alone in that field, shooting, shooting. . . .

It never got really dark, for Mitau acted as a torch and shed a rosy glow on the churned-up snow. The trench mortar went on without intermission. We still had about a dozen

shells stacked in the shelter of the bank of the Aa, near where
the carts were standing with the horses harnessed. At that
moment Lieutenant Kay came galloping on his horse. He
dashed into the yard, just as flames burst through the roof of
the house and the walls crumbled. He shouted: 'Get back at
once! The Letts have got Mitau! We can still break through
by the railway station and get on to the road to Schaulen. The
battalion has gone long ago!' – the despatch rider who was to
have notified us had never arrived.

We went after we had fired the last round of ammunition
from our trench mortar. The mortar itself we dragged on to
the ice on the river, and, while guns and ammunition were
hurled on to the carts, we fired the trench mortar in all directions. I made certain that not so much as a button was left
behind. We piled the dead on to one of the carts. The wounded,
four in number, sat on the same cart. We painfully pushed the
slipping horses and sliding carts over the ice and almost lifted
them on to the other bank. Including Kay, we still had five
unwounded men. As the last shell dropped triumphantly into
the wood, I stuffed a hand-grenade into the barrel of the mortar
and pulled out the pin. Then I bolted. The mortar burst with
a terrific bang. We put the cart with the wounded men on it
in the middle. In front and behind were machine-guns ready
for firing. In this wise we retreated.

The bullets whistled round us till we were close on Mitau.
Then we jogged along towards the town in silence. Soon we
reached the outskirts. Not a soul was to be seen in the streets;
we clattered over the cobbles like phantoms. The noise from
the inner town resounded in the narrow street and echoed at
every corner. Suddenly the front cart put on a spurt. A few
Letts came out of a side street, their shadows dancing in the
light of the burning houses. We tore past them hell for leather.
They opened out and fired after us. At last we got to the railway

station and saw the high road ahead. Kay on his horse raised his arm as though he were giving the order to a whole battery, we whipped up the horses and saw nothing right or left. At the station some Letts were standing about, shouting and yelling, probably drunk. We raced past them.

Just before we reached the high road, I fell off the cart. I picked myself up with some difficulty and panted after the others. The road was unoccupied. The darkness swallowed us up. I must have been the last German soldier to leave Mitau.

CHAPTER XI

MENACE

JUST as a man who has lost a great deal of blood grows unconscious of his own pain and fatigue and is able to take a curiously
clear and impersonal view of his surroundings, so we saw
Germany as through a polished glass, as soon as we had crossed
the frontier. The strangeness of the people and the country
made our resolves seem unreal, and hid the immediate past
from us, as with a thick veil. The heat of our blind rage evaporated in the cool air of Germany. If we managed to keep any
pride or confidence in ourselves during that retreat through the
wide Lithuanian snowfields, it was by the knowledge that we
were only repeating the experience of the armies who returned
from the front in 1918. But we were determined that their
collapse should not be repeated.

We expected to find the land in a state of ferment, to feel
the cities trembling with unrest, to sense the increasing struggle,
the certainty of a speedy change. But the country seemed
quiet, a thin skin had formed over the wound. Our hopes
trickled away like the water in the sluggish canals in Kehdingen,
whither the Government had despatched us. The peasants
trudged over their fields in heavy boots, the cattle were fat in
the stalls. Our quarters were clean, we helped with the work
and adapted ourselves to a life of peaceful productiveness.

In the evenings I often stood on the dyke and looked down-
stream. The girl from my house told me that before the war
the lights of the steamers used to gleam in long festoons up and

down the water. But now the broad expanse was empty, the harbour lifeless, the stream a wide, shining blackness.

'They had to hand over all the ships, you see,' said the girl. 'We all stood on the dyke when they sailed down the Elbe on their last trip; and that was the first time we really knew that we'd lost the war.' We talked a great deal on that wind swept dyke; in its sublime isolation it appeared to me like a bridge that might lead to the new realities. We spoke of this and that, but all our whispered confidences ended in war and revolution, till finally she shivered and said: 'Come on, I'm cold. Let's go home.' I was rather vexed at having spent such a long time talking about these things with the girl; but so it was on this day and almost every day.

We could not escape from our incubus. We could not get rid of it in the stuffy pot-houses, nor in the dancing halls that were crowded every Saturday with girls and lads and soldiers, nor in the well-to-do streets and cafés of Stade, nor in the peaceful farms on the marshes. Something kept us on the *qui vive*, which had nothing to do with the uncertainty of our future, nor with the fatuity of our present employment; we did not know what it was. Some nights we spent entirely in drinking, and if we did not do that, we were in the girls' rooms, and if we were not there, we were gambling away our money. We were waiting and we did not know exactly what we were waiting for. We kept our weapons, not knowing when we should need them again. We lived absent mindedly, we kept on running our heads against walls, we did not belong anywhere, we were strangers in a strange land. We realised that we were required to account for ourselves, but there was nobody to hear our justification; so we grew taciturn and lived shut up in ourselves, carrying a whole load of unsolved questions. We had offered ourselves to Fate unconditionally and Fate had thrown us away like a stone.

MENACE

There was a rumour that we were to be called upon in case of any disturbance. But we had no wish to fight for law and order.

At Bromberg, on the way from Memel to Stade, we had jumped out of the train when we heard that the town was to be ceded to Poland, and would have defended Bromberg and the frontier. But we were not allowed to, and indeed it was only right that we should not, for we knew that they mistrusted us and with very good reason. One day a commission from the *Reichswehr* arrived, and the members of it were much astonished that we did not salute them. We laughed when they, by order of the Government, demanded that we should deliver up all weapons and all equipment and the horses and carts. That night we went to the stables and fetched out the horses – they were ours, we had captured them ourselves and brought them through with immense trouble, there was not a single one of the Government's among them – and those horses vanished and the carts with them and were never seen again. Next day each man was given several hundred marks – from a well-wisher, we were told. The weapons also disappeared, but in this case we knew where to find them. So, when the *Reichswehr* commission turned up, there was nothing for them to remove except a bag of nails.

When the Hamburgers went to the Baltic States they formed a battalion six hundred strong. When they marched into Kehdingen they were a company numbering twenty-four men and a lieutenant. Of these twenty-four men, three had joined at Weimar – Schmitz, Hoffmann and myself. Lieutenant Kay was still with us; but one day in February, 1920, he invited us three to Stade, and when we met there in a grog shop, he told us that he was going to leave us. The good citizens of Stade were having their evening drinks, and they looked at our table disapprovingly. For we were putting away a good deal and Lieutenant Kay had a naturally loud voice. 'We are breasting the stream of life,' he said. 'We have been smitten with a passionate lust for blood – we suck honey from the very marrow of the nation's bones and then smear that honey round the nation's mouth!' He lapped up his grog. 'Future generations will ask us what we did. And we shall answer that we have stirred people's blood. For the soul is the emanation of the blood, and the blood boiled and the stream rose and we stirred it. Then future generations will say: "Well done! Full marks!" But those johnnies over there – here's luck! – they'll be asked too, and they will answer: "We thickened that blood nicely and made soup of it, and it was very good." And the future generations will say: "Rotten! No marks at all!" and then at the last judgment,' and he drank, filled up his glass afresh and dissolved the sugar with great care, 'our bones will collect and form up in parade and they will be told "Fall in on the right." But the dry-as-dusts – Cheerioh! Judge, here's to you – will bow respectfully and say "Excuse us, oh Lord, we can't collect our bones, because we never had any." And they will be told: "Fall in on the left, you goats, where you belong." And I tell you, it will be a clean division.' And we drank and talked very wisely and the other people looked at us furiously but behaved in a most gentlemanly manner. Lieutenant Kay got melancholy drunk and wailed loudly and asked us whether he really had to go and become a crabbed twister of the law, and whether everything was really over. I said no, and stuck to it obstinately. But Lieutenant Kay wouldn't believe it and said all the fun was over and he was going to swot and get through his exams. Then he smashed a few glasses and said: 'Damage to property,' and then he hit an indignant customer under the jaw and said 'Assault and battery!' Finally he attacked the policeman whom the manager had called in and said 'Resistance to authority.' We had some difficulty in quieting him, and he hung out of the window and waved for a long time. I never saw him again. A month later he fell at the Town Hall in Schöneberg. His body was identified by the papers in his pocket, for his head had been smashed to pulp.

A few days later Schmitz departed. I accompanied him as far as the station and he said to me: 'I can tell *you* what I'm going to do: I'm going to the Ruhr to join the Red army. I'm told it's mobilising there.' I nodded and he said: 'We're going to stir a little blood there.' We both laughed, remembering Kay, and then I said: 'Anyhow, *auf Wiedersehen*, and if we meet again on the barricades, we can arrange now that, if it can't be avoided, we'll hit each other good and hard in memory of old times.' Schmitz laughed and said: 'Well, well, wait and see. Nowadays it depends on who shoots quickest!' Schmitz had gone one better than I and I could only remark that I was a damned good shot. We shook each other warmly by the hand and were a little embarrassed over our display of feeling. Then his train drew out.

I could not believe that men and their weapons would no longer have a life in common. The Hamburgers still stuck together. Wuth was continually going from one place to another and at first we thought he'd got a girl in Hamburg whom he was always visiting. However, one day at the beginning of March he collected us all and we discovered why he was about the country so much. He brought fresh air with him, tearing gusts that brushed our faces and made us breathe more deeply. It was as though he had opened a chink through which a ray of sunshine shone and the motes danced.

Something was brewing in the country. There was one army which had to be disbanded on account of the peace treaty, and another secret army which began mobilising. Commissions were abroad in the land, consisting of obsequious individuals in frock coats. Famine, strikes and hatred were in the streets; profiteers with fat pocket-books and burgeoning chins drove about in shining motor cars; fugitives from the districts which had been stolen from us sought a wretched subsistence; foreigners bought up whole towns. Under the thin veneer of peace created by well-intentioned citizens of every class, there was a mad whirl of unemployment and stock-exchange gambling, of food-riots and full-dress balls, of mass-demonstrations and government conferences – there seemed to be nothing that could escape from the general madness, and much that was destroyed by it. Paper rustled over the whole country: convocations and ultimatums, regulations and prohibitions, proclamations and protests, fell like snowflakes over the land, simulating authority where none remained, rousing hopes which ended in despair. There was a great deal of talk about reconstruction, but the materials were shoddy and the ground insecure; there was also plenty of talk of destruction, but somehow the rotten scaffolding held up.

The country was in a dangerous state, when the falling of a stone might precipitate all sorts of calamities and the only question was who was going to drop it. The frontiers were still vague, but when anyone tried to fix them, there were loud complaints, and the new boundaries were like knife cuts, severing whole provinces, like limbs amputated by a drunken man. Little scattered bands of men fought on the frontiers; but when they found that they got no backing, that there was no reserve of strength behind them, they turned on Berlin. From the east came Ehrhardt's brigade from Upper Silesia, and the exiled troops from the Baltic States; Lützow's and Pfeffer's came from the Rhineland and the Ruhr district; Aulock's and Schmidt's volunteer corps were on the watch. They demanded plain speaking from Berlin – Berlin could explain nothing – and the troops stood their ground gloomily but determinedly, with their rifles in their hands.

The *Entente* insisted on the letter of the treaty being

observed. The Allied cabinets sent ultimatums and threatened invasion. They insisted that the remainder of the German army must be demobilized. The German Government gave way. Nobody will ever know whether they did so because they saw no other way out of it, realising that they had taken on too great a responsibility; or because they sensed danger from the irritated soldiery; or because, if they were ever able to take any decision, they were determined to guard the hardly-won victories of the revolution – though it was not originally of their own making – against the machinations of the monarchists. Actually they may have thought that there was some conspiracy behind the advance of the soldiers, some reactionary plot. If so, they were mistaken. It was no inspired, controversial political idea that spurred us to protest. The actual cause lay simply in despair, which is never articulate. But these desperate men were accustomed to make the first move in the face of danger, considering that attack was the best defence.

Power and responsibility seemed all at once to be simple and inspiriting and sweet. We discovered in ourselves a degree of determination which made all things appear easy. We had never learnt to split hairs. We thought that we must act, so as to be stronger than circumstances, instead of allowing circumstances to master us. This decision was made by eight thousand men, no more; yet they were likely to be enough, for they were the only ones who were prepared to face all the consequences of their decision. We knew that there was likely to be a stiff fight, so we prepared everything for that fight. We believed that it was we who were meant to have the power and no one else, for Germany's sake. For we felt that we embodied Germany. We believed that we were entitled to have that power. The people at the head of affairs in Berlin had no such right. For we did not believe that they were working solely for the good of Germany, as we were, who felt that we *were* Germany.

There was indeed a constitution and a treaty: it was just because of these that we proposed fighting them. We thought that when they spoke of Germany they meant the constitution, and when they spoke of the constitution, they meant the peace treaty. Did they hear our menaces above the reading and writing of their shallow programmes and proclamations and debates and notes and newspaper articles? No, we thought, they did not hear them, otherwise their outlook would have changed.

Captain Berthold, commander of the Bavarian battalion, an aviator who had brought down fifty-five enemy machines and had the order *Pour le mérite*, a man who just managed to keep his battered body together with hinges and bandages, was the mainspring of our activities at that time. He had, of course, as a Bavarian, his private dislike of Prussia, but he was undoubtedly the least reactionary of all the officers of the Baltic troops in Kehdingen.

During the time of waiting the companies began to melt away. The towns, and the girls in them, were enticing. The Hamburgers stood firm, as also did the Bavarians, in spite of having nothing to do. But everyone knew that something was in the wind; the men buttonholed their officers and asked them insistently what was going on; the officers lay in wait for the despatch-riders hurrying from Berlin to Stade, and these told tales of dry, idiotic negotiations between General Lüttwitz and Noske, of haggling over requisitions and promises, and of hard-won rights and such like well-worn platitudes. And they described the mixture of conflicting opinions, interests and claims. Things did not look well to our way of thinking, and we were afraid they would end in compromise – but in that case we were ready to march in spite of everything, without Lüttwitz and Kapp. Possibly even – against them.

The harsh, pompous demobilisation order came just at the

right moment. Neither townspeople nor peasants had any further obligation to billet us; the peasants indeed would have been quite ready to keep us, but the townspeople not for any consideration. 'We won't be demobilised,' we said, fetched the weapons from their hiding places, and besieged Wuth and Berthold with questions; they, however, were for the moment as uncertain as we and were impatiently waiting for news from Berlin. The soldiers stood about in close groups in the villages, fully armed. Gradually these groups began to move, without orders, and made for Stade. When we arrived in the sulky little town on March 13th, 1920, at two o'clock in the afternoon, special editions were published and posters were stuck up on the walls.

At an early hour in the morning, the 2nd Naval Division under Commander Ehrhardt, had marched into Berlin and had occupied the Government quarter. At the Brandenburg Tor they had met Ludendorff who was out for his morning constitutional. The *Reich* Government and the Prussian Government had fled. General Lüttwitz and Kapp had formed a new government and had caused posters to be distributed headed 'The Lie about the monarchist *Putsch!*'

All at once Stade was full of troops. Divisions paraded in various spots; isolated companies went through the streets, their packs piled high; motors and despatch riders raced about; tremendous crowds of townspeople, soldiers, workmen and peasants collected at the street corners, in front of the posters and of the newspaper buildings. Hoffman and I spelt out one of the notices over the heads of the excited and gesticulating people. 'Words,' said a workman, 'Words!' and he spat scornfully, but restrained himself when he saw us. Hoffman read and then said, grinning a little ruefully: 'Words!' and we commiserated with one another at having to make these words mean something. We went further and wondered where the little bows in the old monarchist colours had suddenly come from that were being worn, and all the Iron Crosses: these were the same people who had just given us notice to quit.

Wuth arrived at top speed and collected his company. Berthold, he told us rapidly, was coming early next morning with his battalion; the Hamburg and Berlin guards had declared themselves neutral – if we gave them double pay, they'd join us; he had no idea what the *Reichswehr* would do, but he did not think there was much doubt; and finally: 'Listen to me, gentlemen. No more slacking now. Officers are to be saluted. Understand?'; and that he had billeted us in the schoolhouse for the night.

After an excited, wakeful night, we met Berthold. He said that he had put himself at the disposition of the new Government. The Hamburgers placed themselves under his command. Berthold's plan was to go straight to Berlin via Hamburg, without waiting for orders. But the rest of our weapons had to be collected. I was told off to set up and bring over what I could of the six machine-guns that were lying about in a fragmentary state in the neighbouring villages. I rode off immediately. Early in the afternoon I got back with four guns and three thousand rounds of ammunition. The battalion was paraded in the market square ready to move.

When we got to the railway station everything was silent and empty. A stoker came out of one of the sheds, saw us, grinned, spat on to the lines and said: 'General strike!' and vanished. We took possession of the railway station, Berthold enquired for experts, found two men who had formerly been railway employees and sent them to the engine house. The engine they found had first to be fired, then began the wildest shunting with much whistling and shouting and a great deal of laughter from the strikers, who were hanging over the bridge and watching.

MENACE

Berthold walked up and down the platform irritably. He was wearing his blue peace-time greatcoat, had loosened the strap of his sword, which trailed aggravatingly. We had stacked our rifles and were waiting. All in all there were about four hundred of us.

I had procured a pile of newspapers and was sitting opposite Wuth in the waiting room, reading. Who Kapp was, Wuth did not know, but there were a lot of other names as well – Jagow and Wangenheim and the Rev. Traub. Rather a lot of old gentlemen and old names, I opined to Wuth. Lüttwitz was also an old stager. At the end of our time in the Baltic States the oldest man of us all was Bischoff, a young major.

'I'm for Ehrhardt,' I said to Wuth, 'but not for any of the others.' Up to that time I had hardly heard of Ehrhardt, but thought that he must be a young commander.

'Damn all these old names,' said Wuth, 'this is the young people's affair.' He mused for a moment and said: 'We must put a stop to the revolution.'

'We must carry on the revolution!' said I and looked at Wuth and reflected what a gap even five years' difference in age makes.

The train was ready; we climbed noisily into it, placed machine-guns at the communicating doors and in the engine, and then steamed away into the twilight, singing.

CHAPTER XII

PUTSCH

I SHALL never forget how the shadows of the dying day cloaked all the ugliness of our departure. The whole loveliness of the world shone from the forest and in the soft buds of the silver birches, which nestled trembling beside the railway embankment. The earth seemed to be holding its breath, listening for the gentle murmur of awakening life; everything seemed to be glowing with an inner radiance – yes, even the darkness, which came down on us like velvet, appeared but a delusive veil, hiding from us the perplexities of the day – to many of us it gave our last dreams of happiness. We were silent, perhaps sensing intuitively the terror into whose open jaws we were hurrying.

The train drew up on a stretch of open line. Right and left of the embankment rose the dark walls of high gabled houses, which seemed threatening in their very silence. Lieutenant Wuth came down the corridor with long rapid strides and told us that the train could not go on any farther because the line was barred at Harburg station. The command was at once given for us to detrain. We were only to take the guns with us and leave the baggage in the carriages. The night was to be spent at Harburg, so that we could proceed early in the morning. In case the train could not be got past the station, we were to go to Hamburg on foot by the bridge over the Elbe. We carefully lifted the guns out of the compartments, climbed across sharp stones and awkward sleepers, stumbling and swearing, and came to a gate which opened on to a wide street. Here we paraded.

The few solitary lanterns we carried shed a pale greenish light on the dark mass of houses and the guns made a tangled barrier of shadows across it. A few civilians suddenly appeared spectrally on the line of light; they recoiled in amazement, and vanished again into darkness. Along the whole sombre line of houses in that street only one lamp was to be seen. It hung high above our heads and looked quite unreal, apparently entirely detached from the earth. Captain Berthold passed down the line, his sword clanking, and was swallowed up in the darkness. The march began.

We could feel that this town was inimical. We still had in our mind's eye the quiet marshes, the wide calm river, the peace of carefully cultivated land. Here everything was close on top of everything else, black masses of stone grew up in front of us out of the pavements, the streets seemed like dangerous clefts in space, mysteries lurked at every corner. We did not feel as if we were passing the homes of living people, we appeared to be looking at ruins, vast rubbish heaps, with bare, blackened walls, piled-up stones behind crumbling façades of glass, iron and plaster. Disgusting smells seemed to be rising from the cellars; no star pierced the gloom above of this street. We clattered through a mist of smoke, fog and danger; our shadows changed alternately from terrifying giants to sinister dwarfs in the ghostly light; our feet made a hollow sound and it was impossible to keep in step.

The first few groups began a faint, husky song. But it was silenced almost immediately, when a window was thrown open and a burst of wild savage laughter startled the column; laughter that was a scream of mockery, shrilling through the air like a sharp poisoned arrow. It was a woman, or rather it was the town itself, or the evil embodiment of the town. This laughter had to be stopped, it was unbearable. We must howl, sing till our throats were sore; so each sang whatever came first into his head. I felt for a hand-grenade at my belt, and it was all I could do not to yield to my wild desire to take out the pin and hurl the bomb in at the open window. Gradually we began to sing in tune and then we turned into a street bordered by trees, a wide street with low houses and front gardens.

A certain number of people now began to appear. Some were crowding through the door of a café and collected beside the railings. We were received with a buzz of talk; questions were hurled at us. I was the next file to Hoffmann, and a man suddenly stepped up to us, raised his hands and said in a voice which trembled with age, alcohol and joy: 'Boys, are you going to fetch back our Kaiser?'– Hoffmann was really taken aback at this and could not make any answer until we had gone on some ten paces.

'N-no-not that – not that –. . . .' he murmured and looked round as though he had just awakened to a consciousness of his surroundings. I laughed under my breath, amid suppressed curses; but I was almost sorry that we could not say that we were going to fetch the Kaiser – then our performances would at least have had some sense.– But what I was thinking of – was there no sense in what we were doing? This accursed town, this confounded darkness, were robbing us of our feeling of security. In the devilish air, that was a poisonous mixture of fear and hatred and imminent danger, everything evaporated that so lately as yesterday had seemed sure and potent. Fetch back the Kaiser? No. We were concerned with bigger things than the man in Doorn. I tried to make the words of the Kapp programme seem real. But there was the rub! The proclamation began with a justification: that hardly indicated conviction! No, it was not the words of his programme which called us to fight. What was it, then? It was simply that we enjoyed the danger. To march into the unknown was enough for us; for it answered some primal need in us. We did not know what would happen; but how should we ever know except by finding out?

As we arrived at an open square came the command: 'Halt!'

We saw crowds of armed civilians. What were the ones with white brassards? *Bürgerwehr?* And the ones with red brassards? *Arbeiterwehr?* What airs they were giving themselves! Was Berthold actually talking to them? Oh, of course, enquiring about billets. We were to be quartered in the Heimfeld school? That must be the big building opposite. How tired I was! . . . 'By the right – quick march! –'

We stacked our guns in one corner, and piled up the ammunition round them. Some humorist among the Bavarians drew caricatures of Berthold on the blackboard, then we lay down on the hard narrow benches. As I was falling asleep I remember thinking that it was just our luck to find ourselves in the beginners' classroom, where the benches were so narrow that one could hardly move. . . .

In the morning Hoffmann woke me, looking as though he had not slept, and said: 'I don't like the look of this!'–

'What?'–

'Come and see' he said and dragged me up the stairs past the open doors of schoolrooms full of yawning men. He stopped at a corner window. 'Down in the yard there are machine-guns! There, behind the barn, they've been lugging boxes for the last half hour – ammunition, I suppose – men, women and children at it! The streets are swarming with armed workmen. But the best of the lot is over at the back there, in the fields; have a good look – what is it? – Trenches, man, regulation trenches! Not to put too fine a point on it, we are caught in a trap.'–

'How extraordinary! Does Berthold know? And Wuth?'

149

'Of course they do! There's been coming and going for the last half hour of deputations and commissions and parleyings. Workmen and townsfolk and *Reichswehr*——'

'What, they've got the *Reichswehr* here?'

'A Pioneer corps – the 9th. That's just the trouble. The b——rs locked up their officers this morning, opened the arsenal and distributed arms among the workmen!'–

This was really a delightful situation! 'How the devil do you know all this?'–

'I've been running round all the morning. I don't know why, but I had a funny feeling and couldn't keep still. The whole town is in an uproar.'

We looked out of the window. Round our sparse line of sentries was a large crowd of people, unarmed; the armed men stood farther away, squeezing into corners.

'We'd better go and talk to Berthold,' I said.

Soldiers were standing in all the corridors, staring out of the windows with every expression of astonishment.

'I can't think what's the matter with me,' Hoffmann complained, 'I believe there's going to be a scrap and I . . . I don't know. . . .'

'What's wrong with you, man, are you ill? Here, have a drink of water.' I turned a tap in the corridor, it spluttered and gurgled, but the water would not flow. 'Here's a nice mess – look – the swine have turned the water off! Come on, we've got to see Berthold – quick!'

We tore downstairs. 'That's what happens –.' I said angrily. 'What?' asked Hoffmann.

'When airmen think they can take command in street-fighting. Hell! We're well in the soup. All tidily collected in one place. Instead of occupying all public buildings immediately and keeping a strong mobile reserve. . . .' I opened the door and heard Berthold saying to some emissaries from the populace:

'Yes, yes, gentlemen. You are demanding our withdrawal. But I've already told you that I have no intention whatever of remaining in Harburg. We *want* to move, the sooner the better. What the devil should we want to stay in Harburg for? The flag? The flag will be taken down as soon as we leave and not before. We're going as quickly as possible. The men are packing up now. If you hadn't delayed us, we might have been off long ago. Now please go and calm the people, so that no accidents happen! Will you kindly go, gentlemen!'

'Pack up?' I whispered to Hoffmann. He pointed out of the window, without saying a word. The square was black with people. The sentries were closely surrounded where the main streets opened on to the square.

'No, my friend,' I said. 'We shall not pack up anything. On the contrary, we shall place the machine-guns in position; that seems more important at the moment.'

Hoffmann nodded and we got to work. We mounted a gun on each side of the house, and one in the loft. Down below, at the main entrance, the Bavarians had two light machine-guns and a heavy one, but this latter was hidden in a near-by classroom. The main entrance with the big staircase did not face on to the square but on to a wide side street.

The Hamburgers stood at the first-storey windows. I passed round the water-boxes of the machine gun and amidst a fire of bad jokes we filled them in the most natural manner. We lifted the gun on to the benches, so that it should be ready to fire at any moment. The line of sentries had retreated a little. All the windows facing the square were now open, a few heads peered out stealthily; the streets opening on to the square were crowded as far as the eye could reach. There were a great many women, and even some children, and the ceaseless hum of voices numbed our senses. The armed men seemed to be chiefly workmen.

Hoffmann and I stared down into the square. 'They're very silly, after all,' I said, 'What do you suppose they really want of us?'

'Yes,' said Hoffmann and looked at me wanly, 'yes, the workers are fools. We were fools too when we were fighting for law and order. Now they are fools.' Wuth stood behind us. He was wearing his velvet cap. So there was going to be a scrap! Hoffmann said softly but impressively: 'Now, if they only knew it, the moment has come for the workers! If you want to have power, sir, you must know why you want it. We don't know; I don't believe Kapp and the other men in Berlin know either. If the workers are clever, they'll join us, then we'll see that they get what they are aiming for, and they'll show us what justification there is for power these days.'—

'They're not clever,' said Wuth. And I added: 'Perhaps we've got too many old gentlemen on the job!'— —

Yells and whistles sounded in the square. We leant out of the window. Captain Berthold was crossing the small space that our sentries had hitherto been able to keep clear, bare-headed. He approached the crowd, passed the line of sentries, pushed his way through the struggling masses and only halted when he had got well in amongst them. He raised his hand. There was an instant silence. He began to speak. From where we stood we could not hear what he was saying. We saw the throng press close round him. At the back they climbed on to steps and railings. Bands of men with red badges fought their way through the crowd. Berthold's voice was vehement and ringing. They simply had to listen to him. But why were the armed men pushing at the back? What the devil was the reason that all the rifles were suddenly presented?

The Bavarians and the Hamburgers carefully lifted up their guns. Now the guns were facing one another across the crowded square. Berthold talked and talked. A wave of oppressive hatred rose from the masses to us, like the hatred of one race for another. We stared feverishly at the crowd, instead of at our armed adversaries, who were, after all, much more dangerous. Gradually a dusty yellow haze formed over the sea of heads below us. I had a curious feeling of sympathy with Berthold. Suddenly came the shot for which we had all been waiting. One little crack, no more; but it seemed to wake us all from our stupor. Every man's hand went to the trigger of his gun and bullets spurted from every corner.

Hoffmann ran to the other room, where his gun was. I balanced mine on the window-sill and fired. I resisted the furious temptation to fire into the middle of the fleeing, yelling crowd.

At the corner of the main street, into which the terrified masses were pouring, crouched a group of Reds with rifles, waiting for the throng to disperse. I mowed them down with the first turn of my handle. The men lay, neatly picked off, in a row in front of a house. I peppered one window after another of this house, saw the panes smash and little clouds of brick and mortar rise off the walls. In a few feverish seconds the square was cleared of every living soul. While a new cartridge belt was being got out of the box, I leant out and saw dark pitiful heaps strewed over the square – men, women and children. I had a horrible feeling of nausea; I screamed something hoarsely; then, hanging half out of the window, I sought a fresh objective. To the left, in a dark passage, some men were hurriedly training a machine-gun on us. I dragged my gun round, it dangled crookedly out of the window; I set my knee against the window-sill, held on to the wavering machine and fired. Suddenly the gun jerked, reared, so that I almost fell out of the window, boiling water scalded my eyes and face. A terrific impact hurled me backwards. I fell into the class-room among the desks, dragging the gun with me. I put out my right arm to save myself, and met blood and dust. Heavy groans sounded beside me: the Hamburger who had been passing me the cartridges lay there with his face torn and mangled, streaming with blood. There were five shots in the gun-jacket; four men had been killed and the shrapnel had made round holes in the caricatures of Berthold on the blackboard.

The whole house trembled in the hail of bullets which thudded against the walls. Splinters of glass flew into the room, shivered on the floor and gashed the dead and the living. The pictures danced madly on the walls and then crashed to the ground in fragments. Stones and bullets embedded themselves in the walls, the chalk dissolved to powder, floated all over the room and covered everyone and everything with a whitish dust, turning the streams of blood to a sticky paste. We lay pressed close to the front wall, unable to shoot.

The door flew open, Hoffmann came in, threw himself on the floor and crept over to me on his hands and knees. At that moment a shell burst in the passage and the door swung back and forth, as though impelled by a ghostly hand. Hoffmann glared at me with a pale dust-besmirched face, fumbled in his pocket and pulled out a little mirror which he held up to me. I looked in it and saw that my face was splashed with blood. It was flowing from a tiny wound in my temple. I dabbed at it with my dirty handkerchief and smudged it all over my face.

'My gun's bust!' roared Hoffmann. I pointed enquiringly at my machine-gun, which lay where it had fallen. He nodded. Lieutenant Wuth edged into the room, bent double. His velvet cap had got very ragged and a stream of blood was flowing from his forehead. He beckoned us out of the room. We crept to the door on all fours and then slipped through into the corridor one at a time. There we were able to stand upright, sheltered by the thick walls.

'There's no sense in that,' shouted Wuth. 'Only one man

154

in each room; watch by loopholes in the wall; everyone else into the passages. Don't waste your ammunition!'–

The passages were full of dead and wounded men. A Hamburger bored a loop-hole in the wall with an iron bar. Hoffmann and I hauled out the boxes of ammunition. Then we rushed along to Hoffmann's room to secure the ammunition from there. I went to look at each of my guns, stumbled over dead bodies, and hurried into the classrooms. But not a single one of our guns was in working order. Only the one up under the roof was going on firing steadily. I carried up some boxes of ammunition. The wounded were shrieking and groaning for water. The doctor and his orderly bandaged them as best they could, tearing strips off the shirts of dead or living; the supply of bandages had long since given out. The doctor stopped me, pointing enquiringly at the blood on my forehead, but I waved him away.

The school was bombarded from every side. Bullets thudded on our walls unceasingly and methodically. The hatred of the whole town seemed to be concentrated on the building. One of the Hamburgers came out of a classroom and said: 'Now they are aiming at us with their machine-guns from hardly a hundred yards off -- they'll shoot the place down brick by brick!' The whole box of tricks was trembling. When one of the Bavarians fired down by the main entrance, the whole house resounded as though a mine had exploded.

The Bavarians lay silently on the stone floors in the corridors and on the landings. Only the men at the observation posts were in the classrooms. Hoffmann, Wuth and I lay among the rest.

'Where is Berthold?' I enquired.

'At the main entrance,' murmured Wuth.

A young Bavarian officer climbed slowly over the prone bodies, saw Wuth and said with his voice cracking. 'Surely the guard we left by the train will realise what's up? Won't the news have got to Stade? Balla and the other battalions must know that we are in a tight place?'– Wuth shook his head silently. The Bavarian said in a monotonous voice: 'Won't Hamburg send to help us? I don't understand – they can't just leave us to it?'

Wuth got up and took the officer by the arm and led him away.

Someone came and said: 'There's shooting in the town!' At once half the men were on their feet. They crowded into the classrooms again and everybody listened.

'That must be our pickets coming from the train.'

'No, it's from the other direction, it's the Hamburgers!'

I listened with all my ears, but I could hear no diminution of the ceaseless hammering of bullets against the school. Someone thought he heard cheering. Wuth came and said: 'Don't get excited, gentlemen! Back into the corridors!' He looked at me and whispered: 'They've captured the train; and they're waving our flag in the field at the back!'–

'Mightn't it be our own men?'–

'No, they're civilians.'

The bombardment grew fiercer. It rattled like hail on a corrugated iron roof. The soldiers crept closer and closer together. But, as always happens in moments of greatest stress, one man here and there came away from the crowd. We could not keep still; we wandered through the rooms, ran along the passages, climbed into the loft, routed in the cellar, carted about ammunition. Hoffmann and I went round all the entrances. One of the doors led into the playing ground, and this door was in the dead angle. The yard was surrounded by a wooden fence. I wondered whether we could not get to the opposite houses unseen. From there one might perhaps get into the open country: the trenches were farther to the right.

PUTSCH

I beckoned to Hoffmann, who pointed at the machine-gun in the loft, and we climbed up again.

I went into one of the classrooms and threw myself down by the spy-hole. The Bavarian on duty rolled over to one side without saying a word, and laid his head wearily on to his arms. The square was absolutely empty. I could not discover a single one of the enemy's men.

'I'm thirsty!' said the Bavarian.

I shrugged my shoulders. 'You Bavarians are always thirsty.'

'Oh, shut up and don't fool!'– I crawled out again.

Hoffmann said: 'We're running a bit short of ammunition.'

The gun under the roof had scarcely enough cartridges to fill one belt. I went downstairs. One of the windows on to the staircase was still quite whole. It looked on to the yard and was sheltered by one of the wings of the building. Just a narrow strip of field could be seen through this window.

Hoffmann and I approached the window. Down below they were shouting for ammunition. 'We're coming!' I yelled. Suddenly there was an ear-splitting crash, two arms clawed at the air, the gun clattered down the stairs. Something heavy hit me on the chest, my knees gave way, I fell – and lying on my breast I saw a head, and a hideous mess of blood and hair and brains – Hoffmann – Hoffmann!–

Hoffmann was dead. Dead. I laid him down gently. Then I crouched on the landing and stared dully into space.

'Is the ammunition coming?' sounded from below. Wuth passed me like a phantom, stopped a moment, saw and murmured: 'Ensign, the ammunition!' A tremendous noise arose. The Bavarian light machine-gun at the main entrance fired a few shots. I stumbled downstairs.

'They're coming, they're coming!'–

Wuth pulled me down on to the ground, to where the other gun was standing. The Bavarians from the other crew shouted to us that people were coming out of the houses and were now at the dead angle.

We had placed ourselves right and left of the main entrance, on the first landing, about on a level with the upper light of the door. We could only see the ground floor of the houses opposite and a tiny section of the wide street. On the staircase in front of me lay a completely disabled heavy machine-gun, two dead men beside it, both with ghastly head wounds, like Hoffmann's – 'Quietly,' said Wuth, 'quietly!' –

The other gun was firing. A few shots only reached the staircase from outside. I could see nothing. The narrow strip of road was empty. From the square the bullets hailed monotonously on the walls.

Upstairs, people were calling for Wuth. He rose and went rapidly up the steps. Three or four Bavarians asked whether we had heard anything of the men we had left guarding the train and whether reinforcements were not coming from Hamburg or Stade? I shrugged my shoulders.

Wuth came and said: 'Captain Berthold's orders: you're only to shoot when it's absolutely necessary.' He squatted on the stairs and stared straight in front of him with unseeing eyes.

This bombardment had been going on for five hours now. I looked intently through the narrow chink of the door, and thought I saw a shadow moving. Nothing; but in the house opposite there was a movement at the window. My hand went to the trigger.

'Don't shoot!' said Wuth. –

I distinctly saw a man with a rifle at the window, straining his eyes in our direction. I trained my gun on him. He seemed to have seen me – yes, he raised his rifle – he aimed – with lightning rapidity I threw myself to one side, the rifle cracked, and something hit me in the arm. I watched curiously to see my sleeve turning red with blood.

'Wounded?' enquired Wuth and was at my side immediately.

'Look out!' I shouted and pulled him aside with my left hand.–We investigated the wound. It was very slight. The bullet had entered the stone wall beside me, and a splinter had ricocheted into my right forearm. It was bleeding profusely.

'Get along and have it tied up!' Wuth commanded.

The doctor hastily bound a strip of stuff round my arm. He spat some fragmentary words through his teeth and looked absolutely worn out. 'Berthold wants to parley with them – to parley – what on earth are we coming to. . . .'

I walked over to Hoffmann's body. He lay on his back, stretched out peacefully. What – was he moving? Surely I had heard him gasp just now? Hoffmann . . .! Alas,– it was only blood trickling from his forehead and nose into his throat which made the gurgling noise. The dead man snored like this for a long while, and each time I was startled afresh. I could not sit there doing nothing, I had to move; I touched Hoffmann's hand shyly in passing.

Berthold ordered these words to be chalked on a blackboard:

'TRUCE! WE WANT TO PARLEY!'

Ropes were tied to the blackboard and it was hung carefully out of a window. The gun fire was instantly concentrated on this point and in a very few moments the blackboard was shot to smithereens.– I was wandering through the house now with a tall young Bavarian. Up in the loft, the two men with the light machine-gun were sitting peering quietly out into the square. They were both Bavarians. I went downstairs again with my companion. We came to a passage into which bullets were continually whistling through the doors. The Bavarian wanted to show off, so he leapt past one of the doors upright and then laughed and looked round triumphantly at his companions. He did it a second time, but suddenly jerked curiously to one side in the middle of his jump and fell like a log; his rifle slid along the corridor. He was dead.

The little thin Bavarian officer appeared again. 'Surely we shall be relieved?' he said and looked at me imploringly. I was going past him without a word, when there was a shout from below: 'Officers to go to Captain Berthold!' Wuth came towards me. I accompanied him as far as the room where Berthold was collecting the officers. It was a narrow room close by the main door. Wuth and the little Bavarian went in together, and for a second I saw the few remaining officers standing close round the Captain. Then the door was shut. But I could not stay outside, I knew with a deadly certainty that they were considering surrender. I made up my mind, opened the door and went in.

'Sir!' I said hoarsely, the words almost choking me, 'Sir!' and then I clicked my heels and said: 'Please may I come in?' The officers looked round in astonishment and Wuth came over to my side. I looked at the captain. He half turned his head and said: 'Yes, what is it?'

I said: 'Sir, I know what it was like in Halle; surrender is not. . . .' I began to stammer, pulled myself together and said: 'There's another way out!' and went on quickly: 'At the back, the door into the playground is not overlooked, I have had a good look round; there is a wooden fence and nobody will see us until we get to a group of houses on the very outskirts. The trenches are a long way to the right. I'm sure we can get through that way.'

The captain raised his hand: 'How much more ammunition have we?'

Wuth answered: 'All told, about another 500 rounds.'

The captain said nothing. For a few moments there was silence, except for the steady rain of shots outside. Wuth said:

'It's a possibility, sir; but the sortie would have to be covered by a squad of men staying in the place and going on firing.

I said quickly: 'Yes, sir; we still have three sound machine-guns, we can simply stay behind and continue firing until –'

'And then what happens to these men?' the captain enquired and darted his head at me like a bird.

'We can –' I stuttered 'Only a few men, sir; we can probably cut our way through afterwards.'

The captain said quietly: 'No. If the sortie is resolved on, gentlemen, officers will cover it.' The officers saluted.

I said: 'The men won't leave without you, sir.'

Berthold rose and said: 'Then there will be no sortie.' He reflected for two terrible seconds and said hesitatingly: 'If any of the men wish to try and escape alone, they may do so.– That will do, you may go.'

I saluted and staggered to the door, realising with a gnawing pain that this was the only decision possible for Berthold. I found myself back again by Hoffmann's body. The daylight faded rapidly.

We had no ammunition, we had no water; we had so many dead that we counted the living. And we had lost hope. Everything was at an end. What did we care that the bombardment was slackening outside? Wuth came and said that Berthold had got in touch with the besiegers. What did I care? The little Bavarian officer joined us – he stuck to us like a burr. I still had a few cartridges in my pocket. There was a slight commotion down at the entrance. It had already got very dark inside the house. Suddenly two of the Workers' Red Cross orderlies stood before us; they were middle-aged men and asked quietly where our badly wounded cases were. A third man, wearing a red badge came up behind them and said in an undertone: 'We guarantee a free pass out to unarmed men. Please lay down your weapons.' He said 'please'! Wuth smiled sardonically, undid his belt and let it slip to the ground. The little Bavarian said excitedly to Wuth: 'But the belt is my private property!'–

'Put it on underneath your tunic, you damned fool,' said Wuth roughly and turned away. The firing stopped completely.

We collected slowly in the entrance hall. A few of the men were already standing in the square, I was on the steps, looking at the black mass of armed men, when they began shooting again. The men in front ran back. 'Traitors,' they yelled, 'traitors!' and 'The swine are going on shooting. . . .' I tore up at once to the loft to the last remaining machine-gun.

It did not last long. We fired our last cartridge. Two Reds met me in the passage and said: 'It's no use, you men – what's the good?'–

'You b——y swine,' I said and felt myself grow livid. 'Is that how you keep your word?' They said no more.

A heavy reek of blood, sweat, dust and gunpowder oppressed our lungs. Several Reds stepped over Hoffmann's body, carrying rifles. I was mad with rage.

'Down with your gun!' they shouted threateningly.

I threw it aside and said: 'Haven't got any more cartridges anyway.'

One, quite a young fellow, said: 'You're just fools – you've only been led astray. But if we catch any of your officers. . . .!'

At that moment Wuth came round the corner. I dragged him back.

'Take off your shoulder-straps!' I hissed. He looked at me with horror, and I took and ripped the things off his tunic. 'They've got it in for officers,' I said; he shrugged his shoulders. Then slowly and with a terribly sad expression, he took his velvet cap off his head. He was wearing a plain tunic. I stuck Hoffmann's bloody cap on to his head. He started and said: 'Quick – Berthold!'

PUTSCH

Below in the dark hall a wild turmoil reigned. Reds, civilians, our own men and even a few of the *Reichswehr* were mixed in inextricable confusion. We saw Berthold. His *Pour le mérite* shone for a moment. Only a few people stood between him and ourselves. At that moment a sergeant-major of the *Reichswehr* Pioneers seized a greatcoat and flung it round Berthold and whispered: 'Run for it, sir, they'll kill you.'
Berthold turned on his heel and then cried in a loud voice: 'No, I shall stay with my men!'

Wuth pushed through the crowd, he hurled people out of his way, threw himself at the captain, and hissed furiously: 'Get out, Berthold, damn you, get out!' The captain stumbled, Wuth rushed behind him, pushed him out and suddenly they both disappeared.

A gigantic sailor pulled open my tunic and put his hand into my breast pocket. 'Is that a custom here?' I enquired. He pushed me aside without answering and passed on. At last I got to the door. The street was black with people. A narrow path lined by armed men was made for the prisoners. Somebody pushed me, I stumbled and was hit on the head. I raised my arm to shield my face. Blows rained on me, but I hardly felt them, I only took care to keep moving. A tumult arose among the crowd, and I noticed that everybody lost interest in me and pushed off in the opposite direction. The tall Bavarian at my side whispered hoarsely: 'They're killing the officers.'

More and more prisoners collected amid the hideous outcry of the mob. We stood there apathetically – my mind was a blank – I saw nothing but an unspeakably horrible collection of faces. I could think of nothing and I did not want to think of anything. My one conscious desire was for a glass of water. I saw Wuth, standing indifferently among the rest, a few paces from me. Thank God! I thought – and then I realised that

Berthold had probably not managed to get through. Nothing was to be seen of him.

The doctor pushed through towards us, accompanied by the giant sailor, saw me, flung himself at me trembling and said: 'Where is Lieutenant Wuth? Where is Lieutenant Wuth? I must tell him that I've got to attend to the wounded. Where is Lieutenant Wuth?'

The Hamburger next to me fired up: 'Shut up, you idiot! There aren't any officers here, you fool!'

At last the doctor understood, his face went ashy, his jaw dropped. 'Yes, yes, of course, yes, yes – well, I'm just telling you that I'm going to attend to the wounded. Yes. . . .'

Our march began. Close files of armed men went right and left of us. My wounded arm began to be unbearably painful. All my nerves seemed to be concentrated in the one place. We stumbled along by the fence, then turned to the right into a quiet street.

'Halt!' shouted a coarse voice. The front ranks stopped. A sudden electric shock ran through the lines and the Reds turned their rifles on us. I cannoned into the file in front. What could be the matter – was some fresh horror coming? –

'There's your captain, have a look at him –'. What was that? What was the drunken beast saying? – The captain – the captain – ?

'The captain!' shouted the Bavarians, and the sound hit the columns like a blow. The Bavarians suddenly charged, snarling.

There lay the captain. There lay Berthold – in the gutter. He was naked – where was his head? – A bloody, trampled naked body, his throat cut, his arm torn from its socket, the body covered with weals and thick with wounds. Could that really be Berthold? – There lay his head!

The Bavarians groaned aloud. We fought our way towards him. Cudgels were used against us – but our first men had reached him – one or two shots were fired. Nobody should stop us. The Reds pushed forward – the Bavarians at the back followed on, jerking everyone out of the way. The first ranks were urged on by the ones following, crowding to see the last of the captain. But in these few agitated moments the Reds had got reinforcements and interposed themselves between us and him; cudgels were used freely. We were obliged to pass.

A tumultuous mob accompanied us. Women screeched and shook their fists at us. Stones were thrown, sherds and sticks flew through the air. Some of these missiles struck the guards, who shouted at the women furiously. We were quickly herded into a café; the crowd yapped at our heels, but was held back by armed men. We arrived in a dancing hall lit by gas lamps. Cheap, dusty, tawdry ornaments hung on the walls, and the ceiling was adorned with wreaths of paper flowers from which depended coloured Chinese lanterns. We paraded. The guards were shouting confused orders. Outside, the mob was snarling and banging on the door. I did not care what happened now. My arm was agonising – I turned half round: there were, at the outside, a hundred left of the four hundred who had started – and Wuth was not among us. One of the Reds spoke and I boiled with silent fury. What a snout the fellow had! He was quite young, with long black bushy hair, a pair of horn-rimmed glasses, very red lips and a dark Russian blouse. We knew the type! He appeared to be the leader. He went along the ranks and enquired loudly: 'Where's the man with the light cap, who was firing the machine-gun on the first floor right at the beginning?' He stopped in front of me, stared and probably saw that my tunic and riding breeches were of a better cut than most of the others, and said condescendingly: 'Who's this? Are you a commoner?'–

I saw red. 'Not as common as you!' I said, and cautiously raised my leg, ready to kick him in the stomach if he so much as winked an eyelid. However, he passed rapidly on. My wretched light-coloured cap lay in tatters beside Hoffmann up in the school.

We were tired out and lay down on the floor. The mob raged outside. From time to time they yelled and beat on the door. Then the guards hurried off importantly. In the end, Big Snout came back to us, and of course had to make another speech. He invited us to make a free-will offering for the widows and orphans of those whom we had slain. A few of the prisoners groped wearily in their pockets. But I fired up: 'Not a farthing!' I snarled. 'We're not going to buy our damned lives that way!'–

'But if you don't do something of the kind, the crowd will, force their way in here – you must soothe the excited masses!' the fellow said helplessly. I seized a chair and emphasised every word by waving it threateningly in his face: 'If the crowd gets in here, we shall defend ourselves with chair legs and fists and teeth and then you can count how many of you are left!' Big Snout retired. We set sentries so as not to be surprised by the mob. Then we dossed down on the floor. I could not sleep for a long time; my wounded arm had swollen and the blood had soaked through the bandages, making everything stiff and uncomfortable. At last I fell into a sort of half doze.

Early in the morning the door was thrown open, we heard the yowling of the mob which was either still there or had come back again, and then a group of prisoners was pushed in, Wuth among the first. Many of them had head wounds, practically all of them had weals on their faces and their uniforms were tattered. The door was closed hurriedly and we fell into line. I elbowed my way to Wuth and stood next to him. He was very pale and his face seemed to have got terribly thin. The soldiers, especially the Hamburgers, rallied close round him. Everyone knew him – and when he stepped into the hall a breath of relief seemed to pass over all the prisoners. Most of them were eyeing him furtively now.

That beast in the Russian blouse was talking to a gigantic workman, who was armed and wearing an enormous red brassard. This fellow's coat was open, and his bare brown chest was adorned with blue and red tattooings. The noise outside increased. We heard shrill yells from the women. Stones crashed on the door. The fellow in the Russian blouse turned to us and said: 'We know there are still some officers amongst you. You're fools to allow yourselves to be misled by these swine. If any of you will tell us which of the officers is still among you, we'll let you off and send you to Hamburg under safe escort, and set you free there. But if you don't give up your officers, just you wait and see what happens! – Well – what about it?'

I immediately seized Wuth's arm with my left hand and held tight. I felt his muscles stiffening, a shiver go over his whole body. I held on as hard as I could and kept him back. He was striving with all his might to get forward. His idea was, of course, to give himself up for our sakes. Obviously he could not be allowed to do so. He struggled to loosen my grip. I glared at him furiously; he had a drawn look, his skin seemed to be pulled tight over his thin cheeks, but his mouth was set firmly. 'Keep your jaw shut, Wuth!' I whispered. The rest of the prisoners stood without making sound or movement. On the right flank a slight disturbance occurred. I looked round anxiously. It was only Tietje, one of the Hamburgers, who had put his hand on to the back of a chair, playfully and apparently unconcernedly.

'Very well, have it your own way,' said the man in the Russian blouse. The other fellow turned sharply round, stamped his cudgel violently on the floor and went out. The first said: 'You're going to be moved from here. But not for a little while yet, there aren't quite enough people waiting for you outside at present!' He grinned and left us.

The prisoners instantly crowded round Wuth. Tietje said: 'What on earth do the "comrades" take us for?' and waved his chair.

Wuth snarled through his teeth: 'If these people out there make themselves unpleasant, gentlemen, hit back! Don't submit to anything. Take care always to keep next to one of the guards or behind him, so that he gets his share from his own people! Keep close together. The biggest men go in front and at the back; wounded men in the middle. Snatch their sticks from them when you can, but don't get out of line. Keep your eyes on me. I shall be in the front rank.' After a short pause he enquired: 'How many Hamburgers are actually left?'

Somebody answered: 'Twelve.' We said no more.

The tattooed man entered and roared: 'Fall in!' and then threw open the door. For a few moments there was no sound except the tramp of our feet. Wuth was the first to emerge. I followed close behind him.

We ran, ducking our heads, and raising our arms to ward off blows. The crowd made way at once, as though a wedge had been driven into them. We did not know which way we were to go; we did not know whether we had been delivered over to the crowd or whether there was some place of refuge for us; all we knew was that we had got to put up a decent show even if it was our last. A whirl of stumbling feet was before my eyes and my left fist smashed into a face and felt the scrunch of something cartilaginous. A heavy blow came down on my head, its force broken by my arm. A corduroy-covered stomach came into my line of vision and collapsed after a well-aimed kick. A hard black hat fell; and I got a tremendous, if unreasonable, satisfaction out of stamping on it. Something hit me on

the head; something hammered my shoulder till it was sore.
There was a shin – I landed one on it with my heavy boot.
A blow fell on my right arm, which was hideously painful.
This was an unfair game – each of the opponents was only
hit once, but we were struck times without number.

The tattooed fellow was marching beside me. He held his
gun half up, but he was looking carelessly ahead, and allowed
anyone to strike us who could. I saw a labourer swing a long
hose like a cowboy with a lassoo. I leapt back, the hose fell
with a whack and wound itself noisily round the tattooed
guard. He howled with rage, turned round and drove the butt
of his rifle into the labourer's face. Wuth was three paces away
from me boxing scientifically. Some women got at him.
These women hammered us with sticks, stones, pots and ropes.
They were broadly built and wearing dresses made of some
kind of blue stuff, with wet aprons and dirty skirts, their
wrinkled faces red with exertion, their hair tangled and wild.
They spat, abused us, screamed – we reached them – now to
get past them! A little Bavarian, an elderly man, was next to
me, panting with running; and when we got near the women,
I heard one screech: 'What are you hitting the young ones for?
Get at the old goats and swipe them!' The unfortunate little
Bavarian got his share.

In a narrow street through which we passed was a strong
lad, who took his job very seriously. He picked his men and
looked searchingly and carefully along the line before striking.
But then he delivered an upper cut that sent the victim reeling
and covered him with blood from nose to jaw. He lighted on
Wuth; which was a mistake; for Wuth ducked with lightning
speed, the brute stumbled, and Wuth ran his knee into him
below the belt with all his force. He doubled up and fell, but
Wuth fell with him and they rolled over each other. I got to
the spot, seized Wuth by the collar and dragged him up; we

raced on. I no longer felt the pain in my arm; I began lashing
out even when no one was threatening me. Shots resounded
at the back, there were screams and the crowd got restless.
However, a fresh gang came out of a side street, chiefly composed of women. The women were the worst. Men hit, but
women spit and abuse, and it is impossible to plant one's fist
in their faces. All at once I saw – an idyll amid this confusion –
an old woman leaning on her umbrella. She had such dear old
eyes under her bugled cap! She could hardly stand; she looked
at us earnestly and – lifted her umbrella in her trembling
hand, and hit me with it! – Christ! –

More shots. Now we ran for all we were worth, driven by
shouts and blows, the mob in our wake. We came to a high
red wall – a gate flew open – we sped through it. We had
arrived in the Pioneers' barracks. The Reds collected at the
gate and barred the way to the crowd. We stood panting,
wounded and bleeding in the yard. The *Reichswehr* men
showed us the way and hurried us indoors. We were taken to
the riding school, whose floor was thickly covered with pease
straw.

Seven of us had been shot and killed by the mob. Wuth
lying on the floor of the riding school snarled: 'Next time we
come to this b——y town, by God, we'll bring 15 cm. guns!'

However, Tietje, the incorrigible, averred: 'A scrap is
always good fun – even if you get hit yourself!'

We lay in that riding school for three days in the rustling,
dusty straw, irritated, tired, exhausted, filled with a dull,
gnawing rage. One of the Bavarians told us each day in a
monotonous voice how Berthold had died. This man had been
with the captain to the end. Berthold had got to that side street
under cover of the cloak. Then he met a group of sailors and
workmen. One of them recognised him by his *Pour le mérite*.
They attacked him, he defended himself and lashed out in all

directions. A stick hit him on his bare head and he sank to the ground. He managed to draw his sword which he still wore, but it was seized from him. He fought for his decoration, half leaning against a lamp post. He was dragged down, his legs were trampled on, his tunic was pulled off, his wounded arm was broken. Berthold snatched a revolver from one of the sailors and shot him down. They flung themselves upon him, a knife flashed, his throat was cut. Slowly he gasped out his life, alone, fighting to the last, trampled in the filth of the gutter. His murderers divided his money amongst them. The Bavarian lay on a doorstep, wounded and under guard.

One of the sentries from the train told us how they had been attacked and cut up, very few were still alive. The baggage had been stolen.

One of the *Reichswehr* Pioneers told us what tremendous losses we had inflicted on the Harburg men. We told him what we thought of his corps and he retired offended. But the sergeant-major who was our chief warder, told us with malicious pleasure that the Berlin *Putsch* had failed. We listened to him in astonishment. Then Tietje said: 'Yes, quite true, we had an idea of making a *Putsch* – well it's all gone phut and Kapp's bust.' Here we turned our backs on the noble Pioneer and crept into our straw.

Nobody knew what was to be our fate. We sat there and waited and had plenty of time for reflection. The captain's sister came and brought us cigarettes. The Bavarians surrounded her, their faces twitching, unable to say a word. She was quiet and brave. Nobody spoke a word in the riding school on the evening after her visit.

On the third evening I said to Wuth: 'The longer I think about it, the more I am convinced that our war isn't over yet. But I also know that up to now our attempts were bound to miscarry. We shall never be a company again. Each one of us will have to fight his own battles from now on. What are you going to do, Wuth?'

He lay with his head pillowed on his arms, staring at the ceiling, and said: 'I'm going to settle – yes to settle down. My last ten men and I – the last of the Hamburgers – we shall get together and become farmers. Any old where – in Lokstedt or on the heath at Lüneburg or on the Königsmoor at Bremen – we shall settle down, build houses – farmers and soldiers, that's a sound mixture.'

I said: 'Yes, it's a job. But not for me. You see, it's like a disease. I don't feel as if I should ever be able to keep still any more. What we've done up to now hasn't been in vain. Blood is never shed in vain; it always demands its price, which must be paid some time. But this time the cost seems to me out of all proportion to what we have gained. I think the reason is that though we were always in the thick of things, we were fighting for something which turned out quite differently from what we expected.'

Wuth sat up and looked at me. I went on eagerly: 'I mean, the most passive came through best in the end simply because the active ones consumed each other. Nothing new has come out of the November revolution. We haven't witnessed the reversal of things. All the old values still hold good, they never died: church, school, trade, society, they're all there, just as they always were. Only the army's gone phut – and that was the best thing that came out of the pre-war days. And the nobility – well, just look at the names and the faces of the members of parliament and the ministers. We lost the war under the old régime. There's only been a game of 'Puss in the corner,' the new one is the same as the old – and has the same ideals – so this régime can't make good our losses, it seems to me. I don't believe they even want to. It's perfectly true what the Communists say – that the same bourgeoisie is openly in power

172

to-day, which was in power behind the scenes up to November
18th. Therefore we have had no revolution. And are we
satisfied with things as they are now? With their regulations
and speeches and programmes and acts and newspapers? Is
there one name in which we have confidence? Is there one
word that we can believe? Everything was smashed up by the
war first. Very good. That doesn't seem to me to matter much.
But since then, hasn't everything we wanted been scorned and
made fun of? So, if we feel that there is something better to
aim at – what then? If the revolution hasn't taken place yet –
what then? We must just make it ourselves!'

Now Wuth smiled. I cast down my eyes and looked nervously at my toes. I said: 'I have a feeling that there must be
a revolution. Parliamentary democracy – that was new in
1848. They were very decent people then. I daresay in its
day it did good. Marxism? That's a programme that one can
pin one's faith to, that one can make into the bible of revolution.
But the revolution simply hasn't happened. The issue of
1918 was a mixture of 1848, of Wilhelmism and of Marx.
It looks like it, too. All the old stock was taken over by the
new firm!'

'I am damned curious to know what this boy is getting at!'
said Wuth. All the Hamburgers were listening by now.

I said: 'Perhaps I'm not explaining myself properly. I'm
not an orator. But my idea is, that we must make what I
should call a national revolution. Yes; and I think we've begun
to do it. Don't we all flare up if anyone says our *Putsch* is
reactionary? It seemes to me that everything we've done so
far has been a part of this revolution. Perhaps not consciously,
but that doesn't really matter. I mean it this way: all the
revolutions in the history of the world began with the rebellion
of the spirit and ended in hand-to-hand fighting. We have
done exactly the opposite. We began on the barricades. And

we failed. It is a spiritual uprising that I mean when I say that we must make the revolution.'

'My poor child,' said Wuth, 'are you hoping to look for the spirit now? I hope you may find it – and that it may be a good one.'

I said: 'You must excuse me if I express myself badly. But do you know how the Russian revolution began? Do you know how many 'Bolsheviks' there were up till 1917? I mean real Bolsheviks, who wanted this revolution and no other? Not quite three thousand in that whole enormous empire, so I was told, and a good many of them were scattered about in other countries, in Switzerland and goodness knows where else. But they were people who worked tirelessly. They were revolutionaries in theory first and in practice afterwards. Line for line, word for word, idea for idea, it was all worked out to the last detail. They learnt their tactics as well as their strategy. I grant you, they had Marx. But, after all, that only told them *why* to make the revolution, not *how*. We must make the revolution for the sake of the nation and with the nation. So we've got to know first of all what the nation really is. I mean *know*, not guess. We're all of us beginning to guess. And then we must know on what to model this nation that we haven't got yet. And to learn that seems to me our present task.'

I stopped, overwhelmed by the flood of my own eloquence. The Hamburgers were silent too. I stood up. Wuth asked:

'What are you going to do now?'

I said: 'I'm going.'–

'Where to?'

'Away!' And I approached the sentries at the door of the riding school. The Hamburgers watched me.

One of the *Reichswehr* Pioneers' N.C.O.'s had taken a great fancy to my riding breeches. He had already asked me twice whether I would not sell them to him. Now I took him aside and said: 'You can have the breeches.' He asked at once: 'What do you want for them?'

I said: 'Now listen carefully: a pair of old breeches of yours, a belt with a sword knot, a pair of your shoulder straps, and a *Reichswehr* cap with the wreath of oakleaves on it, that you're allowed to wear because you've fought so bravely.'

'Nothing doing!' said the Pioneer.

'Please yourself!' I said and turned on my heel.

'Wait a minute, don't be in such a hurry.' He stood and looked undecided. Then he asked: 'Are they good leather?'

I said: 'A1 leather, much too good for you – you'll only mess them up anyway – He looked and considered and said: 'I'll bring the stuff in half an hour. It's my watch at the barracks gate. But you can't get through here – the workmen have sentries here too.'

'Excellent, my little hero! You've grasped the situation exactly.– See you in half an hour.' Then I went over to the Hamburgers and took off my riding breeches. Wuth understood at once. I said goodbye to the Hamburgers. I shook hands with each one of them and we didn't say very much. 'Cheerio!' and 'All the best!' and then I went and hid in the straw close by the door. The Pioneer came and handed me the things carefully. I gave him the riding breeches.

Then I went to the far end of the riding school where it was dark. There the straw was piled up high under a small window that was half hidden in the wall. Nobody took any notice of me except the Hamburgers. I put on the *Reichswehr* cap, buckled the belt round me and fixed the shoulder straps to my tunic. Then I climbed up on to the window-sill. I turned to give the Hamburgers a last look and waved to them.

Suddenly the Hamburgers began to sing softly. The Bavarians pricked up their ears in astonishment, the guards at the door turned and looked at them. The Hamburgers – the last ten men of the company that had once been a battalion – were singing their pirate song.

I pulled myself up and swung myself through the window. Outside I caught the strong branch of a chestnut tree, let my legs dangle and came down hand over hand. Then I crossed the dark parade ground to the gate. The N.C.O. was there, he stepped back two paces and let me pass without saying a word.

Feeling unspeakably lonely I went towards Hamburg, through the empty, echoing, twilit streets.

PART II

CONSPIRATORS

'Action is never contemptible, inaction always.'

Walther Rathenau in Reflexions.'

CHAPTER XIII

ANACRUSIS

IT only needed the separation from my late companions to bring home to me how very young I was. Though the parting caused me the most acute grief, yet I had the resilience to make my decision quickly, just in the way I had done on that wretched November night of 1918. What disturbed me was the thought that I must have peculiarly adaptable feelings; I was able to give up ideas and take on new ones and do all sorts of rash things without any regrets or fear of the consequences.

Having now to face the world in all its prosy materialism, where life was regulated by apparently senseless but yet inflexible rules, I grasped at books, which had given me my first vague ideas about life. Before I had set out like the 'pure fool' in the legend, books had acted as a barrier between me and the daily tribulations of a somewhat difficult upbringing. So now, when everything seemed colourless and unmeaning, the window of a bookshop awoke in me a longing for the directness of vision which books used to give me, in the days before I tried to follow in the footsteps of my brother fool.

Pushed into the corner of a shop window I saw a rather dusty book, called: *The Future*. Greatly attracted by this title, I went into the shop and treated myself to the book. Then I retired to my attic, lighted my last big candle, sat down in the ancient and rickety plush chair, having first propped it up with an old hand-grenade box, and began to read, shivering. I read all through the night.

THE OUTLAWS

The book was by Walther Rathenau, whose name I vaguely remembered as one of the leading industrialists and economists during the Great War. The very first sentences, which emphasised that, though it treated of material things, these were important only for their reactions on the spirit, gave me a singular feeling of satisfaction: this was just the kind of thing that it seemed to me necessary and right to read at the present time.

The book was strangely impressive though written in a curiously stilted way and quite unemotionally; even the few sentences which were lighted with a serene optimism being tempered by a gentle melancholy. I was eager to hear this impersonal but thrilling voice speak of the future; and I read that the goal is man's freedom. – With a feeling of weary disillusionment, I turned over the pages and saw that it had appeared in 1917; was once again fascinated by the doctrine that the spirit of God is but the apotheosis of the human spirit; read on spellbound and meditated for minutes at a time, wondering whether I had any share in this. There was so much that I could not understand, and then again so much that I had already thought of for myself. I could read and agree with what I read, not once or twice but a dozen times – I could almost see the goal at which the writer was aiming – and then – a bar, and a vague wave of the hand to explain what was to come. It was an extraordinary book and it made many things clear to me; yet it seemed to give but a barren answer to the urgent questionings of youth. I felt that it was spiritually reactionary – written by a man who was born too late and not by one who had come too soon. Its prophecy was criticism, and its claims could be heard at every street corner – people's rule – democracy –. I had a vision of a blind prophet crying in the wilderness and listening for the stones to speak since man was silent. I read and read and neared the end. It all seemed to me like the airy fabric of a dream – life seen through a glass, darkly – like the landscape that I could see through my window now, for the dawn was coming and my candle had burnt low. The uneven line of the roofs was beginning to show up against the velvety background of the sky, and I leant out of my window and looked down into the dark chasms that were the backyards of houses, and felt at any rate old enough to realise that the world needed restraint rather than inspiration. So I shut the book and decided that the shiver which ran down my spine was probably due to the chill of the early morning.

At this moment the French entered the town. I heard the blare of their bugles, raced down into the street and watched. The ideas from the book I had been reading in the night were still revolving in my mind. I put my hand up to my face, as if to brush away cobwebs, and listened to the insulting jubilation of the conquerors, saw their assurance, their smartness, the smiling disdain of those able to dictate punishment and reparation. The town was surrendered to an alien's pleasure, its honour was affronted – it was intolerable that we should have to suffer it. The inarticulate rage of the proletariat rose in me. I saw the little dark officers wearing patent leather boots, I noticed that they had slender waists, I observed their well-tended horses, their look of careless hauteur, their medals; I saw a captain wave his stick smilingly at a girl, who thereupon stepped back hurriedly from a window. The fact that they could laugh when we were ruined, that they could march in triumph when we were crushed, sent waves of hatred surging through me.

I ran about the town all the morning, almost sobbing with rage. The people I met looked pale and walked quickly, even the street noises seemed to be tremulous. French patrols, consisting of three and four men each, were about everywhere. They marched briskly, with distant looks, as if they raised an invisible barrier around them. Large companies wandered round the town, the soldiers examining the place with cheerful interest and apparently finding it to their taste. At certain points, such as the main railway station, the opera, the chief police station, pickets had been placed, machine-guns were posted at every corner, rifles were stacked in little pyramids. Officers with short flexible riding crops strolled up and down the pavements, never singly, always in twos or threes, and the faces of the passers-by grew stiff and expressionless as they met. At one of the hotels the tricolour flag was being run up by officious *poilus*, while the officers hurried in and out.

I tried to bring my ideas into some sort of order. To approve of anything – such as the excellent precision of the military machinery, the good, soldierly appearance of the troops, their clean, fair, cheerful faces – seemed to me treachery. I did not want to approve of anything; I wanted the hatred of our people to build as it were a granite wall round the victors, so that they should feel themselves isolated, continually hovering between fear and terror. I saw a squad of negroes coming along in charge of a white corporal. They had spindle legs, on which their puttees slipped, and they walked with their toes turned in. They grinned, showing big white teeth, looked round unconcernedly, and were obviously enjoying an unaccustomed feeling of superiority. These, then, were the representatives of humanity and democracy, brought from the farthest parts of the world to discipline us barbarians! Excellent! if we were not barbarians now, we certainly would become so. The last wisps of my overnight dreams vanished – this was no time for fighting with spiritual weapons!

The whole town was in an uproar. Only twice before had I seen it in such a state of excitement – in August 1914 and on the day of the revolution. Little knots of people collected at the street corners; they opened out to let the French patrols

pass, but closed in again behind them. A crowd fidgeted
silently and uneasily about a disarmed policeman. Everyone
seemed to be waiting for something to happen, without knowing
what.

A company of soldiers paraded in front of the general post
office. A crowd, with which I straightway felt myself to be in
sympathy, collected at the entrance gates. Something elemental
seemed to break through the crust of everyday respectability.
More and more people collected and waves of scarcely concealed
hatred rose from them. The officer in command walked up
and down uneasily and the soldiers drew closer together. The
officer rapped out an order, the men precipitately fixed their
bayonets. I began a loud caterwauling which was instantly
taken up by the crowd. The officer turned and flashed dark
eyes, trying to intimidate us. The noise increased. He turned
to his company and gave an order. They presented their
rifles, but there was no smartness about the movement. They
had grown nervous and they fumbled, and one man's helmet
slipped. We yelled and laughed, with mingled jeers and hatred,
and a piercing voice, rising to a squeak, cried: 'Present-arms!
Smartly – again!' Howls of laughter came from everyone and
echoed under the archways and in the corners of the yard.
The officer, thoroughly put off his stride, actually did make
them do the movement over again. Now there was no holding
the crowd – they howled and yelled and caterwauled. The
officer turned and all at once the soldiers advanced in close,
determined formation. The crowd retreated before their
fiercely threatening looks; at that moment a strong patrol of
Moroccan troops came along the road and pushed on to the
pavement. The crowd dissolved. At the corner of the side
streets they reassembled into little groups, accompanied the
marching men with jeers and yells, made way for patrols in
one place and collected again in another. A considerable

number went towards the police headquarters, and I followed them.

Crowds surrounded the square. A group of officers stood in front of the Schiller statue; the soldiers were lying on the ground, but soon got up and gathered round their rifles. Moroccans, negroes and white men surrounded the machine-guns. Schiller's long nose pointed unmoved across the square. Opposite the police station, by the ladies' entrance to the public lavatories, was standing a very young French officer, who amused himself by brandishing his riding whip at passers-by wishing to get to the stopping place of the tramway and making them step off the pavement. Towards women and girls, however, he behaved with obtrusive gallantry. The crowd collecting on the other side of the police station stood and watched him angrily.

In the stream of people coming down Schiller street was a young man in a blue suit, of medium height, and with notice-ably large dark eyes. He did not step aside from the open space which had formed round the officer, but went calmly on. He was passing the officer when the latter shouted something at him; the young man took no notice; the officer got as red as a turkey-cock, ran after him and, when he did not even trouble to turn round, touched him with the quivering tip of his riding-whip.

A shout rose from the crowd; for the young man whirled round, snatched the whip from the officer, flicked it once across his face and then broke it into three pieces, which he flung at the Frenchman's feet.

The Frenchman staggered back, the little weal showed white in his scarlet face, then he pulled himself together, took a deep breath and went for the young man with an inarticulate snarl. The latter stood motionless, with his legs planted firmly apart and a dangerous look in his face, till the Frenchman was within half a step of him. Then he flexed his knees rapidly, seized the officer by his tunic and breeches and lifted him up with a flourish. He held the struggling man straight above his head for a moment, then carried him three steps and threw him almost carelessly down the stairs of the ladies' lavatory. Then he turned and walked round the building, straight through the group of French officers, who stepped aside dazedly to let him pass. One of the Moroccans helped up the chastened officer, who dashed excitedly over to his companions. There was a great commotion and immediately afterwards shots resounded from the horse-market. Suddenly the crowd pressed forward. A furious outcry arose. The French ran about confusedly, the sentries began firing. I ran across the square towards St. Katherine's Gate. Bullets thudded on the pavement, hummed round my legs, chipped bits out of the walls. The crowd dispersed hurriedly in all directions. I turned into a side street, but shooting was going on there too. So I ran into the entrance hall of a house.

Something burst through the door immediately after me. I looked up and recognised the young man, who was now calmly leaning on the bannisters with folded arms. I approached him and said enthusiastically: 'That was fine!'

'Don't talk,' he said. 'Help me instead. We've got to rouse this town!'

'You bet I'll help!' I shouted and introduced myself by name.

The young man shook hands, bowed and said: 'Kern.'

CHAPTER XIV

THE RALLY

THE town refused to be roused. After their first show of
barbaric valour the citizens of our diplomatic metropolis
affirmed that the French were also human, against which
nothing could reasonably be urged. Nevertheless no one
seemed to want to associate with the French; they never
succeeded in gaining an *entrée* to local society, not even among
the families on whom they were billeted. No girl would ever
be seen with a Frenchman: the French were completely
ignored. It may be that this coldness was less due to dislike
than to disappointment; such a disappointment as might be
felt by a tradesman if an old and valued business friend became
a competitor and got the better of him by unfair means. For
the town had always prided itself on being cosmopolitan, on
holding liberal views; it was a town which had always considered itself progressive, and in former days there had been
so many points of contact between it and Paris – that radiant
prototype of the art of life. Who could have expected this to
happen: that the town should be occupied by hordes of French
soldiery, brutally enforcing their claims at the point of the
bayonet, in a manner so utterly foreign to real democracy!
The town looked on in silent contempt. And a few months
later, after the *Reichswehr*, which had crushed the rising of
the Red army at Wesel, had evacuated the neutral zone in the
Ruhr, the French vanished away softly and silently, leaving
nothing behind except a few posters saying that France would
keep inviolate all contracts and promises.

THE RALLY

War and the revolution had robbed the town of much of its refinement, but little of its smugness and none of its catholicity. The atmosphere in the town was tense with suspicion, as it was in the whole country during this and the following years. Coming events cast their shadows before; everyone realised that, despite an appearance of harmony, something was out of tune, yet no one dared to expose the fraud. Nevertheless there were dawnings of new ideals. Many were homeless, many as yet had no fixed standards; but again many were ready to acknowledge that with the new era must come new ways of thought and action.

*　　*　　*　　*

After I had spent several weeks in an india-rubber factory on piece-work, stamping out rings for jam jars, the foreman discovered that I had been in the Baltic States. I had almost forgotten it myself by now; it was like the memory of a confused nightmare. But the foreman threatened a strike if I stayed and so I was dismissed. After that I tried my luck as an apprentice to a film company; but I very soon had a difference of opinion with the director, which ended in a threatened and an actual box on the ears. The director threatened. Finally I wrote out receipts for premiums in an insurance office, for eight hours a day. The head of my section praised my industry but complained of my handwriting. I was free from four o'clock onwards.

My companions in the office frequently debated whether it could not be arranged to throw a typewriter at the director's back, with all his sixty thousand Marks annual income, to teach him that we underlings were at starvation point. I urged my colleagues earnestly to fight with spiritual weapons only. I was, indeed, almost always hungry, but the satisfaction of that hunger seemed to me a question of secondary importance.

THE OUTLAWS

I possessed neither an overcoat nor a hat. When I wanted to put on a clean shirt, I had to wash it in the evening and let it dry overnight. My shoes were sound – they were English ones I had looted while I was in the Baltic States. But my trousers were not holding out. I had to mend them every day. My coat, too, was slowly but surely falling to pieces. However, in my tie I wore a huge old-fashioned pin, the last piece of our family jewellery.

My attic was a perfect armoury of weapons which I had collected at the time of the Revolution. Under my narrow iron bedstead lay three boxes of hand-grenades and ten of cartridges. The rifles themselves, tied up in parcels as I had got them, took up pretty well a third of the whole space.

Kern, who was still a naval officer on the active list, came up to see me in my attic about once a month on his way through to Munich, where he attended mysterious conferences. He usually stayed for a couple of nights and slept in a hammock. One day he rummaged among my books. I had knocked up a shelf out of an old box, on which Rathenau and Nietzsche, Stendhal and Dostoiewsky, Langbehn and Marx rubbed shoulders.

'Do you mind if I take this one along?' asked Kern holding *The Future* in his hand.

'Of course, you can take it,' said I, anxious to hear his opinion of it, and glad not to be teased about my rather odd taste in books.

*　　*　　*　　*

A great new national association, which had been evolved from a volunteer corps, was anxious to start a branch in the town. Kern and I went to the inaugural meeting.

All the men wore stiff collars. They addressed one another as 'brother.' We introduced ourselves, and I was agreeably impressed when I found that, in spite of my distinctly shabby appearance, I was treated absolutely as one of themselves. However, there was a reason for it: the very first words of the chairman laid particular stress on the fact that the society considered it to be its special task and its sacred duty to bridge the gulf between the classes. I listened carefully, though I was rather distracted by the waiter who kept on trying to put a glass of beer on the table in front of me. There must have been about forty men in the hall, most of them young and all belonging to the so-called upper classes. The spirit of the men during the war was touched on and the atmosphere grew more genial. Then they talked about the octagonal cross of regeneration, which interested me, because from what I had heard of the symbolism and the practices of this association, I hoped to find in it the dawn of a new chivalry, and the first glimmer of the new mysticism. I leant over to my neighbour and asked him in a whisper what was the idea of this cross of regeneration. He answered: 'I dunno – it's all rot anyway!' I drew back and I must own that I was rather disappointed. Brother Patrol-Leader, which was the speaker's title, was, I discovered in the speech by which he was introduced, the private secretary to a large bank. He was demanding a united Germany and the rejection, as completely opposed to the German genius, of Socialism. The older Brothers nodded eagerly, the younger listened attentively, but in silence. The party-spirit, said the speaker, had led Germany to the edge of an abyss and nothing but a moral, cultural, religious and political revival, in the spirit of this Order, could deliver it from a future of dishonour and ignominy. The applause was great and the waiter tried once more to give me a glass of beer. Someone thanked the speaker for his ardent and illuminating address and declared the meeting open for discussion. Immediately a man with dark curly hair, who had been sitting beside me all the time in an obviously nervous state, jumped up and enquired anxiously what were the views of the Brotherhood on the Jewish question. An embarrassed silence followed; finally Brother Patrol-Leader cleared his throat and remarked that the Order preserved absolute neutrality in religious matters. The tactless questioner sat down again at once. Then he told me that he was a member of the governing body of the Pan-German Offensive and Defensive Alliance, earnestly pressed a packet of leaflets into my hand and poured all the secrets of the Wise Men of Zion into my ear. A membership card lay under his pen, but when I told him my name, his manner grew noticeably cooler and he soon moved to another place and began eagerly whispering to his new neighbour. Meanwhile, various other questions were asked; landlords and industrialists, vegetarians and pensioned majors, all demanded that the Order should help to bring about their ideals. But the Order had in every case decided upon absolute neutrality. I looked at Kern, who had been sitting there all the time without saying a word. Then I rose timidly and asked whether I might be allowed to enquire what were the definite tasks that the Brotherhood had set itself: I presumed that it would begin by instituting a kind of reserve or a continuation of the volunteers, in order to lift the terrible burden of . . .? I was interrupted at this point by an elderly Brother, a University professor, I discovered, who stated emphatically that the Order would only effect its aims by strictly legal methods. I asked what, in the name of goodness, were the aims of the Order? And I felt that I was going the best way to make myself unpopular. However, a man sitting near me suddenly shook me by the hand and introduced himself. He said his name was Heinz and he would be very glad if I would allow him to pay for my beer. I thanked him cordially.

The discussion had come to an end and then Brother Patrol-Leader said humorously: 'And now let joy be unconfined.'

THE RALLY

Gradually the consumption of beer increased. And if class-antagonism was discussed over the first glass, '*Heil Dir im Siegerkranz*' was sung over the tenth. I did not mind that. What I did object to was that the windows were carefully closed before the singing began.

Kern rose. Heinz and I followed. We started on our homeward way in a state of considerable perplexity.

* * * *

Patriotic clubs sprouted like mushrooms. The same mixture of ideas and people was to be found in all of them. Scraps of old ideas and beliefs joined to all the latest catchwords and half truths formed a strange patchwork. From the grey groundwork of theories grew flowers of rhetoric from old and young seeking enlightenment. And the curious medley of the fumes of beer, sun-god-myths and military music was an expression of the confusion of the times. Quotations from Schiller and patriotic songs were mingled with the muttering of spells and the conflicts of race-antagonisn. The wildest chimeras were allied with the crudest civilisation. And everyone indulged in dreams: the Rhine was populated with submarines, the English fleet destroyed by death-rays, and the Polish corridor cleaned up by means of peasants armed with scythes.

These gatherings were symptomatic. People collected here who felt that they had been betrayed and cheated by fate. The hopeful and the despairing came; all hearts were open, ready to let themselves be sucked into the mysterious whirlpool, from which some day might arise that which we call the new era.

Kern had invited Heinz and myself to select the best and most active members of all these patriotic unions, and thus to organise a small but finely-tempered society, which would meet not only to hold 'German evenings' and have pleasant entertainment but also to undertake certain things, which could not be achieved unaided by the best-intentioned patriotic enthusiasm. Kern reckoned that, in the circumstances, the town might become the centre of a wide-spread conspiracy of resistance to the Inter-Allied occupation of the Rhineland. The country seemed to be on the point of going to pieces entirely. It was worth while preparing for the moment of dissolution. We ought to have a hold in every town, every village, thought Kern. Relations had already been established with Hungary, with Turkey and with the oppressed peoples. And soon mysterious emissaries were arriving from Kern, bringing brief news and then going on; carrying messages from town to town, from society to society and from country to country; creating a living network. Everywhere little bands of young men were waiting for the word, prepared to the last button.

*   *   *   *

We gathered our troops. Heinz's head was full of ideas. He had been an officer at an absurdly early age, had been wounded four times, and was now secretly a poet and most undisguisedly an aesthete. Hating furiously all forms of sentimentality, he used to enjoy crushing displays of it with a single phrase full of the cruellest sarcasm. All sorts of scents stood on the table by his bedside – but he had discovered a new explosive made of dung. He wrote excellent sonnets and could hit the bull's-eye at fifty yards.

Both of us joined eighteen societies. Whenever we saw a young fellow bored with the slow progress of events, and with the rivers of talk which flowed from worthy elders of both sexes, we approached him and enticed him to join us. We collected workmen and students, apprentices and shop boys, red-hot idealists and contemptuous fanatics. We organised our people in the various societies without creating a separate organisation, and we founded a Saal Defence Corps without

192

any definite responsibilities. We protected the meetings of the Nationalist parties and fought the Communists who tried to rush them. We went to Socialist meetings with the Communists and helped to break them up. We tried to disturb Communist meetings but quite unsuccessfully! However, the company increased rapidly and the members got to know one another's ways.

The leader of the Communist shock-troops was called Otto and had invented soot-bombs. These were an elegant mixture of plaster of Paris, soot and water, which, when thrown in anyone's face, turned him from a floury-cheeked baker to a blind chimney-sweep. Otto was to be found wherever a row was in progress. We knew each other and used to hail one another when we met in the street or before a fight. We became great friends.

Jörg belonged to the police. Once he cleared a public house, which was full of Polish workmen, by taking the pin out of a bomb and running towards the crowd carrying it in his hand. At the very last moment he threw it out of th window. He joined us, after he had helped us to extract Mahrenholz, the student, from a workers' meeting, at which he had been half killed for saying that he knew very well that he was casting pearls before swine.

We poked about in the most out-of-the-way places. Wherever we found anyone who showed, in however absurd a way, that he was possessed of courage, we approached him and he invariably joined us. We generally recognized such men at the first glance. In every hundred there were three or four who came to us practically of their own accord. Jörg dragged in his friends and Otto his comrades, stout fellows; Heinz got the prize, though: he produced a confirmed pacifist of the most militant kind!

When we had collected fifty men, Kern stopped our enlisting

any more. For the present he considered that fifty men were
enough.

* * * *

For a time I was attracted by political economy. I said to
Heinz: 'We simply haven't the faintest idea of political conditions and forces.' – I said: 'We are talking through our hats!'
And: 'We still have a great deal to learn.' So I attended all
the lectures in the national educational establishments and the
University. I bought books full of statistics and foot-notes
and indications as to sources of information; my pockets
bulged with pamphlets and schedules. I apprehended nothing;
I understood nothing. I knew the communist manifesto by
heart and beat Otto hollow with it in a debate.

* * * *

Then I got religion. 'The revival,' I said to Heinz, 'must
be carried through with religious fervour.' – 'Are we,' I asked
him, 'at all religious? Not in the very least!' – 'And yet,' said I
to him earnestly, 'what drives us is inspired by religion. We
are seekers, but we are not believers yet.' – 'We must,' I affirmed,
'become true believers.' And I visited the churches, Protestant
and Catholic – I was turned out of the synagogue. I was
captivated by the sonorous enthusiasm of the preacher at St.
Paul's; I quivered with awe before the sacred mysteries of
High Mass at the Cathedral; I worshipped the sun in the
Taunus mountains with fair-haired lads; debated with young
enthusiasts of all denominations, came up against Nietzsche,
despaired, grew intoxicated with him, and decided that the
way to salvation lay with Nietzsche.

* * * *

'Literature!' I said to Heinz. 'Why, we have no conception
of what spiritual ideas inspire our deeds.' – 'If we want to
understand what it means to be a German,' I adjured him, 'we

194

must get to know the works in which it is reflected!' And I read. I read with terrific fervour, sometimes all through the night. I was the terror of friends who possessed books, I was a regular visitor at the municipal library, read anything and everything just as it came, from the Edda down to Spengler, was a customer of the communist 'book-chest' in the Passage and at the Borromäus Society. Heinz hurled bits of the *Divine Comedy* at me, I threw chunks of Shakespeare at him. Finally we made our peace over Hölderlin.

*　　*　　*　　*

All through these months I wrote receipts for premiums every day for eight hours. My companions always knew when there had been a political meeting in the town. They used to say that they could tell the views of the speaker by the number of bruises on my head. They teased me about mixing myself up in things which did not concern me in the very least; but they bore me no malice for not taking part in their everlasting discussions about increased pay and so on.

I joined in the life of the town. I stood in a queue at the box-office of the theatre for four hours at a time, so as to get a ticket for the gallery, and thus made friends with the only real experts among the audience. I begged free tickets for the Monday Philharmonic concerts; I slipped in to the Winter Garden without an entrance-card, with the air of one who was a subscriber of many years' standing. At first I was a little shy about the state of my wardrobe, but afterwards I made a virtue of necessity and behaved accordingly. I took dancing lessons. They did not cost me anything, because Madame Grunert, in despair at the few men who came to her classes compared with the number of girls, most kindly and tactfully shut both her eyes.

I fell in love. I fell into the deepest abyss of despair and was at the same time raised to the highest peaks of bliss. At a sign from HER, I was ready to blow up myself, the house, the town, the whole world. Then I bought a little book in the shape of a matchbox, called *Mozart's Journey to Prague*, and wrapped it in twelve pages of foolscap covered with a poem indited by me to HER. I presumed that I should soon have a numerous family to provide for and decided to work overtime at writing receipts – and God alone knows how hard that was! My companions in the office were surprised to see me shaving every day. With the first money I earned by my overtime, I bought a little gold necklace for HER. Then I had a new suit made that was a real work of art. Ten years later SHE became my wife.

*   *   *   *

At about that time, the Government started the great disarmament scheme. Everyone who handed in a rifle was to receive a hundred Marks. As soon as we heard this we raced round the town. We looked up every man who had the faintest reputation of being patriotic, we scoured the neighbourhood, we went into the houses of society ladies, and we begged. We begged for ready money; we lied where people did not seem safe and told them the truth when they abused the Government and the French. Once Heinz was given a sausage instead of money, and one kind-hearted lady handed me a plate of soup in the hall. At patriotic meetings we implored people to give us their guns. Otto appealed to his comrades, but they knew the value of guns as well as we did and kept them. We lay in wait near the police stations and kept a careful eye on the worthy gentlemen who, with their rifles shouldered, came to do their duty as citizens, at a hundred Marks a time; and we drew aside those whose appearance inspired us with hope into a dark corner and offered them a hundred and five.

Thus we wrested numerous weapons from the Moloch of

destruction and took them home. We were not conspicuous, because people in every street were carrying rifles. Otto was the only one who was held up by a policeman, being too well-known. However, Otto looked the man in the eye with every appearance of sincerity and explained: 'I was just going to give it up.' But the policeman insisted on seeing Otto to the police station, and so Otto got his hundred marks and lost five.

But Jörg and his friends took away cart-loads of rifles; so that finally each one of them had a collection as big as mine. The weapons floated from the peaceable citizens to the most active, which was perhaps hardly the result that the Government had hoped to achieve.

*   *   *   *

There was some reason to doubt whether the Government was capable of desiring anything beyond the continuity of its existence. It was the product of a compromise between all the various factions in the country and dared not risk any decisive action, since everything decisive is a risk.

The West was threatening inexorably with its demand for milliards. To say 'no' to them meant opening the sluices of the torrent which had already flooded Poland; to say 'yes' submissively meant death by slow strangulation. The Government could do nothing but wearily clothe its destitution in paper formulae, send notes, resist ultimatums, implore, protest, appeal and disclaim.

*   *   *   *

'We're stifling!' said Kern. 'We must poke holes in the roof, so as to let the fresh air blow through our stuffy German houses.'

He came into my room and told me that he had resigned his commission; that his job now was to prepare the ground for decisive action by hundreds of little individual undertakings. He squatted on the boxes of cartridges, tensely depicting how all over the country in the mass of tired, hungry, exhausted people, isolated ones were preparing, as we were. As yet, he thought, the way and the final goal were not clear. Nevertheless, the cry that was raised everywhere for a strong man showed that people were only awaiting the coming of a leader.

After talking for a long time he rose to go. He took the book which I had lent him out of his case and stood it on the shelf. I looked at him questioningly. Kern only said: 'So much smoke and so little fire.'

CHAPTER XV

ADVANCE

AT the beginning of 1921 a young man called Gabriel came to see us, as Kern, Heinz and I were sitting in Heinz's room. Gabriel said:

'I was told that I should find men here to help me. I come from the Pfalz, and was an officer in a Bavarian regiment. I had a sister. Four months ago I went with her to see some friends and it was late in the evening when we started to go home. Near a barn in a field, some little distance off the road, we met some Frenchmen – a patrol consisting of four men with a drunken officer. They stopped us. The officer asked for our passes. I told him that I thought passes were only needed when we went to the town. I tried vainly to reason with the officer. He shouted at me. I got angry too and asked whether this was an example of the much-vaunted discipline of the French army. The brute gave me a backhander across my face. I kept control of myself as my sister was with me. She screamed. The Frenchman seized her arm. I told him to let go of her. He said that we must go to the guardroom and linked his arm in my sister's. She did her best to pull away. Then the fellow tried to kiss her. I snatched his hand off her. Then the men seized me. They beat me, they dragged away my sister. I could see her trying to escape. They pulled her along the ground to the barn. They kept me there and beat me. I shouted and swore and threatened. They bound me. They dragged me to my knees and tied me to a tree. They stuffed a rag into my mouth. I fought to the last. Believe that, please believe that. The men ran after their officer to the barn. Then I heard my sister scream. I heard . . .'

'Stop!' shouted Kern. He said huskily: 'I've got sisters too.' Gabriel went on quietly: 'She drowned herself a few days later. I went to the district commandant and told him what had happened. He laughed, then threatened, and said something about German tarts. For four months I have been looking for the brute who is responsible for my sister's death. Now I've found him. He's in Mainz. Will you help me?' –

We helped him.

*　　*　　*　　*

A mysterious man came to see us with an introduction from one of our friends in Cassel. He was a portly, upright individual, with a very high stiff white collar and a sunburnt face. He was well-bred and discreet, but carefully let it be seen that he knew about our activities and approved of them, with perhaps some small reservations. He reminded Kern and Heinz that they had been officers and said a few quiet words about the tribulations of our country, about the untiring energy with which serious men and glowing patriots had begun the work of reconstruction in spite of altered circumstances; about the sacrifice which the country demanded from each of us, a sacrifice which might even go so far as to make one collaborate in something which meant the apparent renunciation of one's own point of view . . . 'In short,' said Kern, 'You want us to do something special, Captain?'

The gentleman stopped us in dismay: 'Please, excuse me, not Captain, not Captain now, gentlemen!' And then he explained that he had discovered that the French Intelligence Department worked with an army of German spies. It was necessary to undermine the activities of these spies; and he

wanted to know whether, possibly, we might be formed into
a counter-organisation, a sort of anti-spy system? It would have
to be done secretly, of course, as the peace-treaty had unfortunately forbidden this form of activity to the German authorities – though he could – and there the captain looked round
carefully and leant forward to whisper – he could give us the
assurance that no difficulties would be put in our way by his
superiors. He lowered his voice still more and made a long
speech. Finally he said: 'Of course, gentlemen, your enterprise
would have to be kept secret at all costs. Absolutely secret and
in all circumstances. Even the authorities . . .'

'I understand,' said Kern contemptuously.

Heinz enquired thoughtfully: 'If I have understood you
correctly, sir, . . . our job would be to ascertain the names of
German spies in French pay . . .?'

'And to undermine their future procedure,' said the captain,
with great dignity.

'That is to say,' I added, taking care to give my voice the
proper military ring, 'that is to say, to abolish them?'

The gentleman was pained. 'That is to say: to hinder their
destructive work as far as you can with the means at your
disposal!' he amended.

Heinz cupped his chin in his hand and said: 'Suppose one
of us in the execution of his duty were to come into conflict
with the Law, the . . .?'

The gentleman rose to his full commanding height: 'Gentlemen, you are Germans! We must all make sacrifices. We must
all sink our little personal troubles in the demands of our
great and glorious country! We all . . .'

'Very good,' said Kern, stood up and kept his right hand
obstinately behind his back.

The gentleman left – a burning patriot, steadfast, zealous.

*　　*　　*　　*

THE OUTLAWS

The net was already spread. Gabriel was at work in the Pfalz. His was a dangerous position; for the commandant of his native place failed to return from a shooting expedition and Gabriel was suspect. Little groups had been formed in Mainz, in Cologne, in Coblenz, at Worms, at Treves, at Aix and all over the place. These young men roamed through the towns, through the vineyards of the Moselle and the Saar, through the wide plains of the Lower Rhine, in the villages of the Pfalz, always liable to betrayal, knitting up communications, watching, investigating, reporting. They bored their way into the structure which had been built up by the *Deuxième Bureau* and was kept going by an army of spies of German nationality. They ferreted out the devious paths taken by the nimble franc, they crept round closed houses, behind whose shuttered windows lurked shadows, they lounged in public houses, in which suspicious characters met and took instructions from beetle-browed gentlemen in black overcoats and bowler hats. They suddenly appeared before important corporations, young, bold and undaunted and warned, threatened and advised. They made speeches at meetings of excited workmen, in factory yards, at pit heads, in smoky halls. They leapt suddenly on to the running boards of the motor cars of Separatist leaders, pointing cameras at them; they tore the Separatist posters off the walls, created disturbances at their meetings, as ringleaders of gangs of wreckers.

They were the living conscience of the province. Any girl walking with a Frenchman was afraid of having her hair cut off. Anyone who had any intercourse with the officers of the Army of Occupation was careful that it should be private. The French *gendarmerie* – and not only the French – hunted them. The German Government authorities avoided them like the plague. They were the only real danger to the French. In no town did they number more than twenty men.

ADVANCE

We had all the reports from Rhenish Hessia and the Saar district. Elberfeld was the centre for the Rhine province and Mannheim for the Pfalz.

*   *   *   *

One of our men in Mainz was taken up by the French police. He was beaten at the police station and two teeth were knocked out. They asked him where the ammunition was; and who Heinz and Kern were. He refused to answer. They tore the clothes off the upper part of his body and thrashed him with horsewhips. He set his teeth, bleeding and trembling as he was, and said nothing. One of the Frenchmen lit a cigarette, stepped close up to him and put the glowing end on his skin. He screamed with pain, while the Frenchman enquired with mocking politeness and dotted him all over with the fiery end. But he told them nothing. After three weeks the French had to release him; the German authorities were getting restive.

So we were being spied on! Kern was pale with fury to think that there should be traitors even in such a small community! At all costs we had to find out who was in French pay. Heinz asked whether there was anyone among our men who was in the habit of indulging in smutty talk, find him and we had found the traitor.

*   *   *   *

Kern and Heinz were, as so often happened, travelling on a secret mission. Müllnitz, who was a student, an ensign and the son of a general, came to see me accompanied by an elderly woman. The lady told us that she kept a small shop for laces and fancy jewellery. In the course of business she often had to go into the occupied area, to Wiesbaden and Mainz. In the Kurpark at Wiesbaden, where she was chatting with a business friend, the latter introduced a French officer to her. He was, it appeared, an Alsatian, whose name had originally been

Schröder, and he was now in charge of the intelligence bureau in Mainz. This man, in the course of a pleasant conversation, pointed out to her that the amount she earned in business was small compared with what she might make in another way – in which, incidentally, she could do him a personal favour. The lady was taken by surprise and, being unacquainted with the customs of the lower walks of politics but a good business woman, gave an indecisive but not unfriendly answer. The officer, whose rank was that of a captain, talked to her, dropping pointed, barbed hints, but twinkling his eyes pleasantly, creeping round the kernel of his subject. All that he asked was that she should bring some of her friends to see him – possibly gentlemen who had been in the *Reichswehr* or who were still in that service or in the police, and who would perhaps be glad to earn a little something extra in these hard times – or perhaps even a big something! The lady said nothing. She left the matter open. The captain, not in the least put out about it, gave her his address and said goodbye with the greatest *empressement*. Her business friend urged her not to be a fool, there was nothing in it, the captain was most generous and such a delightful man; she herself had already . . . of course, only in a small way, just as the opportunity arose . . . absolutely safe . . . thousands were doing it . . . The lady, who was a friend of Müllnitz's people, told them all about this conversation, in a great state of perturbation.

We took counsel together. Then I decided to beard the lion in his den.

Monsieur le capitaine begged us to enter. We did so. In the middle of a spacious room stood an enormous writing-desk. The captain, a young, dark, clean-shaven individual, something of a dandy, greeted the lady most cordially.

'I have brought,' she said, 'two young friends to see you, who might in certain circumstances be inclined to be useful to you.

One of the gentlemen,' she indicated Müllnitz, 'is in the *Reichswehr*, the other in the police.' The captain was delighted. He shook hands only with the lady, it is true, but he asked us in the most friendly way to sit down. I sat on a chair close behind the writing-desk, the lady sat on the other side, rather to the back of the captain, Müllnitz exactly opposite him. Müllnitz said haltingly that he had heard that the captain was anxious to have information. The captain took out a blue file, gently raised his hand and asked for our names. I deciphered the words written on the file with some difficulty, as I had to read them upside down; the words were: *Journaux des canailles*. The captain turned to me.

'My name is Schröder.' I said.

The captain started and looked at me keenly. I looked him stonily in the eye and handed him my pass. The pass was made out to Police-Sergeant Schröder and my photograph was on the front page. The captain opened his file and entered my name on a long list. Müllnitz gave his name. He was terribly pale and I saw his hands trembling as they lay on the arms of his chair. The captain closed the file again and pushed it over to the edge of the desk, right in front of me. I glanced hastily at Müllnitz, who understood me at once.

'I am from Schleswig,' I said to the captain 'my home is in Hadersleben.'

The captain replied at once: 'Ah, then I have the honour of addressing a representative of a people that has suffered much from Prussia, and no doubt you are hoping for reunion with your real native land?' Incapable of saying another word, I bowed. The captain spoke German without the trace of an accent.

'And you, Herr Müllnitz?'

Müllnitz forced himself to speak. 'My father is a general, and . . .' What on earth possessed him to say that, I wondered!

But the captain adroitly helped him out: 'I understand, gentlemen, you are afraid for the future of your class; you are impoverished and serving against your own convictions. The Bolsheviks are the danger, and not only for you. The greatest danger still threatening is Prussian Bolshevism! I take it that you are a Bavarian, Herr Müllnitz?' Müllnitz answered in the affirmative. The captain went on chatting briskly, questioning him. He addressed himself almost entirely to Müllnitz. Sticking out of the blue file in front of me was the corner of a sheet of white paper. Slowly I raised my hand, laid it on the table, slid it imperceptibly towards the blue file. Müllnitz halted and stammered, gave personal details and tried to explain why he wanted to get in touch with the captain. The latter was drumming his fingers on the arm of his chair. I looked imploringly at the lady, who was sitting saying nothing. She leant forward and Müllnitz referred to her saying: 'Don't you agree with me?' She made some reply and the captain at once turned politely towards her. My hand began to tremble furiously, I pulled and plucked, and all at once the paper sailed gently to the ground at my feet. I heard the captain make some joke about the franc standing higher than the Mark. I bent down as if to tie up my shoe, seized the paper and stuffed it into my stocking with shaking hands. Müllnitz looked at me, I nodded almost imperceptibly, and had to bite my tongue and press my feet together to still the mad turmoil of my blood. Müllnitz, quickly making up his mind, rose and promised to return with matters of interest. We murmured words of farewell, the captain shook hands with Madame and bowed; we went.

The page I stole contained a long list, the names of the 'canailles.' The gentleman in Cassel had every reason to be satisfied with us.

*   *   *   *

ADVANCE

We waited till late at night for Jörg, who was to come and report progress about a little gun-running affair in a place in the Taunus. Kern was getting anxious, for Jörg should have arrived during the afternoon. It was nearly midnight when he stumbled upstairs and dashed into the room, pale, distracted and exhausted: 'Otto and Mahrenholz . . .' he gasped. 'Both nabbed in Mainz.'

The weapons had been brought safely through the line of demarcation. The recipients, peasant lads from the Taunus, waited at the appointed spot. The weapons were distributed and hidden immediately. Then they all went and had a drink in an inn. Someone must have given information to the French. On the way home, they met a party of Moroccans led by French *gendarmes*. They appeared suddenly from a farm with their rifles at full cock. Our men at once separated; the French fired, four men were surrounded and taken prisoners, Otto and Mahrenholz among them. Jörg was able to fight his way out. He dashed across country into a neighbouring village, borrowed a bicycle from a farmer he knew there, and came to Mainz. He made cautious enquiries all along the road and heard that the four had not been put in prison yet, but that they were at present being kept in the Moroccans' barracks, no doubt in order to be further interrogated.

We dug Müllnitz out of bed while it was still dark and made him knock up his uncle, who had an old, but fast, motor car. I wrote a note to my firm saying, as I had frequently done of late, that I was ill and obliged to stay in bed.

We started out in the early morning, Kern and I in the car which Müllnitz was driving, Heinz, Jörg, two policemen in mufti and a young Communist, a friend of Otto's, by train. Each of us had a revolver in each trouser pocket, and an egg-bomb in each coat pocket. Kern had another couple of bombs in his overcoat.

THE OUTLAWS

Our fellows in Mainz, informed of everything by Jörg on the previous day, had discovered that the prisoners were shut up in an old gymnasium which was being used by the Moroccans as a barracks. Kern got them to show him the position of the place and outlined his plan. Then we started. The car waited near the barracks, in charge of Jörg and Heinz. The Mainzers and the other three divided themselves among the surrounding streets. Kern and I went to the gate of the barracks – our feet unable to keep pace with our racing hearts.

The sentry was a Moroccan. He marched up and down with short, mincing steps. Innumerable French soldiers and officers strolled through the gate. The gymnasium stood detached in the middle of the yard. I stopped near the sentry, both hands in my trouser pockets holding the butts of the revolvers, with my fingers on the triggers. Kern came gracefully round the corner, passed the sentry, politely taking off his hat, and was allowed through without any difficulty. He walked across the sunny yard, his overcoat billowing with the speed with which he walked, kicking up the pebbles under his feet. He arrived at the door of the gymnasium. He put his hand into his coat-pocket . . . .

I croaked hoarsely and took a couple of steps towards the sentry, who turned towards me. Kern took out a hand-grenade, hung it on the door handle and took out the pin. Then he ran round to the side and flattened himself against the wall into a corner.

The sentry looked me up and down in surprise. I stared at him and counted the seconds mentally – one, two, three, four, five, then –

A dull crash. The sentry started and whirled round. I reached him in two steps. I saw nothing except the sentry, who stared at me with wide black eyes, his jaw dropping. He tugged at his rifle. I took my hands out of my pockets, held up the revolvers and yelled: '*A bas les armes!*' The sentry staggered back, his mouth and eyes wide open, uncomprehending staring into the muzzles. Then – steps, shadows, noise. Kern was there with the rest, Frenchmen were swarming to the spot; I ran back and saw Otto hit a *poilu* under the jaw so that he fell into the arms of his companions. Kern was firing shots into the air with both hands. I turned and stumbled and ran as hard as I could.

Damn the pavements in this town! They seemed to be full of people – if they were people and not shadows? On – on – there was Jörg and there the car. The doors flew open, we threw ourselves in; the car groaned and jerked and started.

'To the bridge,' cried Kern, 'as quickly as possible!' The car roared and Müllnitz sat at the wheel as if he were made of stone.

We all lay tumbled on top of each other – Otto, Mahrenholz the two farm lads and I. Kern was next to Müllnitz. I distributed revolvers. 'Loaded and safety-catch up,' I said. Each man held the revolver in his hand ready to fire.

We raced across the bridge – 'The Rhine, the Rhine,' I said and murmured over and over again, 'The Rhine,' till we reached the farther shore. The car seemed to eat up the greyish-white high road.

'Look out when we get to the line of demarcation,' said Kern looking round at us and holding his hat on: 'They're sure to have rung up all the guards.' We nodded silently. The wood slipped past us. Mahrenholz looked at me laughing, nodded, spread out his arms. I understood; he meant to say how lovely the world was.

We came to a group of houses. Soldiers stood in the road. We reached them. They waved their rifles at us and more and more hurried out of the houses.

'Get on!' shouted Kern. Müllnitz stepped on the accelerator. The car leapt forward with a roar. Cracks resounded – shots whistled past us. . . .

And we'd got past – we were safe!

Mahrenholz leant forward. What was wrong? There was blood on his cheek.

Mahrenholz was dead.

CHAPTER XVI

UPPER SILESIA

In the year 1917, the kingdom of Poland was created anew by German politicians, generals and statesmen. In the year 1918, the grateful liberated people turned the kingdom into a republic; and in the German provinces of Posen and West Prussia the proletarian revolution turned into a Polish nationalist rising. In the year 1919, the Polish occupation of these provinces was completed, not altogether against the wish of the German authorities, though there was some fierce fighting with the weak frontier guards; and this accomplished fact was ratified by the Treaty of Versailles. At the same time the Peace Treaty created the Free State of Dantzig, the Polish Corridor and, after taking a plebiscite, the district of Upper Silesia. The German National Assembly and the Government raised a protest against the Treaty but signed it. The little district of Reichtal, to the north east of Namslau, the birthplace of Korfanty, a former member of the *Reichstag*, was included in the new State by the Poles, in the enthusiasm of colonisation; and although the Peace Treaty said otherwise on this subject, no further notice was taken of it. The first Polish insurrection occurred in Upper Silesia, and was suppressed by German volunteer troops and frontier guards.

In 1920, on February 11th, the Inter-allied Plebiscite Commission, called the IAK, took over the government of Upper Silesia under the chairmanship of the French General, Le Rond. In the summer of that year, the Russo-Polish war broke out. The cavalry commanded by the Soviet General Budjonni beat the Poles and pushed through the Polish Corridor, well into former German territory. Poland seemed to be lost. German visionaries, who were laughed at as 'nationalistic Bolsheviks,' hoped that this opportunity, which opened the way to all sorts of possibilities for Germany, would be seized to conclude a Russo-German treaty and that Poland would be destroyed. But in East Prussia and along the frontiers the guards were strengthened, an internment camp for Bolsheviks was formed, and the most rigid neutrality was preserved. In August 1920 the second Polish rising took place in Upper Silesia, after a Polish army, organized, officered and equipped by the French, had succeeded in keeping back or defeating such Soviet troops as were in the neighbourhood. The second Polish rising in Upper Silesia, led by the Sokols, was suppressed by the German frontier guards. After this had occurred, the IAK arranged that the guard should be removed in October, and formed a kind of armed police corps consisting half of Poles and half of Germans, called the Apo. March 20th, 1921, was fixed by the IAK for the plebiscite.

Meanwhile, three conferences, one at Spa, one at Brussels and one in London, which were discussing the question of reparations, had turned out badly for Germany. The *Entente* had occupied Duisburg, Rührort and Düsseldorf, and threatened further encroachment. It was in these circumstances that the voting took place in Upper Silesia. Seventy per cent of the votes were given for Germany. Germany joyfully noised abroad this victory. Korfanty demanded that, on the results of the ballot, the Oder should be the boundary of Poland. Under the very nose of the IAK, he organised the Polish Sokols, raised an army of insurgents, collected regular and irregular troops on the frontiers and so prepared for the rising. At about the same time, the German Government was carrying out its great disarmament scheme and disbanding the various military organisations. On May 3rd, 1921, the third Polish rising in Upper Silesia began. Insurgents, Sokols and Saxon troops pressed forward as far west as the Oder and northwards past Kreuzburg and occupied the country, openly supported by the French, secretly by the Italians, and by the English by a 'wait and see' policy. Alone in the industrial districts, the Apo and similar troops discharged their duty.

* * * *

At the protest meeting against the rape of Upper Silesia, Dr. Walther Rathenau spoke on May 22nd, 1921, just a week before becoming Minister for Reconstruction in the new Wirth Cabinet. He said:

'On August 4th, 1914, a German statesman spoke the most unfortunate word politically that has ever been heard in our land, when he referred to a "scrap of paper" and meant a treaty. A storm blew through the whole British Empire, and this storm led to war. At the time we called it self-defence. But the British Empire said "Treaties must be kept." And rightly. For the only means of defence against unbridled licence is a treaty, and these treaties must be held sacred between nations.

'Such a treaty was made between all the civilized peoples of the world, and signed by twenty-eight nations. This treaty has lasted for two years. What has happened to it? Where is the sanctity of the Treaty of Versailles? It has been nibbled at in the west and broken in the east.

'And who has broken this treaty in the east? Poland! For one hundred and twenty years the Poles have complained in every quarter of the globe of injustices done to them, of oppression. They have travelled throughout the world as delegates, demanding help and justice. And every time this cry resounded through Europe, it found a response. Even in Germany. For the heart of Germany has never been closed against anyone demanding his rights and appealing for justice.

'Poland has once again become an independent sovereign state. Her first act has been to break that very treaty to which she owes her new dignity. Lloyd George asked the President: "On what are you basing your contentions against the Treaty of Versailles? Whose blood was shed to win the war? Was it that of the Poles?" This question was answered at Warsaw by a flood of invective. There was no attempt to give any reasoned reply.

'But it is we who are oppressed. We signed the treaty. And since we are a justice-loving nation, we shall adhere to what we have undertaken. We make no effort to rouse our people to hatred or to revenge. But, in return, we demand justice from the world; and this justice cannot be denied us. Justice has always been re-established on earth sooner or later.

'We have had to endure unspeakable things in Germany. Our country has been mutilated and our resources are exhausted. We can only anticipate a sad future. The appeal for unity which you have just heard is a timely appeal. We are still a country with sixty million inhabitants, and the world shall know that this nation is conscious of its own strength: not for war, but for work; and not only for work, but also for the defence of its rights.

'We shall defend these rights by peaceful means; but no one shall deprive us of them. And if, owing to unfortunate circumstances, irresponsible persons should dare to separate this province from us, then it will be a sin, whose consequences will lie far more heavily on the nations than Alsace-Lorraine. A wound will have been made in Central Europe which will never close and which can only be healed by justice.

'This meeting is our *cri de coeur*, and this cry is addressed to the morality, reason and conscience of the world. One of the speakers to-day has referred to some words of our great poet of freedom. We may fitly close this meeting with another quotation from the same great thinker. He puts the words into the mouth of a people suffering injustice as we are suffering, and he says:

"If the oppressed finds justice nowhere,
If his burden grows intolerable,
He stretches up his hand to heaven
And seizes thence his deathless rights." '

* * * *

On the same day at the same time as the future Minister was making his speech in Berlin, Müllnitz, who was on duty at an outlying post, was attacked by Poles, killed and abominably mutilated. On the same day Paul Töllner, of the Marburg Teutons, fell, shot through the heart, at the attack on the mill at Leschna. On the same day the sound of nocturnal fighting reached us from Zembowitz, and Polish ammunition columns passed close by us on the road from Guttentag to Rosenberg; scouts from the army at Halle crept through the oak forest surrounding a village in Upper Silesia called Leschna, which was in our occupation. On the same day, the situation of the insurgent army was desperate, for the Oberland Corps' attack on the Annaberg had hit the Poles very hard. On the same day, the isolated, struggling but victorious, advancing troops of German youth, the deliverers of Upper Silesia, waited for the command – I mean, waited for the tacit permission of the Government – which should give the Self-Defence Corps, who were waiting outside the debated area, free passage to their distressed brethren; for a German victory was hovering in the balance. On the same day came Briand's sharp note requesting the disbanding of the German Self-Defence Corps.

THE OUTLAWS

On the next day, the Government published the following regulation, under the authority of Article 48 of the Republican Constitution, for the re-establishment of public safety and order:

§1. Any person who undertakes, without the consent of responsible officials, to form associations for military purposes, or who takes any part in such associations, will be punishable by fine up to one hundred thousand marks, or by imprisonment.

§2. This regulation comes into force immediately.

* * * *

Not a single man among those who went to Upper Silesia did so for the sake of upholding the sanctity of treaties. And if any one of them had visions of his deathless rights in heaven, it was of the right of youth to seek justice by revenge. For the first time during the German secondary wars a battle quite free from problems was in progress: this country was German; it was threatened; and we were going to its rescue.

* * * *

I was on sentry-duty and stood leaning up against the wall. Round about the farm were dark lines of trenches. The other sentries were placed along the village street and the field and forest paths, and were hidden by the darkness. We heard faint sounds of rifle fire from the direction of Zembowitz and Rosenberg. The dark and mysterious oak forest surrounded the narrow clearing in which lay the village of Leschna.

I ruminated on how I had arrived at this place, and the world in which I had been living for the past few months seemed quite unreal to me. It was at six o'clock in the afternoon of May 4th that the newspapers had contained the first news of the Polish rising. I stood in the street and read about it, and decided that the time had come. So I went home, packed my rucksack and hurried to catch the nine o'clock train. On the way to the station I met one of the older men working in my office, and asked him to tell the manager that I was not coming back, as I was going to Upper Silesia. The man was astonished but benevolent and murmured 'Ah, yes;' that it was very fine to be young; and of course if one could change and do better for one's self . . . and he wished me luck and hoped I should get more pay in my new job. Obviously my good friend thought that I was going to Upper Silesia to write out receipts for premiums. I did not trouble to correct him, but turned away after a brief farewell. Then I met Major Behring, the leader of many associations, whom I told what I was going to do, and he shook me by both hands with manly vigour and said that as long as Germany bred such young heroes as myself she could never go under. And he asked me to be sure not to forget to bring him one of the Upper Silesian plebiscite postage stamps for his collection, of course with the date stamp of the polling day.

The train steamed away into the night. I stood in the corridor and savoured coming events with the smoke that penetrated every crack. At Bebra a man got in wearing a leather coat, and stepped on my foot. As I kicked back, we fell into conversation, whose tone, however, altered rapidly. He was one of the Elberfeld group and I knew him by name. Reconciled, we wandered through the corridors together. Everywhere, in every carriage, young men were sitting or standing. They were cheek by jowl with snoring commercial travellers and business men munching sandwiches; the railway officials kept a suspicious eye on them; they were dressed in worn field-grey and darned breeches like myself; their fair hair and arrogant faces gave them all a sort of family likeness, without one's being able to say exactly wherein the likeness lay. We recognised each other at once and saluted one another;

we had come from all parts of the realm, scenting fighting and danger, without knowing of one another, without orders and with no definite goal, save only Upper Silesia. In the train we formed the nucleus of a company, a leader was found after a few minutes' talk, immediately and as a matter of course his authority was recognised; a future sergeant-major wrote out the roll.

At Leipzig some young fellows got in, wearing feathers in their caps, talking in the Bavarian dialect and bringing curious luggage: cart wheels, heavy rollers tied up in cloth and odd pieces of iron packed in boxes. I wandered past them, touched some of the rollers and murmured: 'Guns?' The man standing nearest to me grinned.

At Dresden a troop of forestry students joined us, wearing green uniforms, hunting knives and cocked hats. An entire academy was trekking to Upper Silesia, the teachers accompanying them as officers. They carefully stowed heavy washing baskets in the luggage racks and assured the conductors that they contained surveying instruments for the Upper Silesian forests.

At Breslau the station-master announced that the line of demarcation was barred and that Self-Defence Corps were illegal and would not be conveyed further. The travellers got out of our way nervously as we took possession of the train, boarded it, and gave notice that we should smash up the whole station if the train did not proceed immediately. The train went on.

We got out of the train at Namslau, and with the volunteers who were arriving by every train formed a Self Defence Battalion. Men came from all parts of the country, every kind of dialect was to be heard, and many and various badges were to be seen. There were Young Germans, *Stahlhelmer*, Rossbacher, men who had fought in the Baltic States, *Landesjäger*, followers of Kapp, men from the Rhine and the Ruhr, some from Bavaria and some from Dithmarschen. Student Associations arrived complete, Workers' Unions, soldiers, workmen and young business people. Balts, Swedes, Finns, men from Transylvania and the Tyrol, from East Prussia and the Saar district came, all young, all keen. And every third man I had met somewhere, somewhen, during the German secondary wars. And the men I did not know had friends who knew me, or had sometime fought in the same places as myself; after three minutes' talk we knew all about each other.

After a very few days a company paraded ready to advance. At Namslau station sealed waggons were shunted on to a side-line. At dawn we arrived and unloaded them. The lading bill was marked 'machinery – spare parts.' Now each of us had a rifle, but we were still short of ammunition. I met Schlageter. He had come from some place in the south, to smuggle arms and deal with officials, and he took pity on us. That night we broke into the *Reichswehr* arsenal and stole a light machine-gun and a large quantity of cartridges.

Schlageter told me that he had seen Heinz, who was busy among the towns down in the industrial district, in connection with the special police. Then I heard that Müllnitz was with a neighbouring troop and Otto near Oberland in the south. I met Jörg a few days later; he had been commissioned to bring a big gun from Waldeck-Pyrmont to Upper Silesia. So he and three other policemen took French leave, requisitioned a lorry from a carelessly guarded brewery, loaded it with ammunition, tied the gun on behind and drove straight across country quietly looking for Upper Silesia; and, being policemen, were not stopped by anyone. I began to be afraid that my usually keen instinct, which had hitherto led me to the decisive places, was going to let me down, since I had arrived in the north of the province and the fighting was going on in the south.

THE OUTLAWS

We heard various rumours from the direction of Oppeln; from Löwen Castle, where lived General Höfer, the leader of the Self-Defence troops; from Cosel and Ratibor and Beuthen. We knew that negotiations were in progress; and we knew that at these negotiations nothing would be discussed except ourselves and the country; and we knew that every hour that we were fighting was important.

A light wind swept over the grass. A part of the parapet crumbled and rolled gently down to the bottom of the trench. I listened anxiously and strained my eyes into the darkness. Nothing was to be heard in the forest; from Rosenberg the faint sound of rifle fire came a little more plainly. The first blow had been struck here in the north. Kreuzburg had been relieved, Sausenberg and Schloss Wendrin taken by storm. Now they were outside the town and could get no farther, while we lay scattered in this forest and could not move either. No one explained to us why we were stuck here. We were bound by an order, nothing more; for the Poles hardly put up any resistance; but here we were, giving them time to re-form their scattered sections. When we advanced over the boundary at Konstadt, the Italian guard vanished into their houses, as if at the word of command. The English, who raced up and down the roads in their rapid cars, saluted our columns. Shortly before Schlageter left us again to fight his way back into the towns, he talked to some English officers, who lumped together their allies – the French and the Italians – with the Poles as white niggers. The English did not like their own part in this affair. They muttered through their teeth that we were damn well to send all these white niggers to hell. We began on this job at Sausenberg. We were to have taken up our position at once, occupied Leschna, guarded the line of communication between Rosenberg and Zembowitz and the road from Rosenberg to Guttentag. And now here we were, tucked away in the middle of the forest, and had been for the last four days.

I heard the breech of a gun rattle and wondered where the sound came from. The day was dawning. I could see the sentry at the inn. I waved to him. He was fumbling with his rifle, into which he seemed to have got some grit. When, four days ago, just before nightfall, we had emerged cautiously from the forest, we heard music and shouting from the inn. We crept carefully through the empty streets of the village. For the Poles were supposed to be in Leschna; and, besides, the whole village had, with a single exception, voted Polish; and the people had attacked the Germans in Sausenberg at the beginning of the rising and had killed and mutilated a great many. For the rising had happened in this way in the north: the local Sokols seized the power, the German villages were attacked by the Poles, and they could not keep up the defence for very long, because regular Polish troops were following behind the insurgents. The Poles denied this and we were anxious to prove it true. When we had heard the music, we had taken it for a trap; and a few shots were fired. We had advanced rapidly and had seen a crowd of young fellows dash out of the door of the inn, armed, and run shouting towards the forest. We had fired at them, but on getting to the inn we had discovered that a wedding was being celebrated; the whole village had been assembled: we found only crying women. The bride had come towards us, pale, still wearing her high green coronet, an erection of fir and oak leaves, trimmed with red and white ribbons. The tables had been covered with food and drink; remembering Seydlitz near Rossbach, we had quickly sat down to the wedding feast; some of the Polish girls were not at all unfriendly, it seemed to us, though of course the bride was sobbing and furious. Next morning early the Poles had attacked.

They had fired suddenly and unexpectedly out of the under-growth, but a strong patrol of our men attacked them in the flank and our machine-guns, mounted on a roof, did consider-able damage. They had been obliged to retreat but had left their wounded, among whom was the bridegroom. He had a nasty thigh-wound, and we rather nervously carried him into the house in which was his bride, still in her wedding dress. Then we sent the doctor in and waited about outside. How-ever, we had not heard the bride scream, as we had feared, and a little later, when the company commander went in to interro-gate him, the young wife, though pale and red-eyed, was sitting quietly at his bedside. The wounded man was tall and slim, with a fresh, open intelligent face, the son of one of the richest farmers in the place. He told us, with a curious pride, that he had been a soldier, and had seen active service with a well-known German regiment. When we asked in surprise how he came to be among the insurgents, he told us that he was a Pole, though he spoke German better than Polish and had never been in Poland; that he had liked being a soldier; and that his brother was a loyalist. The doctor, a medical student in his fourth year, asked that his patient should be allowed to rest, so we went away. Then had come the second attack.

We had been attacked twice every day. We had dug trenches round a farm at the southern end of the village, set sentries and sent out patrols in all directions. On the second day Töellner had fallen at the counter-attack on the Leschna mill, which lay in a wooded hollow quite close to the road. We had been obliged to retire a little way and when we had advanced again, we found that the body had been stripped and mutilated. So we decided that the only prisoner who should live should be the wounded bridegroom. That same afternoon we had attacked a Polish column, defeated them and taken two prisoners. They both belonged to the regular Polish army and had Polish equipment and French rifles. Here we had proof that regular Polish regiments were being used against us, and I contended hotly that by shooting these two men we should destroy their value as evidence; hence for two whole days I had been suspected of having humanitarian tendencies. The prisoners had been sent to Sausenberg.

There must have been a good many Polish corpses lying about, for while the sun was shining, a heavy stench drifted in our direction. But we had not troubled to go and look. All day long we had lain stripped to the skin in the burning sand and baked ourselves in the sun. When we were attacked during the afternoon we had not had time to get dressed again, and the sight of so many naked men standing in trenches and firing must have been astonishing. Later we had attacked in the same state, carrying only rifles. It had been the wildest, maddest attack in which I ever took part.

It was now broad daylight. Dew was glistening on the grass and the white sand was damp. Nothing moved in the trenches, in which the company lay. It struck me afresh how strange it was that we had all collected here. There lay Lindig, a blacksmith's apprentice, and Busch who was a lieutenant in a famous regiment; there lay Nawroth, a miner from Upper Silesia and von Unruh, the son of a former Imperial Minister; there lay Kenstler, the son of a Transylvanian peasant, and Bergson, a Baltic student. We came from every district and yet were not strangers to one another – we were intimately acquainted and always had been; for we all subscribed to the same code.

The undergrowth crackled, and I heard faint sounds among the trees. I hurried through the trenches and grunted into each dug-out: 'Here they are!'

We heard their shouts – '*Na bravo*' – '*Na Lewo*' – and saw them preparing to attack. They had to hearten themselves by chattering, and to still the trembling of their limbs with valorous words. This habit of chattering before an attack is a characteristic of the soldiers of small nations. The Esthonians, the Letts and the Lithuanians used to chatter in the same way. These peoples had been oppressed for so long that they had forgotten how to take decisions quietly.

The company commander hurried along the trenches. 'Not a shot to be fired before I give the order!' he said. I placed the machine-gun in a dip in the road, beside the wood. Then they broke through the edge of the forest.

We fired.

*　　　*　　　*　　　*

We could not understand why we were ordered to go back instead of going forward. The Poles bolted whenever we came across them; the Germans cheered us when we came into the villages. And now we were to retire, back to our old quarters in Konstadt, hang about and wonder and be condemned to a life of restless stagnation – all this in the very moment of victory!

Heinz arrived, sick and feverish, with a wounded arm, and explained matters.

The Oberland Corps had made an attack from Neustadt on the Annaberg in the early hours of May 21st, 1921. This was the key to the insurgents' front line. The Oberlanders had dashed through the woods, across the valleys, over the hills, in three groups, surprised the Poles, who were expecting the attack from the south, and climbed the heights under a fire which rained on them from every bush and every house. By noon the Annaberg had been in German hands, but twenty-five per cent of the Oberlanders were dead.

After that, Bavarians, Tyrolese, Silesians, soldiers from all the Germanic races, had pushed into the country, hased fleeing bands of Poles – and in hundreds of places bells had rung and German flags waved. They had hurried on and the land had swallowed them up. For nothing followed.

When they had had time to stop and think, they had found themselves alone. And before them, the insurgents were re-forming their battle front.

The German Government had barred the western boundary of Upper Silesia. At the moment when victory seemed secure, the German Government had sent companies of armed police and threatened with imprisonment and arrested such of the Self-Defence Corps as were camping at the Oder. Meanwhile every man was needed on our front. The whole situation depended on our being able to rush up more troops and make good our victory by sweeping all the insurgents out of the country and liberating the towns. One last thrust, with fresh troops, and the country was free – and on the western boundary these troops were raging and cursing and unable to move. The Italians and French never kept the frontiers guarded as these policemen did.

The Annaberg troops knew that they had been betrayed.

*   *   *   *

When we were preparing to attack Rosenberg, a French division marched past ourselves and the Rossbacher and occupied the town. The mayor, with his maids of honour, received them ceremoniously and praised the 'Deliverers' with fine words – the Poles fled unhindered.

The French made a new boundary and created a neutral zone, two and a half miles wide. In this zone the Poles were allowed to roam at will and we could only fire at them after we had wormed our way through the chain of French sentries.

The Korfanty line was destroyed by our movements. The Poles were unable to hold any of the northern part of the province. Our line had not advanced as far as Pless and Rybnik in the south; the Poles were definitely in possession there. But in the towns the fight continued to rage.

Little groups of our men – deserted, hunted, betrayed – roved through the towns, over which hung smoke and famine and despair. They fought the insurgents of the IAK and the French patrols. But, one after another, they vanished. The Hauenstein people, known to the authorities as the Special Police, almost despaired when, day after day, news came and they heard how our troops were melting away – how one was found shot, another beaten to death with cudgels. An army of spies buzzed round the lonely men, prisons swallowed them up, walls were splashed with their blood. Bergerhoff fell and Krenek, Hauenstein was rescued from prison at the last moment, Schlageter fought his way through three times, Jörg extricated Otto from a mob of insurgents, but Otto died the next day of a wound in the abdomen. But the others, Eichler and Becker, Fahlbusch and Klapproth, and all the rest of them, held their ground.

The places where our men were absolutely wiped out were abandoned to the Poles by the French. But where our men held their own, the IAK remained and the towns were kept free of insurgents.

Thus the new line, called the Sforza line, because it had been elaborately planned by the Italian Commissioner Sforza, was drawn obliquely across the coal district, across the province, ratified by the League of Nations, recognised by our Government, and grumblingly accepted by Korfanty and the Poles. Curiously enough, this line was practically identical with that made by the German front line after the Annaberg and Rossbach incidents. Also, Beuthen, Gleiwitz and Hindenburg remained German, in spite of the fact that Sforza's line included them among Polish territory; and that because the remains of our troops had held them in spite of betrayal, in spite of the gnawing, vain hope of German intervention. The Self-Defence Corps reclaimed two-thirds of the province for Germany; the last third could not be reclaimed because a German regulation destroyed the Corps.

While the fate of Upper Silesia was being bewailed in gin palaces and beer shops all over Germany, we tried to save what could be saved by hiding our arms. We had to smuggle them through the western frontiers, for the Prussian police watched our doings with even greater suspicion than did the IAK. We buried them in the woods, gave them into the hands of loyalists, despatched them with peaceable-sounding lading-bills into the Ruhr district and the provinces where we guessed they might be needed.

For two more months we stayed in Upper Silesia. We were supposed to be volunteer agricultural labourers, and so we tied up sheaves, piled them on to unsteady carts, threshed and mowed all through the day. At night we smuggled arms and guarded the Polish frontier.

But during the heat of the dry summer of 1921, a spectre arose amidst the blood and confusion and danger that was born of the hideous harvest of our experiences. It was told of in whispers, unbelievers were silenced, the guilty carefully effaced themselves. A threat dropped like molten lead into the hearts of men:

Traitors will be dealt with by the Vehm!

CHAPTER XVII.

O. C.

It began in Munich. A representative of the Independent Social Democrat party, by name Gareis, was found shot dead in the street, quite near his house, on the day after he had made revelations concerning the secret survival of military associations among the townspeople. His death occasioned a great stir, but the murderers were never brought to book.

A few weeks later, Matthias Erzberger, with his friend and colleague Diehl, was walking in the Black Forest, at the foot of the Kniebis, near Griesbach. Two young fellows overtook them, turned and enquired whether he were not Erzberger. He admitted it with some astonishment, and the young men pulled out revolvers and shot Erzberger, while Diehl, who ran for his life, was wounded in the arm. Two ex-naval officers, former members of Ehrhardt's Brigade, were alleged to be the perpetrators of the crime.

The police, in making tremendous efforts to elucidate the mystery of the murder, found clues which led to Munich, to Upper Silesia, to Saxony, to Hungary, to the Rhineland, to Frankfurt-on-the-Main. They succeeded, by unremitting labour, in arresting large numbers of people, who all had subsequently to be released. But they never succeeded in capturing the two culprits.

The indignation felt by a great many people at this shameful deed was demonstrated by the offer of an enormous reward which was advertised in all the newspapers and by public placards. The police discovered a document, which appeared to prove the existence of a secret society, called O.C. One of the statutes of this association was: 'Traitors will be dealt with by the Vehm'. When this discovery was made public, the offers of reward became fewer.

The people who had seen with surprise how within a few days a German army had appeared in Upper Silesia, armed and ready for action, without the slightest rumour of mobilisation in Germany, were no longer surprised when they discovered the existence of a secret society. Nor were they surprised when obscure information came from Upper Silesia, whispered intelligence, strange enigmatic tidings. Their astonishment, indeed, gave way to an awe-inspired silence. For the power of the O.C. soon grew terribly manifest.

Murder crept through the streets: poison, daggers, revolvers and bombs seemed to be the tools of a gang of pitiless criminals. Men well-known as leaders of the people fell. The masses, starving, intractable, embittered and on strike, began a vague agitation. In furious demonstrations, they protested against an intangible terror which threw very distinct shadows before. Soon there could be no further doubt that everything was being done in accordance with a uniform, enigmatic plan. The O.C. was apparently carrying on its nefarious work quite openly. Excitement grew and with it horror. But at the same time a curious fascination developed, and drew more and more people into the whirl of crime which was forming under the surface. It was like a plague afflicting peaceable citizens. It attracted even those who were recognised as law abiding. Numerous choral societies, for instance, felt themselves to be the organs of the mysterious power, and thought they were chosen to be the liberators of their country. There were whisperings in beer-shops and cellars and attics. Moreover, the song of the Ehrhardt Brigade, which was sung to an old

English musical comedy tune, was heard in every street. Children sang it, patriotic societies shouted it on their 'German evenings,' and at places of amusement the bands played it in response to very frequent requests. The mystery surrounding the society and its doings, lent the song the glamour of defiance and rebellion. The men were legion who aimed at notoriety and who tried to establish their claim to it. They whispered the magic phrase: 'Chief's orders!' – no one dared to enquire further and obedience was ensured. Whenever a story of gun-running was told, or of a bombing outrage, or of a murder, everyone decided at once that the O.C. was at the back of it. It was strange, too, and rather sinister, that indignation was, too soon and too frequently, mingled with a secret enjoyment, the terror was pleasurably titillating. There were moments when the most peaceable and loyal junior clerk felt excitement rise in him as the foam on the beer rose in his glass, at some mysterious tidings of the O.C.

Quite soon it was considered a distinction to belong to this secret society. Many boasted among their intimates that they were members of it – many even boasted of it openly. There were men who were well known to be high officials in the O.C., and wonder alternated with indignation at their not having been arrested and imprisoned long since. The affair grew to be an open scandal. The sharpest orders and decrees of the authorities, the most severe prosecutions, produced no result. The poison penetrated even the highest circles. It was felt that something must be done to stop it. All the responsible elements hailed with joy the fact that the police did at last proceed to make arrests in several notorious cases.

However, it was just here that the O.C. showed how danger-ous it was; for in no case could the delinquents be brought to confess. Fifth form boys who, among their fellows, enjoyed the reputation of belonging to the O.C., grave majors, and respectable patriotic directors of industry, about whom rumours were rife, insisted that they had nothing to do with the O.C. Men who had belonged to the Ehrhardt Brigade, who kept in touch with their friends in Munich and the rest of the country, who openly spoke of their 'Chief,' told the police blankly that they did not even know what O.C. meant. In the police stations and on editorial tables lay mountains of material; people were continually being stirred by fresh news, facts, clues, suspicions; in the newspapers were paragraphs saying that first in one place, then in another, a corpse had been found in mysterous circumstances; and since there was no other evidence as to the identity of the murderer, the crime was fathered on to the O.C. The papers told how in different parts of the country suspicious members of suspicious societies had been arrested and the organisations dissolved, and that it was most probable that they were somehow connected with the O.C. But no positive result was achieved. People began to ask themselves how it happened that this mysterious power was able to envelop itself in silence – how it was that people, who had possibly been brought to admit that they were members of the O.C., were yet unable to say who were their brethren, who was the Chief, and what was the aim of the association.

The spectre rattled its bones audibly; the plague spread; the Republic was in imminent danger; everywhere plans were discovered which boded revolution and civil war; everywhere secret preparations were being made. The whole country was in a state of ferment; unions and societies worked themselves up into a fever, the authorities to dismay. From London and Paris came, at first amicably and then with veiled threats, the question: 'What on earth is this O.C.?' Appeals in the Press, questions in the parliaments, were multiplied. But the subterranean power of the O.C. grew and grew.

*　　*　　*　　*

THE OUTLAWS

'Primitive natures' said Kern, who was rather fond of lecturing occasionally, 'have to solace themselves by giving names to unknown powers – it robs them of a good deal of their terror. It is not improbable that the first dawn of organised religion can be traced to that need in humanity. The god who can be addressed by name, to whom altars are built, whose image can be made and adored, loses the greater part of his demoniacal nature. From being a revengeful god he becomes a law-giving god. Satan banned to his kingdom, hell, furnished with hooves and a sulphurous smell becomes a household demon. Lightning isn't anything like as terrifying since we know that it's nothing but an electric spark, which anyone can manufacture on a smaller scale. Now that we can all say simply "William of Hohenzollern" instead of "His Majesty," the Emperor has completely lost the aura of the divine right, to understand which was obviously not everybody's business, and which therefore kept its tremendous power to the last. The incomprehensible, happening here and now, becomes ordinary and respectable, if you only know how to classify it: as, for example, the Wise Men of Zion, the world-conspiracy of the Jews, of Freemasonry, of the Jesuits, in short of the super-national powers. How simple the world is when you understand it! And so it seems to me, that if people hadn't already got some conception of the O.C., they'd have to find one. Think – here's a secret society consisting of men who are ready to fight for power with every weapon, loyal to one another, bound to their superiors by vows of silence and obedience, with the death penalty for traitors – a society with mysterious rules, a conspiracy with local branches, with a chairman and a cashier – and yet secret. Splendid! Since the danger is recognised, isn't it already half overcome?'

Kern said: 'I suppose life itself sets about breaking loose sometimes. The good folk who feel the urge of primitive energies, imagine that they are serving them when they try to materialise them. They feel something that they don't understand and they want to estimate its value: they hope to get round it that way. But it's no use – it has to be faced. At bottom, these people are only defending law and order, not moral principles. But are there any principles to be defended? A bad conscience tries to exorcise the power that threatens it. It creates a bogey that it can make faces at and thinks safety is thereby assured. And what about the other people, whose sympathies are with the O.C.? What else are they doing but trying to insure themselves? If I meet a man who says he belongs to the O.C., I know he's either a fool or a liar or a member of the C.I.D. It's a help to know that. It's a help when your adversary is led astray by the appearance of things and thus mistakes their nature. It's useful to have a sceptical mind and so avoid confusing life itself with one of its manifestations. The power of suggestion is enormous. It creates the veil behind which people like ourselves can work comfortably. We have to thank that document for rousing the plot-complex to such heights – it has of course been helped in its work by the kindly co-operation of our excellent, though intellectually somewhat neglected, police. Incidentally, the man who composed this interesting paper and played into the hands of the police, is a very near relation of mine. Unkind people say that he has a weakness for practical philosophy.'

Kern said all this comfortably sitting on a little safe in my exchange-office, speaking more to Heinz than to me. Heinz was leaning up against the low door, and I was counting a packet of dirty notes at the counter; for since my return from Upper Silesia I had been occupying a little wooden booth in the middle of the station, making profits out of the inflation for a firm of Berlin bankers. Apart from a narrow table, a chair, the telephone, a file and the safe, nothing was in the office;

there would not have been room for anything more anyhow. When Kern had finished his harangue I asked him if he would mind holding down the hook of the telephone receiver, when I had to telephone for a customer. At that moment a customer did come and wanted to change dollars. With a great show of efficiency, I promised to get him the latest exchange and lifted the receiver. Down the now deaf machine I enquired for the exchange department and asked for the latest rate. 'Specie or notes?' I enquired; 'eighty-two, thank you,' I said, and hung up the receiver and gave the delighted customer far less than the current rate.

'But that's cheating!' said Kern astonished and taken aback, while Heinz grinned. I assured him that it was indeed cheating; that everything that I was doing in this little office was cheating; cheating to order; very honourable cheating; cheating which was the soul of this business. And I told him of all the edifying tricks, of the little meannesses that went on, such as entering a big deal as several small ones, because any exchange of over three thousand Marks was taxed; and how I made the customer pay the tax all the same and the firm pocketed it. I told him of the ring of exchanges which kept the official rates down by buying and screwed them up by selling. And so on.

I said to Kern: 'One has to be capable even of that. We still have a great deal to learn before we are ready to take up arms against the destructive powers of civilisation.' – I continued: 'You told me a little while ago that the men in Mainz were complaining of being hindered in their freedom of action by a want of money,' and I pushed a bundle of notes over to him. He drew back and said sharply: 'If other people are blackguards that doesn't seem to me any excuse for your being one too.'

'It would appear,' I said and counted out some money to a Pole with dirty finger nails, 'that you are still infected with bourgeois sentiments. It would appear,' and cashed a beautiful crackling ten pound note for an elegant silent Englishman, 'that even if everyone else were playing fair, the fact that the Mainzers are held up for the want of money is enough excuse for me' and flinched somewhat at the cloud of scent which emanated from a no longer young Frenchwoman, who was greedily counting her notes, 'to have no consideration,' and did a suspicious Dane out of at least ten per cent., 'either for the profits of my highly respected firm or the purity of the moral principles of my unprotected youth.' And I gave a little lady of the nocturnal Kaiser Street the only fair exchange of the day for her Dutch gulden.

'It would appear,' said Heinz, 'that certain things can only be said in stilted language.'

'I can't take the money,' said Kern obstinately.

'If I had made this money by cheating instead of by speculation,' I said offendedly, 'you may be quite sure that I shouldn't have told you anything that might have led you to dangerous conclusions.'

'The confusing of emotions' said Heinz, 'seems to me to be the most effective weapon of the O.C.'

*   *   *   *

My office soon became the Finance Institute for the Rhineland. Even Heinz had to make up his mind to work to bring his share of the money necessary for our activities in the occupied area to me for safeguard. We were able by daring speculation to create a fund, not indeed inexhaustible, but still sufficient for our modest needs. For we had had much to do since our time in Upper Silesia.

The 'Activists,' who had collected in Upper Silesia, thenceforward separated and were able by co-operation to give greater power and greater importance to the isolated exploits of their members. In the months following, a tough invisible net was formed, of which the individual threads reacted whenever the signal was given at any point. This happened without any compulsion whatsoever, without any association, plan or programme – simply by the action of a spontaneous and natural community of interests. Every association, every Party, every profession contained some of our men. They played into each other's hands, shared information, warned one another, gave useful tips and worked in the thrilling knowledge that the same thoughts and ideas, the same aims, the same situations, were arising in a hundred different places at the same time. They were bound by fetters far stronger than any vows and rules could be. They behaved as men of a single race – felt the same enthusiasms and the same doubts – and were glad to find that they all had the same conflicts and found the same solutions. They forced themselves to the inexorable conclusion that it was not enough to offer their lives: they must offer what was more than life – their honour and their conscience.

One event followed another. We lived double lives. What we earned by our hated, though necessary, toil during the day, enabled us to have our free times and to carry on our real work at nights. We went from one excitement to another. We heard of each other during hasty meetings. Gabriel and his men snuffed out the beginning of a Separatist movement in the Pfalz through sheer bloody terrorism, though of course it was impossible to smash the well-organised French machinery. The Elberfeld men, spied on by suspicious Communists, by Separatists and the French as well as by the German authorities, and always alive to the danger, which had threatened for years, of a French occupation of the Ruhr, laid the foundations of an unremitting resistance, supported by Schlageter and his men, who had changed their base of operations from Upper Silesia to the Bolshevised towns of the Ruhr. In the frontier States, in the eastern Provinces, in Brandenburg, Schultz was creating a hidden army of defence – the black *Reichswehr*. In Munich, our men were engaged in a wearisome war with mawkish patriots. They had their fingers in every pie – they investigated all grades of politics, without finding that it aroused any sentiment in them beyond one of disgust. They found time to make an end of the French-inspired machinations of the Bavarian Separatists; they made enquiries in Austria, conducted researches in Hungary and Turkey, and fed the sources of Southern Tyrolese unrest. When Kern was on the move, we inferred his stopping places by the news which filtered through from all sides – news of gun-running in East Prussia; of the police being led astray in their search for the murderers of Erzberger; of the enlistment of six thousand Dithmarsch peasants; of the capture of a Separatist leader near Cologne; of the organisation of German Bohemians; of somewhat coercive conversations with *Reichswehr* commanders; of men rescued from prison in the occupied area.

Thus Kern became in a short time one of the leaders among the Activists. Whether it was a case of gun-running in Danzig or a bomb outrage in Hamburg, he was called in to direct operations. Very soon he was surrounded with a halo of legends. He always had at least three new plans simmering in his mind and one in his pocket ready to be carried out; he was always on the move and brought fresh air with him; he glowed with an inner fire, whose intensity suffered no lukewarmness in its neighbourhood. This broadly-built man of middle height, with his open countenance and dark eyes, radiated strength, both physical and mental. He was as unsparing in his demands on others as he was on himself. He was always prepared to defend passionately any idea that seemed to him to have value, until he proved it to be worthless, when he lost no time in throwing it overboard. Nothing gave him greater *élan* than the premonition he had of his early death.

Our group meanwhile was becoming well-known and even popular in the town. Each week-end saw us at Mainz or in the Taunus mountains or at the bridge-heads. The number of those who were posted as deserters in the roll of the army of occupation in the Rhineland grew apace, and the Intelligence Bureau in Mainz kept an even stricter watch on us than before. Very soon spies turned up in our most secret coverts and announced themselves as loyalists, which roused our suspicions from the very outset. Very soon anyone turned to us who had a blood-feud, or who wanted help for some private activities, or who was in possession of information on which the German authorities could not act. Very soon the authorities themselves came to us. At times we were the ball and at other times we directed the game.

*   *   *   *

Official affairs had long since ceased to interest us. The troubles of representatives and voters, parliamentary debates, the enactments of ministers, the conferences of Powers, could not touch us. For we lived below the surface, and nothing that came from above was capable of stirring the waters to their depths. Though we boldly took a part in the events of that other world, because we were determined to avoid no difficulties, we knew that there could be no compromise between us and it. And therefore we sought none. Thus we were unable to answer the question that was so often put us, as to what were our real aims.

The country lay open before us like a tilled field ready to take any seed; and we were not prepared to allow any other seed to be sown than the ideas which came to us in our dreams.

The country was in that condition when anything was possible. It was in a state of cold stagnating fluidity, which needed only the addition of something to make it freeze. If we could not supply that something, all our doing was in vain.

O.C.

So we looked round to see where we might find a man to speak the word for us. But wherever we searched among the men of the new German upper classes, we could only look and pass on scornfully. Where might we find a man, apart from the silent Seeckt, with character enough to make a historical figure? Perhaps in the shrewd Ebert or the pursy Scheidemann? The modest Hermann Müller; the venerable Fehrenbach; Wirth, who was honest to the backbone? Or – Rathenau?

*　　*　　*　　*

Rathenau was speaking in the Municipal Education Hall. Kern and I only just managed to squeeze into the packed meeting and lean up against a pillar, ten feet from the speaker's desk. Among the crowd of frock-coated men who sat round the committee table, the Minister stood out by the nobility of his bearing. When he stepped to the desk, when his thin, aristocratic face with its noble brow appeared above the lectern, the buzz of talk in the hall died down at once, and he stood in the silence for several seconds, with his dark, wise eyes and a certain indolence of carriage. Then he began to speak.

What surprised me was not the tone of his voice: that was just as I had imagined it from reading his books – cool and warm at the same time. What surprised me was the passion which infused the opening phrases of his speech, and the absolute conviction that this passion was sincere.

'Filled with sadness,' said the Minister, 'we watch the unravelling of the Upper Silesian drama. . . .' And he pronounced these first words softly and most impressively, so that one could really feel the gloom which oppressed him. The reason for his sadness was the infringement of the principles of justice.

The first phrase was the key to the whole theme of the speech. The Minister did not take things lightly, he spoke as a man agonising for full knowledge, driven by a sense of responsibility and a desire to serve, and almost reluctantly giving

239

the results of his conscientious enquiry, whose lodestar had been an ideal recognised as absolute. And yet the assurance of his arguments must have given him confidence – a confidence which led him to use as an illustration of his thesis the historic proclamation, made before the French National Assembly in Bordeaux in the year 1871, by the members from Alsace-Lorraine as they said farewell to France. This speech was directed against a victorious Germany, and began with the words: 'In despite of all justice. . . .'

From this aspect, that is, with the premiss that justice existed, that this conception was not imaginary, everything that the Minister said was logical and conclusive. He seemed to be impregnated with an idea, which was not new, except as the predominant motive in the mind of a statesman; and this idea gave German politics what had been so long missing: fulness and aim and reason. For justice, regarded as an absolute good, demanded absolute equality for all classes. In order that we, who were conquered, arraigned and under suspicion, might be admitted to this equality, we must gain credence. In order to gain it, we must fulfil our promises. By this fulfilment our goodwill and its strength would be demonstrated. According to the measure of our strength, justice would give us freedom. No link was missing in the chain of arguments. The broken bond was reunited and Germany was once again a part of the civilised world and of democracy, gaining fresh glory by sacrifices, atonement and faith.

The Minister addressed his speech like a message to the townspeople, who listened with interest and with their attention pleasantly riveted. He abandoned himself to his eloquence and expressed himself with ease, enjoying his own ideas. He spoke with a full realisation of his powers and excited by the wave of warm appreciation which rose to him from the hall.

O.C.

His magic could indeed work nowhere so well as here; for the citizens of this town were proud of the spirit which informed it and which was embodied in the two great names which are always associated with it. Rathenau had in him something of that which had made both these names great. He himself had once indicated what seemed to become truth in himself, when he said that a statesman should be a mixture of two opposites: like Napoleon and Bismarck, he should be half a Roman and half a Levantine – half god and half devil. This mixture of two opposing forces was the secret of his personality; in him were mingled what seemed to the citizens of this town – who were sometimes in doubt which to rate higher – to be characteristic of both the local great men: Goethe and Rothschild.

While I was amusing myself with my ideas about this man, though I was following his discourse carefully, I suddenly realised which way his sympathies lay. He had said that our thoughts were polar and had tried to prove to us that the ultimate opposing elements were courage and fear. But what he sought to conceal in his speech showed itself in the tone of his voice, in his gestures, in the question in his eyes: the fact that his heart was with the coward.

When I realised this, my gaze involuntarily left him and turned to Kern. He was standing almost motionless, leaning against the pillar beside me with his arms folded. Then an extraordinary thing happened. It occurred while the Minister was speaking of leadership and confidence, while his voice rang through the silent hall, cutting across the fog of material comfort which lay over the assembly. I saw Kern, leaning forward and not three steps away from Rathenau, drawing him under the spell of his eyes. I saw the paleness of his face. I saw his concentration; the hall vanished, so that nothing remained of it but one small circle, and in that circle two men.

The Minister turned round doubtfully, looked towards that pillar, first vaguely, then in surprise; he halted in his speech, tried to regain the lost thread, found it and then passed his hand confusedly over his brow. But from now on he spoke to Kern alone. Almost imploringly, he addressed himself to the man standing by that pillar and grew weary as he did not change his position. I heard the end of his speech without taking in a word.

As we elbowed our way towards the exit, Kern passed close by the Minister. Rathenau, surrounded by a chattering mob of people, looked at him questioningly. But Kern pushed past him – unseeing.

CHAPTER XVIII

ACTION

IN July, 1918, U-boat 86, under the command of Lieuten-ant-Commander Patzig, sighted the British steamer *Llandovery Castle* in the English Channel. The boat was a hospital ship and flying a Red Cross flag. However, Lieutenant-Commander Patzig thought he could distinguish guns and, remembering the Baralong affair, he ordered the steamer to be sunk. This was done. Lieutenant-Commander Patzig failed to return from a later expedition.

The German people had not protested against any of the terms imposed on them by the armistice and peace treaties as furiously as they had against having to hand over the so-called war-criminals. Everyone will remember that storm of indigna-tion, one of the many which raged through Germany. The *Entente* decided that it would be dangerous to draw the noose too tight; and, knowing the German character, they were not afraid of creating a precedent. They were therefore inclined to give way on this point. No one had, indeed, expected the German people to raise so unanimous and determined a protest against this particular proviso. But at that time they would have felt that they were contemptible if they had not been prepared to sacrifice everything for the honour of Germany. However, the Government, realising that honour would not feed the hungry, decided to compromise in the matter, and celebrated as a victory the fact that the Allies agreed that the punishment of German war-criminals should be left to German Courts. Lieutenant Commander Patzig was one of the names on the English list of war-criminals.

THE OUTLAWS

Since Patzig was dead, the German Government felt that something should be done in the matter, and haled the other two officers of the submarine, Lieutenants Boldt and Dittmar, before the courts, though their names were not on the list. The State Prosecutor Eebrmayer felt it to be his duty to make a special effort to demonstrate to the whole globe the German Supreme Court's love of justice. So he ordered the two lieutenants to be handcuffed. The English officers, who had been sent to Leipzig to observe the proceedings, received this mark of well-bred courtesy with unmoved faces. The Supreme Court condemned the two officers, whose crime was that they had obeyed their superior's orders unquestioningly in face of the enemy, to four years' imprisonment for conduct unbecoming officers and gentlemen. For the Supreme Court is a court dealing with externals – and Brutus is an honourable man.

*   *   *   *

Kern, Heinz and I were present at a meeting of some patriotic society on the occasion of a passionate recitation by an elderly man of a poem dealing with this decree, in which there was a great deal about smirching the shining 'scutcheon of Germany's honour. During the moments that elapsed between the end of the recitation and the furore of clapping that ensued, Heinz could not resist shouting: 'Waiter – a beer!' Having thereby somewhat disturbed the solemnities, we repaired to my office in the station and discussed how to rescue Boldt and Dittmar from prison.

Since it was to be supposed that every malcontent in the country was making some such plan, haste seemed indicated. I stoutly advocated that we should move at once, since both men were still in the cells of the Supreme Court and therefore might both be rescued at once. A pregnant silence followed my remarks. Then I heard with astonishment that several naval officers, among whom were Kern and a man from Freiberg in Saxony named Fischer, had driven up in a car one evening recently to the prison in Beethoven Street in Leipzig, dressed in police uniforms, had shown a cleverly forged removal-order, and demanded that the two prisoners should be handed over as quickly as possible, as they had to catch the night train. They added that everything was to be done most secretly, as there was reason to fear that a rescue of the two men would be attempted by the O.C. However, the Saxon prison officials did not walk into the trap. They rattled their keys, made a great show of willingness and hurry, and secretly gave the alarm to the police. They, not being anxious to meet sinister powers anywhere but in the open, first of all turned on every light in the neighbourhood so that the square was as light as day. Kern and Fischer smelt a rat, climbed into their car and dashed off at top speed. Later we discovered that the plan had been betrayed, and Kern thoughtfully prophesied that, after the wave of anti-Semitism which was stirring our beloved country to its depths, there would certainly be another wave, one of anti-Saxonism.

Since the first attempt had failed so dismally, they were obliged to share the secret with others. We had to wait and see to which prisons Boldt and Dittmar would be transferred. However, a plan could meanwhile be discussed in its broad outlines. Kern, as a matter of fact, was of opinion that the liberating of the war-criminals was an affair of honour for the navy, and determined that Heinz and I should take no active part in it. At first we were inclined to challenge him to a duel with pistols, but finally yielded on condition that some other affair should be handed over entirely to us – and were roundly abused for having bargaining natures.

*　　*　　*　　*

The Boldt affair went off very smoothly – some of the junior officials in the Hamburg prison had been in the navy and later in Ehrhardt's Brigade.

Dittmar had been incarcerated in Naumburg on the Saal. After lengthy preparations, we managed to smuggle a steel-cutting apparatus into his cell. Some of the naval officers wanted the rescue to be effected on the birthday of the All Highest Naval War Lord, that is to say, on January 27th, 1922. But at the last moment the man who was to have driven the car in which Dittmar was to escape fell ill, and Kern, not knowing where to turn at the eleventh hour to find a substitute, chose as chauffeur an individual of the name of Weigelt, who had come from Thuringia and represented himself as an officer in the Flying Corps. The affair was undertaken a day later than had been planned, that is on January 28th, 1922.

According to the reports, the rescue of Lieutenant Dittmar was effected in this wise:

Adjoining the wall of the prison at Naumburg was a nursery garden, and the window of Dittmar's cell was visible from this place. In the evening the rescuing party crept into the garden and climbed the wall; they let down a rope-ladder into the prison yard and held their revolvers ready to fire. Sentinels were placed all around the prison; the car waited in a side street. Weigelt, the chauffeur, turned up drunk. Dittmar cut through the bars of his window and to the stumps he fastened a long rope which he had made by twisting strips of his blue checked bed cover. The rounds of the warders had been timed very carefully. As soon as they had disappeared into the building, Dittmar, watched breathlessly by his comrades and his young wife, squeezed through the window and let himself down from the third floor.

As he moved, the rope began to swing, and his body hit the wall several times. He tried to keep clear by planting his feet against it – and put his leg through the window of the cell below him.

The whole prison began to hum. Dittmar, sliding down as quickly as he could, put his foot through another window. The prisoners, filled with envy that one of their number should be getting away, shouted that the war-criminal was escaping. Glass crashed, the prisoners raged, doors banged, lights were turned on. At that point, Dieter, late Lieutenant-Commander in the Imperial Navy, created a diversion by making a noise at a far corner of the wall. The warders hurtled out of the building, hesitated a moment and finally ran towards the place where Dieter was making the disturbance.

Dittmar had slidden down as far as the top of the first storey when the rope broke. He fell and crashed heavily to the ground. At the same moment Kern jumped off the wall into the yard. Fischer and the brave young wife crouched on the wall, their revolvers in their hands. The warders were still quite happy investigating Dieter's hubbub. Kern and one of his companions lifted Dittmar, who had hurt his spine, carried him to the rope-ladder and hoisted him up with considerable difficulty. At the same instant that the officials saw the rope hanging from Dittmar's cell and hurried up swinging their rifles, the prisoner vanished over the wall.

When rescuers and rescued reached the ground, panting, the whole district had been roused. However, our sentinels who had kept a careful watch, hurried round and guarded the street. Dittmar had already been packed into the car and Kern had climbed in beside him, when Weigelt, looking pale and nervous, said that he could not start her as the engine had got cold. Fischer leapt across to the driver's seat, held a revolver to Weigelt's temple and said 'One – two – ' At 'three' the car moved. The pursuers rained bullets at our departing backs.

THE OUTLAWS

No nation in the world has such a highly developed sense of duty as the Germans. The police got tremendously busy. All high roads, railway stations and frontiers were immediately barred. The telegraph wires hummed, as is usual in such cases; every kind of police – and there were many – was in a fever of excitement to capture the criminal Dittmar and to hand him over to justice once again. A warrant was issued and his description was posted.

While the frontiers were being watched, Dittmar lay hidden in Saaleck Castle, hardly a mile from the prison, awaiting his own recovery and the end of the railway strike.

*   *   *   *

I sat peacefully in my office changing money. Travellers were streaming through the station; porters hurried by; there was continual coming and going. There were, however, two men standing at the chief entrance to the platforms, who had come but who did not go. One of them was wearing a bowler hat, the other a light travelling cap. Both had ordinary overcoats and completely expressionless faces. I was convinced that I had seen these two men before. I rapidly put up a notice saying: 'Closed for family reasons,' locked up my office, and rang up Heinz. 'Yes,' I said, 'C.I.D. – detectives. These people aren't here for fun – their pay isn't good enough. Dirty work at the cross roads! I expect every man that has legs to do his duty. Stop.'

Ten minutes later the first of our men arrived. Heinz told us at once that Kern was travelling – he was probably arriving to-day and most likely Dittmar would be with him. We ascertained that every exit was watched by C.I.D. men – there were two at each entrance to the platforms but only one at each of the gates out of the station itself. Heinz looked up the trains from Thuringia, and discovered that an express was due in a few minutes. Very soon some twenty of us were posted unobtrusively about the station. I took a platform ticket and went through the barrier. The train drew in.

As soon as I saw Kern I dashed at him. Dittmar was close behind. We pushed through the barrier. For some reason there was no detective here. Close by the main entrance was a board for official notices on which was a red placard with a description of the wanted man. A group of people was standing curiously in front of it. Kern steered straight for the warrant.

'Abominable!' he shouted. 'This man is being hunted as a criminal,' he roared, 'for simply doing his damned duty. Down with the rag!' And he tore down the notice.

The travellers crowded round in a moment. The two detectives first of all followed Kern with their eyes, then with their heads, then with their shoulders, and finally with their legs. One of them stopped again immediately, but pursued his colleague with anxious looks, as the latter pushed his way through the crowd. Kern swore horribly. The detective came closer. Just then a green uniform sped into the throng, buttons glittered brightly, and a policeman laid a heavy hand on Kern's shoulder.

'You come along with me to the station!' he said firmly. This policeman was Jörg.

Reassured, the detective turned back. And Kern, casting a lightning glance round and seeing Dittmar in the act of slipping out between the two officials who were oozing efficiency at every pore, suddenly calmed down and went along beside the consequential Jörg with a hangdog look. As Dittmar went out by the main entrance, the ring, which had formed close round the detective there, slowly dissolved.

Jörg said anxiously to Kern: 'I hope those C.I.D. fellows won't enquire about my report!' However, they did enquire, and Jörg was ejected from the police force.

*　　*　　*　　*

Dittmar, Kern and the young wife were sitting in the express for Bâle. They were going to communicate with us as soon as they had crossed the frontier. Our men were at every intermediate station through which the train passed, ready to lend a hand if the C.I.D. was too active.

One member of our band was a traitor. We had had plenty of proofs – for instance, Jörg had discovered at the police headquarters that Dittmar's presence in the town was known. It was, therefore, essential that his departure should be hastened. Somebody told how Weigelt, when he had assured Kern of his readiness to help in the rescue, had said as a particular proof of his trustworthiness that he knew all about the abortive attempt in Leipzig. A little matter of gun-running from Saxony to Czechoslovakia for the German Bohemians had to be stopped at the last moment, because certain worthy gentlemen in celluloid collars and shabby overcoats, who alleged that they came from the housing office, made awkward enquiries as to Fischer's occupation and the reason for his continually changing his address. Heinz had already twice been arrested on remand and questioned twice. Various files of documents in various towns all over the country had names on them which were not, indeed, spelt Kern, but which all began with the letter K.

It was hard enough to find fifty reliable men among the half million inhabitants of our town – but it was harder still to find five who could keep their mouths shut. Hitherto our company had found no clean-cut line of demarcation, no code, which was in every way better for us than the serviceable ethics of the world. Nevertheless, we very soon felt the need for isolation as an essential in our fight, which was a fight for our own existence. Traitors must be suppressed.

The first telephone call came from Heidelberg, telling us briefly that Dittmar's train had passed safely. Gabriel was talking about the Fascist methods. The Fascisti were just beginning to become famous in Italy. Traitors among them were punished by being bound to a post in a public place in their home town with their trouser legs tied up, and having a dose of castor-oil administered to them. We thought it was a good idea in so far as it precluded any possibility of the victim's setting up as a hero and martyr; but it seemed to us too humane, and not suited to the German character whose idiosyncrasies would not lead one to expect that the culprit's embryonic sense of shame would make him keep quiet about the reason for the proceeding; and therefore further treason would not be out of the question.

When the telephone call came through from Karlsruhe, we had to get a fresh supply of drinks, and the conversation turned with unexampled ferocity to all the several forms of death that might follow the different varieties of treason. Heinz illustrated his bloodthirsty impulses by quotations from the works of modern German poets. However, we refused to admit their authority, since the gentlemen in question enjoyed the protection of the State, and therefore had unquestionably neither drawn their information from real life, nor used it in any way except to uplift the morals of the community. Still, we got a few ideas from Heinz's quotation.

Then the message came through from Freiburg. The train must be getting near the frontier. The name Weigelt cropped up again in the buzz of conversation. There was a sudden silence. One man had a letter of Fischer's which he proceeded to read aloud. According to that, the car which we had used to effect the escape had not been returned. The car belonged to a well-to-do manufacturer from Halle, who was a sound man in spite of his opulence. Fischer had been to see Weigelt, who said that he would have to clear out, because rumours were beginning to float round Thuringia concerning the rescue of Dittmar, which would soon lead to police investigations. Weigelt had owned to Fischer that he had made no secret of his part in the affair to some little ladies in a bar which he frequented. Fischer had insisted that Weigelt should return the car, but had given him quite a large sum of money, so that he should not be without means in his flight. The girls had had that money. Weigelt indeed had vanished, but several land-owners in Thuringia recounted a few days later how a young man, an ex-Flying Corps officer, had turned up, telling them that he was Dittmar's rescuer, and asking for money and assistance.

A letter of Dieter's was also read. Dieter had been enquiring into Weigelt's past, and had established that he had never been in the Flying Corps, but in the A.S.C. He was 'wanted' by the *Reichswehr* because a train of waggons which had been entrusted to him had disappeared. He had been dismissed for irregulari-ties from another post. He was probably on his way to the Rhineland now.

Gabriel interrupted at this point. Weigelt had been to see him and Kern, dressed in a fur coat and a monocle, and had unfolded to them his grave fears that, if he were not supplied liberally with money, he might easily fall into the hands of the police, and then he could of course not guarantee that the Dittmar affair and other interesting matters would not be disclosed, and sundry names brought to light during the enquiry. Kern had handed out various small sums to him, and then, in response to continuous pressure, larger amounts. But Weigelt had informed him that he would require more in the near future.

All at once we were very cool and silent. According to the time-table, the train must by now have arrived in Bâle. We emptied our mugs, and determinedly washed down all gloomy thoughts with the last drops. We cast furtive glances at the telephone. The ticking of the clock grew agonising.

ACTION

Suddenly the nerve-shattering silence was broken by a shrill ring. Heinz jumped over two chairs and seized the receiver. 'Trunk call from Bâle . . .'

We leapt on to the tables and smashed the glasses against the wall.

* * * *

A few days later, Gabriel, gloomy as ever, haggard and fanatical, came to my room, where Kern and I were sitting. Silently he laid on the table a list which he had got from the anti-spy organisation in Cassel and had distributed among the Activists. He pointed carelessly to one name. Kern read it, jumped up, and walked up and down the room for a long time with a set face.

I looked at the list and said: 'Of course there are various possibilities. One might challenge Weigelt to a duel – but he'd probably funk it. Or one might have him up for blackmail and treason. But one can't very well make use of civil courts when one is fighting them. Or again one might get him into trouble with the French, by whom he seems to be employed, by a little clever work on the part of our anti-spy people – and they'd deal with the matter themselves. But I suppose that's hardly done! – Then, of course, there is a fourth possibility. . . .'

CHAPTER XIX

THE VEHM

IT was not difficult to persuade Weigelt to make an excursion into the mountains – it was much harder to induce him to come out of the night-clubs of Wiesbaden, which he made for unerringly as soon as they came in sight. It was late in the evening when we started on the homeward way. We walked through the Kurpark. It went against the grain to make any kind of preparations for our sinister work; I felt towards this man as I should feel towards a bug – that it had to be destroyed. Therefore Kern and I took the first path we saw, having no definite plan, but keeping Weigelt between us, and waiting for the psychological moment.

A light mist hung over the sky. Isolated lamps shone with a pale greenish light on the dripping trees. Weigelt shivered, took my arm and tried to hurry on, jabbering unceasingly.

The dark path through the park seemed to lead to nothingness. The leafless branches of the bushes stood out threateningly among the dark shadows of the trees. Weigelt pressed his arm to my side, and remarked that the place was positively uncanny. I suddenly had a mysterious impulse of terror, that almost choked me. The thought rose in me that according to human ordinances the deed towards which we were heading through the shadows was accursed. To vindicate myself I argued that we were acting in a judicial capacity; yet I instantly realised the weakness of this argument. Responsible only to a narrow group, we must not seek to justify ourselves before

the wider circle of humanity unless we were prepared to admit
that its ways were right. Devil take these brainrackings! How
did our present doings concern the rest of the world? We
were approaching the end of an episode which concerned only
ourselves. The traitor was to be dealt with by the Vehm.
That we happened to be carrying out the sentence was a
matter of luck – who could say why one should lose a throw at
dice? Whose fault was it that he interfered in our affairs?
He walked along beside me gabbling, a mean, shallow creature,
repulsive as vermin.

He stumbled and clung to my arm. I jerked away roughly.
There had been enough of play-acting! Why should we be
concerned for his life, since he himself was only wasting it in
feeble dissipation? At one place where the path went close by a
lake, Weigelt stood still and listened to the water lapping
against the bank. His eyes suddenly sought Kern and he asked
hesitatingly, almost plaintively, whether we intended throwing
him into the lake. Then he began to laugh. Kern looked at
him, before growling that it was an idea worth considering.
Weigelt went on hastily, pulling at my arm. Soon he was singing and bawling again, was cheered by the sound, and bounded
along gaily, eager for drink and girls.

In a way he seemed to be fascinated by our warning. Knowing his danger, he refused to admit its imminence. For an
instant I felt sorry for him. Secret doubts assailed me; but I
told myself that once our decision to make an end of this man
was taken further moral questionings were absurd. A sharp
gust of wind dispelled the mist; it hung in wisps over the lake
and passed in clouds over the pale crescent moon. The shadows
of the trees appeared and disappeared. The distant, lights
shone across the lake. A branch cracked loudly somewhere
near us and Weigelt started at the sound. He sang boisterously
in a raucous voice, and we guarded him inexorably. We

increased our pace without having any idea in what direction
we were heading until in the end we were almost running. A
passing car dazzled us with its head-lamps, then raced by
beyond a clump of trees. Evidently there was a road there.
Windows reflected the light and we saw dark solid masses,
presumably houses. Weigelt sang to free himself from bleak
cold terror.

A backwater stretched up as far as the slippery path, and a
low railing was mirrored in the water. In the far distance
shone a solitary light. Weigelt began to recite in a loud tone.
He stood still suddenly and said, beating time with uplifted
finger: 'A lady who wore a red hat . . . ' But he was not given
time to finish the filthy rhyme; for Kern raised his fist and
brought it down like a sledge-hammer on Weigelt's head.
Weigelt crumpled up, fell prone and lay still. His hat rolled
down the incline and his glasses splintered against a stone.

Kern looked at me with wild eyes. His figure was sharply
silhouetted against the dark water, and his coat bellied in the
wind. I leant over Weigelt, who raised his head, muttered
something and tried to rise. I knelt beside him. Bewilderment
showed in his wide-open eyes. He recognised me, scrambled
up suddenly and stood there, swaying. Before Kern had time
to turn round, Weigelt raised his arm and for a moment it
poised threateningly over Kern's head; in his fist was a life
preserver. I shouted, hurled myself at him and seized his hand.
Kern spun round. But the leather thong held the weapon in
Weigelt's grasp. He jerked himself free of me and his arm shot
up; then the bludgeon swung into my face. I felt the cartilage
in my nose give. Blood streamed into my eyes and mouth. I
went for him blindly, and felt his elbow through the heavy coat
he was wearing. I clutched at his arm, seized the cold hand,
felt for the weapon and with great deliberation loosened
one of his clenched fingers. I bent it back till it broke, and then

his grip slackened. 'You swine,' I gasped, 'you swine!' Weigelt screamed shrilly for help.

Streams of blood were pouring down my nose. I loosed my hold on Weigelt and rubbed my face, which had lost all sensation. Beside me raged the contest.

It was in vain, I thought, for him to try to defend himself, the dirty dog. I pulled myself together, looked up, saw Kern stumble and Weigelt standing over him. I kicked him in the stomach, and he howled: 'Help, murder!' His screams echoed through the trees and across the lake. Then I went for him, seized him by the throat, clawed at his eyes, crashed my fist in his teeth, choked the voice out of him. I wanted to push his teeth down his throat. But he spat blood and teeth in my face – straight into my mouth, and I was nearly sick with disgust, as I tasted the thick, sweetish, warm slime. Then he collapsed, and I staggered back exhausted.

The whole place seemed to be astir – his shout for help had wakened all the ghosts. I thought I heard steps – but what did I care for steps – let anything happen that would! Weigelt was once more on his feet. Kern instantly knocked him down again. I felt that I had to make some remark, so I gasped: 'He's damned tough!' Kern kicked Weigelt, who suddenly rose to his knees and raised his arms imploringly.

'Fight!' shouted Kern, in a ringing voice.

'I will,' babbled Weigelt, 'and I'll never give away anything again. . . .'

'Fight!' I shouted.

Weigelt suddenly ran towards the light at the railing beside the lake. Kern reached him before I realised that Weigelt had pulled out a revolver. I suddenly saw the barrel in his hand. I was able to knock up his arm, before the shot was fired. Weigelt held on to the railing with his left hand and kicked wildly at us. I hurled myself at him and threw both arms around him; he again spat blood at my mouth. Then he managed to kick me; I loosened my hold, but Kern had by now got possession of the revolver.

Weigelt shouted; and every one of his cries raised the tide of red fury in us. We dashed at him; he struggled, he hit out. Kern seized his leg as it was raised to kick, jerked it up and pulled, and suddenly Weigelt's whole body slipped over the railing and fell. With a rushing sound he slid into the water and the spray splashed into our faces.

I leant over the railing. Bubbles were forming on top of the water. A little way farther down the bank Weigelt's head came up. His mouth came out of the water, hideously distorted, and he flung his arms into the air. And then a cry of utter terror broke from him, rose up in entreaty to God, drove panic into our hearts, called on the water, on heaven, earth, woods and men to witness his unutterable anguish. Kern fired the revolver into the noise; he shot across the water, once, twice, held the revolver with its barrel up, and then collapsed beside the railing.

Weigelt paddled towards the shore. I twisted the revolver out of Kern's hand and ran along the steep bank, knocking my head against trees, getting tangled up in bushes, stubbing my toes and knees on roots and stones and boughs. I ran panting, seething with a primitive lust to kill, to the shallow place where Weigelt was trying to climb out.

When I reached him, his body was half way out of the water. As I came, he raised both arms. I leant well forward and seized his coat, and deliberately put the revolver to his head. He groaned heavily, and raised his bleeding face to me as though he were pressing it resignedly to the cold muzzle of the revolver. He murmured something, his injured mouth forming the words with difficulty. He raised his eyes painfully, looked at me unseeingly, and tremblingly held up both his hands. He whimpered; I found it difficult to understand him. He said: 'Please, please, please, please . . . .'

He gasped for breath and said: 'Mercy, have pity . . . .'

He murmured: 'Life, life . . .!'

'You cad – you swine – you traitor!' I spat the words at him.

He moaned weakly in a piping voice: 'I won't give away anything. I'll never betray anything again. I'll do everything you want me to. Only let me live – live – '

Slowly I pressed the revolver closer to his head. 'You miserable worm,' I said. 'You traitor! You shall . . .' And then I felt suddenly terribly tired. I looked numbly at his distorted face and said: 'Get away!'

He stammered something that I did not catch. I turned and went slowly back.

Kern was still in the same attitude by the railing. As I leant beside him, my arms hanging limply by my side, the revolver heavy in my hand, he roused himself. There was a long silence between us. Behind me I could hear groans and splashes. Kern said bitterly: 'Damn it, I don't feel much of a hero!'

Considerably relieved I muttered: 'He's alive.'

'I know,' said Kern.

He took a few hesitating steps and then turned along the path towards the town.

Hour after hour we walked. We had to cross the whole of the Taunus to get home. Shivering, we turned up our coat collars. We staggered along the road almost blind with headache. Neither of us spoke a word. The smell of blood was nauseating. It had soaked through all our clothes right down to the skin. We washed ourselves as best we could in a mountain stream, but the blood flowed again as we got hot with walking and formed a horrible layer over our skins, slimy and sickening. In the early morning we reached the first tramway and squeezed into the darkest corner on the outer platform. As we arrived in the town, exhausted but upheld by the tension of recent events, a crowd was coming out of a fashionable dancing hall. The men had crumpled white shirt fronts and top hats set aslant, and were whistling for their cars. Three girls in marvellous evening wraps, accompanied by elegant young men, passed by us. They were in fancy dress and wore silk breeches; their bare shoulders gleamed among soft dishevelled fur. They were boisterously singing the latest comic song, in slightly alcoholic voices.

CHAPTER XX

KERN AND I

AT that time, when we scarcely had time to draw breath between one fierce battle and the next, we had to simplify our conceptions and look at life in clear broad outlines. Though we were not experienced in that method of fighting, which is certainly the one that presents fewest inconveniences and which was referred to with great relish in the newspapers as 'war with spiritual weapons,' we nevertheless took some pains in the short time that was left to us for reflection to fish in the chaos of words for those that would express our ideas. Yet we felt most definitely that that power which impelled us was not really an emanation of ourselves but rather the outcome of mystic forces which it was impossible for mere human reason to grasp. Each one of our deeds, however unpremeditated, however little practical result it might show to the eye of the materialist, at least furthered the development of our individuality, at least stirred people up more than the old conferences and regulations, the speeches and decisions and promises of Parties and Societies. Every deed of ours shook the structure of the old system, and provoked reactions, which inevitably led to fresh activities on our part. We realised fully what we were doing, we accepted the curse under which we had fallen – that violence breeds violence, and that we could not withdraw from our chosen path. Indeed, we felt a sense of duty in carrying out a historical purpose, which, while it relieved us of no personal responsibility, gave our actions an added excitement. The will to create, which did not hinder us from destroying, which indeed made destruction right and necessary, led us to touch on higher things in our nightly conversations in which the consonance of our thoughts and speech were made intoxicatingly manifest. We sought to express the final cause of our mission, and how best to accumulate and direct the forces which gathered from all quarters.

The nearer we got to the centre of the vortex, the harder it grew to take decisions. What at first had been almost a game, the merest reaction of lively minds, because nothing else was conceivable, demanded our complete surrender, as our conception of the code to which we subscribed grew clearer.

Not all of us admitted the impalpable constraint; so it was not easy for Kern to enforce discipline on certain members of our company who were hatching a plot to derail the train carrying the Soviet minister Chicherin to the conference at Genoa. I had told Kern about this when he was in town for a few days. He immediately stopped the proceedings; but our men were overcome by a lust for blood, as we had been in the early days of fighting in the Baltic States, and would have accused anyone but Kern of weakness and cowardice. Kern gave no reasons for stopping them. That evening he came to see me.

We sat and talked far into the night. I said slowly, feeling my words drop uncertainly into the silence:

'I have never had the feeling so strongly as in the last few days that all events are concentrating on one point. Perhaps I am under the influence of a universal mood, born from the innumerable hopes and wishes which are agonising for the great change. But if the decision really comes now – what is our position?'

Kern said: 'No real decision is uninfluenced by the forces to which we subscribe. There can be no real decision depending

on men who are the result of an epoch which could not sustain
its one real test, the Great War. The world would never have
had any meaning if it had chosen as its heroes such characters
as fell short even of the standards that they themselves helped
to set up. They can quarrel and make treaties, they can
negotiate and command, they can write and make proclamations,
but their call never takes men out of themselves. The places
they fill with confused noises are not the fields where decisions
are won. These still lie virgin, beyond the dense thicket
through which we are thrusting our way.'

'What gives us the right to our arrogant claim? Are we the
chosen – we, who have no power of ourselves; who have no
talents save for shooting; no understanding save of plotting;
no experience save of our failures; we, who are pursued and
pursuers; who are even filled with disgust at our own deeds?'

'We are not chosen to bring into being the ultimate visions;
not to gather the harvest. But does the issue concern us? What
concerns us is the work. No, we have had no result; we never
shall have any result. We have created an organisation in whose
suffocating atmosphere we are now gasping for air. We began
the advance towards the east, and did not get to Warsaw; we
failed before Riga. We carried our flag to Berlin and brought
it back again. We swept Upper Silesia cleaner than it had ever
been, only to leave it a prey for the first comer. We practised
naked anarchy and are no further on than before. We were
told that we were defending a forlorn hope, and had nothing
to answer save that that was no reason for deserting our post.
You ask what gives us faith in spite of all this? Nothing but
our deeds, the fact that we are able to work, that we are fit to
work. We may consider ourselves symptomatic. When did it
ever happen that any decisive change took place without men of
our stamp being concerned in it? I cannot believe that our
generation, which has been hurled into war, educated and

hardened by it, should now be fated to renounce war in obedience to the feeble commands of those who are afraid of the
consequences of their own actions. I cannot believe that a
force dies before it has been used up.'

We were silent. I could only see Kern as a silhouette against
the white-washed wall. I got up and threw myself on to
the bed. I said:

'I want more. I don't want just to be a sacrifice. I want to
see definite results. I want power. I want some aim which
will engross my life. I want to savour life whole. I want to
know that all this has been worth while.'

Kern leant back into his corner.

'What do you mean by that big word "sacrifice"?' We don't
sacrifice and we aren't sacrificed. I can only conceive of myself
in relation to the surrounding world. I'm afraid you conceive of
the surrounding world only in relation to yourself.'

'No; because I don't want to be shut out from the world
around me. What is given into our hands is not enough for
me. I want to take part in some achievement, which helps on
not only myself but the whole nation. You want that too. Out
there, they're struggling for power. Perhaps no one who seizes
it is worthy of it, or indeed can be worthy of it. But they have
control over the machine. Those whom we are fighting, and
whom we despise, hold in their unworthy hands an instrument
which can only be beneficial if it is used with reverence and for
a high purpose. Every little day power is being fought for.
What ought we to do?'

'To pass by the little days, in order to prepare for the big
one.'

'That simply means that we've got to go on living under this
terrible pressure and –?'

'Waiting.'

'I can't wait, I won't wait.'

'Occupation neurosis?'

'No. We can't do enough, we can never do enough. What we are doing now doesn't satisfy me.'

'Of course, Napoleon was a Brigadier-General at twenty-six.'

'Hell! Shut up pulling my leg. Tell me, if you know, which bit of God's mantle we must snatch at if it is wafted by us?'

'Hell! Shut up asking questions. Tell me, if you know, a greater happiness, if you are asking for happiness, than that of discovering what makes life so glorious for us. What is it but the courage to face life wholly? How otherwise can life be consummated for us, and through us the fate of the nation?'

'What makes our life so full is our duty to the nation. Others feel it besides ourselves. Are you so soon satisfied? You say "fate" where others would say "hunger," if they wanted to prophesy.'

'I say "fate" because I must conceive of the nation as a force and not as matter.'

'Then the nation isn't your final goal?'

'Have you never started up from dreams whose deepest meaning you realised when you were awake? If we are chosen, we are chosen in order to preserve in our hearts what has come down to us through hundreds of years, what has been preserved through every accident, what first made us worthy of being a nation. No nation striving for fullest development refuses to rule, as far as its faculties permit. I recognise no submission save to this power.'

'Well, then, in which dream is the fulfilment of this power shown?'

'In the domination of the world by Germany.'

*   *   *   *

There were many things over which we disputed that night;

and we found that we always had to get down to first principles before we could agree. It no longer satisfied us to know that we were separated from the rest of the world by our attitude to life. We asked for the 'Why.' And since we knew that this question was arising among all the youth of the nation, we felt that we must ask it even more insistently, for we had lived our lives far more intensely. That could only mean that we must be equally radical in our questioning, that is, to get down to the radix, to the root, of the matter. And therefore we submitted to the tyranny of words, as indeed we were prepared to submit to any tyranny under which we could grow strong. And Kern said:

'There is one tyranny to which we can never submit – economic tyranny; it is entirely foreign to our being, and we cannot develop under it. Its pressure would be unbearable, for it is too narrow and too contemptible. This is a fact that each man must sense intuitively without seeking to know the reason. One is conscious of the pressure and therefore it is impossible for one to stretch out a hand to those who deny its existence.'

I said slowly: 'Those who speak of understanding, set economic tyranny high in the scale of things.'

'Those who speak of understanding, also speak of reconciliation. But if a wide river of blood flows between the two parties, a reconciliation is only possible when the combatants are capable of recognising each other's innate worth.'

'Those who speak of reconciliation, believe in absolute worth.'

'That's where we differ from them. What can these men who are travelling to Genoa contribute to the sum of knowledge? They speak the opponent's language; they think the same thoughts. Their weightiest argument is always that to harm German economic life is to harm the economic life of the whole

266

world. Their chief ambition is to be reinstated among the Western European Great Powers. And when I say "Western" I mean the Powers who have submitted to economic tyranny because it gives them their power.'

'If I am correctly informed, Chicherin is also going to Genoa.'

'If I am correctly informed, Chicherin is going to Genoa in order to meet the western nations on their own ground and to claim a hearing for Russia as a nation for the first time since the establishment of the Soviet Union.'

'Bolshevism as a claim to nationalism? I shall become a Bolshevik to-morrow.'

'If you do so, I shall look on you as a Russian. It is that that makes me convinced that nationalist evolution points to the path before us. Make war on an idea and you will suddenly find that you are making war on a country. The Russia of Chicherin is, like ourselves, fighting for its freedom, which it will accomplish in discovering its own peculiar civilisation. Throughout history Slavism – like Teutonism – has had to guard itself against foreign influences. Only it seems to me that the Teuton individuality always held up the Teuton outlook on life as a standard in the fight, whereas in Slavism a sort of civil war arose between one foreign influence and the other. But what can one say when the Slav, in order to defend himself against western influences, accepts the support of an ally which, though born of the west, is inimical to the west. That is the same as if one called on the Beelzebub of Marxism to throw out the Devil of Capitalism. Well and good. But it is significant that this Beelzebub has stuck a Russian cap on his head and that under his domination the Russian has grown more powerful than he ever was before; and it is still more significant that nowadays an attack on Bolshevism is also an attack on the national independence of Russia. Since the differences in

Russia were sharper than anywhere else, so the warfare to which they gave rise was fiercer. Hence it came about that the Soviet Union – a union of national republics organised on a strong hierarchical basis – found in Bolshevism its suitable constitutional form – a thing the German Republic did not find in Weimar.'

'These peculiar nationalists speak of "world revolution".'

'They say "world revolution" and mean Russia. A people and its ideas are as great as its strength. The Russian idea of world revolution always reached so far that they wanted to clear their country of foreign troops, to dare an invasion into Poland, to frighten the West with nightmares and to mobilise at no cost to themselves in every country in the world a zealous and faithful army of irredentists.'

'Let's join this army of irredentists.'

'We cannot join the German Communists because they must not be allowed to achieve power at the instigation of Russia. They must not be allowed to succeed, because after their victory they would turn into Russian irredentists and would be compelled to go through the same process, the process of the evolution of primitive forces which, expressing itself in Bolshevism, has for the first time made of Russia a nation. For this reason, we dare not allow them to prove successful, since they deny their own nation.'

I said excitedly: 'But it's a matter of war against the west, against Capitalism. Let's become Communists. I'm ready to make a pact with anyone who will fight my battles. I have no interest in protecting the propertied classes, since I am not one of them.'

'It isn't a matter of interest. The Communists are concerned with interests. If we quarrel with them about it, it's not because it's theirs, but because we can recognise no other interest than that of the nation. If instead of "Society" or

268

"Class" we speak of the "Nation," you will understand what I mean.'

'But that represents Socialism in its purest form.'

'It does, as a matter of fact, represent Socialism and only in its present form, that is to say in the Prussian form. A socialisation of everything by means of which not only the economic tyranny will be destroyed through a collectivism that will give the last farthing of value to every member of the nation, but also a socialisation through which we shall regain that intellectual unity which was stolen from us in the nineteenth century. It is for a socialisation such as this that we are fighting, and the enemy is every man who refuses to share in the fight. They're all *such* good Germans – such warm patriots! But when they pronounce the word "German" with all the fervour of which they are capable, what they really mean is that social organisation, that civilisation, which was the distinguishing mark of the last century. And after that they are thinking of that which the Great War broke up. Never by any chance do they mean that which is our inspiration. How could they? Between them and us no agreement is possible; for they are no longer capable of the final sacrifice. If it is indeed a power that we are undermining, that it is our task to destroy with every weapon that comes to our hands, that power is those in the nation who have allowed their Teutonism to be submerged in a flood of western culture. They utter the word "Germany" and mean "Europe" – their true motherland. They shriek aloud in fear of the very subjection they in their hearts desire. They want us to survive and are ready to sacrifice the last remnant of Teutonism to obtain the only dictatorship of which they can form a conception. They are surprised that the Germans continue to be feared! It is not they who are feared – these men who are ready to submit – it is not because of them that the Germans are feared – it is because of us! It is because in us and in a hundred thousand others like us, the war and the events of the post-war years have re-awakened those qualities which first made us dangerous to the west. And that is good – that is a hundred times good. Since we are at one with our age and our age with us, therefore the possibility remains open to us of making good our mistake in remaining passive at the very time when everything around us called us to be active.'

'Rathenau has begun an active policy. It is for the further-ance of his active policy that he is going to Genoa.'

'Rathenau? Hm – Rathenau – '. Kern rose and leant against the window. 'He is our hope, for he is dangerous.' Kern began to walk up and down the room. In the darkness he stumbled against a box of bombs, against rifles that were stacked in the corner. He began to speak softly and insistently:

'He has more power in his hands than has been given into any single hand since November 18th. If ever Fate came to a man with a demand, with a passionate demand, it is to this man, who has shown himself the fiercest critic of his contemporaries and of his age. Nevertheless he is a man of his age and is moved by the forces that govern this age. He indeed is the finest and ripest fruit of his age. He unites in himself everything in this age that is of value in thought, in honour, and in spirituality. He saw what nobody else saw and he made demands that nobody else put forward.' Kern went to the window, threw it open and looked out. Then he turned round. 'But he has never taken the last step, the step that would make him free. I feel in every sentence of his speeches and writings that he is waiting to take this final step until the time comes when it will prove to be decisive. I think the time has come. I think he will prove himself equal to the emergency. For us all that matters is whither he leads.' I rose and came to meet Kern in the middle of the room. Kern said:

'I couldn't bear it if once again something great were to

arise out of the chaotic, the insane, age in which we live. Let him pursue what fools call a policy of fulfilment. That's no business of ours. We fight for higher things. We are not fighting to make the nation happy – we are fighting to force it to tread in the path of its destiny. But I will not tolerate that this man should once again inspire the nation with a faith; that he should once again raise it up to purposefulness and give to it a national consciousness. For these things belong to an age that was destroyed in the war, that is dead, dead as mutton.'

'In that case,' said I, 'we know who is our enemy. It only remains to decide where he is most vulnerable.'

*　*　*　*

I asked Kern: 'How is it that you, as an imperial officer, were able to survive the ninth of November, 1918?'

Kern replied: 'I did not survive it. As honour demanded, on November 9th, 1918, I blew out my brains. I am dead. What still survives is another thing. Since that day, I have lost my ego. But I will not be other than the two millions who died. I died for the nation; and all that is surviving of me lives only for the nation. Were it otherwise, I could not bear it. I follow my star. I die daily, because I am mortal. While my actions are the sole motive force within me, everything I do is the expression of this force. This force is destructive – hence I destroy. Up to the present, it has desired only destruction. Who sups with the devil, must have a long spoon. I know that I shall perish in the moment in which this power no longer has any use for me. Nothing else is open to me than to act as the whole force of my will orders me to act. Nothing is left to me except to reconcile myself to the noble suffering imposed on me by Fate.'

CHAPTER XXI

PLANS

A TELEGRAM of Kern's took me to Berlin. There I met him and Fischer in a small secluded boarding-house. Kern was in good spirits, and thousands of plans and possibilities were surging in his brain. He was almost pleased at the failure of the attack on Scheidemann. He had, he told us, always been in favour of trying out the cyanide mixture, which was finally used in the little indiarubber ball, in a closed room. The cool audacity with which that aged tribune of the people had gloried in his escape in a long and eloquent speech before assembled multitudes, half an hour after the attempt had been made on his life, filled Kern with the kind of surprised interest with which one would observe the habits of some strange exotic creature. Fischer, a quiet, thoughtful young man, an engineer from Saxony, the type of regular officer who could conceive of no conditions of service save one in which the rank and file had confidence in their leader, asked me to take over one of the many affairs which had been planned, so as to relieve him and Kern. The Weigelt episode had become notorious; I hoped to be able to carry on the work in Berlin. My wish to be allowed to join in when the rooms of the Inter-Allied Military Control Commission in Berlin were raided, was negatived by Kern; and Fischer thought that he had enough men for the new attempt at gun-running from Freiberg to the German Bohemians, which had been betrayed the first time. I therefore chose another gun-running affair that was to end up in Pomerania. But Kern asked me first to help him with the preparations for the rescue of some German Activists from the French military prison in Düsseldorf.

The work in Berlin turned out to be harder than we had anticipated. We were obliged to carry on with an incredibly small sum of money. We had not been careful enough to finish off the ends of some of our affairs. Cases of disloyalty were cropping up with increasing frequency. Episodes which were not under Kern's direct supervision seemed to go wrong from the very beginning. We were suddenly confronted by a collection of tasks which we were simply incapable of carrying out. News and calls came from every part of the country. Every day mysterious unknown people came to see Kern. It was not always easy to direct them, since we changed our habitation every few days. Every glance at a newspaper showed us that a heavy storm was threatening.

In the middle of the month of June, 1922, Kern's enthusiasm seemed suddenly to falter. He grew more cautious than we were accustomed to expect of him. He cancelled a number of affairs for no reason and postponed others. He spent a great deal of time alone with Fischer – and Fischer himself began to brood over things. Sometimes he said nothing but what was absolutely necessary for days at a time; and very often they left me at home when they went to listen to debates in the *Reichstag*. They always came back irritable and disappointed.

The succession of bombing attacks in Hamburg seemed rather pointless to Kern. He asked me to go to Hamburg to stop the business. At the same time I was to look round for a chauffeur to drive the car, which we had not yet got, for the rescue of the men in Düsseldorf. When I came back, Kern was more annoyed with me than I had ever seen him. He pronounced the chauffeur to be quite unsuitable, and sent him back. He spoke of having already despatched someone from the Ehrhardt Brigade, Ernst Werner Techov, to Saxony to fetch a car. At this point I rebelled. I demanded to be told what plans were being made. He contended that they did not concern me. I pressed for an answer, fearing that he had lost confidence in me. At last Kern said that he had not wished to involve me in an affair whose results I could not foresee. I refused to admit the objection that I was too young.

On the evening of one of the following days, Kern, Fischer and I were sitting on a bench in the Zoological Gardens, waiting for the car which was due to arrive from Saxony. Kern said he had put off everything that had been planned in order to be able to concentrate on this one affair which should prove decisive in more ways than one.

He sat leaning forward, with his arms resting on his knees, watching the people strolling in the soft twilight. Fischer was quietly sitting back, looking at the pale evening sky through the tree tops. Sounds of distant music reached us faintly. *Reichswehr* soldiers passed. Kern followed them with his eyes. He told us how they had marched into Berlin along this road in March 1920, and that it had been the best day of his life. He said he knew that what he was going to do now would mean that he broke faith with someone. But he would still be loyal to the idea which forced him to carry on at whatever cost. Duty was no longer duty, loyalty no longer loyalty; and honour no longer honour – what remained was action.

Kern said: 'If this final act is not attempted now, it may be impossible for decades. We want a revolution. We are free from the hindrance of plans, methods and systems. Therefore it is our duty to take the first step, to storm the breach. We must retire the moment our task is done. For our task is attack, not government.'

Fischer sat motionless. A policeman passed slowly and looked us up and down. Night came on. Kern said: 'The

274

desire for change is here, everywhere. It has stirred whole nations. For those who seek to advance and who are not cowards, it is the only real reason for life. The situation cannot be controlled by any one man. But each individual can determine its tendency by his own action. What we have done up to now has strengthened the position but is not enough. We are attacking what is material; and that is, after all, embodied in man. We have destroyed limbs but not the head and not the heart. I intend to shoot the man who is greater than all those who surround him.'

My throat grew dry. 'Rathenau?' I asked.

'Rathenau,' said Kern and stood up.

The car did not arrive until we were in bed at our lodging in the Schiffbauerdamm. Ernst Werner Techow told us that he had had a breakdown on the way. He knew nothing as yet of Kern's plan; for Kern was determined not to allow his assistants to be in any way responsible for the deed. He only mentioned Rathenau if it could not be avoided. He feverishly prepared everything that was connected with the deed. But he procured neither money nor passports for himself. When I finally enquired what he intended doing when his task was accomplished, he answered: 'Not what you think. We shall try to escape to Sweden. If the act leads to no decisive result, we shall return at once and attack the next man. I cannot believe that our deed will not be at least a beacon to rouse men to further action. When the end is to come does not rest with me.'

Hardly any of our preparations went right at the first go off. Something was wrong with the car. The expected Lewis gun did not arrive; we had to get another one; and it missed fire several times when we were testing it. Fischer was trying for days to find a suitable garage, and he eventually got it with the help of a man who had untrustworthiness written all over his face. When, finally, we heard that Rathenau was going away from home, Kern said to me dispiritedly: 'It seems as if the very stars in their courses were fighting against us.'

Kern had to suppress a plot which was being planned by a seventeen-year-old schoolboy. He roughly refused any help from me. He made Fischer take lessons in driving from Techow, so that Techow might also be eliminated. On the other hand, he contemptuously made much use of the services of a boastful and psychopathic student.

Fischer was of an equable temperament. He was the centre to which Kern always returned. If he noticed that Kern was wasting his energies over details, he took him for long walks. One day on a sudden impulse he took us into a cinematograph theatre which we happened to be passing. 'Dr. Mabuse, the Gambler' was being shown. We did not manage to get seats together. When the interior of a prison was thrown on to the screen, Kern shouted across three rows: 'I say! That's the cell we got Dittmar out of!' People said 'Sh!'

Kern and Fischer went to the *Reichstag* one day when Rathenau was speaking. On the way home, Kern stood for a long time looking into a photographer's window on the Unter den Linden in which was a portrait of Rathenau. The strange, dark, eager yet self-possessed eyes looked at us out of the narrow aristocratic face almost searchingly. Fischer after a long scrutiny said: 'He looks a decent sort.'

On Saturday, June 24th, 1922, at about half-past ten in the morning, the car stood in a side street off the Königsallee in the residential suburb of Grunewald, near Rathenau's home. Fischer kept watch at the corner where this street opened into the Königsallee. Kern fetched his old waterproof out of the car. Techow was engaged at the bonnet; he told Kern that the oil-feed was broken, but that the car could do a short quick run,

PLANS

Kern was calm and cheerful. I stood by and watched him. I was trembling to such an extent that I felt as if the engine against which I was leaning had already started. Kern slipped on his coat. I wanted to say something – something warm and reassuring. Finally I asked: 'What motive shall we give if we're caught?'

'If you're caught,' said Kern cheerfully, 'you can throw all the blame on me – obviously. On no account tell the truth – say anything – Lord, it doesn't matter what you say. Say anything that the people will understand who are in the habit of believing what they read in the newspapers. For all I care you can say he's one of the Wise Men of Zion or that his sister is married to Radek, or any rot you like. Anyhow, whatever you say, make your statement as bald as possible. That's the only way they'll grasp anything. They'll never understand our real motives; and if they did, it would be a degradation for you. Mind you don't get caught! Every man will be needed soon.' He pulled the leather helmet over his head, and his face looked gallant and honourable in the severe brown frame. He said: 'The Düsseldorf affair mustn't be given up. Yesterday I had news that somebody has blown the gaff about the Freiberg gun-running business again. The men must be warned – don't forget. You must clear out of Berlin at once. Tell the Elberfeld people to be careful of Matthes, the Cologne man; he's planning a *coup* for his Separatists. Gabriel must not leave the Pfalz if the row begins. If Hitler is the man I think he is, he'll realise his chance now. A year later will be a decade too soon. Say good-bye to the other fellows for me.' He lifted the Lewis gun from under the seat and put it ready in the front of the car. He turned and looked me full in the face: 'Stick to it, old chap; you're a useful tool – mind you don't let yourself get rusty. I want to ask one thing – let Wirth live; he's a good fellow and not dangerous.' He leant forward took me by the lapel of my coat, and said softly: 'You can't think how thankful I am that everything is behind me.'

At that moment a little dark red car drove quietly up the Königsallee. Fischer came and climbed into our car without a word. Techow was sitting at the wheel; his face had suddenly gone grey and hard as if it were carved in wood. Kern shook hands with me briefly, got into the car and stood upright for a moment with his coat blowing in the breeze. The engine began to quiver. I flung myself at the door and stretched my hand into the interior – nobody took it. Kern sat down and the car started.

The car started; I wanted to hold on to it; it slipped away humming. I wanted to scream – to run – but I was paralysed, vacant, petrified, utterly forsaken in the grey street. Kern looked round once more. Once more I saw his face. Then the car disappeared round the corner.

CHAPTER XXII

MURDER

'MURDER OF WALTHER RATHENAU

'Berlin, June 24th.

'IT is officially announced that this morning the *Reichsminister* Rathenau, shortly after leaving his villa in Grunewald for the Foreign Office, was shot at and instantly killed. The assassins overtook the Minister's car, in another motor car, in which they made their escape after the murder.'

Notice in the *Berliner Tageblatt*.

Krischbin, a bricklayer, told the story as an eye-witness to a reporter from the *Vossische Zeitung*:

'At about a quarter to eleven two cars came down the Königsallee. In the back of the first car, which kept more or less to the middle of the road, a gentleman was sitting. We recognised him at once because the car was open. The second, which was also open, was a dark grey six-seater, a powerful touring car. Two men in long, brand-new leather coats and helmets were in it. The helmets left their faces exposed and we could see that they were clean shaven. They were not wearing goggles. A great many cars come along the Königsallee in Grunewald, and one doesn't notice each one that passes. However, we all noticed this one, because the magnificent leather coats caught our eyes. The big car overtook the smaller

one, which was driving slowly and almost on the tramlines –
no doubt because of the large double curve which is just ahead
– and cut in on the right side, so that it forced the little car to
go towards the left, almost to our side of the road. When the
big car had got about half a length ahead, and the passenger
in the other one was hanging out to see if the paint had been
scratched, one of the men in the leather coats leant forward,
seized a large revolver, whose butt he put in his armpit, and
pointed it at the gentleman in the other car. He did not even
need to aim, they were so close. I looked him straight in the
eye, so to speak. It was a healthy, open face; what we call
"an officer's face." I took cover, because the bullets might have
hit us too. The shots came quickly, as quickly as a machine-
gun. When the one man had finished shooting, the other one
stood up, pulled the pin out of an egg-bomb and threw it into
the small car. The gentleman had already collapsed in his seat
and was lying on his side. Now the chaffeur stopped, quite
near Erdener Street, where there is a rubbish heap, and shouted;
"Help! Help!" The big car suddenly leapt forward at full speed
and went off down Wallot Street. Meanwhile, the car with
the dead man in it stood by the curb. At that moment there
was a crash as the bomb exploded. The gentleman in the
tonneau was actually lifted up into the air – and the car itself
seemed to give a jump. We all ran up and found nine empty
cartridge cases on the pavement and the pin from the bomb.
Parts of the car had also been blown off. The chauffeur re-
started the engine, a girl stepped into the car and supported
the gentleman, who was unconscious and probably already
dead. Then the car drove back as hard as it could along the
way it had come, as far as the police station, which is about
thirty yards from the end of the street.'

*   *   *   *

MURDER

'What have you done? You have lain in cowardly ambush and murdered the noblest of men. You have laid a terrible blood-guiltiness upon the People whom this man always served with every fibre of his being. It is the nation itself whom you have shot through the heart. Your accursed deed has not only struck the man Rathenau; it has struck Germany in her entirety. Deluded fools – you have slain one man but you have wounded sixty millions. A whole nation bewails the criminal madness, whose victim has been the deliverer of the People. The whole world turns in horror and loathing from a country in which a spirit such as yours could grow and ripen. You have destroyed at one blow what this man built up painfully throughout long years of self denial. In this man you have betrayed the fate of our people. You have shaken the foundation of all communal life – confidence. You have struck at Bismarck's work and the future of Germany. You were not worthy to live in the shadow of such a man. May your end be as shameful as this deed – death shall bring you no honour – no punishment that strikes you can be heavy enough.'

* * * *

Rathenau wrote in his *Mechanism of the Spirit*. 'We only realise death when we look at a single part instead of at the whole. The ancients likened the decline of man's life to the falling of a leaf; the leaf dies, but the tree lives; if the tree falls, the forest lives; should the forest die, the earth is still green; and if the earth should come to an end, a thousand sister planets arise in the rays of new suns. Nothing organic dies – everything is renewed; and the God who watches it from a distance sees the same life and the same picture after thousands of years.– We cannot point to anything destructible in the whole visible world. Nothing which is mortal could be born. Everything that is striving towards a goal, that is fighting and working, becomes worn out, and thus a material organic world is only conceivable on the presupposition of eternal change, whether it be in the mechanism of the human body or in that of the atom. But this change is no more like death than is the evolution of a plant, which would be impossible without change of substance. The idea of death has arisen from a mistaken point of view – from the fact that the eye concentrates on the part rather than on the whole.– Nothing that has being in this world is destructible. And if we would express in terms of death the Power, which defines the limits of the worlds in their corporeal existence, the glorious Genius appears as the Guardian of Life, as the Lord of Transfiguration, as the Witness of the Truth.'

CHAPTER XXIII

DEATH

An icy breath pierced all hearts like the stab of a knife. As the newspaper vendors cried the tidings in hoarse voices, as the noises in the street died away for appreciable seconds, only to swell again to a diapason of horror, it seemed as though the sound of the distant shots rang menacingly in every ear. People stood in confused knots unable to realise what they had just heard. After a few moments they moved on again rapidly as if in flight before the terror that was hunting them, and yet knowing that they could find nowhere to hide, because Mystery was closing all doors to them. Everyone had fallen victim to this secret terror at the same moment, felt the same and feared the same, and sought a way out of the confusion with the same tremulous haste. Hence a kind of quivering mist brooded over the crowd, the precursor of panic and madness.

As at the word of command, the masses thronged into the streets, filled the towns with the thunder of their steps, and the air with the rushing wind of their fury. Hundreds of thousands went out from their homes, seeking to lighten the monstrous oppression with which the deed filled them. As I saw them wandering confusedly about the streets, driven by the sudden collapse of their well-ordered world, the fire of uttermost agony burned in me, I longed that I might be the spark that set off this potential energy. Trembling, I felt for my revolver, but I could find no definite target among the sea of faces; with chattering teeth I telephoned round among the Activists, but the mysterious power held them in thrall too; I raced through the streets, boiling with hatred, ready to kill the next man, myself, the whole world, but the flying seconds tricked me of the final impulse. I wanted to pick out my victims from among the throng of the nameless – Ebert or Wirth – but then one idea froze my blood and I leant against a wall bathed in a cold perspiration and thought: 'Kern,'– I could think of nothing but 'Kern.'

But Kern had vanished.

Kern and Fischer trod an unknown way. They roamed through the world, bearing the brand of Cain, knowing with a deadly certainty that they must in the end be themselves swallowed up by the spectre which their deed had evoked. Sparse news came to their friends after many days, a few poignant words, handed on by word of mouth.

This is what we heard:

The car stopped a few hundred yards from the spot where the deed had been committed. Kern threw the Lewis gun over a wall into a garden full of flowers. Techow pulled open the bonnet of the disabled car. They tore off their leather coats and helmets, and saw their pursuers already turning the corner. The police, crouching over the handle-bars of their motor cycles, only noticed a car standing peacefully by the roadside and went past.

At the demonstration in Alexander Square, they stood wedged in among the crowds who were cursing the murderers, and saw cars full of armed soldiers ready for pursuit. They listened to the threatening words of the excited mob, raised for a moment above its ordinary preoccupations, only to fall back into them at once. They even penetrated to the offices of the police commissioners.

They met Techow once more at the Wannsee, and sailed

284

far out on to the sunlit lake. Then they disappeared from Berlin.

The motor boat, which was to take the outlaws to a sailing ship on which passages had been booked for them to Sweden, was to await them in a heavily wooded bay close by Warnemunde. The boat was there at the agreed time. But Kern and Fischer in the confusion of their flight mistook the day, arrived twenty-four hours too soon, and found no one there. They thought that they had been deserted and turned back.

And since they knew now that there was no hope for them, they made the fatal decision: they would return – they would dare once more – they would see one more opponent fall before they fell themselves. They would return to their friends, arm themselves once again. But Fate denied them everything.

They acquired bicycles. They spent the nights in lonely farms, in game-keepers' huts, and with friends from the long-past, happy, seafaring days. But the time soon came when people were afraid; pale faces called to them from behind closed windows to go on – that nobody would betray them, but neither could anyone help them. It happened that they were resting as guests in the house of a former comrade, when a man walked through the village carrying a notice which said that the murderers of Rathenau were in the place. The inhabitants crept into their homes and bolted the doors.

They roamed through the great forests of Mecklenburg and the Mark. No one knows how they renewed their spent powers; no one knows of the whispered conversations, of the nights spent under starry skies, of the quiet softness of the approaching dawn.

As the boatman was setting them over the Elbe and they were half-way across, the pursuers appeared on the bank they had just quitted. The posse of men cried 'Halt!' to the boatman; and Kern and Fischer sat wearily on the benches, staring into the water. Nevertheless, the boatman grumblingly finished his journey and landed the fugitives before going lazily back. So the pursuers lost the trail.

They begged for food. They crept round farms and gazed through the windows into low rooms where people crowded round the lamps. They gathered berries and fruits, they dug roots out of the fields and rubbed corn in their hands. Once a gamekeeper fired a charge of shot at their backs.

They ranged in the gigantic forests of eastern Hanover. News got round that they were hiding in these woods and the greatest police *battue* that has ever been known took place. A chain of guards surrounded the forest; all the neighbouring provinces sent out their men; every bush was searched separately. The enormous circle narrowed down and down towards the centre. But somehow Kern and Fischer escaped the net, and nobody knows how it was done.

They lived in the forest like wild beasts and they were hunted as such. They descended on startled friends who helped them on their way, and who told afterwards how Kern had been unaccountably cheerful and unembarrassed. They must have gone like the wind from the Elbe to Thuringia, for, two days after they had been seen at Gardelegen, they threw their bicycles into the Saal, and came to Saaleck Castle.

*   *   *   *

The Government set a price of a million Marks on the heads of Kern and Fischer. Many newspapers, who had made it their sacred duty to defend the laws of humanity, of mercy, of the dignity of man in their columns, were ready to give up their ideals for the time being. They spurred on the nation and indicated where the subscriptions might be deposited which were flowing in freely to provide a reward for whoever would deliver up the outlaws to earthly justice. In inverse ratio to the moral sense of the citizens, the blood-money rose to four and a quarter million Marks. The *Reichstag* decided at once to pass a law for the protection of the Republic and instituted a special State tribunal. An army of officials was occupied in trying to track down the criminals. The police secured the persons of all the Activists that they could lay hands on, and took particular pains to attach all available documents, in the totally unfounded expectation that Activism must pour out its feelings on paper.

The *Reichstag* met while the murdered Walther Rathenau still lay in state in an open coffin with his shattered chin bound up in a handkerchief. The majesty of Death remained within the silent house in Grunewald. Rathenau was of too high a type for either the hate or the sorrow of his friends to do him justice. He was remote even in death.

*   *   *   *

I wandered aimlessly about the town in the mad hope of finding my two friends. I roamed through every street that we had ever been in together, I visited every place that I had ever visited with them. I passed blindly by the funeral *cortège* that followed Rathenau's coffin – the people seemed to me like wraiths, seen through a bluish mist. I turned over the pages of the newspapers, seeking tidings of the fugitives, and the first time that their names leapt at me from among the welter of print, I leant up against a tree trembling and dazed in the midst of the busy traffic, felt for my revolver and then ran – anywhere – wandered restlessly through the streets till I could bear it no longer and raced to the station.

I begged money, I procured passports for Kern and Fischer, which were forged and yet genuine. I pored over the notices that were issued by the Berlin police in the style of the daily *communiqués* of the Great War. When the two were said to be in Mecklenburg, I went to Mecklenburg. I went to Holstein, to Thuringia, to Westphalia; I whipped up our distracted men and sent out Activists to search. Generally by the time I arrived in any town where my two friends were supposed to have been seen, the name of another, far-distant, town stood in the police *communiqués;* a map had been found which must have belonged to the culprits, or a collar stud, or somebody pretended to have recognised them. I never stayed in any place longer than two hours. I suddenly turned up at the houses of our men, and searched; I despaired at the apathy of men grown suddenly cautious. On one day I pulled down seven official placards. I pored over the atlas and marked every place at which they had been proved to have been. I sent news to likely halting places on their presumable road. But no path led to them. No rumour proved to be truth. No help reached them.

Sometimes I changed my route half way through a journey and then feeling wretched and embittered spent the night sitting in a little waiting room at a table stained with beer and tobacco. I was hag-ridden by the idea of finding them. I murmured the name Kern over and over again and felt as if I gained strength from it. I thought that if I concentrated on him hard enough I should eventually arrive at being corporeally near him too. I knew that the bond between us was unbreakable. I refused despairingly to believe that I could fail to reach him. I was afraid to sleep, lest at that very moment he should be wandering in the neighbourhood seeking help. I recalled every word that he had ever said. I thought over every deed that bound us together. I imagined the most improbable situations: I visualised him coming into the room, into the compartment of the train; I thought that the man in a blue coat who was walking just ahead of me and whose face I could only see indistinctly, would turn round and prove to be Kern.

DEATH

I stood for a long time before a notice that bore his photograph, as a young naval officer in the white summer uniform, and on which was a facsimile of his handwriting, upright, clear, unpretentious. I pulled down the notice carefully and hid the bad reproduction of his features in my breast pocket.

I went to Erfurt. I wanted to look up Dieter, because I had heard that the two had been seen in Thuringia. I went to Dieter's lodging, but the landlady said surlily and suspiciously that he had left the day before and she did not know his new address. I wandered through the town, searching every street. I even dared to go into the police station, expecting every moment to be arrested, but Dieter's change of address had not yet been notified. I bought a newspaper and read that all efforts on the part of the police had ended in failure at Gardelegen, but that Kern and Fischer had apparently gone towards Hanover.

I took the train to Hanover, and, as I had been doing for the past three weeks, carried the money and the passports for them both in my pocket, and the clothes and boots in my trunk. The train steamed through the Thuringian mountains and I looked out of the windows without seeing anything. Just before we got to Bad Kösen and Naumburg I got suddenly nervous. I stood up, opened the window and leant out. I watched the river Saal and looked for the hill which rose almost perpendicularly beside the railway embankment, and on top of which were the two massive grey weather-beaten towers of Saaleck Castle. My thoughts went back to the time when Dittmar was there, after Kern had rescued him from prison, and I felt a longing to get out at Bad Kösen and visit the castle, to tread the paths that Kern had trod, where his spirit must surely linger. But I believed that I ought to overcome this wish, that I ought to go on to Hanover; I thought that perhaps at that very moment Kern was in great distress and that I

289

should regret every wasted second. As the train stopped at Bad Kösen I was once more overcome by the almost irresistible desire to get out, but I fought it down and went on, looking sadly and longingly at the castle.

Yet at this very time Kern and Fischer were in the castle waiting for help. At this very time Dieter had a letter from Kern in Erfurt, but had neither money nor passports nor all the things that I was taking to Hanover.

It was not to be.

Once more they were alone between wind and sky. They lived in the top floor of the castle, outlawed, deserted and lost. Out of the window they could see the trees and the gentle landscape, broken only by the defiant walls behind which they found their last refuge. They saw the Rudelsburg rising steeply up out of the valley, the Saal flowing peacefully between wooded banks, the village which nestled down at the foot of the mountain. They heard the wind rustling and soughing in the trees; and since nature knows neither sloth nor haste, only the expectation and the overtones of great movements and quiet work, there could only be present in them a reflection of that deep merciful peace. That ultimate peace had surely spread its wings over them. Strength must have flowed to them from stars, plants and stones, from the great unity which they had served; and with it the stimulation to and the desire for the hour of their confession of faith. They were very near a union with the spirit; they were very near to that harmony for which they had battled. They had lived. And because they had walked through trespass and tribulation, through affliction and through privation, they could despise easy solutions and cheap devices. They welcomed the flame, which at one time spurred them on to action, and at another time purged their souls of dross, and at last gave them the boon of death. And their death was worthy.

DEATH

This was the manner of their dying:

Two contemptible creatures, whom life had spawned in a gutter, saw that the castle was inhabited in spite of the fact that the owners had gone away. They crept round the towers, recognised Kern and Fischer and betrayed them. Their names shall not be told, they shall be neither cursed nor hated – they are not worthy of a revengeful thought. The police, knowing that the tracks had been lost, did not believe the report. But the men insisted on their right to the reward. So two C.I.D. men from Halle were sent to investigate.

Thus Kern and Fischer were discovered. The officials forced their way into the inhabited tower. As they came up the stairs, the door opened above; Kern waited for them with a pistol in his hand. He drove the men before him and they fled. One of them implored Kern not to shoot, crying that he had a family. Kern murmured something about 'Pack of cowards,' giving his soft-heartedness a cloak of pride, and vanished back into the tower.

But these men went and fetched assistance. In a few hours, the castle was surrounded by at least a hundred policemen.

This was on July 17th, 1922. Two days earlier a storm had gathered which now rose to its wildest fury. Vapour scudded across the hill and the towers which were veiled by the massy grey swirling clouds driving before the raging tempest. The gale tore whole branches from the trees, beat down the ragged bushes and swept leaves and twigs down the slope in a mad vortex. The landscape was shrouded and lost in mist. Nevertheless, there were plenty of sightseers who came from the village and surrounded the castle. They stood dotted over the hill, crowding the lightly wooded slopes, wandered round the base of the frowning towers, in one of which they supposed Kern and Fischer to be trembling at the approach of doom. These two appeared once more; they showed themselves on the battlements of the eastern tower. They leant down above the prying mob, which stared up at them fascinated, contemptible in its smug unworthiness. And into the faces of the uncomprehending throng proud words were thrown with an infinite defiance like that of the storm. 'We live and die for ideals!' they cried. 'Others will follow us.' They gave a cheer for the man whom they had honoured as leader and who, like themselves, was an outlaw. They threw down scraps of paper weighted with stones on which their last messages must have been written; but the storm was so violent that not one of these could be found. They watched the papers as they were blown away. Then they vanished from the roof into the interior of the tower – and no one saw them alive again.

The C.I.D. men, however, 'in order to demonstrate their courage and resolution,' as they stated in their reports, opened fire on the top window from the safe shelter of the uninhabited West tower. One shot hit the window – it was fired by that very man who had begged his life of Kern. Kern must have been crouching near the window, for the shot, which smashed through the glass close by the window-sill, hit him in the head between the right temple and the ear. He died instantaneously. Fischer evidently tried to bandage his fallen friend; he had torn strips of linen and had staunched the blood. When he saw that it was in vain, he lifted the dead man and laid him on a bed. Since the dead man's shoes sullied the bedclothes he carefully placed a piece of brown paper under Kern's feet. He folded his hands and closed his eyes.

Fischer sat on the other bed. He raised the revolver, put it to the same spot as that at which Kern had been hit and pressed the trigger.

CHAPTER XXIV

FLIGHT

NEVER had I felt so strongly that my two friends were near me, as during the time I spent in the bright and rather tiresomely clean town. The fact that I met none of our Hanoverian comrades almost seemed to be a good sign. I was sure that Kern and Fischer must have found some safe refuge. Feeling relieved and cheerful, I walked about the streets, certain that I should find them; and even the prison, which I passed in my wanderings, failed to damp my spirits. I no longer felt uneasy and, for the first time since the day of the murder, I fell asleep without the numbing fear which disturbed my slumbers with wild dreams. But in the end I had a horrible nightmare after all: I was suddenly obliged to flee from a vague creature that waved hundreds of feelers at me threateningly from a dark corner. No way of escape remained to me but to go down a steep winding stair, leading to a bottomless pit. The creature was swifter than I – its arms came nearer and nearer; my legs almost refused to function as I kicked at it blindly, the ground gave way under my feet and I tried to scream but could not. Just when I thought I was lost, however, I remembered thankfully that I could fly and that I only had to raise my arms and beat them up and down in order to soar above the ground. My body, indeed, no longer had any surplus energy; I had to draw on my innermost reserves of strength in order to rise. I took a few staggering steps, as probably storks do before swinging into flight, and then I rose and floated a few feet above the ground at a tremendous pace in the dim light of the house. All at once I found myself in the open air and passed over a rugged landscape above the heads of my enemies into which the vague demon form had changed. My body was continually sinking and threatening to fall to the ground, but with a despairing effort I forced my arms to move once again and found that my body immediately shot up with the fresh impetus. The air seemed to be compressed below me and I was wafted higher and higher. When I came over the dark sea, I saw the demon in the shape of a horrible polypus moving on the bottom of the water and watching me mockingly with a round eye which goggled at me from the middle of its spongy belly. Although I was flying at a great height, one of my feet dragged in the tempestuous waves, and I felt myself becoming waterlogged. I made one more tremendous effort to rise into the air, and was in fact able to do so, when my body gave way in the middle and I crashed to the ground in a spinning dive. At the same time I heard wild shouts, which, however, died down again at once and came faintly through the closed window as I opened my eyes painfully. Newspaper sellers were crying some news down below. I got up quickly, with a desperate headache, dressed rapidly filled with a curious sense of terror and hurried into the street through the little hall of the hotel. A crowd of people was standing at the corner looking into the window of a newspaper office. I pushed through and read the blue characters of a telegram which announced the death of Kern and Fischer.

Though I never for a moment doubted the absolute truth of the bald statement I thought that it was all still a part of my ghastly dream. I was still falling, spinning round a sloping axis at lightning speed, and the momentum of my fall tore the clothes off my body. At the same time the friction of the air heated my limbs to burning point, wrapping me in a glowing incandescence which gradually consumed me, until with stinging horror I felt myself carbonizing, and my head, now separated from the rest of my body, rolling away by itself. My head was the first to come to – it rested on the cool iron of a bench and a policeman was bending over it.

I pushed him aside and stumbled through the park with bowed shoulders. I stopped by a pond and heedlessly threw some pebbles into the water. They fell heavily to the bottom, throwing up little clouds of mud as they vanished. Small fishes darted towards them and shot away again as suddenly. The policeman approached and I went on. A vague agony was gnawing me; it bored its way into my skin which was numb and paralysed as though with a local anaesthetic, leaving only my mind to ache with the thought of the irreparable loss. I felt I must make absolutely certain; that I must read the news once more; find in it the live torment for which I was yearning. In the booking hall of the railway station people were again collected round a placard and I elbowed my way into the crowd. What was hanging there was not the telegram but a warrant for my arrest.

I had some difficulty in realising it. It was not made out in my own name but in the name under which I had been living in Berlin. However, the clothes I was wearing at that moment were described and any available information was requested. I slowly wormed my way out of the crowd and half an hour later I was sitting in the train.

A hideous caricature of a face seemed to be grinning at me through every one of the dirty, half-obscured windows of the station. The strident noises that filled the place set all my nerves on edge, so that I had a sudden almost irresistible desire to drink a large bottle of some really strong brandy. I staggered to the bar and bought a bottle, ignoring the newspaper sellers who were crying their journals and shouting the

death of my friends into the rushing unconcerned clamour.
Yet when I had taken the stopper out of the bottle in the dim light
of my compartment, the smell of the alcohol sickened me and
I leant back exhausted, feeling that I must not stupefy myself,
that it would be unworthy not to face what I must now bear.
So I threw the bottle into the luggage rack and crouched numbly
in my corner until the train moved.

A stout man unfolded a newspaper. I read the names – I
read them over and over again – as they stood in large type at
the head of the columns. I read them quite dispassionately, as
though they did not concern me in the least; but I was just
waiting for this fat man, with the gold watch-chain across his
pendulous stomach, to make a single derogatory remark about
my friends! I was almost sorry when he turned over the pages,
sucking his teeth, and buried himself in the financial section.
I had been deprived of the relief it would have given to my
feelings to hit him across his vibrating cheeks. Three men,
apparently commercial travellers, who were playing cards over
by the window, were telling each other stories while they
shuffled and dealt. One man with a black moustache and
a Saxon accent said: 'When Rathenau got to heaven, he met
Erzberger. "We must have a bottle of wine on this!" cried
Erzberger and called St. Peter. But Peter said he was sorry,
he couldn't give them any drink because Wirth (the innkeeper)
hadn't come yet. . . .'

'How dare you . . .?' I shouted jumping up. So this was
what Kern had died for! Just so that these miserable wretches
might make their rotten little jokes, I thought, and I shouted
again: 'You cad! I'll push the words down your filthy gullet!'
and leapt at him. But I fell back weakly and heard them say:
'He's drunk!' I tried to say that I was not drunk but I swayed
and fell.

'It's all right – keep quiet – I'm a doctor,' said the gentleman, as he pressed me back on to the seat, and the rattling of the train hammered in my throbbing head. He said: 'Man, you've got a high temperature. You mustn't go any farther. You must get out at the next station and go to a hospital.'

I drew away; the compartment was empty, the blinds were drawn across the windows looking into the corridor. I rebuffed the doctor's efforts, refused to let him take my pulse, and tried awkwardly to rise. He talked to me soothingly. But I shook my head and stood up. The coat which had been lying over me fell to the ground and the revolver slipped out of the pocket. I seized it hastily, fell on to the bench again as I stooped, and put it back. The doctor saw the weapon, looked at me searchingly, then let me go. I walked along the corridor steadying myself by the walls, staggered into the lavatory, saw the hectic flush on my chalky face in the mirror, and was desperately sick.

I had to struggle with the fever all through the journey. I fixed my eyes on one spot until the dancing faces kept still again. At the moments when I collapsed entirely everything passed through my mind that had made life worth while for me. Now nothing was left. Rathenau was dead, so there was nothing to fight for. Kern was dead, so there was nothing to live for. Nothing remained for me to do but to quit this life in as seemly a manner as possible. Nothing was worth while. . . . I had never been ill before, and now at the moment of my friend's death I was smitten; and the fever that was scorching my very bones appeared to me symbolic. I was burning because everything that was combustible must burn. This gross, abominable world must be annihilated 'Annihilate, annihilate,' said the train as it crashed over the rails.– There were not even any real people left in the world – only hideous phantasms. There was nothing to be done but to fire into the middle of the whole pack and destroy them, coldly and systematically. The earth should bear no more devils – they should fall to their master, Satan, like rotten fruit, when he set up his kingdom again. Why should not I sign a compact with the Lord of Evil? My wish should be for invisibility – if only there were yet some means of achieving it – some magic ointment, or a ring that one could turn on one's finger – a cap of invisibility, dedicated not to Siegfried but to Hagen – perhaps the philosopher's stone, which one could put in one's mouth –. Kern should be as a lighted torch, a beacon, shining over heaps of ruins –. Fires should be kindled up and down the streets, and plague bacilli thrown into the wells. The God of Revenge has his angels – I would enlist in that company! No streak of blood on the lintels of the doors should be any safeguard. Explosives should be put under this decayed, stinking farrago, so that the force of the blast should hurl the remains to the uttermost ends of the universe. How would the world get on without humanity? I would wander through the smoking places, through the stark, lifeless towns, in which the smell of corpses would stifle whatever still breathed. I would set in motion all the machinery in the deserted workshops and let them roar to destruction. I would fire two railway trains, let them meet and rear and fall and crash down the embankment; ocean liners, giant ships, those marvels of the modern world, I would set at full steam ahead and drive them into the harbour walls, so that their shining sides should be riven and they should vanish in a boiling maelstrom. The earth should be utterly destroyed, so that nothing remained of the work of human hands. Perhaps, then, a new, nobler race would appear from the moon or from Mars to repopulate the earth; well, let them come – there might be some hope for the earth then.–

At the station at Munich stood Treskow, ensign in an infantry training college and a former schoolfellow of my cadet days. He saw my condition, took me through the streets to the barracks, and put me to bed in his room. Friends came to visit me. I saw the uniforms, and tried to rise to get at my revolver to defend myself. They held me down. Burning and twitching, I shouted Kern's name. They set sentries in the corridors so that no officer should come into the room. Treskow brewed a mixture of pepper and spirits, and they poured it down my burning gullet.–

I awoke feeling very weak but still quite clear in the head. I could not stay in the college – my friends were risking their rank and their profession. Treskow got a family he knew to put me up. I slept in a different place each night. I really was able to sleep again now; Treskow's infernal concoction had driven the fever thoroughly out of me.

What remained was a restless hunted feeling. I realised that sooner or later the end must come; but, for that very reason, I wanted to make the most of every second and felt that I must crowd the whole gamut of experience into the small space of time that remained.

I tried to look up my old friends – not because I was afraid of being alone, but because I felt that I must not allow myself the joy of being submerged. But I only found very few of them, and they were, like myself, fleeing from the police. The army which Kern had hoped to raise by his deed was destroyed by it. The individuals recovered by slow degrees; but the structure, that had grown almost of its own accord during the months of combat, was destroyed. The Bavarian Timber Dealers' Association no longer existed. If they had never had any timber to deal in, they had now lost all their personnel as well, from the manager down to the meanest understrapper. The Credit Society had lost all its credit since the police had tried to investigate the non-existent books. Thus the distressed little groups of men, haunting outhouses, farms and shepherds' huts, were thrown absolutely on their own resources, sought for opportunities to escape from the whirlpool of flight, and found them in the decision to undertake fresh actions.

Since Bavaria resisted the demands of the Central Government to recognise the Supreme Court for the Defence of the Realm, the Prussian Secretary of State for Home Affairs sent his spies to Bavaria, who were known as Weismann-spies and who searched even the mountain valleys for Activists. This hunt had to be countered by a *quid pro quo*, and so I went into the mountains and loafed around farms, spent the nights in game-keepers' huts, and the others with me, each one choosing his own beat. Soon it happened that more and more of the outlaws found their way to us; and we lived in colonies together, sharing money, stores and clothing – everything except girls – and making the country unsafe from the Lake of Constance as far as Reichenhall. A good many of our men branched off, and went to Hungary and Turkey, to return when the time should be propitious. Quite a number of them crept back into Germany, and a great many never reappeared at all.

One man came and told us about Kern's grave in the shadow of the Castle walls. He said that Dieter had faithfully packed up two suits to bring to our two friends, but that he had looked for them in vain when he got to the castle. The place was shut up and no one came in answer to his call. So he laid them in the western tower where they were afterwards found and led to Dieter's arrest. A great many people were arrested, nearly all those who had been connected in the remotest degree with the crime; and besides these anyone who had ever been suspected of being an Activist. But they were still looking for the unknown man who had been with Kern and Fischer up to the moment when the crime was committed.

As I heard Kern's name I, who was always thinking of him

but somehow could never trust myself to speak of him, realised that my flight was desertion, that I must not shun the light, that I must do what he had done. So I collected what money I could induce my companions in the mountains to part with and returned to Munich. There I opened the doors for travellers who were going to the Passion Play at Oberammergau, carried luggage for bespectacled scarecrows, and directed stout Dutchmen to places where they could get good food, and shrill-voiced Americans to the *Hofbräuhaus*. I speculated on the exchanges and saved the smallest sums, for a forged passport was not a cheap thing to get, and I must at least have my fare to Berlin as well as the expenses of my stay at Bad Kösen.

During the agitating days of preparation it became absolutely clear to me that anything that I could do now was utterly senseless. I supposed that I must first earn the right to do what Fischer had done; and it seemed to me that it would be sheer snobbery to wander round the country as they had done. I had played too small a part on the stage of life for it to be granted to me to have the full dignity of flight. A man at the next table to me in a café had been talking all along about balancing accounts. It was time for a line to be drawn under my sum. The disproportion between the expenditure and the result seemed to me too great.

I had collected all the newspaper reports of the murder. I could have borne it if hatred had flamed against us from the whole wounded pride of those whom we had attacked; but what actually arose did not touch the root of things, it was mean, it was naked and ugly in all its conventional pathos, it was simply a polemic against old enemies. Rathenau died. These worthy souls went on living. Rathenau was dead; the others cleaned up their shoddy, worn out goods for the hundredth time and put them in the show-windows. Rathenau fell; those who called themselves his friends took a fresh inventory, but there was nothing new among the rubbish. Was it worth while to attack these people? No, it was not. Thus we had become superfluous – and therefore we must pass away and without any demonstration. All over! *Finis – exeunt omnes.* The world wanted time in which to rot comfortably.

The waitress came and whispered to me that Herr Treskow had asked her to say that two Weismann spies were standing at the door watching me. I looked up and saw Treskow sitting at a distant table. I induced the waitress to help me. She agreed at once to take me up to her room. I got up and followed her unobtrusively. Then I sat, almost choking with disgust, up in her room, alone, hiding, humiliated. I was afraid that fear would overcome me. During the last few days I had been surprised at the number of policemen who were about. No, it was not for us to creep away like this. I would not flee perpetually from these underlings; I would not spend my time looking round trembling lest I were being pursued. Up and doing! I must have been mad to have given way. What had we got such an efficient police force for? I was a taxpayer too. I would give them something to do! I counted over what cash I had; it must suffice. I must keep my excitement within bounds. There was no more time to waste in brooding.

I had got so far that I was sitting in the train. I never for a moment thought I was being anything but unreasonable. To hell with reason! I sat in the crowded compartment and fed my hatred and disgust on the smells of the other people. They were talking of their business, of money-making. Here was a cool million to be had for the asking – if these miserable wretches only knew! The district inspector came to look at our passports – what a sell for him that mine was in order! I got up and went into the corridor, opened the window, and stood for the whole of the journey gazing into the night. I wanted to go home once more. I wanted to change my shirt.

FLIGHT

I had been wearing it for the last three weeks and it had got torn and dirty. I smiled wryly at my niceness, but got out when the train stopped at the familiar station.

Another young man was sitting in my office changing money. I thought of Kern who had so often sat with me in that narrow wooden box. I went to my home, tore my clothes off and dropped them about the floor – all except the coat in whose pocket was my revolver: I hung that carefully over a box.

While I was washing myself down, I heard sounds at the door. I squinted under my arm and saw the police on the threshold. A wild exultation possessed me. So it had come! This was the end. I cried almost exultantly: 'One moment, please!' ran to my coat and put my hand into the pocket. At that moment an arm was thrust over my shoulder and the weapon was twisted out of my hand.

PART III

CRIMINALS

The ruin of his hopes leaves the steadfast man undismayed.

Ernst Jünger

CHAPTER XXV

CONDEMNED

'. . . to five years' penal servitude and five years' loss of civic rights.'

We stood to hear the sentence, which condemned each of us to long years of paralysing inactivity and which deprived us of our civic rights. Unheeding, we heard a murmur rise from the court, as the judge read our sentences from a crackling parchment; we saw him look round the court with that appearance of mild severity which became him so well and then continue the monotonous recital composedly, raising his voice a little at every name, and carelessly proclaiming the figures, which meant so much to us, as a man throwing a ball, with the half-triumphant ejaculation: 'Catch!'

We were condemned. And we did not realise it, for we were incapable of realisation; we were not even excited, for we were filled with a sick longing for green fields and the open air. During long days, we had watched the grotesque legal procedure; we saw men dressed in shabby old-fashioned black robes, sitting in an imposing hall, which was decorated with the portraits of the German Emperors; men who exuded mediocrity at every pore and whose stupid, expressionless faces and bleary eyes were lighted by nothing but cold, contemptuous hatred. We saw the representative of the State, the Public Prosecutor, who in the old days of the Empire had acquired power, honour and respect, and now was vociferating raspingly of ideas which could only be born of a brain which had no conceptions beyond formal logic. We saw women crowding into the auditorium, dressed extravagantly and covered with diamonds; who only stopped sucking sweets when things got really exciting; who crossed their silk-clad legs provocatively and watched the accused, whose fate hung in the balance, through lorgnettes and opera glasses, as they would have watched fierce, beautiful animals, who were safely housed behind bars. Sitting at the Press-tables we saw narrow-chested, spineless boys and worthy, spectacled nonentities, in whose dull faces we could see the sort of stuff they were ladling out to their faithful but heartily despised readers. We saw witnesses standing up in their Sunday best, stumbling through the oath with or without reference to God, in voices that trembled with excitement and making statements in which they contradicted themselves in every other sentence, with nervous looks at the prisoners in the dock. We saw self-confident figures march up, exchanging glances of understanding with the barristers, and trying to give their accusations at least the appearance of truth by speaking in loud and decisive tones.

We, meanwhile, sat on our benches looking at the rays of sunshine that every now and then shone into the gloomy court through the stained-glass windows, which bore the arms of the various German towns. We sat and listened to pleas and counterpleas; we replied reluctantly and half-choked with rage to questions which seemed to us utterly unimportant and beside the point. Our heads ached dully, we felt tired and wretched, but just occasionally we got a certain pleasure from giving a crushing answer to a particularly silly question.

We had been imprisoned on remand for months. When we were thrust into the bare cells, each one of us, with the first instinct of a prisoner, as soon as the door had shut, rushed to the window and shook the bars. Then the greyness overcame us,

and what even yesterday had been real and living and impera-
tively engrossing, vanished and came to us like the vague sounds
that penetrated to us over walls and courtyards when the lights
were out and only the restless steps above us, beside us, gave
monotonous evidence of life and humanity. Slowly the whirl
in our minds settled down. We did not try to justify ourselves
but were determined to defend ourselves with all the means
which we could command.

Foxy-faced men came to see us – police inspectors, judges,
lawyers. And the ostentatious friendliness which they demonstrated roused all our suspicions. They were so human and
sympathetic – they referred to our youth, to the keen
enthusiasm which indeed did us credit but which was dangerous
in a world that was so full of hard materialism. They enquired
anxiously after our well-being; they exhorted us earnestly to
open our hearts to them. All this had no result beyond putting
us into a state of nervous tension which made us suspect evil
everywhere and showed us exactly what was true and what was
false – we recognised the truth of their indifference and the
falseness in their cowardly flight before a real conviction and
their fear of coming out into the open.

The examining magistrate came to visit me. He was an old
friend of my father's, and had in former days visited at my
parents' house. Now he spoke warmly of the deceased and
implored me to tell him, my father's friend, the truth, the
whole truth, so that I might find lenient judges. And this man
went, wearing the frock coat of ceremony, to see my mother,
murmured tenderest words of condolence and assured her of
his faithful help. But he said nothing about being the magistrate who was to examine me; all that he said was that he must
know the whole truth in order to be able to help, and listened
with great emotion to what the old lady told him, pressing
his hands as her faithful friend, her eyes streaming with tears.

Then he confronted me with it word for word at the trial and made abundant use of it in his report of the proceedings.

As we walked up and down our cells during the long nights, six steps there and six back, unceasing, we knew that we should never again be at peace. We realised that there was no deliverance for us, that beyond every fence that we broke through full of hope, a fresh land would lie spread out before us with fresh, richer promises. We should be eternally restless. For flight was impossible, and it was impossible for us to compromise with a world afraid of itself. Our sickness was the sickness of Germany – we felt the process of change as if it had been a physical pain. And thus, placed between two orders, the old, which we were destroying, and the new, which we were helping to create, without being able to find room in either for our own essential being, we became restless, homeless, condemned to be for ever seeking that form of life which could give us peace and never finding it. We were an accursed generation.

And when we realised this with the clarity born of long nights of brooding wakefulness, we scornfully recognised the impotence of those who thought to sit in judgment over us. We could not demand justice, since we had never acknowledged justice to be a moral claim. No law court in the world could lay a punishment on us that would strike at our innermost being. What could be inflicted on us that we had not already inflicted on ourselves?

On the day of the trial, we greeted one another in the passages gladly, but with a certain embarrassment, took our seats in the dock and examined the apparatus which had been set up to deal out a justice in whose righteousness we were totally incapable of believing. For it was not a case of the right or wrong of a particular action – it was our whole existence which was in question. A wave of sullen enmity met us, and we felt completely at ease in it. For this hostility had not the courage to show itself openly. We watched the judges arrive, their faces so paralytic with gravity and dignity that they looked like masks. We felt that here was the mask of justice hiding the face of brute force.

We were fascinated by the beautifully designed machine. Although we knew that anything which either we ourselves or the lawyers said would make no more difference to the final result than if we threw peas at the wall, yet we marvelled. Here was an apparatus which ran as if it were a thing apart, beautiful in form and absolutely unswerving. The buzz of the flying wheels drowned every sound of the outside world, blotted out the background as well as the foreground, bade human weakness as well as human desires die away before the breathless play of matter.

The only moment which we all feared, though we did not acknowledge it even to ourselves, was the instant when Rathenau should stand up in the court, a menacing shadow, compelling silence. But that moment did not arrive. The Minister was the unnamed person whose death called for atonement, nothing more. Once it seemed as though a note of respect crept in between one question and the next, but the judge waved aside the awkward interpolation and the machine went on.

It all seemed so unreal, that we did not grasp what exactly it was that decided our fate. We sat and wondered, and a secret wish rose in us to learn the rules of the game, so that we might be able to understand these extraordinary proceedings. The thought never once rose in me that every word that was uttered might influence my liberty for years.

The question was whether my journey to Hamburg to fetch the motor car which was to be used for the murder constituted aiding and abetting within the meaning of the law. And the

Public Prosecutor cited a case in which it had been ruled that it was to be considered as aiding and abetting, if a girl's fiancé provided her with an instrument to help her procure an abortion, even though she made no use of that instrument. Dr. Luetgebrune, a man obviously of lower Saxon peasant stock, bringing a whiff of freshly turned earth into the stuffy, oily, dusty atmosphere, rose and with the polite insolence of the experienced lawyer drew attention to a similar ruling, volume so and so, page so and so, according to which what his learned friend had just said was, of course, true; but in the case where the girl definitely refused to take the instrument the fiancé could not be called an accessory. The Public Prosecutor drank a glass of water and continued turning over the pages of the statute book.

In the nights following the days of the trial, when we gazed with aching eyes at the narrow, barred square through which the night air came into our cells, we were overcome by a choking terror of the unknown, lying in wait for us at every corner. So long as we could meet life, we did not flinch before any of its manifestations, and if it threatened us, we could defend ourselves and had already done so gladly. But what was coming now – was that life at all? Was it not rather something that was altogether outside it; something that was neither life nor death and yet partook of both? Freedom was the one thing we had treasured beyond all else – and now we were being deprived of freedom and no one knew for how long. Suddenly we were at the mercy of others – naked to the world; we had become simply a number and could have no will beyond that of the gaoler. We had perhaps never felt our individuality so strongly as at this moment in which we were about to lose it. Now we had to hold our own against deadly isolation – and for whose sake? For our own? We were not in the habit of working for our own ends. And now even the power of action was being taken from us. We were to be resigned – and resignation is senseless. Nay more, resignation is shameful – yet the shame must be borne. Perhaps even it might help us to develop – it should help us! We must not succumb; not that we personally mattered, but destiny must be fulfilled.

So we heard our sentences. We were led away. As we stood in the corridor, the warders put handcuffs on us for the first time. They separated us brutally. I was able to wave goodbye to Techow, who bore his fifteen years' sentence as though it were an honour, and found opportunity to throw down the cameras of two sensation-mongering photographers.

We were taken back to our cells in the prison van. The smart police officer who had hung about us almost awkwardly, as though he still felt that we were in some sort comrades, arranged for our stricter supervision. We were squeezed upright into a sort of cupboard closed by a shutter – the product of the most scientific prison-technique – in which we could not move, were almost suffocated and were thrown against the sides of the van at every jolt, with burning hatred filling our hearts. Back in our cells, we were deprived of every one of our possessions, which had grown dear to us through the long months of internment; the doors were trebly locked and bolted as though we were pariahs, ruffians, an innately low and criminal gang, not worthy to see the sun and not worthy of the companionship of other men.

We were fettered. A chain was passed round our bodies, of which one end was fastened to our hands, and the other end held by the warders, of whom a host conducted us through the streets to the station, to the train; warders who kindly and condescendingly assured us that in their hearts they were on our side, but that they must do their duty – their duty! – and then forbade us to smoke, and poured forth floods of ultra patriotic oratory, in order to make the time pass quickly and agreeably for themselves and us. After an endless journey, after a last glimpse of wide green fields and dark slender fir trees, we were delivered at the prison, taken in charge by indifferent officials, who rattled bunches of keys and chewed the remains of their breakfasts as they took down particulars of us, with a derisive grin when we said: 'ex-lieutenant.'

Then the door of the cell clanged behind us.

CHAPTER XXVI

PRISON

'YOU are a prisoner. The iron bars across your window, the locked door, the colour of your clothes tells you that you have lost your freedom. God would no longer permit you to squander your liberty in sin and evil-doing. He therefore deprived you of it and said to you: "Thus far and no farther."

'The punishment meted out to you by a human judge, is imposed on behalf of the Everlasting Judge, whose ordinances you have neglected and whose commands you have disobeyed. You are here for correction, and all correction is felt as a misfortune. Never forget that it is your fault and yours alone.

'But this chastisement is intended to be productive of good for you: you must learn to master your passions, to overcome bad habits, to obey promptly, to respect ordinances divine as well as human, so that you may, by sincere repentance for your past life, gain strength to lead a new one, acceptable to God and man. Submit, therefore, to the law of the realm. Be obedient, also, to the rules of this establishment, for its regulations must be obeyed implicitly. It is better to obey of your own free will than to be punished for stubbornness. You will have a sense of well-being in doing so, and the truth of these words will be established in you:

'"All chastisement while we are experiencing it seems to be not joy but sorrow. Nevertheless, a calm reverence for justice will be born in those who profit by the experience."

'So help you God.'

THE OUTLAWS

These words stood at the beginning of the blue book of rules, which contained, in unnumbered paragraphs and in not always perfectly grammatical language, prohibitions for pretty well every form of human activity except breathing and working; prohibitions which I was determined from the very outset to disobey or to circumvent. The book hung next to a dustpan and brush and duster on a narrow ledge above a bucket, a brown earthenware vessel, in a triangular wooden frame that was always wet. This bucket, which was closed by a lid, had according to the regulations, to be cleaned daily, inside and out, with sand. Beside the bucket stood a spittoon and a box for toilet articles. Opposite this malodorous corner was the stove, a brick erection, with a sloping top, which was heated from the passage outside, and was unbearably hot on warm days and impossible to warm up on cold days. Next to the stove hung the bed, chained to the wall, consisting of an iron frame across which were placed rough wooden laths, three mattresses stuffed with seaweed and a pillow covered with some blue checked washing material; a horse blanket served as cover. During the day the bed had to be slung up to an iron hook; to use it except during the time set apart for slumber rendered one liable to 'disciplinary correction'. At the head of the bed, at about the height of a man, hung a small cupboard, which contained a food bowl, a spoon, a salt cellar, a drinking cup, a soap dish and a wooden comb. On top of the cupboard stood a small wooden wash basin and water jug, underneath it hung a towel. Opposite the bed a carpenter's bench took up the whole length of the cell as far as the bucket. Underneath this stood a box of tools, which had to be handed out in the evenings at lock-up time; and the wood which was to be shaped lay in rough blocks piled up beside the pail, with a swab and a low four-legged stool. A Bible and hymn-book lay on the carpenter's bench, and above it was the gas jet, covered with a wire guard,

which was lighted in the evenings by the attendant whose
business it was to keep the corridors clean, heat the stoves and
distribute the food, and turned off again at seven o'clock sharp.
This was the inventory of the cell, which was six paces long,
not quite three wide, some ten feet high and whose floor was
covered with worn boards. The door, which on the inside was
perfectly flat and covered with a strong metal lining, was a good
six inches thick and had on the outside a clumsy lock to which
was fitted an enormous key, a wide steel bolt in the middle, a
chain bolt top and bottom, and a little glass-covered peephole,
through which no doubt one could look in from the outside,
but which gave no view from the interior. In the other narrow
wall, which like the others was whitewashed, was the window.
This, however, was placed so high that one could only just
reach the sill by stretching up to it, and it was only about three
feet wide and some eighteen inches deep. The lower half was
made of frosted glass; the upper half was transparent and
could be opened half way. The bars, six in number and with
two rows of cross bars, were inch-wide, rectangular steel rods;
outside these was a close, rusty wire netting. Outside the
window, let into the outer wall, was a reflector made of strong
opaque ground glass, higher and wider than the window itself.
So it was impossible to see more than a tiny bit of sky. The
cell was always wrapped in a sort of disheartening twilight.
It was as fusty as the opening words of the introduction to the
prison regulations, and the 'calm reverence for justice' did not
seem to grow from very pure soil; if at all, it was born of the
mixed smell of gas, sweat, excrements, dust, bugs and food
which filled the cell.

* * * *

No sound from the outer world came through the thick walls.
The place, built in the thirteenth century as a convent according

to the rule of St. Hedwig, reared its gigantic grey pile in the middle of the little town; a gloomy fortress, inhabited by five hundred ostracised men, guarded by sixty subordinates armed with swords. The town was strange and far from my home; I only knew it as the place where a battle was fought to the great glory of a king of Prussia during the second Silesian War, and as the birth and death-place of one of my favourite poets, whose works I sought vainly in the prison library. It may be that the events which were convulsing all Germany were felt even here but if so nothing of them penetrated my cell. Nothing reached my cell but the feeble effluence of an utterly unreal and preposterous authority, to which I had to submit without in any way recognising its title, without feeling the faintest quiver of agreement with it. I could not feel that there was the slightest connection between myself and any of the things which surrounded me – I could not understand them in relation to myself nor myself in relation to them. I was lonely to a degree which lay well under zero in any scale of temperatures.

I walked up and down. I picked up objects as I passed and laid them down again. I wove little dreams – six paces long – from which I awoke as soon as the rattle of keys sounded in the corridor, as soon as I turned towards the door of my cell. I was waiting, without knowing what for. I sat by the table in a waking doze, I stood by the window and stared at the scrap of cloudy sky. I counted the boards and the number of steps I took on them. I reckoned the time by the position of the ray of sunshine that shone into my cell. I looked forward to my dinner, although I knew that I should not enjoy it. I looked forward to the daily exercise, although to take it under the eyes of armed overseers was positively a torture. I looked forward to the night, although I knew that I should not sleep. The least interruption was welcome. When the barber came to cut my short hair still shorter, the pleasure of being able to exchange a few surreptitious words overcame my detestation of his cold, soft, damp hands fingering my face and neck. I longed passionately for the visit of the librarian, though I knew that this time the choice of dog's-eared and rubbishy old books would be no better than any other time. When the attendant went down the corridor, I hoped he would pass me a clandestine note from one of the other prisoners, or the screw of chewing tobacco, which I rolled in lavatory paper and lighted over the gas jet when that was burning; when it was not burning I induced a spark with a flint, a steel button and a slow match. I leant against the door, so that a tiny crack appeared at the top, through which I could push some little object as a signal to the attendant to whom in return for his services I gave the cake of good soap that I had managed to smuggle in or a piece of pencil or drafted a petition or a complaint. Everything, however negligible it might appear to outside people, grew to have a great value for me to whom it was prohibited. Everything was prohibited to me.

Work, however, was not prohibited; it was prescribed. Payment for a day's task was a half-penny, of which half was allowed me for the purchase of stamps, tooth paste and chewing tobacco, while the other half was kept back and credited to me, so that I might be able to pay my fare home when I was released. It was not this that made me avoid work like the plague, nor because it was so utterly and designedly stupid, as if it had been specially planned to turn one slowly into an idiot. It was simply because it was smugly eulogised and prescribed with threats, as a heaven-sent means of wholesome correction and amendment. I jumped up after every five minutes' work and tore up and down my cell, filled with an indescribable loathing, not a loathing of the particular job, but a loathing of work in general. These were some of the tasks imposed – I leant over the carpenter's bench, planing square blocks of wood into shafts for hammers – seventy had to be done in the day; I plaited bast, making long ropes of the coloured strands, which were stiff, damp and evil-smelling from the dyeing – seventy-two yards a day; I sat at a rattling sewing machine, mending old unwashed military garments left over from the Great War, the stinking pile in front of me, rotted, sweat-soaked scraps strewn about the cell – two-hundredweights a day; I sorted bristles, picking half a pound of white pig's bristles out of two pounds of black with a pair of wooden tweezers; I stripped quills; I hemmed handkerchiefs; I punched leather. The daily drudgery in my cell seemed to me, like everything that was not done with conviction, with an inner urge, as despicable as the cowardly feeling of satisfaction when the work was done seemed to me contemptible. I never for a moment doubted the hypocrisy of those who talked about work as a blessing and then prescribed work as a punishment. My cell taught me a horror of things which were artificial and not natural; taught me to understand the hatred which drove the oppressed to value freedom from thraldom above everything, to think materially when they should think ideally, to dream of happiness when they should dream of destiny.

I awoke every morning from horrible nightmares to a weary day, that seemed to me much more unreal and much greyer even than the visions that came to me in the night, and made me feel happy in spite of their confusion and in spite of their terrors. In my dreams I at least had visions of doing something; and in a curious way, I enjoyed the terror. For the knowledge that I could not escape from the four walls of my cell allowed me to glide into sleep without releasing me from consciousness. I never got free of the cell in my dreams – it was there as the inescapable background; it reflected its terrors into the wild doings, terrors that I welcomed because they were vital. Often when the sound of the hated bell, which regulated the day and whose strident note I shall never forget, startled me out of the strange and yet familiar regions of my dreams, I felt actual existence to be only a confirmation of the mysterious flights I had taken while my thoughts circled the walls of my cell, seeking an exit, and finding adventures in the process. I ranged through populous towns, past greenish lamps and flowering gardens; I lived on tropical islands; I climbed up steep gorges; I wandered through echoing castles; I saw men as shadows, houses as fortresses, trees as menaces; yet I never for an instant forgot that I was in the cell, that I was a prisoner, and that I had to put the bucket outside the minute I was waked. I was fleeing, I climbed over fences and walls, hid in backyards and lofts, saw the swearing officials hurry past me and return, felt them tearing along behind me – and if they caught me, a mad joy rose in me, for I had hoaxed them, I was in my cell and their questing had been just as vain as my flight. Very soon all my desires took refuge in dreams, as all my fears had done. I fought the battles that the cell tried to prevent my fighting, I walked the paths that it would have prevented my walking. And the rectangle divided by bars through which the night came in grey waves, and which I recognised afresh in the short spells of consciousness between one vision and the next and carried over into the following dream, intensified the excitement; it gave me the certainty of living in two worlds, a conviction which forced me to take decisions which life very seldom offered.

At one time an indifference had discovered itself in me which was dignified because it ignored small things, because the battle to which I was vowed rejected everything that did not fit into heroic surroundings. But in my cell I sank into a state of indifference which was disintegrating, because it sprang

from the lack of great things, because it was grey and feeble
and was dictated not by rebellion but by resignation. But I
must not drift – I must not submit – I must not bow down.
I had only one aim – to guard myself. And I could only do so
by defiance, by stubbornness, by a guerilla warfare against the
hateful, clinging net of authority and against the people who
served this authority.

Once upon a time I was free. Now I was a prisoner. Once
I attacked, now I had to defend myself. However, I was at an
advantage with a force which understood all the ordinary
criminal instincts, but which was powerless before those who
are impelled by an inner conviction. Hitherto every phenomenon, every change, every situation, had brought me fresh
experience. I was locked into a cell; but perhaps even here I
might find something that would develop some part of my
mind.

A warder roared at me, because I did not keep the regulation
distance when we were out for our walk: 'Get into your place,
and be damned to you! – Do you hear me? – Perhaps you haven't
washed your ears lately? – Refusing obedience? Aha! That
means being reported. Just you wait, my young friend!'

I was brought up before the committee of prison officials.
The head warder instructed me to enter the room and indicated
that I was to stand in front of the horseshoe-shaped table at
which the chief officials were sitting. There was the governor,
a small stout man with a broad and fundamentally good-
humoured face and eyeglasses, the files lying in front of him.
There was the chaplain; he had been a prison-chaplain for
seventeen years and was the coldest of Pharisees; in his opinion,
the only prisoners that were worth taking any trouble with
were Poles. Then came the cashier, a member of the local
choral society, always cantankerous, as pedantic as his business.
There sat the supervisor, a sneak, long, tough and lean, with a

melancholy beard straggling over his wrinkled neck. Then the steward, stout, good-humoured, called 'Barley Chopper' by the prisoners. There sat the secretary, a rough, thick-set, hypocritical man, with a red face and prominent eyes. There they were – a collection of nonentities, whose power of command arose simply from the assurance of their inviolable position over against the despised and despicable prisoners.

And the Governor said:

'You have been reported again; this time for refusing to obey orders. That is the fourteenth time you have been reported in the three weeks you have been here. – Stand up straight and take your hands from behind your back! – What's the idea – do you imagine that you're here for amusement? – Silence. You will only speak when you're told to. – I'll have you put under arrest at once if you're not quiet. If hitherto you have not been subjected to the severest punishments, it has been on account of your youth. Remember that you are going to be here for five years – Silence! Oh, you refuse? But I'll break your will, if I have to put you in irons for a month! You may depend on it, I shall break your will!'

I said, 'Go ahead!'

CHAPTER XXVII

1923

NIGHT after night one of the prisoners sang the *Internationale*. The song rang through the passages, echoed in the courtyard, and rose up like a promise in the accursed building. It was always the same solitary voice and as often as not one of the other prisoners would yell at him that he wanted his night's rest. The man who sang was a Communist and an unacknowledged political prisoner called Edi.

The day when he and I first came across one another was dreary and oppressive. I was taking the daily walk along the narrow, uneven path, one of a long line, with a distance of eight steps between myself and the next man. There was a high wind; it came whistling round the corners, carrying smuts from the coal dump and white powder from the lime-pit, bringing all the smells from the wash-house, the kitchen, the vegetable store and the workrooms, blowing dirt from the gas-works into our pale faces, cutting through us and buffeting the walls. I turned round to escape its fury and saw him shuffling across the yard. He was dragging an enormous black bucket. The warder signed to me; I caught hold and the two of us carried the huge swaying load of stinking excrements, under the supervision of a uniformed individual armed with a revolver, a sword and a bunch of keys.

When we found out about each other we at first hesitated a little, because we had neither of us quite shaken off the prejudices of a world of which we were no longer a part. But the voice of the warder, who roughly reprimanded us and sent each to his cell, tore down the barriers and revealed us to each other as sufferers in a common cause. We were living in a world where everything was inimical to us; we needed to find human companionship in that wilderness of stone and iron. The time came when nothing separated us from each other save the wall between our cells.

In the evenings, directly the warders had made their final round, I heard his knock. I heard him climb on to the stool and then on to the window-sill and open the window. And I sat clinging to the wire-netting and squeezed my head between the bars, while whispered colloquies flew back and forth. I heard about the life of a miner in the Ruhr, of the life lived for days on end amid darkness, dust and sweat, in a continual state of harassing anxiety; of existence on bread and potatoes and gin, with few and scanty hours of leisure. I learnt to understand the immeasurable embitterment, the defiant pride, the sullen determination to fight against all who were not of the working class. I told him why I, a soldier, felt the bond between us, why my battle was his. Our conversations were curious. He told me about his comrades' methods of fighting, which were new to me and which did not seem to me to be very efficient, considering that they were dealing with masses on whom they could not rely very definitely. But he pointed out to me that it was essential to have an absolute theoretical system from which the masses could not deviate; and drew my attention to the efficiency of the widespread organisation that could even survive inadequate leadership for a considerable period. I countered by standing up for the individualists, who from their very loneliness grew to value the joys of comradeship. We spoke as if we were going to lead the revolutionary armies to war; and drew near to each other in our common Napoleon-dreams and Lenin-visions, our hot heads pressed between the bars.

THE OUTLAWS

Edi had taken part in the Red campaign in the Ruhr, as leader of a scratch troop. One day he had had to take news of a *Reichswehr* attack on his company's position to headquarters and, since time was pressing, he had seized a horse from the stable of a local landowner and gone off on it. When he had had no further use for his steed, he had auctioned it and spent the proceeds on drink. And since this was rapine and pillage and altogether a disgraceful performance, he was given six years' hard labour and loss of rights and police supervision and was not treated as a political prisoner.

We were separated when our first joint attempt at escape miscarried. We were separated not so much because they were afraid that we should try again, as because no intercourse was permitted except for mutual spying. I only met Edi occasionally after this: when we were taking a douche in the steam-filled bathroom, when we were called up before the committee, in the sick-room, in church, or when we went to get clean clothes; and we were never able to exchange more than a few words. But in the evenings I had a sense of companionship as the faint sound of the *Internationale* came to my new cell, which was in a dark passage in another wing opposite the arrest cells, and which was secured with an immense padlock to which only the head warder had the key.

*   *   *   *

Though the rigour of my first year's imprisonment had been softened by those few weeks of companionship, it seemed all the more bitter now. The cell seemed to exercise an almost physical power of oppression. The process began from the first moment. Every individual article in the cell seemed to emphasise it as a place of punishment. Nevertheless I realised even more strongly than before that every experience could only enrich life.

NINETEEN TWENTY-THREE

Once I had overcome the deadening influence of the cell I was determined to defend myself against lethargy at all costs. I began to doubt the value of anything which could not withstand the constraint of the cell and was inclined to throw it overboard. Everything was purged by the loneliness; and I felt more strongly everything that had ever moved me, now that I had time to savour it and it was not lost in the whirl of continually succeeding experiences. I frequently found myself still leaning against the door, when the first pale streak of dawn crept into the cell, and I determined not to make things too easy for myself, lest after all I should lose my soul.

I had the portrait of my friend, which the governor allowed me to keep, because he saw that I was prepared to go to any lengths in order to have it. There was not a moment of my waking hours when the picture did not speak to me, driving out every cheap feeling of sorrow. My friend was dead and I had not been able to follow him. How would he have borne to walk among the degraded, how could I bear to stay, when he had found an end which to him was no end save of his own life? And if his death was fulfilment, action and symbol, exhortation and necessity, if his death was all things save one – atonement – what remained to us, but to continue in the path which he had shown us? Nothing could separate us; and his death was the one thing in this cell which raised me above the desires of the day and which gave me strength to hope for new beginnings whenever there seemed to be an end.

And so I did not fear the visions of the night, even when those other eyes looked at me out of the darkness. Indeed, I welcomed them, if only for the violence with which I bade them begone. I felt that I was fighting a battle which would be waged all my life and which must never be won if its value was to remain. I often heard the sound of the gentle voice of the nurse who had got into the car where Rathenau lay dying and who had related during the course of the trial in soft, halting words, how he had opened his eyes once more and had looked at her very strangely. I knew that puzzled look – I had met it when we were running to an attack; it lay behind the half-closed lids of friends who had said the last farewell; that look must have moved Fischer to try and staunch the blood in Kern's head in the tower. I could hardly bear it. I could hardly bear to have to give those eyes an answer. I was guilty; but I would rather be a murderer than a judge or an executioner.

At times I felt a curious pride in my miseries. My sweating body, my brain plagued with feverish pictures, my heart in which desires and wishes fought furiously for expression, everything lived concentratedly. The judge's indifferent voice had simply announced five years – the space between one date and another. I was horrified when I looked back through the years: five years ago I was still a cadet in the lower fifth form, starving during the war, a pale, delicate boy of medium capabilities, wearing the imperial uniform with immense dignity and afraid like my schoolfellows that the war would be over before we were old enough to join in. I could not realise that the same gulf which lay between that misty figure and myself, the prisoner, now stretched ahead of me. To be imprisoned for five years; five years with nothing to do but to wait. And outside, life was going on feverishly, my friends were grappling with the problems that alone made life worth while.

* * * *

My raging fear that I should be left out of a decisive action, rose to fever heat when news came of what was going on in the outer world, either through a grudging hint from some official, or from reading a torn newspaper that the wind blew across the yard, or from the letter which was allowed once in two months. These scanty tidings came to the exile in his direst loneliness like the lights of a distant army and showed him that he was not altogether deserted. I felt that I was progressing step by step with the companions of my recent past; and since the motive power for us all still remained what it had always been, I was convinced that it was not simply the result of the ravings of a crowd of lunatics; nothing had been in vain; nothing could happen which had not been pre-ordained by some unknown tribunal. Yet it was bitter to have to take a solitary post. I wanted to be free, to get away from the inexorable walls of this infernal place, which fettered me and bade me wait, when the only crime that my friends or I could commit was to wait.

The vague letters left me plenty to guess at. Time passed; I knew that every movement was pressing onwards irresistibly to some goal while I sat and hoped and brooded and despaired. The day seemed interminable. The minutes dragged out to long spans; and when I measured the period which I had already passed in the cell and compared it with what was still to come, I might well be filled with horror without accusing myself of weakness.

When letters came, which told everything that was worth telling between the lines, I noticed that the stamps had a different impress every time. As the nominal value of the stamps rose from hundreds of thousands to millions and from millions to milliards, I got a good deal of satisfaction from watching the agitated officials who stood about the yard or the corridore rattling their keys and looking at thick wads of tattered notes with an expression in which excitement, despair and an utter lack of comprehension were curiously mirrored. If they spoke of anything beyond strictly official matters it was of inflation, a word which I am sure conveyed no more to them than it did to me. I had only experienced the inflation in its early, innocuous and technically explicable beginnings. Now it appeared to be an independent occult power. Money had no more value? Splendid! Its basic absurdity was manifest? Excellent! If the powers of the day, after they had conquered everything that could be conquered, now came into an empty space in their mad lust for expansion and found that nothing was left to them except to attack and destroy each other, who, among those who had steadfastly refused to bow to their rule, would not be pleased at this, which was after all a hopeful sign? Nature abhors a vacuum – it always sets about filling it. The advance guards of the renaissance would find a clear field and behind them would come the masses who would be satisfied only by victory.

And that victory seemed to be announcing itself one evening during the first days of November, 1923, when suddenly, after the sentries had gone their round, Edi's voice called my name. I hurried to the door. The call came from one of the cells opposite and I answered him. Edi shouted that he was in an arrest cell, that another attempt at escape had failed. He shouted that he had had the news that things were moving at last and that something was brewing in Bavaria.

We shouted to one another through the closed doors, across the echoing passage. We were both full of the wildest hopes. Mouth and ears pressed to the iron doors, we quarrelled about Marx and Bismarck, about the masses and individuality, about distribution and conditions, about world-revolution and the rising of the nations. We roared insults at each other, half in jest and half in anger, and finally the *Internationale* pealed from his cell and I sang the Ehrhardt song in opposition – till the warders banged on our doors with clubs and shouted something about reporting and arrest. So we said good-night to each other somewhat sobered; but I paced up and down far into the night.

The officials really did report us; and when the Governor

said with a tolerant smile that he had always tried to do his best for me, I knew that the rising had begun – but when three days later he said harshly that I was the most insubordinate prisoner he had had in the establishment for the last twenty-five years, I knew that the outbreak had failed.

CHAPTER XXVIII

A LETTER

ONE day I caught the supervisor stealing material for shirts from the store room. Having this hold over him, I was able to make him help me to get into communication with my friends. It is part of every sound system of punishment to cut the prisoner off from the evil influences of his former surroundings. I was therefore only permitted to communicate with my nearest relatives by letter; and every question that I put and all information that they sent which were concerned with those things which lay nearer to my heart than the little everyday matters, were carefully blotted out. So I sent out an urgent call for this other news, without giving the Governor the trouble of censorship; but I got no answers; nothing beyond hints in the official letters which were designed to give me hopes which I was not in the least anxious to have. The letters said that I was certain to be free soon, that I was to be patient and that our affairs were going well. But I felt the pity that prompted these utterances and I had no use for them. In February, 1924, the supervisor came to my cell with an air of great importance, carefully looked up and down the passage, and then quickly stuffed a closed envelope containing a thick wad of paper under my coat.

That was shortly before lights-out. I raged up and down my cell, hugging the letter under my coat, and the warder had hardly growled his 'good-night,' the door had hardly banged, the bolt rattled, the light gone out, before I dashed to the window. I fixed the mirror to the wire netting, so that it caught the light of the lantern in the yard and reflected it in a tiny square into the cell. I knelt on the stool, pulled open the envelope with trembling hands and read:

'. . . When the French occupied the Ruhr our men were prepared. We took the German proclamation of passive resistance to be a bad joke and not weakness. But very soon we noticed that all the government orders sprang from the very spirit against which we had been fighting. So we decided to pursue our policy of resistance in the usual way. There was some hope that we might manage to induce practically every one who was at all worth while to join us, and so eventually to force a change in the situation.

'There was only a handful of us, and we all knew each other. The most energetic men came from all over the kingdom. They formed an extraordinarily militant collection, some of them pretty wild, old front line men and some from the secondary campaigns, of whom each had had his baptism of fire. There was not much to be organised. Every day had its own task, which arose almost spontaneously. Schlageter said to his men who appeared from Upper Silesia in answer to our call: "Upper Silesia was child's play to this." We wandered from one public house to the next as out-of-work miners from Upper Silesia, asked for work and scratched up ammunition as the opportunity arose. We slept in workhouses, in charitable institutions and thieves' dens. We did a little gun-running and brought fugitives into the country across the new borders. We spied on the spies and practised a severe jurisdiction over that part of the country. We blew up things at Hügel and at Calcum, in the Upper Ruhr, at Königsteele and at Duisburg. At night we crept along the permanent way of the State Railway, laden with explosives, we cleared awkward sentries out of the way, we lay beside the sleepers and the searchlights passed across our motionless bodies, we waited up to our waists in water, we appeared from the bushes and exchanged shots with patrols; we watched our opportunity for hours at a time and fought our way through the troops who rushed to the spot as soon as the charge had exploded. We derailed coal and transport trains; we sank a steamer in the Dortmund-Ems Canal and a coal-barge in the Rhine-Herne Canal.

'I had just come back to Essen with Gabriel – we had blown up the lock gate, at the place where the canal goes over the Emscher into an aqueduct, cut the conduit to the lock and thus lowered the level of the water till it was no longer navigable – when we heard that Schlageter's troop had come to grief.

'The police authorities – the German police authorities from Kaiserwerth – had issued a warrant for Schlageter's arrest on account of the bridge which had been blown up at Calcum. We were not altogether unprepared for it, because the German authorities were just as keen on our tracks when we crossed the border as the French in the war area. Sometimes when our people were caught with ammunition on them, the magistrates used even to hand them over to the French. There were posses of German police who worked hand in hand with the French to arrest us. Schlageter was betrayed to the French by the Germans. He was arrested, and with him Becker, Sadowski, Zimmermann, Werner and a couple of others. Hauenstein was taken by the German police and imprisoned.

'We tried our level best to get them out again. But Hauenstein, who had the whole affair in his hands, money, plans, everything, was not released – more particularly when he asked over and over again at least to be given leave of absence to help Schlageter's escape.

'We were on the go day and night. When we had eventually located our men in Werden and had concentrated all our forces there, they had been moved on to Düsseldorf. We heard of their being abominably ill-treated in the Essen Coal-Syndicat,

334

where the French Headquarters are. We were told that they had been thrashed with whips and clubs. In Werden we had got into the prison yard, but we did not manage it in Düsseldorf, because the German police kept a much stricter eye on us than the French. We tried to organise a mass attack on the prison and Gabriel asked the Krupp workers, of whom thirteen had been shot down by the French in March, to join us. But it was all in vain. We approached the mayor, who shook like a jelly when we appeared; Gabriel went to Berlin to interview the Government, and was turned down with jeers and recommended to apply to the Red Cross.

'On May 26th, 1923, Schlageter was shot by a French firing party on the Golzheim heath near Düsseldorf, just three hours before we were going to make a last, despairing, furious assault on the prison. The rest of them were taken off to the Island of St. Martin de Ré and were to be transported to Cayenne from there. . . .

'. . . . Gabriel took over the direct control in the whole of the occupied area. Heinz was in Frankfurt, Hauenstein in Essen, Treff in Cologne. But I had to relieve Treff, for he was suffering from a serious wound in his hand, which he had got in February, when he had sought out the leader of the Separatists in Cologne and had shot him. In his flight he had fallen through a skylight. To "convalesce" he went to the citadel in Spandau, where a battalion of the Black *Reichswehr* was living, making fresh plans for the campaign of the Ruhr. But he was not there for long. In June he and the rest went and fetched the captain out of the State Prison in Leipzig.

'It seemed as if at long last everything was coming right again. The whole country was in a state of uproar. What held it together was nothing but fear of the chaos from which the German revolution must grow. But the inflation, the downward rush of the Mark, of values, which bound each individual

335

to the things which made his life safe, his daily bread, law and order and so forth, created an atmosphere in which what had been faith became fatalism, and fatalism despair. Very soon each man fought for himself alone; the nation was simply a disintegrated mob, the raw materials for a revolution, for which everyone seemed to be waiting and which everyone seemed to be ready to follow.

'But we, the friends of God and the enemies of everyone else, had to slay inexorably whatever tried to come in our way. For years we had been absolutely alone; now everyone who still had any hopes for the future collected round us. There were even times when we could depend on having a crowd of determined men at our backs when we advanced. The Separatists were to discover that in Düsseldorf, in Aix, in Krefeld, in Bonn. One shot fired by us was enough to rouse the whole populace. Armed with hoses and clubs, with stones and shotguns, we attacked and killed, fired on by the French, organising the revolt till everything had been destroyed that opposed itself to us. That was in the parts round Honnef and Aegidienburg, in the narrow strip between the bridge heads of Coblenz and Cologne which is free of French occupation, where Gabriel led the main attack. He managed to entice a crowd of about fifteen hundred Separatists from the occupied area there, while we lay in the woods and watched their arrival. The blighters came strolling along, dragging their rifles upside down in the mud, ragged, untidy, dirty, with vicious faces. They pushed their way into the villages, shooting and yelling; they dragged the beasts out of the stables, slaughtered them in the open street, plundered, drank and burnt. Then we called on the peasants to rise. The bells clanged, beacons were lit on the hills and we broke out of the woods in wild hordes, armed with scythes, pitchforks and flails. Suddenly the whole valley was alive. The peasants, sweating and splashed with blood, raced in among the clumps of men, killed, hunted, raged – it will be a long time before the Westerwald peasants forget the battle in the Seven Mountains.

'The signal for our last effort was the Government's abandonment of the policy of passive resistance. Everyone rushed to Berlin. The secret army had formed almost of itself. The burden of waiting grew well-nigh intolerable. The Black *Reichswehr* was vegetating in its inadequate barracks, under the shadow of demoralising obscurity. And the dammed energies simply drove the various forces to beat up against one another to their mutual destruction. The men who were gathered there had learnt to be merciless to traitors. The Black troops were already in Coburg, prepared to move into Thuringia in the direction of Berlin. Armed and uniformed troops marched along the streets in Bavaria, no one hindering them.

'On November 8th, Gabriel and I came to Munich. The town was in a state of indescribable confusion. Hitler was proclaiming the National Republic – it actually happened in the Bürgerbräukeller. And on November 9th, the police and the *Reichswehr* shot at the advancing men and thirteen were killed; all fellows who had been with us in the Ruhr, incidentally.

'Then the devil took a hand in the game. It was all of no avail. National anthem and flags were produced – but they could not hide the mess. It was an opportunity such as a people has once in a century – and we – what about us?

'Gabriel allowed us no rest. We tried to assemble, but we found suddenly that nobody remained. There were just a few in the Pfalz, who formed a little troop under Gabriel's leadership. He seemed to be absolutely burnt up inside. What he did, drily and hollow-eyed, seemed to be done by a machine. His methodical, absolutely passionless conduct of

337

affairs, which could almost always be relied upon as a guarantee of success, had nothing left to link it with the mad fury, thirsting for revenge, that characterised his early days as an Activist. We grew to feel him almost uncanny. Ideals alone give courage. But he refused to let ideals have anything to do with his work. He only laughed when we sat round and, as he said, "saved Germany" again. He said coldly into the talk, during which the queerest plans were propounded, that we must necessarily come to grief and that he was glad of it. He grinned derisively when he said "Germany." But he gave the troop the job of shooting Heinz-Orbis, the Separatist leader and Prime Minister of the "autonomous Pfalz."

'In the evenings the Prime Minister used to sit drinking at the Wittelsbacher Hof in Speyer with his friends and with French officers. The place was crowded to overflowing when we pushed in and pulled out our revolvers and the French officers obediently put up their hands. The hall was absolutely still and hundreds of eyes stared at us. Then the shots rang out and Heinz-Orbis and five of his friends collapsed. We shot down the candelabra and cleared out; but Treff got a shot in the back and as he died Gabriel said: "Yes, yes – we shall all come to it."

'Those who went to Pirmasens with us knew about it. Death and the devil had not agreed about us. The devil was at large in Pirmasens. God with us – but we had always felt most comfortable in the devil's company. It was the irony of fate that we had to drive him out now! Once before we had fought for law and order; and we had vowed never to do it again. Now we were doing it again after all. It went badly against the grain. But we were determined that so long as there was any fighting we would be in it.

'We found the citizens of Pirmasens in exactly the right mood. The Separatists had plundered the shops of food stuffs, had

destroyed some houses, stormed the town hall and taken poses-
sion of the police court, which they made their headquarters.
From there they fired merrily in all directions. This was the
situation on February 12th, 1924. The Separatists were requested over the telephone to leave the building. They refused.
Then we marched up, a handful of boys, a good many Pirmasens
men and most of Gabriel's people. The Separatists fired and
threw bombs at us; at the first attack we were unable to dislodge
them. Now Gabriel roused the town. The bells rang a tocsin,
the fire-brigade arrived. We raced through the streets and
roared at the townsmen to join in the battle. We surrounded
the space in front of the police court. The fire-brigade sent
streams of water against the windows, but were not able so
much as to smash one. So at about six o'clock in the evening
we put out all the street lamps and fired on the building. As
we were preparing to rush it, Gabriel fell.

'He was shot through the head and died instantaneously.
Yes, yes, we shall all come to it. We shouted the news of his
death to one another and then nothing could hold us in check.
I saw many who were foaming at the mouth and yelling with
chalk-white faces as they raced forward. We dashed at the
building and smashed the windows. We threw paper, tow,
wood, petrol and hand-grenades into the rooms on the ground
floor. We hurled brands into them, so that a munition dump
exploded. We crashed against the heavily barred door till it
burst and leapt up the steps and fetched them out one by one:
and any that escaped alive from us were killed by the mob
outside. We stood among the fumes, frenzied, gasping, possessed, we raged through the rooms, found the leader and laid him
out. Outside were the French, not daring to move.

'And then we discovered for the first time since November,
1918, that there was nothing left for us to do. Even the
question: "What next?" stumped us. We dispersed miserably.

'We are not going to make any plans. It is all over. It was great – and it is finished. We shall never again march together as we used to. Our mad crowd doesn't exist any longer. One or another is somewhere about the country, and soon we shall know no more of one another than what remains as a common memory. Perhaps – no certainly – the big account will be balanced again. And the few men who remain will be there again, each one alone or perhaps each with a fresh group. Perhaps – but then it will be a different war with different rules.

'I could count those who survive of the old crowd on my fingers. Those who are not dead or in prison or leading the life of fugitives across the border, have just settled down into the mud that seems to lie over everything. A good many have drifted away, have grown indifferent, and a number are adapting themselves to fresh ideas and are waging a sullen war in new places. Heinz is being dragged from one prison to another. Jörg has been locked up, because he tried to overthrow the Government with ten men and was arranging to occupy the Ministry of the Interior as his own future domain. The two who killed Erzberger are still wandering distractedly about Germany, casting longing eyes at the country for whose sake they risked banishment. None of Kern's companions have yet escaped from prison. Techow wrote from Sonnenburg, in the name of you all, to say that you preferred not to be rescued so long as there was something more urgent to be done. There isn't anything more urgent to be done, but there's nobody to help you. You'll have to help yourself. Perhaps, even, prison will be your best way of getting across the morass. Put your passions on ice. Save up your hatred. There will be very few who will be able to feel that nothing is in vain in this world.

'Meanwhile, I am allowing myself to be catapulted into the

air every day with a few yards of cloth and wood. I went to the Rhön flying station directly after Pirmasens and was in the air for the first time just a week later. And then? – There's a nigger-sheik in Morocco called Abd-el-Krim, who is supposed to be planning a revolt against France – and airmen are useful everywhere . . .'

CHAPTER XXIX

1924

THE time came when raging terror overmastered me, when all the ghosts in that accursed place seemed to be wailing in the wind that howled round its grey walls. During the first year of my imprisonment I had still felt that I was in some sort of touch with events in the outside world, and even that I had some share in determining their outcome. But now I was utterly remote. I was so lonely that I could not bear it when the Governor humanely tried to establish some sort of contact with me; I could not bear the sympathy of the chief warder; nor the soothing tone of the occasional letters; nor the furtive questions of the other prisoners; nor the gentle warmth of the first days of early spring. I entrenched myself within the four walls of the cell I loathed; and hated the warder who opened my door and the attendant who brought my food and the dogs who scuffled outside the window. I shrank from any enjoyment. I hated the almond tree at the entrance to the yard, which was covered with pink blossom and which filled the yard with indescribable glory. I detested the great chestnut tree in the middle of the path with its opening buds, and the row of miserable lime trees, in whose branches starlings and finches roosted. Every joy seemed to me deceit and mockery.

* * * *

As time went on I had various opportunities, even in prison, of getting into closer contact with humanity. The Governor

342

often came into my cell but his visits never lasted long and he had a devastating way of planting his hat on his head with a little jerk and bidding me a gracious farewell as he left. Many of the officials used to stand for a minute or two when the cell door was unlocked and exchange a few words with me. But what they had to say showed such a circumscribed outlook that, in my opinion, they represented the atmosphere of prison far more nearly than did the other prisoners; so on the whole I was glad to be spared the humiliation of their condescending sympathy, as well as their well-meaning warnings to me not to get too friendly with the criminals; yet I felt that I too was regarded as a criminal by them, less comprehensible, perhaps, than most, but no less contemptible. No less contemptible and certainly more dangerous. For I was under double supervison and whatever I did was discussed and re-discussed. Yes, I was a criminal in their eyes, nothing else. To these men who ranked as honest and were entitled to pensions, I was an alien, as at bottom I was an alien to the prisoners. I resisted the idea that I was a criminal until one day I read Goethe's remark: 'There is no crime which I cannot imagine myself committing.' I was taken aback by this statement; I read it twice, thrice, I impressed it on my mind. Then I submitted myself to a rigorous self-examination, which was painful because in my desire to be absolutely honest with myself, I found that it was horrifyingly easy to imagine myself committing any crime. In fact, there was no crime which I could not conceive of myself committing; and I could only bear this idea because I was convinced that its origin did not spring from any fundamentally humanitarian motives, implying an acceptance of the intolerable theory that to understand all is to forgive all, but from a strong sense of the inevitability of all things.

I got to know more than was ever told to an examining

magistrate. But the word 'criminal' was considered to be the worst term of abuse; and if ever it was uttered among the prisoners – whether it happened in the yard during the daily walk or in the workrooms or in the dormitories or in the cells for three where the psychopaths were put – wherever it occurred the injured man sprang at the throat of the one who had insulted him. Confused knots of men collected round the combatants and the row ended with arrest cells, to which the Governor condemned everyone concerned. Nobody would own to being a criminal – whether he had simply stupidly blundered over to the wrong side of the law, or whether he discussed the offence for which he had been imprisoned coldly and cynically, or whether he was vindicating a profession that was not always profitable and was certainly dangerous. The first had done it because he was destitute, the second in a fit of passion and the third because he had never been used to anything else. But none of them felt that he was responsible to a higher power or that he was bound by any laws beyond those which forbade his deed and prescribed the punishment. None of them felt guilty. In fact, they all maintained that they were innocent; they insisted on it even when they confessed. Not one but had a bad conscience when he owned to being guilty in response to pressure; for none of them understood the meaning of guilt. Hence they all bore the yoke of punishment sullenly, they hated the judge and the prison officials, they accounted the warders contemptible, and it gave them a kind of sour pleasure to think that if these same warders were put into the prison uniform they would look exactly like themselves. They felt that they were oppressed and downtrodden by man and not by God, by an accursed system and not by a living law. I could never be anything but alien to them.

*   *   *   *

NINETEEN TWENTY-FOUR

The time came when I took refuge from the confusion of doubts in a kind of curious pride. For since everything which I encountered in my strange path could only serve to enrich my stock of ideas I believed that I was justifying my life. There was no pain which did not serve as a warning for the future, no fear which did not give a fresh impetus to courage. It was not the peculiarity of my situation as a political prisoner which raised me from the very outset above my fellows, nor was it the greater severity to which I was subjected; it was something different, something that I had felt, in a way, all my life. All those with whom fate had thrown me were having the same experience as myself. But that was just the point: an experience is never decisive. Anyone may have it; it comes to a man indifferently, whether he is prepared or not. What is decisive is how the experience is sublimated in the individual. And that was what raised me above the others – that I was not afraid to take the consequences, that I had the courage to call myself a criminal.

I never had a single thought which was not an attack on the customs and morals which had established this place; and I took no decision which did not contain the seed of anarchy. The generality of the prisoners, however, had submitted. They lived in a dull, animal state; the occasional ones whose hatred burst its bonds and who answered a humiliating word by smashing everything within reach, were nevertheless part of the crowd, were either supported by it in their short out-bursts of revolt, or were betrayed by it for the sake of small, ignominious advantages. What vegetated round about me in the cells and workrooms was not the scum of a respectable world, it was itself respectable to the last degree. No spark of revolutionary fire lived in these people, no ideals possessed them, they were not inspired by defiance to established codes nor by the pride of exiles. Yet the particular attribute of crime

345

seemed to me to be that it was intended to destroy the existing system and not to be used as an illegal means of adapting oneself to it.

* * * *

The time came when rumour flew through the institution, whispered from one to another, carried from one cell to the next. Whispers full of hope and joy, seasoned by the hints of graciously oracular officials, arose in the dormitories and workrooms. It all began on the day when the flag on the tower was flown at half-mast. The President of the Republic had died, so the chaplain announced from the pulpit, and as soon as he told us, the whole place was in a fever of restlessness. Not one of the prisoners but had the same idea: if the President had died, a new one would be elected – and then there would certainly be an amnesty. And very soon it began to be rumoured that the matter was being discussed in the *Reichstag*.

One of the attendants whispered to me that a third of everybody's sentence would be remitted, no matter what his crime had been. The infirmary warder had it on absolutely sound authority that on the day that the new President took up his duties, everyone who had served two-thirds of his sentence would be released immediately. A prisoner who worked in the Governor's office told everyone who would listen that the officials were already preparing lists, but it was a quarter and not a third of the sentence which was to be remitted. Edi passed me a newspaper cutting, which said that a committee of the *Reichstag* was considering the suggestion of an amnesty for the forthcoming election, by which the now consolidated Republic would let everyone start afresh with a clean sheet.

Edi was full of hope. He and I met in the supervisor's office when we were changing our working clothes. It was full of prisoners jostling one another, and the air of the little room was an oppressive mixture of smells from the wash-house, the boot racks and the piles of clothes, of the effluvia of half-dressed men, of sweat, dust and moth balls. We crept out and up the creaking stairs, till we came to a window that opened on to the open country round the prison and stood there dumbly.

Edi clenched his hands on the bars and pressed his forehead to the grating. His face had got terribly haggard with his lengthy sojourn in the arrest-cells and his bloodshot, fevered eyes looked hollowly from his greyish-yellow skin. We began to speak softly.

Edi said something about the amnesty and I laughed. I could not believe in this amnesty; and if it did come, it would leave a nasty taste – mercy would be thrown at us as a bone is thrown to a dog. 'If one could only respect them,' I said to Edi and gripped his arm. 'And I could respect them if they had condemned the lot of us to death as we should have condemned them if the cases had been reversed. Then I could have respected them – but as it is – and then to have to accept mercy at their hands!'– Edi turned his face towards me and said quietly:

'I've been here for four years.'

We were silent again. The little town with its jumble of low red roofs among the trees and rank bushes looked inconceivably peaceful in the valley. Hardly a sound was to be heard, only from afar came faint rhythmic beats as of a drum. They approached nearer and nearer and as we listened we heard scraps of shrill melody. It echoed from the house, we could not tell whence it proceeded. Suddenly it sounded loud and clear, we held our breath and then it came round the corner. The *Reichswehr* was marching past. I could just see the tops of the helmets and the rifles above the invisible ranks. Then we heard the roll of kettledrums and the music pealed forth. It leapt like a shout to the heavens, the blare of bugles

347

rent the air, as the *Hohenfriedberger* the march of the
Kings of Prussia, crashed out – the march which recalled all
the filth and agony of battlefields, all the standards and glory
of the Bayreuth regiment. It was the triumph of action, the
exultation of courage and sacrifice; it was victory and revolt
together.

Every note seemed to burn into my heart and I swayed,
clutched at the grating, my nerves in shreds – oh, to be with
them, I thought, to be with them, to be free – all my defences,
that I had built up so carefully, collapsed. Outside they were
marching to – what? And I – ?

Below, the supervisor stormed and cursed and shouted. We
stumbled down the stairs.

After this I was just as greedy as all the others for news
of the amnesty. Very soon we heard that instead of an amnesty,
anyone who had a good record was to be released without
further delay. Then came the first election which led to no
result. After that we heard that the amnesty only applied to
certain offences. Then came the day when the Field-Marshal
assumed the highest dignity in the realm. We waited in the
greatest tension. We heard that at any rate political prisoners
would be pardoned. We heard that perhaps even those who
had committed certain crimes would come under consideration.
We heard that the decision would rest with the prison officials –
that everyone who had a record of good conduct could count
on it – we heard that the old Field-Marshal's wish was. . . .
We heard that, broadly speaking. . . .

A great many packed their belongings. The committee was
overwhelmed with requests. The Governor was importuned.
The warders' smiles were full of promise.

And when, long weeks after the election of the President,
the feverish excitement, the trembling expectation, had risen
to their highest pitch – at last, at last, came the edict.

NINETEEN TWENTY-FOUR

And not one, not a single one in the whole of that damned place, came under the ridiculous, grotesque amnesty.

*   *   *   *

Edi and I were sitting in the pale autumn sunlight behind the wood shed, talking of freedom. The branch of a tree thrust over the wall and the faint sound of distant music came to our ears. The voice of the chief warder raised in abuse sounded from the yard above the tramp of many feet. Edi said: 'I've been here for four years now.' He said: 'My wife's waiting for me; she works in a factory.' And then: 'If I were free now. . . .'– I listened as he told me of a tiny home, far away, in a high block of dwellings, among a forest of tall factory chimneys, smoky, noisy, constricted; and suddenly he jumped up, ran at the wall, lifted both fists and hammered frenziedly on the cold stone shouting: 'I want to be free! I want to be free!' And I, strung up, maddened with his anguish, rushed over beside him, hurled myself at the wall, raving, frantic, gasping, kicked it till it crumbled and beat on it with bleeding knuckles distracted, despairing.

'Just like wild beasts,' said the chief warder, as he put us into solitary confinement, shaking his head, 'Just like wild beasts.'

CHAPTER XXX

A CRY

NOBODY was present when the affair occurred which the secretary called 'a violent personal assault.' I might have lied. It is true that my evidence would have been of no account as against an official's. On the other hand, no one had been present except my adversary and myself, and I might have demanded that he should substantiate his statements. I did not lie. I owned up at once and unhesitatingly. I would not lie, on principle, to escape the consequences of any act as long as I was in the institution. If it had been a fair fight between two equals, a fight in which we made use of all the spiritual weapons, finesses and definite rules; if it had been a matter of stalking one's enemy, of dodging and tackling, of measuring each other's strength – in short, a fight – then why should I not lie? But here and now? Prisoners never in any circumstances tell the truth, or only if it is absolutely forced out of them. I was determined not to come down to their level; nor to admit an official as my equal. I told the truth and the astonished faces of the committee proved to me that they were being confronted with a new phenomenon and that they were impressed by it. I was determined to take full responsibility for my action – my attitude was one of defiance. To lie would have been too cheap, would have been flight.

'Seven days strict arrest,' said the Governor, and I was removed.

350

A CRY

We went through long, dark, echoing passages. My nailed boots clattered on the stone flags and I swung my arms with as devil-may-care a mien as possible. The warder walked ahead of me with a severely official expression on his face and kept the distance between us ostentatiously exact. A silent hope rose within me that I might be allotted one of the front cells, because they were warmer and lay rather higher and were in the same passage as the other cells, which gave one some feeling of being in touch with the world. The other arrest cells were deep down in the basement and right at the back of the building. They were only heated from the outside, and it was the month of December. The warder went past the cells to which I had pinned vain hopes, and I was filled with confusion at having hesitated slightly as we passed them. We went downstairs, the warder turned keys and pushed bolts. He deliberated between the various cells and finally opened the farthest, darkest and coldest.

The room was small. The white-washed walls and the grey iron bars made me shiver. The window frame was made of white corrugated glass protected by wires; and the bars forming the cage stood up straight and fierce in the twilight. The cage – for the room was divided down the middle along the darkest wall – needless to say, not the one which abutted on to the heating apparatus – was placed as far as possible from both door and window, surrounded by an iron grating making a square whose side was the same length as the plank bed which was let into the floor and which was the only piece of furniture. The door of the cage was thrown open with a clatter and I went inside. The warder removed my braces and my neckcloth and slammed the door of the cage. He locked it top and bottom, then he fastened an iron bolt and finally affixed a padlock. He went all round the cage and tapped each individual bar with one of the keys, to make sure that they were all sound. He

walked to the door of the cell and back, tested the window pane
and looked at the thermometer which hung on the wall nearest
to me. Then he went out and locked the door of the cell above
and below, pushed the bolt and snapped the padlock. I heard
his footsteps as he tramped along the corridor. The door of
the passage clanged. Once more the keys rattled. Then all
was still.

I sat motionless on the low plank bed for a long, long time.
I could not think, it was too cold for thought, too silent. Nothing in the room was alive, except myself – and was I alive?
I considered my hand which looked pale and bony as it lay on
my knee – like the hand of a corpse. There were black edges
to my bluish finger nails. I seemed to smell corruption.

I was the central point of the room. If I could not manage
to irradiate my being to the farthest corners of that wretchedly
small space, I should be crushed. Seven days I was to pass
here   seven days and seven nights. That was the time it took
a liner to go from Germany to America. I sat on the bed and
tried to imagine myself taking such a voyage. I combined it
with a life of comfort, interest, wide views and freedom.
Freedom! I stood up and leant against the bars. They were
icy cold and I stepped back from them, holding on to my
trousers, to prevent their slipping. I wandered round and
round, imagining myself on the promenade deck: I was well
dressed, I heard music and the sound of the waves, and I
talked to beautiful women and clever men. I dreamt – but
each dream was no more than two steps long. Each thought was
just two steps long. Then it was interrupted and something
quite different took its place. I seemed to be living in a whirl
of events. At the same time, I never for a moment forgot that
I was a prisoner, that I was under strict arrest, that I was walking in circles round a cage, holding up my trousers. If only
it were a little warmer! I stretched my arm through the bars

and tried to reach the warmer wall. It was no use – I could not get anywhere near it. I sat down again on the bed, and wondered how long I had been in this cell. Surely it must soon be dinner time – I was getting hungry. I had been brought here at nine o'clock. I dug my fists into my eyes, held my breath and counted my heart beats so as to find out how long a minute was. A minute was a terribly long time. Then I tried to remember when it was that I had sat counting my heart beats before. Once before I had been in a cramped space, afraid of time. I was sitting in a trench and shells were bursting overhead. One crashed into the ground – too far. A second came with a deafening roar – too short. The third – the third was bound to get our range. I sat and listened to the beating of my pulse. The third never came. How interminable a minute was! I looked up and counted the bars. There were fifty-eight. I got up and counted the planks in the floor – sixteen of them. I put one foot in front of the other – seven times I could do it and then came the grating. I was pleased about the seven. Now I added them all up – $58+16+7=81$. Square root – nine. Did that portend good luck or bad? I was born in the ninth month of the year and the square root of the date of my release was also nine.

I smiled and was ashamed of myself – how absurd I was being! I comforted myself by thinking that most people were absurd when they were alone – really alone. I should love to see the secretary, the man on whose account I was here, in the same situation. What an obstinate, square, red face he had. His head sat right down on his shoulders. The scrubby moustache on his puffy upper lip seemed to exude a kind of sullen servility. How I hated that face of his! 'Violent personal assault!' Well, I was glad of it. I did not regret it for one moment. How taken aback he had been! He had gasped for breath and shouted: 'I'll have you put under arrest!' And he did. Now he was triumphant, I supposed, now he was patting himself on the back and solacing his wounded pride with the feeling of power! No, I did not hate him, I thought. If I hated him I would acknowledge it. I laughed. I really laughed – and the sound echoed round the cell. It ricocheted from the walls and whispered in and out between the bars. I listened in astonishment. I laughed again, artificially, convulsively. The cell replied – jeeringly, it seemed to me. I stopped, shivering.

Still not midday? I could not hear a sound except my own breathing. My breath steamed as I exhaled. I filled my lungs and blew a cloud into the air. I breathed on my hands. I fastened up my trousers as best I could and did knee-bending – one – two – three – four – exactly as our drill sergeant had taught us at school. I did it fifty times, till my legs began to tremble; I wondered how high the cell was and tried to measure it by my own height. I climbed up one of the bars, but quickly jumped down again; for I suddenly saw myself like a monkey in the Zoo, bow-legged and clinging to the bars. I felt humiliated. Man feels a sense of shame when he sees the ape. Can it be true that we are descended from apes? I thought that a man left alone in a small space would soon turn back into an ape. I remembered a book I had read recently in my cell called *Tarzan of the Apes*. It had disgusted me – it was such hopeless rubbish. A man, a white man, descended from men, falls among apes and becomes one himself – becomes one consciously and is proud of it. Could one retreat from humanity among apes? So much the worse for us if it were so! And yet – I dwelt among criminals. I was living with them, speaking their language, enduring the same miseries. I had to obey the warders, although I despised them –. What absurd ideas I was beginning to have! – Would it never be midday?

Up and down – up and down – round and round. I was

determined to tire myself out. It was three years since I had slept properly. What would it be like at night? How wonderful it would be to sink into blissful nothingness, to feel everything fade away utterly, to be submerged – to sleep. The weary day could not tire me. My brain was dull and exhausted. But my body was wide awake. My legs jerked in time to my pulse. I could not keep my arms still – it was agony not to move them. What would the night be like? I should not be able to sleep. How I wished the long night were past – all the seven nights.

Would midday never come?

How slowly the day went. What a lot of things one could do in a day. What a lot I had formerly packed into my days. They used never to be long enough. At that time I lived in a whirl – I followed a star. Yet, had there never been moments when I was worse off than I was now? And I answered 'never' with absolute conviction. Whatever situation I had been in – whether I had been exposed to raging artillery fire – or had waited with every nerve strained, a revolver in my hand, ready to kill or to be killed – or had stood before the tribunal, while my fate hung in the balance – there had always been something stronger than myself which raised me above the torment of the moment, which gave my actions point and aim and reason – but the present was utterly without reason. I simply existed and had to resign myself to circumstances. There is no sense in resignation. There is some sense in expiation, but none in resignation. Had I made a mistake in telling the truth? No, that was not a mistake. I was suffering because I could not bear the idea of appearing to these people as a liar and a coward. Resignation was sweet after all.

Devil take it, how contemptible everything was. I was contemptible myself: brooding was demoralising me. I liked people with spirit – men – the kind who recognised no problems – the kind who took life quietly but purposefully. What was the

matter with me? I called myself 'milksop'; I *would* be reasonable. I laughed in order to hear the sound pass between the
bars.

Surely it must soon be midday!

Why was I waiting for midday? Was I hankering for the
piece of dry bread? Was I looking forward to seeing another
human being? What I was looking forward to, was some
interruption in the monotony.

I heard the outer door in the passage being unlocked and
steps approaching. Something rattled outside the door of my
cell. The warder opened it and the attendant slipped in. I
stood numb and sullen, without looking at him. He pushed a
piece of bread between the bars and a jug of water. Then
the warder condescended to unlock the cage. The attendant
put a dirty bucket with a badly fitting lid inside and laid some
pieces of paper beside it. Out of the corner of my eye I saw
that it was printed paper, a newspaper cut ready for use. It
was all I could do not to dash at the bits and snatch them up.
The keys were rattled vigorously and I was alone once more. I
looked at the pieces of paper. Nothing but advertisements – wait,
though, what was on the back? I stood and read. The sentences
were all cut short, for the paper was divided down the middle of a
column. I spread the pieces on the floor and tried to fit them
together. To my great disappointment I found that a good
many were duplicates. However, I managed to get about half
a sheet to fit, and I read that. It was only a local paper and had
nothing world-shaking in it – but it was so long since I had
seen a newspaper that I enjoyed even the rubbish. This was
last year's. I read it all the same from the first line to the last,
and then I began all over again. I read the advertisements:
a stud-bull was for sale; there was a dance at the 'German
Emperor' Hôtel – mine host had much pleasure in issuing
invitations; Rosenblum was showing the latest Spring models

at his emporium; at the movies Pola Negri was making positively her last appearance. My eye was caught by one line:
'Write on business, write to friends, MK Paper serves your
ends.' I read the rhyme once and again, and was pleased by
its absurd rhythm. 'Write on business, write to friends . . .',
the thing seemed to set itself to music. I sang it as I imagined
it should be sung. I could not get the rhyme out of my head.
It went with a swing; and I had invented a rousing tune, like
a Prussian military march. 'Write on business, write to
friends. . . .' I walked round in circles again, whistling my
tune. I picked up the bread and attacked the awkward triangular chunk. I chewed in time to the tune. It was perfect
nonsense, of course – but that man understood the art of
advertising. I thought I should never forget that rhyme. So
midday had brought me something entertaining after all.
My pleasures were very humble – yet this little distraction gave
me fresh strength. I thought of the letter which Techow had
written from the Sonnenburg prison. In it he mentioned a
visit he had received and said: 'It gave me the strength to
make another effort.' A good sport, Techow. I should be
allowed a visitor soon. Very soon; directly I got out of the
arrest cell. It would be Christmas in a week's time.

Christmas, Christmas – that would make the third Christmas
I had spent in prison. I could not bear to think of it. Certainly the Governor did his best. He wanted to help the
prisoners to forget for this one day. But I was determined not
to forget. I'd be damned if I forgot. I was determined to
forget no injury of word or look or deed. I was resolved to
remember every meanness, every word that hurt or was intended to hurt. All my life long I would bear malice. I would
not forget – except the few good things that happened – those
I would forget.

It had grown dark in the cell – December days soon came to

an end. The long night was beginning. I walked round and round till my head started to whirl. I sat on the bed again and knocked my head painfully on the ring that was rivetted into the wall. Refractory prisoners were laid in chains which were fastened to this ring. I was filled with a cold rage. That such a thing should be possible in an age overflowing with talk about humanity and the brotherhood of man! I could understand that in times when men owned to being harder-hearted they should treat rebels and criminals with severity. But nowadays people acted with just as much ferocity, while talking glibly about love. Nowadays people acted brutally and pretended to understand psychology. Nowadays men were laid in chains, while their jailors talked about discipline. Force is never so base as when it is concealed under a cloak of hypoc-risy. They had not put me in chains – it was enough to have put me behind five locks. I had been spared the final degrada-tion. I am convinced it was because I had unhesitatingly owned up. A prisoner who was locked in this cell and also laid in chains would surely go off his head. Was that any help in keeping him safe? That iron ring in the wall was the last refinement of hypocrisy. It concluded the work of destroying a man's self-respect. I am sure that a prisoner who had once been put in chains would be for ever filled with cold hatred. Some of the first words in the regulations for prison authorities are: 'The prisoner is to be treated reasonably, justly and humanely.'

I was lying stretched out on the bed, waiting for the piece of bread that would be given me in the evening. My head lay uncomfortably on the wooden rest. My whole body ached every time I moved. The cell was quite dark, though a pale glimmer of light shone through the window, probably from the lantern in the yard. I lay and meditated; and the absurd verse, which had pleased me so much at first, kept on running in my head, till I thought I should go mad. I remembered once reading about a Chinese torture, in which the culprit is fastened under a tap out of which a drop falls at regular intervals on to his shaven head. Who could endure it? But after all, there was no comparison between the harmless rhyme and that succession of drops. Nevertheless, a suspicion rose in me. Idiotic as this sequence of ideas was – was I really still capable of connecting ideas? Was not everthing that passed through my mind a confusion of disconnected thoughts? I had now been in prison for two years – two years! Into what a state of chaos would my mind gradually sink!

The warder appeared. How I loathed the harsh tone of the key grating imperiously in the lock. Although I heard it daily, I never got used to it. The attendant lounged in and threw a hunk of bread into my cage as if I had been a wild beast. What the devil – the fellow was a tramp, a loafer, with seventeen previous convictions. His foxy face was for ever appearing about the prison corridors. He had the cunning look of an old lag. He tyrannised over any prisoners who could not stand up to him. He used to wait round corners and carry every word that he overheard to the authorities, usually twisted out of all recognition. The blackguard – no doubt he felt that he could domineer over me now. He was under protection of the authorities. He could carry on his dirty work and he knew it. I lay on my bed and scrutinised him. He went into the corridor and routed in a pile of damp, smelly old blankets. I was allowed one blanket for the cold night. He picked out the very worst, the meanest, the most ragged. I could see him in the light that shone from the passage. He pushed the blanket through the bars. I stood up and said: 'You swab, get me a different blanket!'–

'What's all this?' interrupted the warder, 'we haven't got any different blankets.'

THE OUTLAWS

The attendant grinned. I boiled with rage. The attendant said: 'Under arrest and still talking so big?'

I sprang at the bars and shook my fist: 'May the Lord have mercy on you – damn you!'

He leapt back and grinned again. The warder took him out; the door clanged; and I heard the attendant abusing me foully. I caught the bars and shook them in blind fury. The swine, the swine, the swine! To-morrow he would heat the cell as little as he possibly could; he would pick out the worst piece of bread for me; he would let the water get brackish before bringing it. And I was helpless. He was covered, I could prove nothing against him, his word would be taken against mine. It was no use hoping to catch him unawares, he was never alone – the warder was always with him and the warder would intervene immediately; and for me . . . more arrest. I might complain – I should only be laughed at. I had no defence – I had called him 'Swab.' He was in the right – that ridiculous right. . . .

I was filled with a galling rancour. This was the last degradation. This scum was triumphing over me. He jeered at me like the low-minded beast he was, always trying to find something weaker than himself to tyrannise over. I would not think of him any more. I wrapped myself in the blanket and lay on the bed. It was bitterly cold. Christmas would be here in a week. In a week's time I should be allowed a visitor. I was allowed a visitor once a year. The blanket which I had pulled up to my neck stank abominably. I thought of the delicate scent which had seemed to linger for days after my last visitor. The book she had brought seemed to hold it in its pages like a breath from another world. I could hear her voice and see her eyes. A year ago – ah, if you knew, if you could imagine what it was like! I had lied. I had said in an aggressively cheerful way that I was getting on splendidly. She was not to worry, everything would come right soon. I had laughed and joked. I had stroked her hand with trembling fingers and lied and lied. She had looked at me doubtfully, and after several minutes' silence had said softly: 'Why don't you tell me the truth?' I had looked despairingly at the warder who was sitting there comfortably and apparently taking no notice of us: 'I am telling the truth,' I had lied; and I tried to pacify her by a flood of untruths. If she only knew – but she should not know how I had been humiliated. In a week – I should lie – I should lie. . . .

It was pitch dark. The happier memories refused to stay with me. I got up and considered the situation. My bones were sore and I felt as if I were bruised all over. Perhaps I should be more comfortable if I stretched the blanket as a hammock between the bars? We had often used our ground sheets as hammocks during the various campaigns. I tried to fix the corners firmly to the bars. I thought I might manage if I curled up in it. I climbed in, but the rotten blanket tore with a rending noise and I fell on to the floor with a bump. Furiously I beat the blanket against the bars – and then I was ashamed to be wreaking my vengeance on an inanimate object. I was in despair. The night was so long. I thought back and remembered how long the day had been; and that was only one seventh, no, one fourteenth, of the time that I had to spend in this place. I wondered why it was so dark. A glimmer of light had surely come through the window before? Then I realised that the attendant had closed the wooden shutters. They were creaking in the wind which howled round the yard. They were creaking unbearably. There seemed no chance of sleep. Formerly prisoners had been confined in the dark. That was why there were shutters to the window. How appalling – to spend days and weeks in the dark. I remembered reading about a man in the days of Louis XIV who had spent sixty years imprisoned in darkness. He had somehow got hold of twelve pins. These he used to scatter all over the floor and then he used to look for them again, crawling about the cell on his hands and knees, groping in every spot, every corner, every cranny. He looked for them day and night, all the time he was awake. It used to take months before he had collected all his pins. Then he threw them about the cell again and began his search afresh.– It was an old story; and it went on to tell that that was the only way the man had managed to prevent himself from going mad.

What was I thinking of? How long could I bear it? I was a coward – Techow would be in prison longer than I – three times as long. Everything that I had experienced he must have experienced; and would go on experiencing for years after I was free again. I cursed myself for being faint-hearted and cowardly – a despicable object. I was ashamed of myself. And yet, and yet – no, I could not bear it. This was ghastly. My head was so heavy – my fate so weary. If only I could make an end of things. They had taken away my braces – I still had my underpants – I might twist them into a rope. Then I could fasten it to the top of the grating. Suppose I were to climb up the bars, put the rope round my neck and then let myself drop? I lay on the plank-bed and considered it. I thought it over quite seriously – but all the time I knew that I should not do it. I was too cowardly. I had not the courage – yes, I had the courage – but not the energy. I was quibbling over words like a pettifogging lawyer. After all – should I do it? Then I should be found in the morning with my trousers sliding off, or just in my shirt, my head in the dirty noose . . . no, no, no! Not that way – not that way! It would not be honourable – I must not end in despair.

I should survive that night; and I should survive the following days and nights – and all the long years. I was ashamed of the ideas I had entertained.

I grew calmer. What would happen next? To-morrow would pass as to-day had done, as so many days had already passed. To-morrow I should go for a quarter of an hour's walk in the yard. The next day – no in three days – I should be given a warm meal. And a real bed at night. In three days I should have a real bed in that cell. How absurd to be looking forward so keenly to a warm meal and a bed. How often I had done without things as a soldier and gladly. As a soldier, yes – but this was punishment. Who dared to claim the right to dispose of me in this way? Where did it come from? Was it from heaven? Did they get the right through personal excellence, through sacrifices, through incredible deeds? No – it was their trade – their wretched, plebeian trade. They were paid for it. They had posts and titles. They were exposed to no danger – they had no responsibility. Disgust nearly choked me. Their respectable laws! They said I had broken them. They were in the right. How I despised that right!

I tossed from side to side. How long the night was. Everything was deathly still except that every now and then a shutter creaked. I wondered what time it was.

Then I heard a scream. It came from somewhere along this passage and echoed through the building. Did it not come from the cell next to me? Again! Long and loud. It set all my nerves on edge. I leapt up and hammered on the wall like a lunatic. There was an answering bang. Another scream – echoing – I filled my lungs and bellowed with all my strength. I screamed, hammered, raged. I could not help myself. And as I screamed, my tense nerves relaxed. I screamed wildly, reverberatingly, extravagantly, violently, passionately. Oh, how it did me good – how it relieved me! It chased the night, the misery, the loathing back to their dark lairs. I screamed and I grew strong.

CHAPTER XXXI

1925

ON the morning of New Year's Day, 1925, I awoke feeling so wretched that I did not trouble even to think about it. The sensation of having an empty brain and hollow bones, my utter hopelessness, the thought of my depressing position, made me absolutely certain that from that moment onwards it was impossible for me to continue in the deadly routine of the prison. I felt an inexpressible abhorrence at the idea of getting up for no particular purpose, of dressing, walking up and down and waiting, sitting at the table, standing by the window, listening by the door – in fact of doing all the things that I had been doing regularly for over two years, day-in, day-out, without knowing why.

I made no effort to rise from my bed because I was convinced that every attempt would be vain. I lay bathed in perspiration, disinclined for everything, and gazed at the green and violet circles which formed before my eyes. The attendant ran into the cell to light the gas, stared at me, roared 'Get up!' and clattered out again with his smoky torch, leaving the cell in the pale glare of the lamp. The warder came and shouted through the open door. He came into the cell and seized my arm. Barking 'No nonsense!' at me, he shook me. Then he left the cell muttering.

After that, the chief warder arrived. He carefully felt my forehead before saying anything. Then he made a long speech of which I only took in scraps, such as 'no nonsense,' and 'make short work,' and 'arrest.' He went out again slowly and re-turned with the Governor. The latter stood by my bed shaking his head and his words reached me faintly. 'You must pull yourself together,' he said. And then: 'A young man like you musn't let himself go to such an extent.' He enquired suspiciously: 'You're not being simply obstruc-tionist, I suppose?' The Governor vanished and the chief warder of the infirmary threw open the door, stood on the doorstep and bellowed: 'The Doctor.' The doctor looked at me for several minutes without moving; then he said: 'Prison psychosis,' turned on his heel and departed.

The two infirmary orderlies appeared, sniggering as they put me on to a stretcher, and transported me to the infirmary.

'You'll manage to put it over on them all right,' said one; and the other said:

'So long as you keep it up!'

I remained in the infirmary for eight months.

*　　*　　*　　*

For three weeks I lay in bed, taking no interest in anything. I had no temperature, but had no desire to smoke, although tobacco was easier to get and of much better quality than that supplied in the cells. When at last I made up my mind to get up, I was surprised how my whole life seemed suddenly to have simplified itself. I no longer had any desire to search for reasons, and gradually I got interested in the busy little domain of the infirmary. The doctor wanted to keep me as third infirmary orderly, so I was transferred to the orderlies' cell which was open during the day-time. I was allowed to move about freely within the infirmary. I helped in distributing the meals, cleaning the excrement-buckets, bandaging the sick and making their beds; I helped to cook the invalids' food, to pre-pare the baths, to polish the floors and to swab the passages; I ran from one sick-room to another, from the tubercular ward to that for convalescents, from the mental division to the epileptics'. For the first time since I had been imprisoned I could speak without being stopped or watched, and move about without being limited to the six paces which were all my cell allowed.

I was put in charge of those prisoners who were segregated for observation of their mental state. About twelve of them lived in a not too roomy ward into which opened a door with a glass pane secured by a strong wire netting. So long as they imagined themselves unobserved, they lay about on the beds, smoking or playing games with cards they had made themselves or managed to smuggle in, ready at any moment to manifest their mental instability by mad and usually very ingenious sayings and doings. I was surprised at the cool matter-of-course way in which they immediately admitted me into their plot. They discussed amid shouts and laughter what particular 'line' they should take up, but afterwards they were so concerned to play the part well that they threw themselves into it with an incredible enthusiasm; and very soon they lost themselves absolutely in their chosen rôle, and were unable to distinguish between what was real and what was fictitious. No matter how different the manifestations were, the process was nearly always the same. These malingerers were really ill: the decision they had taken when they were in their right minds to take refuge from the isolation of the cell in a grotesque dream signified the loosening of their grasp on sanity. I was horrified at the consequences of this proceeding: they played a desperate game in order to save themselves from going mad in their cells, and it led them into the very lunacy to which the cell had paved the way.

I was surprised to see Edi when I went into the ward one day. He came to meet me laughing, then drew himself up

majestically and said, while the others howled their applause:
'I am the Sultan of Morocco!' and then continued explosively:
'I'm not going to lend anyone any money!' I sprang at him
and shook his arm: 'You're crazy!' I shouted, while the others
laughed and slapped their thighs. Edi looked at me in astonishment. The chief warder came to lock the room again; but after
that I spent every spare minute standing by the door beside the
peep hole, which could be opened half way, talking to Edi in
whispers.

'I can't stand it,' said Edi. 'I must get out of this.' He
suddenly roared at me: 'I don't see the fun of masturbating
to death here! I've been messing about with myself for four
solid years – it's damnable!'

'I know,' I said to Edi. 'It's the same for all of us Each
one of us will suffer for it all our lives. You can't do that for
years on end and expect to get off scot free. That's just it –
we've grown proud instead of humble, vain instead of modest
– we've learnt to consider ourselves the centre of the world.
We have grown shameless. We have lost all sense of continuity, we can't follow up things any more, and nothing seems
real. Nothing touches us directly. We only get at ourselves in
a roundabout way via the cell. And all the time we realise it –
we know what is happening.– If only one could pray!'

'If only one could smash up the whole caboodle!' said Edi.
'But what would be the use? What is doing us in, is something
intangible.– I want to get things clear again. I want to lead
my life as I think best – even if I go to .he dogs in the end.'

I had no words to express what I wanted to say to Edi. My
experiences were still too recent for me to be able to talk about
them. It was all so near and the mass-suggestion emanating
from this collection of lunatics was so strong that often enough
I was dragged into the whirl, and shouted and yelled with
them, and adapted myself to the rôle of an Arab sheik, for

which they had cast me, though without my consent, with a ponderous gravity of which I never repented till it was too late.

One night I was wakened by the other orderly, who told me that somebody was seriously ill in the 'loonies' ward'. Edi had a high temperature, jumped up from time to time screaming, and hoarsely croaked scraps of revolutionary songs. The others were dancing round his bed, holding him down when he tried to get up, and goading him to fresh efforts when he fell back exhausted with his face glowing and his head hanging over the side of the bed. The night warder unlocked the door for me and I dragged Edi into the ward reserved for the bad cases. I took my bed into the same room and lay all through this and the following nights, never more than dozing, and listened to the heavy tramp of the warders going their rounds, to the groans from the sick-room, to the vapourings from the mental ward, to the occasional dripping of the tap, to Edi's irregular breathing. When Edi was better the first orderly relieved me. But in the middle of that night he came to my bedside, shook me and said: 'Come on – drinks to-morrow!'

I jumped up, startled; for the orderlies were given a glass of brandy when one of the patients died and the body had to be washed. 'Edi?' I asked, seizing the sleeve of his linen tunic.

'No,' said the orderly, shaking me off. 'Two lots of brandy to-morrow. Old Fritz and old May are both dead.'

*   *   *   *

On the day I entered the prison, I was sent to the infirmary to take a bath. An old, bowed prisoner was in the bathroom running the water into the tub. This was old May. He looked at me with his rheumy eyes. 'How long are you in for?' he enquired. I said gloomily: 'Five years.' He began counting busily on his crooked gouty fingers, lifted up his hands and said: 'There you are – I've been here six times as long.'

Old May had been condemned to fifteen years' hard labour in 1875, for killing another man with a beer bottle. When he came out in the year 1890, he went back to his wife who had been unfaithful to him once before. They lived together again, until old May found out that she was once more deceiving him. May was a coachman; and he took the man who stood in his way to a public-house, made him drunk and then tied him to the back of his cab by the legs and dragged him to death in a mad gallop. He was condemned to death but the sentence was commuted to one of penal servitude for life. When he had served another twenty years, there was some talk of his being released. But there was nobody to take him in, so he remained in prison, which he preferred to a work-house. Consequently, by the time he died he had in all spent forty-nine years in prison and was seventy-four years old.

He was not liked by the other prisoners, because he reported everything that he heard or saw to the officials, in order to improve his own position. It was said that by reason of his extraordinary physical strength he had in former days tyrannised brutally over anyone who had been obliged to live with him. There was one prisoner especially whom old May ill-treated whenever he got the chance. This was old Fritz, a miner from Upper Silesia, with twenty-seven previous convictions for thieving. The two hated one another passionately – they used to go for each other whenever they got the chance. There was no keeping them apart; they always managed to find some means of getting together again. When old May had a stroke, old Fritz fell ill too. Now they lay side by side in a room alone.

Old Fritz had roughly refused to hand in a petition for release. He was seventy-two and suffered from dropsy. One day when I was passing the door, old May croaked something at me. The room was not locked, so I went in and saw old

Fritz lying stiffly in bed staring at the cover with half closed eyes. Old May grinned triumphantly as I called the chief warder of the infirmary. He came, gave one look at old Fritz and ordered his night-shirt to be taken off: it was one of the economical arrangements of the place that dead prisoners were packed naked in a box to be sent to a hospital dissecting room. However, as the attendant was drawing the shirt over the dead man's head, the corpse sat up and growled with a furious look at old May: 'Blast you, it hasn't come to that yet!'

When the Governor heard that the two were on the point of death, he came over to see them. He spoke encouraging words to the old men and then asked whether they had any special wishes that he could grant them. Old Fritz asked for a little hay for his cow, pulling out his chewed pipe from under the bedclothes. Old May, on the other hand, wanted a decent-sized bit of liver sausage. Both declined to have the priest come to administer the last sacraments.

During the night, the first infirmary orderly who was on night duty and sitting in the next room with Edi, heard a hum of conversation from the room of the two old men; he rose, crept over and listened by the open door. Old Fritz was muttering feebly to old May: 'You mangy tyke, you're going to die just as bad as you've lived!'

And old May said: 'Ya – you b——r, damn you, you've spent your life thieving and now you're going to do yourself out of your own salvation.' A little while longer the whispering went on and then there was silence. When we arrived, both lay dead, with their faces turned towards one another. Old May still had a bit of half chewed sausage in his toothless gums and old Fritz's pipe had fallen from his mouth and a few crumbs of glowing tobacco lay gently smouldering on the blanket.

NINETEEN TWENTY-FIVE

We washed the bodies and then laid them out beside one another among the buckets in the lavatory.

*　　*　　*　　*

When Edi recovered, he never mentioned the Sultan of Morocco again. He spent a few more weeks in the isolation ward and when the time came for him to be dismissed from the infirmary, he told me he was looking forward to getting some rough work to do again. I asked the doctor to take me off the mental ward, and so I was transferred to the epileptics.

Among the epileptics was a man called Biedermann, the son of a respectable civil servant, who had been sentenced to fourteen years' hard labour for robbery with violence.

'I've been blighted by little devils,' he told me. His attacks were worse then most of the others', who accepted them as part of the natural order of things. He often talked about the little devils by whom he was possessed and who made his life a burden: they had prevented him from ever achieving anything great in life. Actually his first crime coincided with his first fit, which he got while bathing in the Oder. He kept a very careful watch on himself, kept account of his attacks, and tried to record what he felt while they were in progress. He could prove that before his apprehension he had had on an average some eight fits a year; but during the first year of his imprisonment he had had one hundred and seventy.

In one corner of the room was a padded cell, a large cabin made of strong boards, thickly padded inside. If one of the prisoners had a fit, he was simply chucked into the cabin and left to fight it out, where he could not hurt himself. Biedermann asked me not to put him into the box, but to throw him on to a mattress and then to hold him down; he said that tossing about in the box exhausted him so terribly. When he felt an attack coming on, he used to come along to the orderlies' cell,

which was always open in the daytime, sit on the bed and begin
to talk. The nearer the fit came, the more he talked. His
speech grew every moment more vivid and had a fantastic
expressiveness whose clarity was astonishing. He spoke
rapidly and unfalteringly, he threw himself into what he was
saying with unconscious enthusiasm, stood up slowly and walked
up and down gesticulating slightly. He wrote some of his words
in the air with an impressive forefinger, then forgot to wait
for an answer; picked up things as he passed and put them
down again; then his head began to shake gently, his fingers
twitched, he got red in the face, suddenly stopped talking and
ran up and down more and more quickly, looking straight in
front of him. He took no notice if he was spoken to and began
trembling violently, with a definitely sensual look in his face.
Then I fetched the mattress off a bed and laid it on the floor.
Biedermann took no further notice of anything, began to sway,
stumbled, raised his arms and fell forward. I caught him and
threw him on to the mattress and clung to his limbs. Suddenly
he started up, his distorted mouth open to emit a ghastly,
shrill scream, foam splashed from his blue lips, he fought with
all his might against my grip, his body jerked like a fish, his
head beat up and down in time to his screams, he tried to bite
me and spat foam into my face. I had to exert all my strength
to hold him; the attacks sometimes lasted for as long as a
quarter of an hour. At last he lay exhausted and quiet, I let
go of him and gave him a drink of water. Then he lay for a
long time in a semi-conscious state; I made straight for the
epileptics' ward, for if the screams had been heard there
three or four others invariably had fits too, so that the padded
cell was not large enough to take them all in.

Each one of these attacks put me into a state of the utmost
agitation. For a long time afterwards, when Biedermann was
already occupied peacefully in twisting up a screw of tobacco,

NINETEEN TWENTY-FIVE

I ran up and down the long coconut-matted corridor of the infirmary. I felt that I was directly affected by these fits; I was hardly surprised at what Biedermann had once told me shortly before one of his attacks: why he had asked me not to put him into the padded cell but to hold him.

He used to excite himself with his talk, in which his whole being took part, to a state of perfect ecstasy. Then he felt that all his veins were bursting and the devils who had been raging inside him for a long time beforehand, got free and leapt from every drop of blood to overpower him. He felt a sensation of the most utter weakness and in it lost consciousness. If he knew that I was going to throw myself on him and hold him down, he believed that the devils by whom he was possessed might be exorcised before they overcame him or else could be destroyed by me by some secret process.

The doctor advised me to continue holding down Biedermann – that the padded cell was a positively mediaeval appliance. But Biedermann's attacks grew steadily worse. He often had two fits in a day. He attached himself to me increasingly. When he first told me that he proposed to commit suicide, I found plenty of reasons to urge against such a proceeding. Biedermann was waging a tough fight to get himself released or at least to get himself transferred to a hospital. He had, however, served only two years of his fourteen years' sentence, and knew that even if he only had to spend a part of this time in prison his health would be broken for life. Neither the Governor nor the doctor could help him – epilepsy was no ground for release.

When, after six months' struggle, Biedermann begged me to procure poison for him from the medicine chest in the doctor's room, I had long since been prepared for the request; and had made up my mind what to do. It was not difficult to steal the little bottle from the cupboard. I gave him the poison.

That night the doctor had to be fetched. Biedermann had a bad attack with quite fresh symptoms. The paroxysm lasted for several hours and was accompanied by vomiting and foaming at the mouth to an unusual degree. Biedermann had screamed wildly and writhed for a long time before he had lost consciousness and really fallen into the fit. He howled that he was burning inside. The doctor could do nothing and was obviously much relieved when the attack ultimately followed the normal course.

On the following morning the doctor sent for me to his office. I saw that the door of the medicine chest was open. The doctor said that it was about time I went back to the ordinary cells.

A little while afterwards, Biedermann was transferred to a convict-hospital.

*　　*　　*　　*

Towards the end of the year I was back again in my old cell. Every morning I was filled with an inexpressible repugnance to the idea of getting up for no particular reason, of getting dressed, walking up and down, waiting, sitting at the table, listening at the door; in fact, doing everything that I had been doing now, day-in, day-out, with the exception of the time I spent in the infirmary, for nearly three years, without having any idea of why I did anything.

CHAPTER XXXII

GUERILLA WARFARE

I HAD read practically every book in the prison library, and I longed to break through the rules and have a book of my own in the cell – one that brought a whiff of the outside world. I wanted something that had not been simply allowed me by some minor official, but a book which seemed to have some life of its own and came to me as a present, a greeting, something personal and not impregnated with all the gloom of decades of prison life.

The chief warder was a particular friend of mine. I recognised his step in the corridor and the way he fitted the key into the lock. He used to bring my occasional letters and I knew that he was one of the few to whom I could talk openly, without the fear that everything I said would be somehow used against me. He entered my cell with a brief greeting and looked round. He examined the glass and ran a finger over the table, according to the regulations. In his hand was a bundle of letters and a book – a book! It was bound in red leather and had gold lettering on the back. My eyes fastened on that book – I knew it was intended for me – I trembled with joy and anticipation. I wanted to hold it in my hand and run my horny finger-tips over the red leather. The chief warder's hand was clasped firmly round the book. He said: 'No post for you this time.– There's a book come for you; but I don't know if you'll be allowed to have it.' Then, seeing my look of anguish, he added encouragingly: 'The Governor will decide about it.' He turned to go and I stopped him, stepping in front of him and nearly choking with agitation: 'Please, Sir, please . . . the book . . . when will the Governor . . . can't the decision be hurried up. . . ?' The chief warder said he had a lot to do, he was rather displeased, he could not understand why I made such a fuss about this book. He looked reprovingly at the row of books which stood in my cell; a book, this book – surely I could have a little patience – personally he did not care for books –'when you think of all the nonsense that's written in them!'– Well, well, he would tell the Governor – to-day was Friday; if I applied on Tuesday, the Governor would see me on Thursday, and then I could ask him about it myself. He went off slowly and with dignity, somewhat disapprovingly and a little impatiently, but full of kind intentions. The door shut slowly and I caught one more glimpse of his hand grasping the red leather binding of my book.

I was alone. I had forgotten to enquire who had sent the book; I knew neither the title nor the author nor the subject. I had no eyes for the little collection of thumbed and dirty library books on my table. I walked up and down trembling with pleasure and in a fever of impatience. I must have the book now, at once, to-morrow at the latest. To-day was Friday, and the next chance of my seeing the Governor was on the following Thursday – but that was impossible – a whole week – and then he would only give his decision and I might have to wait days before I actually got the book.

I decided to see the chief warder again. I had at least to know who had sent the book – to be able to make the most of the thought that I was not altogether forsaken. That book became the thing around which all my thoughts revolved – something had come into my life which gave it some reason – it was an oasis in the desert of my days, a sign, a shining token.

GUERILLA WARFARE

I stood at the door of my cell, hoping to hear a warder's footsteps; I climbed up to the high, narrow window, squinted through the bars into the yard, and saw the chief warder just disappearing through the door into the infirmary with something red in his hand. I knocked at my door – dead silence. I banged hard with my knuckles. Keys rattled in the corridor; a warder unlocked the door surlily. I enquired when the chief warder was coming back. Not to-day. So there was no hope for that day!

The day passed; I waited. I knew it was absurd – but is the sick feeling of expectancy ever cured by that knowledge? I kept on hearing steps and each time hope rose in me afresh. After lights-out I lay on my bed and tried to remember how often it had happened during the past years that the door had clanged open again after locking-up time and the warder had after all brought what I had been waiting for all through a wretched day. No one came. I was tired. I was filled with a mad fury. These walls, this door – they prevented one's doing the most ordinary things. Why on earth could I not simply go to the Governor – a few words, a couple of minutes, and everything would be straight.

It was dark. I lay awake for a long time, worrying about that book. If only I had it! How often I had fastened the mirror to the top of the window, so that it caught the light of the lantern outside and reflected it on to the table. By that wretched glimmer I had read all through long sleepless nights books that I almost knew off by heart. To-day I would have taken the red leather book close, quite close, to the mirror and turned over the pages and lost myself in a world that was unutterably far away – and which began just the other side of the wall.

I went to sleep and my last thought was the book. I woke up and my first thought was the book. Until a few hours ago

377

I had not even known of its existence. Now it had become the centre of my life. The day passed on leaden feet. I had asked to see the Governor first thing in the morning. But I could see him just as easily on Monday as to-day. During the walk in the small dusty yard I peered round every corner to see whether the chief warder did not happen to be passing. The warder in charge noticed me and kept a specially strict eye on me, ready to interfere at once if I tried to talk to the man behind me. In the cell I squatted on the stool, working nervously and indignantly tugging at each piece of bast that came into my trembling hands. Noon passed. The afternoon passed. I looked out of the window innumerable times. I listened at the door. I enquired of the officials in the passage; no, the chief warder had not yet passed on his daily round.

Evening came. To-morrow was Sunday and none of the senior officials appeared that day. I knew I should spend the whole of Sunday in just such a fever of impatience as to-day. No, I could not put up with the inevitable. The book meant a great deal to me – at that moment it meant everything to me. I tried to persuade myself to see reason. What did that book matter? I must be able to control myself. I had had to deny myself so much. I could not have the book to-day or to-morrow – perhaps in a week's time – and what then ? No, I did not mind at all about the book. But it was just the absurdity of the system which annoyed me. Why should I wait, since there was no reason, absolutely none, for waiting? Why should a wall be built up between me and this little wish – a wall which was unnecessary and distressing? I was wretched for the whole day – I worked myself up into a state of unreasoning bitterness. The whole thing seemed very simple to me – and these people were making it complicated. I was helpless, was utterly helpless, in the face of everything that was done to me. I was at their mercy, the power of decison had been taken from me. I was emasculated – I was no longer a man, I was a thing, a number, not allowed to have a will of its own. In my cell I was a microcosm since I was the only living thing it contained – outside I was nothing. Number 149 wanted a book? What for? Number 149 was in the cell. Number 149 had no concern with the world beyond.

Sunday. In the chapel up above, they were singing the *Te Deum*. The organ wheezed and its notes came faintly through the walls. I did not go to chapel. I sat at my table, shivering and cross, turning over an old magazine of the year 1886. But a smell of decay rose from its pages, which were yellow and thumbed. I had already looked at this volume countless times. Out-of-date pictures, childishly naïve, sickly sentimental. The stories in it were shatteringly insignificant, some 'news from far and near,' which was hopelessly uninteresting – as though the world of 1886 could be anything else to the prisoner of 1926. Thoroughly fed up, I shut the book and wandered up and down. To-morrow was Monday; to-morrow I might be able to see the Governor. If only I had my book now, a real Sunday book in its luxurious binding; if only I could get absorbed in some fate that was not my own; if I could feel a hand slipping into mine and leading me out of the cell, away from all the exasperation and hopelessness – it would have been *my* Sunday; as it was, it was only another prison-Sunday. And this day was wearier than all the other weary days.

How slowly the hours crept past.

Monday. The warder came and I was taken to the Governor's office. I had to wait in the passage, one of a long row of fellow-prisoners. We stood in a line at a distance of three paces from one another and the warder observed every glance that we threw at each other. We shivered as we waited; each man had got ready his request and was preparing the words in which he was going to utter it. Some of them had been reported for punishment and were standing there with anxious or defiant expressions, nervously twiddling their caps. The chief warder appeared, carrying a bundle of documents. He looked along the row searchingly. He asked me what I wanted. I said I wished to speak to the Governor about the book. He said that was utter nonsense; that I surely knew that for this special interview only important requests might be proffered and such as could not be delayed; that it would be arranged on Thursday. He thought I was making too much fuss about it; suppose everybody were to come about such trifles! So on Thursday, that would be all right – 'warder, this man can go back to his cell.' What was the book, I enquired quickly and who had sent it? He did not know, he had other things to think of; it was time I stopped this nonsense; he would speak to the Governor without fail. He went; and the warder took me back to my cell. The prisoners watched me curiously. I entered the cell, the door banged, and I felt a wild desire to smash up everything.

Tuesday. A grey, grey day. I waited. I put down my name for an interview.

Wednesday. To-morrow I should know. If all went well, I should have my book by Saturday.

Thursday. I tidied up my cell most carefully; I put on my heavy shoes; I kept on re-knotting my neckcloth; I washed my hands three or four times. I listened at the door; I stood by the window. Hour after hour passed. I picked up my work and dropped it. The barber came to shave me. I had to take off my coat and necktie again, and I sat on the stool patiently. The warder at the door went away for several seconds. I quickly asked the barber where the Governor was. In the first division, said the barber who went about all over the building. He whispered that 'the old man' seemed to be in a bad mood. The two carpenters from the fourth division who had fought the other day had been put under arrest and had been relieved of their posts. The warder reappeared. The barber finished his work. I was alone again. It would not be long now before the Governor came. He appeared and was not at all in a bad mood. He greeted me jovially: 'How are you? Well, what is it you want?' The chief warder opened his note book and sucked his pencil. I wanted the book, I said; and could I not have it handed out extra quickly?

'Oh, yes; the book. Yes – yes, I'll let the chaplain have a look at it. – Good day.'

Days passed – three whole days. Three times I asked the chief warder. The chaplain had the book. The chaplain had taken the book home and could not be got at for the moment. The chaplain was going away for several days directly after the service on Sunday. The chief warder waved me away irritably when I approached. He hurried down the passage when I knocked on the door of my cell.

On Tuesday I applied for an interview. On Thursday I saw the Governor. The chaplain still had the book. I should hear, all in good time. I did not hear. I lived in a state of tension: hour after hour I waited for some communication. I was lazy and bad-tempered over my work. Each unoccupied moment gave me a fresh opportunity to inveigh against things. I heard from an attendant that the chaplain had come back. I applied for an interview with the chaplain. Days passed; I waited. I was taken to his room. The chaplain was standing, and appeared somewhat astonished that I, who had been entered on the books as a Dissenter, should wish to speak to him. He looked at me over his spectacles. Oh yes, the book; well, he had not had time to read it yet. He would give the Governor his opinion. He turned away towards the writing desk and began unpacking his lunch; I was dismissed.

I waited. I was oppressed, filled with bitterness. In the

evening I banged on the wall of the next cell The man in it climbed on to the table and came to the window. I poured out my woes to him in a whisper. Yes, that was how it was, he said; surely I had been in the place long enough now not to be surprised. All I could do was to go for an interview every week and keep on reminding them about it. The 'old man' was not a bad sort, but he could not always do as he liked – it was the system that was at fault. Had I nothing left to read? To-morrow morning when the water jugs were put out he would lay one under my dustpan – a splendid story, he said, 'The Circus King's Daughter.' No, I said, thank you very much. I had read that one – and besides it was not simply for the sake of having something to read. I wanted my book, this particular one, with its red leather binding – it had been sent from home. Yes, yes, he could understand and – 'Look out, 149!' he said. The warder came round with his dog and shouted 'Silence there!'

It was Thursday again. The Governor came for the inter-views. Ah yes, the book. He must tell me that the book would not be given to me. The chaplain did not think it was suitable for prisoners. It was immoral. I sat up at this, and listened tensely. I enquired with elaborate politeness whether the Governor could tell me who had sent me the book. The Governor looked questioningly at the chief warder. He cleared his throat and said yes, it was from a lady with whom I was closely connected. I got the Governor to assure me that this lady who was so closely connected with me counted as a relative according to the prison regulations. I said, and every word was coldly deliberate, that I must consider it an unjusti-fiable insult to my relatives on the part of the chaplain, if he characterised any book they sent me as immoral. My relatives did not send me immoral books. My relatives were morally at least on a level with the chaplain. Besides, I should like to

enquire why the chaplain had any authority over me, considering that I was a Dissenter. Of course, said the Governor, it
was not meant that way. Immoral! Well, well – the book
simply was not suitable for prisoners in the chaplain's view;
and he must agree with this view. He knew the book and it
contained passages which might excite me, as a prisoner,
unnecessarily. That must be avoided for the sake of the peace
of the establishment. The chaplain had given his opinion in his
capacity as an official, not as a curator of souls. 'You must be
sensible,' said the Governor. Look here,' and he appeared
slightly embarrassed, 'we want to do the best we can for you.
You are a young man, you see, and this kind of book . . .' I
said I quite understood, and I requested to be transferred to a
juvenile institution. Though I was young, I had been subjected
to the most rigorous punishment; and if I was too young to be
able to read books like this, I was also too young to bear the
full punishment. The Governor was pained. He turned away.
'I cannot give you the book,' he said shortly, and the chief
warder made a note of it. I pulled myself together and asked
for a complaints form. 'Very good,' said the Governor to the
chief warder, 'give the man a complaints form.' And then he
went and with him the chief warder, whose face wore a severe
official expression. The door banged more sharply than usual
and I was alone.

I wrote my complaint on the slate. It had to be short; it
must not be worded in any way that could be interpreted as
an affront, it must be formulated as a request; the official to
whom the appeals went was most particular. The instructions
said: 'Unfounded complaints render the prisoner liable to
disciplinary punishment.' Was my complaint unfounded?
Undoubtedly the Governor was within his rights in refusing
me a favour. He might even do it without giving reasons.
There remained the chaplain's insult to my people. But the

Governor had said that it was not meant that way. My complaint was unfounded. Could I withdraw? I wrote it all the same.

Two days later the chief warder came and brought me a form; but he did not bring a pen and ink. The chief warder was not wearing his official expression this time. He sat on the table, smiled and dangled his legs. He said I was a bit hasty, and hadn't I better reconsider the matter. He said he was speaking unofficially for once. What was the point of the whole affair? Good Lord, couldn't I get the damned book out of my head? After all I had to spend years in the place, and there was no point in getting across people; didn't I want to be let off any part of my sentence? He said my complaint was utter nonsense; did I expect that a state official would undermine the Governor's authority by reversing one of his decisions? Here was a form, but I was to be sure to think it over very carefully again. Just on account of a book! He had always thought I was more or less reasonable; and, after all, I made pretensions to some education. Well, he would give me time – his intentions were good. He went without having cast the usual look round the cell.

For a long time I sat undecided. Yes, my complaint was absurd. But I wanted my book. For weeks this book had been the pole to which my every thought turned. I longed for that book. Whatever could it be? Immoral? What did the chaplain call immoral? What would the other officials call immoral? I simply had to have that book. Should all my efforts go for nothing? I knew I should have no peace until I felt that red leather binding in my hands, until I looked through the pages. So I wrote my complaint. I sent for pen and ink and wrote. I considered every word and forgot neither to leave the regulation margin, nor to end up 'Your obedient servant,' nor to grin derisively at myself as I did so. Then I waited for the chief warder to fetch the form.

GUERILLA WARFARE

Days passed. I was taken up to see the chief warder. I stood in the passage in a long line of other prisoners. My turn came and I walked into the room. The chief warder was sitting at the table writing. At his feet lay the watchdog. The chief warder kept me waiting. My eyes wandered round the room and I saw – my book. It was lying on the shelf among the things that were done with. There was no doubt, it was my book. The red cover shone enticingly. I looked at it, fascinated. I tried to decipher the title. The chief warder made a movement and I felt as if I had been caught in the act. He asked after the state of my finances; he enquired about one thing and then another; but he said nothing at all about my complaint. He made notes about various things. Then the point of his pencil broke. He rose, went to the window, turned his back to me, intent on sharpening his pencil. I took a deep breath and one step sideways. My heart beat madly. I snatched the book, my red book and stuffed it under my coat. With my left hand I twisted the tail of my coat behind and I blew out my chest, to keep the book in place. The watchdog followed my movements with almost human eyes. I had stolen my book! I stepped back, pale, shivering, terrified. The chief warder turned. I looked fixedly at the corner and he said: 'That will do; you may go. Next man!' I stumbled to the door and pressed the book to me under my brown uniform. I went back to my place in the rank, feeling a sensation of enormous joy and relief. The warder took me back to my cell, he unlocked the door and locked it. I dashed over to the table, piled the library books one on top of the other, extracted my book with numb fingers and laid it behind the pile, ready to cover it at any moment if the necessity arose. I stroked the binding with the back of my hand. I opened the title page and read: *Stendhal, Red and Black.*

CHAPTER XXXIII

1926

ONE'S memory of any period in life is a sort of mosaic of tiny daily events, like a painting whose stiff lines and pale colours on a dusty grey background show the subject in no strong relief. The slow succession of days grew to be so unreal that there seemed to be no beginning and no end. There were often times when I was unable to prevent myself from feeling that things would go on in the same way for ever – that I should never be free. A day had, indeed, been specified when sentence was passed upon me, on which I was to be released at 3.10 p.m. But this date, as the end to a particular period of time, had grown to have no meaning for me, because I was utterly incapable of realising that outside the walls the world was wide and full of movement.

Existence in the cell had grown to be shadowy, because everything that occurred was related to definite presuppositions. The cell permitted no deviation from this, no excitement, no exaltation, no fervour, nothing of all that made life really worth while. Its pressure destroyed will power by making everything seem contemptible, by beating down every in-dividuality; it prevented impulse, quenched passion, and left as the sole fixed point a vague, delusive hope of freedom, which gradually lost its distinct outline.

If the aim of this process was punishment, then the punish-ment had no sense. Nobody could 'gain strength by sincere repentance' through it; no one could achieve a 'calm reverence for justice'; and none of those who decreed the punishment believed in it either. The Governor and the chaplain and every single official from the highest to the lowest were carefully evasive when I asked them during conversations which were graciously vouchsafed to me whether they really believed that this form of punishment had any sense. They cautiously entrenched themselves behind paragraphs and laws, and unanimously declared that they were only doing their duty; and acknowledged equally unanimously how uncomfortable they felt in carrying out this duty. Something was wrong here. The punishment was not logical. It might be serviceable or convenient for those who prescribed it and for those who carried it out, it might be sanctified by tradition or endorsed by experience – and not even a part of this was the case – one thing it was not: it was not the avenging power of an ethical principle which is promulgated and executed by a higher unity than that of a disunited people. For that reason the punishment was not logical, for that reason it was fruitless and irrational. Moreover, the conditions in which it was carried out were so unbearable, that one's natural instinct was to defend oneself against it.

Rumours of a fundamental reform of the prison-system had been prevalent. Not punishment but education was henceforward to be the central idea. Nobody had any further details as to the exact form this education was to take; the warders needed some time before they could bring themselves to pronounce the word 'progressive,' and still longer before they got any inklings of what it meant; they were never induced to look favourably upon it. When eventually the first instructions were issued, enormous care was taken to avoid giving the prisoners information as to their intention and tenor. However, enough filtered through to fill the workrooms and dormitories with eager surmises. Conjectures went so far, hopes rose so high, that bitter disappointment was bound to follow when the

committee slowly and carefully decided only to put into opera-
tion a part of the new regulations. One of these regulations
was that every prisoner on first arriving was to be put into the
first grade of a progressive system; if he behaved well during the
first nine months, he might be transferred to the second grade
at the discretion of the committee; prisoners could only reach
the third grade if they had never previously been convicted,
if they had served half their sentences, if they had been for
at least nine months in the second grade, if they had behaved
so well that not the slightest adverse criticism could be made of
them, and if the committee had decided unanimously and
finally that there was no chance of a relapse. The first grade
was to wear one green stripe on the sleeve, the second two and
the third three. The first measure taken by the prison officials
was to order green stripes to be provided; and everyone received
one green stripe. Nothing further happened for nine months.

At the end of the nine months, I was summoned before the
committee and the Governor informed me that I had been
promoted to the second grade on his recommendation; my
report had not, indeed, been altogether free from complaints,
he said gravely, but he hastened to add the emphatic assurance
that he did not consider me really bad. A second green stripe
was sewed on to my sleeve. Nothing further happened for
three months, except that I was allowed to spend a greater
proportion of my earnings on tobacco than was permitted to
prisoners in the first grade. In order to make the most of this
privilege I took to chewing tobacco.

Of the three hundred and fifty prisoners some thirty, among
whom was Edi, had been promoted to the second grade at the
same time as myself. I got into clandestine communication
with Edi, and between us we advised each of the prisoners in
the second grade separately to request an interview and to tell
the Governor as far as possible in the same words that the joy

of being promoted to the second grade was not at all overwhelming. The Governor kept strictly to the rule that the privileges were not to be granted all at once but gradually, according to deserts. So Edi and I induced the others to demand an interview every Thursday and to ask for a fresh privilege each time. When I had completed the nine months in the second grade, the Governor was able to point proudly to the fact that I was enjoying all the privileges allowed in the second grade: the light burnt for an hour longer in my cell; I was allowed to write and receive a letter once a month instead of every two months; I was allowed visitors more often; and within limits I was allowed to have books of my own. Within limits, that is to say, exclusively such works as would help the prisoner to improve his technical knowledge. I explained to the Governor that I had decided that authorship was a profession both lucrative and suited to me, and that I intended to devote myself to it strenuously. There was, in consequence, no book which was not calculated to improve my technical knowledge.

The committee then met in solemn convocation to bestow the signal honour of the third grade upon six prisoners. The third grade, said the Governor, was the bridge to freedom. He said that he hoped we should prove ourselves worthy of the great favour that had been conferred upon us, and he particularly expected – at this point he looked at me sharply – that the man who had been promoted to the third grade because he was a political prisoner, would not forget that anyone who expected to be treated decently must also behave decently. The third grade, he said, was an effort to awake an appreciation of higher things in the minds of the prisoners. It was up to us to prove that this was possible. Besides, if we had any special desires, we could always turn directly to him with absolute confidence. I promptly turned to him with absolute confidence and asked that Edi should also be promoted to the third grade: if I were to be treated as a political prisoner, he might surely claim the same right. Then I heard that Edi had been pardoned.

I met him in the passage. He hurried past me breathlessly. 'Pardoned,' he gasped and waved at me with an utterly helpless gesture. He ran on headlong, trembling, laughing, stammering, shouting at every convict and every warder, picking up things, throwing them down again, in haste and fear. In fear, for he was afraid of freedom; he was bound to be afraid of it, as I was afraid of it: as of something quite incomprehensible, something strange, to which one would be handed over even more unconditionally than to the cell. Would he really be free, I asked myself? He was going from a narrow cell into a dusty factory; he escaped from cramping bonds only to be faced with others no less oppressive. He ran along the passage and before he stepped into the office he turned once more and waved for the last time. I never saw him again. Years later I read his name in a newspaper: it stood in a list of other names, as a victim in a collision between the police and the unemployed. A letter which he wrote to me after his discharge was not given to me, as containing 'insulting and scandalous expressions.'

A period began for me that was a shade brighter than the four years which had passed. The Governor was very much in earnest about the new regulations, as indeed he was about every regulation, but by far the greater number of the warders did not take them seriously. It was of course absurd to expect them to develop an aptitude for pedagogy – honest fellows, who had been at their trade for decades. They had grown to be a part of the prison as they had of their curved swords and their gigantic bunches of keys, and they looked at one another shaking their heads dubiously, as the prisoners in the third grade took their weekly gymnastic class, skipping over ropes, bending knees, jumping over boxes and so forth. They grumbled that

that was the way to teach the blighters to climb over the prison wall and to bolt from the police. They complained at having to turn out the light an hour later in six cells, they jeered at the pathetic pictures and threadbare curtains in the common room, in which the six third-grade men were occasionally allowed to assemble. They did their best to play off mean tricks on the third grade wherever possible, and were utterly dumbfounded when they discovered that the Governor no longer unquestioningly accepted the warders' word, if it came to a dispute between them and the third-grade prisoners. Finally they withdrew sulkily and left us in peace, but did their best to catch us out and took opportunities of setting the other prisoners against us.

The prisoners in the first grade inveighed passionately against those in the second grade, until they got into the second grade themselves. Anyone who saw no prospect of getting into the third was from the very outset an opponent of progressive sentences, as a grossly unjust system. 'There goes the murderers' class!' said one of them, as we were once in the yard during our extra free time walking side by side instead of one behind the other. As a matter of fact, although the selection had in no sense been made dependent on the crime but entirely on a man's personal character and behaviour, not a single member of the third grade was in prison for any act against property or morals. There was a cobbler who had been sentenced to twelve years because he had killed a peasant in a hand-to-hand fight for making love to his wife; a sergeant-major, with a life-sentence, who had lain in wait for a tailor and shot him for declaring in an inn that he had stolen supplies during the war; a clerk sentenced to fifteen years, because he and his brother, who had died in prison, returning from the war and looking for work, had attacked a mine-owner and in fleeing from pursuers had shot a night watchman; a tramway conductor, in for ten years, because his loving wife had said on oath that he had put rat poison into her food; an engineer, twelve years, because he knifed a policeman in trying to prevent his father being arrested on what turned out later to be a false charge of stealing. All these men were very decent sociable fellows, whose only desire was to be left in peace to get on with their jobs. They could not understand why they should be treated as criminals and their talk turned on pretty girls with pleasantly rounded forms and the preparation of lavish meat dishes. When we met we played Halma or backgammon, and were agreed that the best-intentioned prison-system was not calculated to educate grown-up people to conform to an ideal type or to become loyal citizens, and that it was a meritorious procedure to procure tobacco by foul means as well as fair. In spite of its being forbidden, we smoked chewing tobacco and seaweed, and were determined not to give up this pleasure, even though we were running the risk of being pushed back to the infernal regions of the first grade if we were caught. Apart from that, the most jealous warder could hardly have anything against us, for we were up to every dodge and knew a good deal too much about most of them.

The permission which had been accorded me to have as many books as I liked had given more interest to my days. Now that I was no longer permanently tied to the cell, I buried myself in my books during every spare moment. I threw myself into a world which had grown strange and unspeakably precious to me; I read everything that came my way, pell mell, without plan or system, learnt English and Spanish on the Toussaint-Langenscheidt method, without succeeding in mastering the pronunciation to this day – '*era ciego de naci-miento*,' I shall never forget that first sentence in the Spanish primer – I read till my eyes ached after the light had been put out, by the pale gleam of the lamp in the yard and missed more sleep than ever. Sometimes I rose from the bed on which I had tossed throughout the long hours of the night as soon as the first streaks of dawn shone in the sky to do physical exercises till I trembled in every limb. Then I set to work and, by the time the attendant was clattering the coffee-urn round the passages, I had read a good many chapters and my only feeling was of annoyance at being interrupted. The Governor came to see me more often, to tell me how pleased he was that I had now created a world of my own. Even when I pointed out that he might have given himself this pleasure a great deal sooner, his imperturbable mildness suffered no diminution and his benevolence began to make me quite uncomfortable. He said he had never done anything but his duty and it was now his duty to exercise an educative influence over me. I did my best to disabuse him of any idea of the possibility of moral improvement in myself or my fellow-prisoners, but somehow our long conversations always ended in the astonishing mutual discovery that at bottom we were both quite decent conversable people, and that this fact could alter nothing of the sense or nonsense of the now sacred principle of education in prisons.

One day the Governor sent for me and when I stood before him, he asked me to take a seat. I was considerably taken aback, but the Governor insisted, and when I had sat down on a real upholstered chair with an altogether surprising back to it, he disclosed to me that he could give me the joyful news – I sprang up full of excitement, but he looked startled and motioned me to sit down again – that it was not beyond the bounds of possibility that within the next few weeks an official notice might arrive concerning my pardon and release. He could prophesy the most favourable outlook, for a Nationalist Government was at the helm and a far-reaching amnesty was in preparation.

After lights-out I lay on my bed with my arms crossed under

my head and stared at the ceiling on which were thrown the shadows of the bars in the trembling light of the lantern outside. I asked myself over and over again if it were really possible, if it were conceivable that a day would come, and come soon, perhaps even to-morrow, when I should not take down my bed in the evening, in order to woo sleep wearily and reluctantly; a day when the world would open out before me, a manifold world with women and ideas and movement and claims; a world which would be paralysing in its abundance, full of strong colours, of trees and houses and railways, of mountains and rivers, of men wearing real white collars, no dingy brown uniform, of animals, and an atmosphere that turned misty blue in the distance, a world that contained nothing of what surrounded me at present. This much was certain: the glory of this new world depended on its having nothing, absolutely nothing, in common with my present surroundings.

I tried to recall what life used to be like. But it was all pale and confused and the images came up with the vagueness of dreams; the faces of companions appeared – moments in the Baltic States – where on earth had that old peasant hut been – who was it lying in the ditch groaning – when had those shots flashed and quivered in the marsh – nights in a phantasmal attic, in which rifles were piled in a corner . . . it was all unreal, it meant nothing now, it was all strange and far away and no longer had any hold over me. And Kern – did he mean nothing to me either? No, by God – I rose and looked closely at the picture which had hung on my wall for four years – at whatever cost, I must be honest, I thought, and shivered a little. Was I posing about Rathenau too? I went back to bed and considered.

I forced myself to think of other things; I pondered over the last four years, ranging back and forth in them. So that had been my life for four whole years: screams from the arrest cells night after night, one took no more notice of them now; a

warder came, unlocked the cell, put his head round the door
and said: 'Pack your things!'; he banged the door and returned
after a quarter of an hour and said: 'Come on'; one went and
enquired where to and why; the warder said: 'Shut up,' opened
some other cell and said: 'In here!' the door banged and one
was left in a whirl of questions to which one never had an
answer; that was how one changed cells. Nobody knows
whether an animal that is moved from one stable to another
questions the reason for the proceeding. Anyhow I did.
Prisoners were never given a reason for anything that occurred
in their daily lives. At first I obeyed the most natural reaction
and did as Edi did – where was Edi now? – I refused to do what
I was told, until, after a fearful uproar that roused the whole
prison, the warders appeared and took such disciplinary
measures as are authorised by the regulations, spiced with the
not altogether friendly expression of the personal feelings of
unnecessarily alarmed officials. Later I delivered a lengthy
discourse to the astonished warder which had as its theme that
any order was a bad order whose reason was not at once
obvious, and anyone who gave it was not a good superior.
Faces appeared, sharp faces above brown uniforms. There was
Biedermann and old May and the infirmary orderly, and the
attendant from the arrest cells, and there was – now who was
that? – yes, it was the fellow who had sneaked on me when I had
passed Edi a screw of tobacco; and what was the name of the
brute who had given away my attempted escape, so as to get
himself pardoned? It had all passed. Nothing was real,
nothing permanent. The nights in the arrest cell – the time
when I had watched by Edi in the infirmary, the one-two-
three-four different pipes that I had managed to procure and
which had all been confiscated, and the fifth that I now kept
hidden among my books. By my books was the packet of letters
– how passionately I had longed for each one of them – and

each one had after all been a disappointment – among them was the one which had given me the last news of the outlaws. Where had I lately been reading about outlaws? Oh yes, in the Icelandic Sagas. There the outlaws were men who refused to conform to the ruling of their kindred and who therefore were driven out of the kingdom; they were allowed to keep their weapons, but anyone who was stronger than they might kill them. However, it had always been the most forceful men who refused to bow to authority and who therefore were outlawed; hence the situation was gradually reversed, because the respectable families weeded out their more vigorous elements and so in the end the outlaws broke out of the woods and became masters in the land. There were no penal institutions in those days – what was the use of these boyish dreams – ? There had been hours of raging despair; had I not held splinters of glass in my hand after my first attempt at escape had failed? Why on earth had I not done it then – just a little nick in an artery – why – why? And why did Senta bark, the watchdog whom I always heard scratching among the bushes at night outside my window, whom I had fed with bits of meat from my Sunday dinner so as to get him accustomed to me – why did he bark when I had got into the yard with a hook in my hand to help me climb the wall? – At Christmas I was always allowed a visitor. How I dreaded the moment when I should be fetched into the visitors' room by a warder, and how I longed for just this moment all through the year. How it had hurt when I turned once more and yet again and waved, and then looked down the long corridor, until the iron grating was closed and the inner door banged and then the outer and I stumbled back into the cell and threw myself across the table and – damn it. 'Awake, downtrodden of this earth,' Edi used to sing in the evenings when a distant scream broke the silence – someone was being given the cat in the arrest cells. And once Edi sang the song during the Christmas festivities instead of the Chorale and was removed. That service at Christmas! How furious I used to get when some of the prisoners began to howl; how indignant I got over the garlands and candles in the prison chapel and over the gaily coloured 'Glory to God in the highest and peace on earth, goodwill towards men.' Goodwill towards men – these tender appeals, how I loathed them; how I used to look for them just for the sake of working myself up into a rage over them. The chaplain, for instance, said one day from the pulpit that really at bottom the prisoners could not be blamed overmuch – it was just that they had been set a bad example – even children saw their mothers misbehaving with the night lodgers . . . Afterwards I demanded of the Governor that the chaplain should be compelled to state from the pulpit that at any rate he had not been referring to my mother. How he had screwed up his face when he came to me afterwards to apologise and to assure me that he had not meant anything of that sort. Hundreds of pictures, and not one of them really vivid – representing four years of my life. And none of this would go on when I was free, free. . . . Soon, incredibly soon.

Filled with raging unrest, I stood at the door for half the day now, listening whether my name were not being called, whether no one were coming to fetch me. I calculated day after day, night after night: now the petition must be with the Minister of Justice, now it would go to the President of the Republic, now to the Attorney-General. . . . The Governor visited me when anything occurred. He said that at a conference in Berlin which he had attended he had talked about my case to one of the officials of the ministry who had been present; that I might hope for the best. Another time he said that I had better be getting ready, the pardon might arrive any day. He arranged for my suit to be pressed and repaired; the supervisor came and took me up to his office; I spread out my things so as to get the smell of moth balls out of them. Then one day I was told that the Governor wanted to speak to me at once.

I ran so quickly that the warder could hardly keep up with me. One of the prisoners shouted: 'Congratulations!' warders laughed, the sun shone into the passages. The Governor said: 'Come in.' He did not offer me a chair. He was turning over papers in a file and his face was very pale. He looked at me over his glasses, cleared his throat and said: 'A fresh warrant has been issued against you. You are accused of the murder of Lieutenant Weigelt. To-morrow you will be taken away for trial.'

CHAPTER XXXIV

TRANSPORT

THE day dawned slowly. I drew back from the window shivering. The night had come to an end at last. I heard a sound in the passage. The key was inserted carefully into the lock, the door was opened. Thank God, something was going to happen. The chief warder whispered: 'Good morning.' I smiled and said: 'I feel as if I were going straight off to be executed.' The chief warder shook his head and muttered: 'Come, come, it's not going to be as bad as that!' I slowly picked up my little black cap and followed the chief warder. I had never seen the passages so utterly deserted as they were in the wan grey light of the dawn. We walked on tiptoe. A muffled figure passed us – the night watchman. On the warders' floor a single gas jet was burning. The chief warder said under his breath: 'The Governor wishes you the best of luck.' He did not look at me as he spoke. He opened the door into the office. Within stood the warder who was to accompany me. I threw a rapid glance at the transport paper – it was red, so I was to be handcuffed. For a moment everything in me revolted. Then I quietly held out my arms. The bracelets snapped. I put my arms up to my face and tore off the green stripes with my teeth. The chief warder raised his hand deprecatingly. We turned to go – the chief warder stretched out his right hand, then he looked at the handcuffs and dropped it again. A door was closed, a second, a third. We stood at the main gate, the night watchman unlocked it, we stepped out into the road. I turned once more and looked up at the grey walls of the prison. Over the Gothic arch of the gateway were carved the words: 'AVE MARIA.'

The streets were empty, the windows closed, the curtains drawn. A waiter came out of the 'German Emperor' Hôtel, wearing a dirty white apron. He saw me, and the hand which he was just raising to his mouth to cover a yawn stopped half way. A number of men emerged from a café. They stood still and looked at me. I shut my eyes and passed on. Their eyes seemed to be burning into my back, so that I voluntarily ducked my head. We came to a wide road planted with trees. The giant elms spread their branches over us in the morning sun. I took a deep breath. The morning air swept the dust of the cell out of my lungs. We walked more rapidly, our steps crunching on the ground. 'Where is the Castle Hill?' I asked. I knew that there was a Castle Hill somewhere near the town. The warder jerked his thumb over his shoulder. I turned; there lay the town, a jumble of brown and black roofs, and in the middle of it a high grey wall broken by innumerable little black rectangles. The streets in the outskirts seemed to be groping like long feelers far out into the gently sloping country. To my disappointment I could see no hill. A workman came towards us on a bicycle. He turned to look at me; I stared back at him and he rode on for some distance with his head turned to watch me.

The station, a small red roughly plastered building, stood among trees. The warder rushed me through the barrier, holding me by the sleeve. A woman with a big market basket drew aside. Railway officials passed slowly up and down. Travellers appeared with boxes and bags. We stood behind a pillar. The grass between the stones was full of dew. The train came thundering into the station, the prison van stopping exactly opposite to where I stood. A door was thrown open, I climbed up awkwardly, my handcuffs were taken off. I found myself in a dark narrow corridor on both sides of which were numbered doors. One of these was opened, the train warder gave me a little push, I went inside and the door was shut. The space was just big enough for me to sit on the narrow bench. If I stood on the seat with my knees bent, I could put my head against the close black wire netting and look out through one of the narrow vertical interstices. The train steamed off.

I pressed my eyes to the grating and clung to the wall with my hands. Very soon my legs began to tremble. Farmhouses flew by, bushes, long rectangular cornfields, ripe and yellow. We came to a level crossing, a cart was standing by it and the farmer in charge was smoking a pipe. I saw the top of a church tower above the trees. We passed little stations whose names I could not read. Every time the train started, my knees gave way and I nearly fell off the seat. Soon my eyes began to ache, for the draught was strong. I rubbed them and regretted it immediately. I had missed a big motor van, I could see the grey tarpaulin cover vanishing in the distance. Advertisement hoardings rose among the fields. We clattered past fences and the red walls of a factory. There were no human beings in the landscape. The distances were lost in mist.

Long trains of goods waggons on side lines proclaimed that we were coming to a good sized town. We had been travelling for about an hour. The brakes squealed. My door was suddenly opened, I shot round and tumbled off my bench. 'Get out,' said the warder.

'Aren't we going any farther?' I asked in astonishment. The warder did not reply. I climbed out of the van. Three policemen were standing outside and a man with a sheep-dog. While the handcuffs were put on me again, I looked along the platform. A great many people stared at me inquisitively. We passed the barrier; a policeman took me by each arm, one walked in front, and the man with the sheep-dog went behind me, so close that he trod on my heels every now and then. I held my arms stiffly in front of me and kept my eyes fixed on the ground. We walked very fast.

We went through a park. The people made way for us from afar when they saw us coming. I had the feeling that they were all standing still and watching me. I tried to look about me cynically, but not with any great success. If they had at least known who I was, I thought; I blushed and tried to get my hands up to my cap to pull it farther down over my face. The policemen immediately tightened their hold on my arms. 'Is this Liegnitz?' I asked. No answer.

A lady with two greyhounds stopped and shortened the leash. She was wearing a light hat which shaded her face – I wished I could have seen her face. We crossed over a square. A tramway passed along a narrow track, the conductor leant over the railing at the back and stared at me. Very soon I felt that I could not bear it any longer; I avoided everybody's eye, and the people passed by me like shadows. But that seemed to be degrading me still further; so I pulled myself together and looked a man straight in the face: He turned away. After that I looked everyone straight in the face and felt better at once. A little girl aged about six and wearing a white frock came out of a gateway. She stopped, looked at me, suddenly pointed a fat finger at me and said: 'There goes the bad man!' God bless you, you little fair creature, and may you be married to an honest baker some day.

The police lock-up was in a narrow dirty side street. A warder took me up the worn steps of a rickety staircase into a big room full of beds, took off the handcuffs and locked me in. I went straight to the window. It was large but heavily barred. There was nothing in the room except the beds, on which lay dirty grey straw mattresses covered with sacking and full of the strangest bumps. I pushed one of the beds over near the window and climbed on to it, so as to be able to see out better; but my eye met only a wall. I wandered up and down.

Everything was cold and dead in me. My brain registered what I saw but it conveyed nothing to me. There must have been bugs in the room, it smelt so horrible. Not that that was anything new; there had always been bugs in my cell. Every now and then when the morning's bag got too big, I used to complain and then one of the other prisoners came and ran the flame of a soldering lamp along the cracks in my bed, so that the smell of charred wood and burnt paint filled the cell for days afterwards. The same thing had evidently been done here. Prisons smell the same everywhere.

A warder brought my dinner, a kind of thick tasteless gruel, no meat. I left it, I did not feel like eating. In an hour's time the warder returned and silently removed the full bowl. After a while he brought me a newspaper. 'Here's something for you to read,' he said and departed rapidly. It was a Catholic Sunday paper; I read it from beginning to end: a moment later I had completely forgotten what was in it. I walked up and down.

Towards evening there was a great commotion and a crowd of men carrying sacks and bundles appeared. They filled the room with shouts and curses and at first took hardly any notice of me. Some of them had no shoes on, their unspeakably dirty feet emerged from ragged stained trousers, which were hardly holding together. They were talking Polish of which I could not understand a word. After a while they began to get more and more excited and I inferred that I was the cause. I leant against the wall and took stock of them. A penetrating smell rose from them. 'Got any tobacco?' one of them enquired. I shook my head silently. They jabbered again. Finally one of them knocked at the door; the warder appeared; they all began talking at once, and finally their spokesman said in broken German that they were not criminals, they were Polish casual labourers, who were only being turned out of the country, and they could not be expected to spend the night with a convict. The warder awkwardly told me to follow him. He took me into another smaller room, in which an old man with bare feet was sitting on one of the two beds. This old man had been taken up as a vagrant. I asked him with elaborate courtesy whether he had any objections to spending the night with a convict. He grinned at me and the warder muttered that unfortunately none of the single cells were vacant.

The window in this cell was small but open. I leant out as far as I could, and looked into a narrow street of low, neglected houses. Children were playing in the gutter. Every now and then a workman passed. A cart clattered round the corner. A woman stepped out of a dark doorway and called: 'Siegfried!' in a querulous voice. The lamplighter appeared, turning on the gas jet with a long pole, which he re-shouldered as soon as the wan light had flamed. I saw his shadow again when he got to the next lamp. It grew dark. The old man still crouched motionless on the bed. I stood at the window for hour after hour. The children disappeared; the lights in the houses were extinguished; a girl slipped out of a side alley, looked up and down the street and then stood in a dark corner under my window; I could just see her in silhouette. She was wearing a handkerchief over her head. For a long time she waited without moving; then a step sounded along the dark road. The girl softly called a name which I did not catch. A figure ran towards her; they met and embraced. Then they walked up the street slowly, their arms entwined. From time to time they stopped and kissed, finally they vanished in the gloom. I turned back into the cell and groped for my bed. I lay down on the sack and pulled the stinking horse blanket over myself. Then at last the old man stirred. He put his legs up on to the

bed and stretched himself out. His breath came in snorts.
Up to now he had not spoken a single word. I said: 'Good
night.' Silence. Suddenly the old man said into the darkness:
'Anyone who likes can lick my arse.'

Morning. I got up and washed in a small dirty basin with
no soap, and used my handkerchief as a towel. The old man
lay curled up under the horse blanket, making no movement.
A warder came in and asked: 'What's your name?' I told him
and he said: 'Come on.' At the door the same *cortège* awaited
me as on the previous day. I was handcuffed and we proceeded
through the town. We met a long train of school children; a
good many of them stopped, the teacher signed to them and
they went slowly on. There were men with despatch cases,
women with shopping bags. The morning sun lay on the
streets, tingeing the grey with gold. The traffic increased. A
great many motor cars whizzed past us, with long shining
bodies. Every face was turned towards me. I said aloud:
'Anyone who likes can lick . . .' 'Shut up!' the policeman on
my left interrupted gruffly. We arrived at the railway station
and pushed through the barrier. The train was already standing
at the platform. A number of sea-gulls were flying across the
lines, swift, white, fluttering shadows. Some of the passengers
were feeding the birds. They stopped when they saw me. I
scrambled into the gloomy prison van, squeezed into my
compartment and climbed on to the seat. After a time the man
who had accompanied me with the dog came and brought me a
hunk of bread and a piece of bacon wrapped in paper. The
train-warder brought me a mug of thin hot coffee. The train
started.

With my knees bumping against the side of the cell, I tore
scraps of bacon off the piece and swallowed them. In the next
cell someone was humming a tune. Whenever the train stopped
I heard the prisoners talking to each other through the bars.

THE OUTLAWS

It was oppressively hot. The air quivered over the fields. I felt as if I had never seen so much sun before. 'Sagan,' shouted the guard. Suddenly there was an uproar in all the cells. 'Hullo, sweetheart,' shouted the man in the next box. I strained to see on to the platform. Some policemen were walking up it with a girl between them; a girl wearing a coarse brown dress and a shawl, a prisoner. The girl had little curls over her ears; she threw a lightning glance up at my window, smiled and passed on. Directly afterwards I heard a noise in the corridor. The prisoners were yelling aloud unchecked. 'Baby!' one of them called, while in the cells at the end someone sniggered. 'Damn fine girl,' said my neighbour loudly. The train squeaked and jerked as it got slowly under way.

At a small station surrounded by woods we stopped. Apparently our coach had been slipped. I could see a bush directly in front of my window and a pile of tree-trunks from which resin was oozing slowly. The forest radiated a hot, aromatic, stupefying scent. My clothes were sticking to me with the heat, and I took off my coat and waistcoat. My neighbour knocked on the wall. 'Where are you from?' he asked. I told him. He came from the prison at Görlitz and was going to Cassel in answer to a summons. He had done three years already and had another four to go, apart from what he might get in Cassel. I told him my name and enquired for one of my friends who was also supposed to be in Görlitz. Yes, he was there, library attendant. Excitedly I asked for further details. The heat grew unbearable. I stripped off my shirt too and sat there with nothing on but my trousers. The warders took no notice of our conversation. My neighbour asked aloud what the girl was in for. 'Perjury; two years,' came the answer. 'Hullo, ducky!' – 'Hallo!' The girl had a clear voice. She laughed. She was going home soon, she said; had been summoned to Halle as a witness. My neighbour asked if she wouldn't like to sleep with him? 'I don't mind,' she answered merrily. 'if you'll marry me afterwards!' The prisoners grew clamorous, groaned over the heat, and laughed at the girl, who had a saucy answer for each of them. We were held up for four hours, and the noise died down gradually.

At last we went on again, past woods and wide fields, moorland and heath, and occasional villages, which seemed to be flattened down to the earth. At Kottbus I heard doors being unlocked along the corridor. I put on my clothes at top speed. There were heavy steps and the rattle of keys. A warder unlocked my door and asked: 'What's your name?' I told him. He said: 'Come on.' I climbed stiffly out of the van. The others were drawn up in two lines on the platform, the girl alone at the back. Some were wearing their own clothes with tidily pressed shabby trousers, others were in the brown prison uniform like myself. I was the only one who was handcuffed. 'I suppose he's dangerous?' I heard the girl say. I turned and laughed. 'Very dangerous indeed,' I said. 'Rape and murder three times.' The girl recoiled somewhat, then she said sturdily 'I don't believe a word of it.' She looked at me and asked: 'I suppose you're a political?' The warder hustled me away. We stumbled across the lines and went along a waiting train. The windows of the compartments were immediately full of heads. 'Shut up grinning!' said the warder to the prisoner behind me. We came to the new prison van. I was the first to get in and I looked round for the girl. 'Hurrah for Moscow!' she cried suddenly. The warder gave me a push and locked me into a cell. The walls in the new cell were scribbled over closely, one name directly beside another, written in pencil or scratched with some sharp object. After a good many of the names was a swastika or a Soviet star. I read them carefully, running my finger along every line – and suddenly I found Jörg's name. Beyond question it was his handwriting. I felt enormously cheered. I pulled a button off my trousers and laboriously scratched my own name immediately under Jörg's. I wondered whether to put any sign after it. Eventually I added the day's date.

So the monotony of the journey was broken. Suddenly I began to take an interest in life again. I sat on the bench and shut my eyes which had got sore from looking out of the window. I sat there for hours and hours.

It had grown dark. We had been travelling for a long time. Scraps of talk still passed between the cells. We were apparently arriving at a big station.

The warder came and asked: 'What's your name?' I told him. He said: 'Come on.' How sick I was of the whole procedure. Some policemen were waiting outside. Policemen are alike everywhere. They say the same thing in the same tone of voice and they have the same turn of the wrist when they are putting handcuffs on a man. We went through the crowded station. Even stations are alike everywhere and people. The green van was waiting by the exit. We got in, the girl sitting in a separate division. I chewed a bit of my bacon. We clattered away; distant sounds, the bells of trams, the hooters of motor cars, reached us faintly. We were unloaded in a dark yard and hastily searched for contraband. Then we were taken to a large cell, in which we saw by the wan illumination, a row of low camp beds, without any covers and with straw mattresses which were spotted with blood. In one corner stood a high tin bucket which smelt unspeakably foul. There were six of us and I recognised some of the voices. One of them introduced himself to me politely. He was the man who had been in the next cell to me on the train and who was going to Cassel. He said he was a manufacturer of vinegar. It turned out that his factory consisted of a basement in the north of Berlin, in which he and his brother brewed vinegar. He entertained the whole company, who lay on the beds swearing at the bugs which appeared from every fold of the mattresses. They talked about the public prosecutor, prison officials and women. The topic 'woman' is inexhaustible. One of them told dirty stories in a thick, coarse voice: it sounded as if he were dribbling at the mouth. At last the manufacturer of vinegar said: 'We've had about enough filth.'

I kept on waking up. Groans and curses came from the beds. The air in the room was heavy and stuffy. My head buzzed and I felt desperately ill. I staggered over to the bucket and was very sick. One man jumped up and hurled his mattress wildly on to the floor, stood beside it like a shadow and stared at the window. Others tossed restlessly from side to side. I went to sleep again and awoke at dawn. Very soon we were all up. One of the men twisted a screw of tobacco and it was passed round. I took a puff of it too, to get rid of the nasty taste in my mouth. Then we drew lots for turns to use the bucket. It was so full that the contents splashed over the top when anyone went to it now. Every time the lid was raised, a wave of the most pestilential stench went through the room; and the window would not open. We sat about dazedly, unwashed, weary and hungry, our faces etched wanly against the gloomy grey morning light.

Gradually there began to be signs of life in the passages. We heard dragging footsteps and the clatter of pails. From under one of the beds which stood by the wall a brown stream suddenly trickled into the cell: apparently the passages were being swabbed. We moved the bed and found a small square ventilator leading into the passage just above the level of the floor. I bent down and saw a pair of thick legs encased in coarse grey woollen stockings and ending in clogs, and heard giggles. The vinegar manufacturer threw himself down full length on to the floor and called to the women through the hole. They were prisoners, cleaning the passages. The vinegar manufacturer whispered eagerly through the hole to the women. 'Come here,' he cried suddenly, urgently, 'Come here, nearer . . .' he put his arm through the hole and began to groan. Little hoarse cries came from outside.

Instantly all the prisoners hurled themselves at the hole as if at a given signal. They threw themselves on to the filthy floor and pushed each other aside violently, one of them jumped on to the vinegar manufacturer's back. Now there was a jumble of men on the floor by the hole, their bodies and limbs twitching, and a wild scrimmage began. 'Is it a young one?' gasped one craning his neck; he was pushed aside but forced his way in again his eyes glittering with desire. All hands were thrust through the hole. . . .

Suddenly they scattered; the door was thrown open and a warder came in. 'What's your name?' he asked me. I told him. 'Come on,' he said. I accompanied him without troubling to give so much as one backward look.

The train jogged through the valley of the Saal. I did not take my eyes from the crack in the window. We came to Naumburg and I tried to see the prison and the former Cadet School. I knew we could not be far from Bad Kösen. I stared at the wooded slopes and was filled with indescribable emotions. My lips were dry and my head burning. I clung to the wire grating. At last we came to Bad Kösen.

There was the path which led through the woods to the Rudelsburg. The gently rounded heights swung past. There was the Saal again. I pressed my eyes so close to the rusty wire that the whites were almost touching it. There was the Rudelsburg, growing straight up out of the yellowish rock. Now now . . . I stared up . . . the Saaleck . . . two grey shadows, the towers reared their stately height, we passed slowly round them and they were gone.

TRANSPORT

'Kern!' I screamed . . . gone . . . gone.

I fell back on to the seat and my head crashed on the wall. The warder unlocked the door and looked in. 'I'll give you a little fresh air,' he said and fastened the door with a short chain so that it stood a hand's breadth open. I sat on the bench without moving a muscle.

At Cassel I spent a restless night alone in a clean cell.

The train stopped at Marburg. The warder came and asked: 'What's your name?' I told him. He said: 'Come on!' Two policemen handcuffed me and took me between them. We walked along the platform. Students in coloured caps were standing about everywhere. We went straight through them. They fell into an embarrassed silence as we passed, stepped back a little and stared at me. I looked at their faces carefully. There might be one I knew amongst them. There – why, surely, I knew that one – the fat one with his face so hacked about? Surely we had been in Upper Silesia together? Of course, that was he. I passed close by him as he stood with his follow-students. I looked at him woodenly. He glanced at me in surprise. Then he recognised me, recoiled a little, his hand went up, stopped – suddenly he turned away with a shrug and stared into space. As I passed I said aloud: 'He's going to be a public prosecutor.' The policeman said: 'Shut up.' I climbed wearily into the new train and sat without moving till we arrived at our destination.

The next day I was questioned for eight hours on end by the examining magistrate.

CHAPTER XXXV

1927

I was brought up for examination a great many times, I answered a great many questions, and I signed my name to a great many affidavits. Every time the examining magistrate stepped into the room, the thick bundle of papers which he carried under his arm had increased in girth. When he finally collected his papers after the last interrogation and packed them away into a blue file, he tapped the collection triumphantly and said that the preliminary examination was now over, as he had an exact description of the events in question. I had no confidence in his smug assurance. I had plenty of opportunity to realise the curious difference that existed between what I had prepared through the long wakeful nights and what was finally written in the reports of the examinations and signed by me. The record contained in the three thousand pages of yellow foolscap in the bulging blue file, had no doubt been put together most carefully; there was indeed evidence and to spare from the statements of witnesses, from police reports, from statistics; this narrative followed the action in every detail, yet it was not in the least like what had really happened. Nothing of what had lived and moved in those inexpressibly confused times was resurrected, but a counterfeit arose to have a phantasmal life of its own, conceived in many minds of which each one changed events to suit his own preconceived notions. Thus I failed to recognise the deed in this dry reproduction and the examining magistrate erred just at the very points where he thought his information was most accurate. Of one hundred and twenty eye-witnesses, sixty said exactly the opposite to what the other sixty said; the bill of indictment turned out to be a document revealing extraordinary credulousness, and in the course of the trial, the drama turned to comedy.

For the murdered Lieutenant Weigelt suddenly appeared in the court, bearing no kind of resemblance to the body of a drowned man, and made his deposition. During seven days of the trial he stood at the bar, his head bowed, never once looking at the dock, answering reluctantly and haltingly the questions which the judge and the public prosecutor and the counsel for the defence put to him. He admitted that he had dragged himself as far as a water-works of which the light was visible from the scene of action, yet in spite of the searching questions put by the judge, he failed to explain why he had told the gate-keeper, to whom he had appealed for help, that he had been the victim of an attack by unknown robbers. The public prosecutor sought to discover by a severe cross-examination on what grounds Weigelt had departed for an unstated destination from the hospital to which he had been taken, two hours before the police enquiry was to take place, and had thus left the authorities for nearly five years in the most mortifying ignorance of the mysterious events of that night. Weigelt protested that he had only the foggiest recollection of the details; he then went on hastily to relate how he had spent two years working as an ostler under an assumed name, and was now the chief engineer in a large works. He protested in answer to a mild question put by the counsel for the defence that he had no interest in having the matter brought up again; on the contrary, it was extremely painful to him, which, with the exception of the public prosecutor, everyone in the Court seemed ready to believe.

Nevertheless, the public prosecutor, hair and robes waving

wildly, defended his documents for seven days. He referred
each of the principal witnesses to the fact that the story sounded
quite different in the documents; but each time he only elicited
the gentle reproach that there might be a variety of interpre-
tations. He bounced out of his mountains of books and papers
like an india-rubber ball, making confusion yet worse confounded; but he sank back again and rustled his documents
when the defence with a few deft touches presented events
in a more favourable light. He fought as a lion in the wilderness
of politics and law, roaring his anger at the depravity of the
world; but the thunder of his rhetoric availed as little to extin-
guish the tittering in the Court as did the judge's appeals to the
public not to behave as if in a theatre.

Nevertheless, I felt as if I were at a theatre. I sat in the dark,
taking practically no part in the proceedings, and filled with
astonishment at finding how little I was really interested in
what was going on! I had made my deposition to the inkpot
which was standing on the judge's table. Now I listened to the
sounds in the stuffy court into which I had suddenly been
thrust, and the pleasure I felt at having an interruption in the
humdrum life of the cell was stifled in the helpless feeling of
being at once the chief actor and the victim. What concern
had I in the talk going back and forth between the prosecutor
and the counsel for the defence? I pulled myself together and
listened, stood up and asked questions, explained and interrupted. After all, I might as well defend myself, I decided,
and delighted in the chance to take an active part in something
again: annoying the public prosecutor and the jury, who leant
forward and stared at me frowning, and confusing the witnesses
for the prosecution. Undoubtedly what was being done
here was of considerable moment to me; but it had nothing at
all to do with the act for which I was being tried. Hundreds
of pairs of eyes were staring at me from all over the Court, an

excited gentleman in a black robe and wearing pince-nez was gesticulating violently, officials in green uniforms and with mighty moustaches were listening interestedly. A man in a biretta was reading charges from crackling parchment and a stammering youth was taking the oath with his hand raised. But what had all this to do with the act itself? The counsel for the defence turned over mighty tomes containing the decisions of the Supreme Court, a juryman took notes, the special reporters sat at the Press-table, writing that the criminal tendencies of the accused were obvious from the structure of his retreating forehead and the fact that his eyes were set close together; or they drew their readers' attention to the truth that had been established by the depositions of the witnesses: that the accused had in his earliest youth stolen apples from neighbouring gardens.

Then my late companions came into the Court one after another; I hardly recognised them and they seemed hardly to recognise me. They came, throwing a rapid glance in my direction, and stood up before the judge and said their say. I looked at them and could see no trace of what had once bound us together. These were well-shaven men in black coats; they announced themselves as having sedate, respectable employments and appeared to be quite ready to leave out of account the witnesses' fees which were their due. They sat on the witnesses' bench when they had finished, and looked at me as furtively as they greeted me when I looked at them. When I was being taken back to my cell, they stood about the passages of the law-courts and nodded to me and shook hands when it was practicable, and then went off to lunch. There was Weigelt who sat in his place rather forlornly; I passed close by him when I was taken out. Weigelt – well, yes. He was quite considerably involved in the affair.

The Court planned to have an exact reproduction of the

scene. On the same date on which the deed had taken place five years earlier, at the same time of the night and at the same place, I stood with Weigelt and was ordered to re-enact exactly what had happened. I seized him and pushed him over towards the railing and the dark water lapped against the bank. Kern had stood there . . . and I had held Weigelt so . . . .

As I pressed his head down to the railing and he raised his leg to kick, he twisted in my grasp and looked at me for the first time and smiled a distorted smile. At that moment a spark of recognition leapt between us and we realised that what had happened concerned only our two selves. There was no question of laws, of murderer and victim; how could the law now seek to avenge the deed and punish the murderer? Weigelt freed himself with a quick movement and said aloud to the crowd of men representing the law that now he perfectly recollected that at that moment I had stepped back and desisted from my attempt to kill him. . . .

Three days later I was condemned to another three years' imprisonment for assault with intent to do grievous bodily harm.

*　　*　　*　　*

My second sentence was to be served in the State prison. This was a newer building, with rather larger cells, built in three wings which could be controlled from a central hall. The same type of warder was here, the same smell in the passages, and the same assortment of prisoners running about as attendants from cell to cell. My surroundings were those to which I had long since grown accustomed, and very soon I felt as though nothing had altered nor ever would be altered. I exchanged the same few words with the warders from time to time; the daily work was brought to my cell; I waged the daily war for little privileges, for a piece of pencil, a book, a letter; I ended the daily walk with the usual little sigh. And the daily rumours of a fresh amnesty were present too.

The Governor was much exercised as to whether he should allow me the same walk as the third grade prisoners; for a number of Communists was immured here and the Governor could not refrain from warning me against them. They were quite uneducated people, he said, and they only roused unrest among the prisoners, and I was on no account to get too friendly with them. But I insisted that I would not be singled out in any way, and assumed from the outset that the Governor had warned the Communists against me in much the same words as those in which he had warned me against them.

During our free time, the Communists went about in small close groups and were recognisable by the fact that they did not wear the badge of the third grade. I looked at them curiously during my first walk, but they did not seem to be interested in me. However, later, as I was walking a little more slowly, they passed by me, engaged in quiet conversation, and one of them raised his hand to his cap in an almost military salute saying with friendly intimacy: 'Good morning, Ensign!' I looked at him in surprise and he screwed up his face and said: 'I rather think, Ensign, that you and I have been in the same mess together once before!' Then he linked his arm in mine and said: 'It's not nice of you to have forgotten old Sergeant Schmitz!' I protested vehemently that I had not grown too proud to walk arm in arm with a damned convict, if he happened to be an old friend from the Baltic times, and we went off together in perfect accord, while the warder watched us dumbfounded.

Schmitz had got four years' penal servitude for a contravention of the Explosives Act. I asked him if there was more doing on the Red front than in the Baltic States, and he answered imperturbably that if there were not more going on, at least it had more sense. We began a dispute over this, and went on quarrelling about it for days; we accused each other of having bourgeois minds and he quite calmly illustrated his points from Holy Writ while I equally calmly made my points by reference to the Communist Manifesto. We were still quarrelling on the day for which we had both been longing with the same burning hope, though without acknowledging it to each other – the President's eightieth birthday. I said it would be inconsistent of him to accept the pardon, and he said it would be bourgeois pride to refuse it. However, when the decree of amnesty was published, I waited at my cell door, vainly hoping that I should be called to the Governor's office; I waited trembling and despairing, though I did my very best to reason myself out of it; and I hardly knew whether to laugh or to cry when I saw Schmitz and his companions walking across the yard towards the gate in mufti, carrying boxes and suitcases; when directly afterwards I heard the blare of the Red band and the warders told us grinning that the Communists had been received outside with bouquets and laurel wreaths.

*   *   *   *

The bell in the tower rang three times. I got up from my stool, and standing by the door, ran my fingers idly across its iron covering. In the passage doors were banging and steps shuffled past. I chewed nervously at my piece of bread; the singing would begin directly; every Saturday before lights-out, the holiday was ushered in by the prison choir. If only they would not sing such sentimental songs – 'Home sweet home', or 'Where is my Wandering Boy to-night?' – and I was annoyed with myself for listening with my ear pressed to the door, never moving till the song had ended. Then they struck up the Old Hundredth. . . .

I leant my forehead against the wall beside the jambs. The cold stone made me shiver a little. I looked at my fingers as they lay pressed against the door: they were white and thin and the black rims to the nails made them look curiously dead. I looked carefully at my hand – it was that of an old man. I tiptoed over to the mirror while they were singing outside and looked at myself. My hair had grown thin and lifeless, disclosing a high expanse of forehead; my face was grey, the skin leathery, and there was a network of fine lines round my eyes. I opened my mouth – my teeth were yellow and decaying, my gums pale. I sat on the bed which I had unhooked and wondered how it was that, though I was tired all day long, I could not sleep at night; and why I had a numb spot in the small of my back, which ached from time to time. I wondered how old I was, calculated, and was rather taken aback at the result. 'I am twenty-five years old,' I said aloud and then I lay on my bed.

The singing was over, the attendant pushed the bolt and the lights went out. In the woods which covered a gentle slope just beyond the walls an owl hooted dolefully. Ten years ago I was still a cadet. In those days I lived within the red walls of the house at Lichterfelde – nowadays the walls surrounding me were grey. My life was a pretty senseless affair! No, damn it, it was not senseless – the circumstances of this life were senseless, but after all circumstances were not decisive. In the interval between the end of the interrogation and the beginning of the pleading of my cause, Weigelt had come to the cell and had said breathlessly that he wished me the best of luck, that that shot had been a warning to him, and that he had become a decent man now. He had become a decent man – so had all my old companions. The public prosecutor, who had urged in the interests of right and justice that I be condemned to five years' penal servitude, who had demurred to my being pardoned, had come to see me in prison before I was removed and had said that he was thinking only of my good, that he was only doing his duty. The public prosecutor was a decent man too. They were all decent – there were only decent people in the world. It was pure imagination to think that there were any scoundrels. I tried to remember whether I had ever known a scoundrel. No, I had never known one – not among my companions, nor among my enemies, nor among the prisoners, not even among the warders. Man is noble, I thought, and enjoyed the loftiness of my sarcasm. Man is noble, and cannot help being so.

The trial had convinced me of one thing – that the outlaws' campaign was at an end. The public prosecutor had conjured up the most desperate background, he had referred to the O.C. and everybody had laughed, as if at a children's bogey: the audience had laughed, and the witnesses and my old companions and the policemen, the Pressmen had grinned like Cheshire cats and even the Commissioner who had been sent from Berlin to watch over the proceedings had chuckled. It was all over and it had all been in vain.

I rose and walked up and down. Then my life had been wasted too. Had it been wasted? It had been extraordinarily rich. I would not have missed a moment of it. The only thing that stuck in my throat and nearly choked me was the fear that there might be nothing left for me to do. It was that same fear which caused all these good people to take refuge in what they called doing their duty. What we had done was not enough – either that which we had already done led to fresh work, or we had been mistaken. I knew that we had not been mistaken.

I knew that we could not have been mistaken, for we had lived according to the spirit of the times; and there had been justification for our actions everywhere. We had lived dangerously, for the times had been dangerous; and since the times were chaotic, so everything that we thought or did or believed was chaotic too. We were possessed by the spirit of our day, possessed by its destructiveness, and also possessed by the pain which made this destruction fruitful. We had lived up to the only virtue demanded by our day, that of decision, because we had the will to decide. But the decisive moment had not yet come. The world was still afraid of itself.

No, the fight was not at an end yet. Everyone felt that it could not be at an end; even if our world, the world of the outlaws, had vanished because it was no longer needed, still the task remained. Once upon a time we had called ourselves revolutionaries, as we had the right to do; we who were fighting for a change in the position of Germany had more right to call ourselves that than had those who were only fighting to alter social conditions. They were fighting because they refused to recognise any authority that was legitimate, we because we would not recognise any that was not legitimate. But the authority which it was and always would be our duty to attack was illegitimate, because it was based on a recognition of values which were dictated by the needs of man and not by the eternal higher power which made those needs necessary.

We had always appealed to that power and to nothing else. We had never been concerned with parties and programmes, with banners and symbols, with theories and dogmas. If our position indicated that we were prejudiced, it was because we aimed at upholding reality against appearances, life against theories, honour against happiness, substance against shadows: it was because it did not satisfy us to enquire into the reason for what was coming, but we also enquired into the standards.

That was our task. There was only one crime – not to fulfil it. The field was wide and open in which the battle of God and the Devil was being waged. The call to take part in this battle came to each individual armed with power, faith, the will to conquer and the strength to take a great decision.

I went to sleep feeling greatly comforted.

CHAPTER XXXVI

FREE

EVERY morning for five years I had the same feeling: 'This is the wretchedest, the most hopeless, the gloomiest day that I can ever experience.' The only reason for living through each day in those five years was that it brought me one step nearer to freedom. For five years all my thoughts centred round this first day of freedom, round the first twenty-four hours and their overflowing measure of sun, space and life.

The shrill clang of the bell from the central tower startled me from my dreams. I heard its leaden after-tones rending the heavy air in the building. Feeling fagged and limp I sat up, looked dully at the dark walls and the grey rectangle of the window intersected by bars. I wondered what I could do to liven up the day. Perhaps the doctor would spend five minutes with me – I might ask to have the sleeping draught renewed. I staggered over to the window and opened the upper light. But the wave of cold air could not clear my head, which was stupefied with sleep and its nightmares, the musty smell of sweat, and a nasty taste in my mouth, so that it hurt me even to think. In the passage doors were banging, the clatter of the attendant's clogs was mixed with the dragging of the baskets of bread and the clatter of iron pots. I groped over towards the bucket, lifted it out of its fixture, and stood by the door holding my breath. The bucket was full, the lid swimming on top. I put my mouth to the crack of the door and drew in a cool breath from the passage. The key rattled in the lock.

FREE

The warder turned on the light, dazzling my eyes. I put the bucket outside the door and took the bread in my dirty fingers. The door banged, I slipped into my clothes, the grey and white striped uniform, the clumsy boots. After a perfunctory wash in the inadequate basin, I tidied up the cell, as I did every day, I hooked the bed up to the wall and sat on the stool. I slowly ate some of my bread in order to avoid chewing tobacco on an empty stomach. I had to hurry over the day's task: the seventy-two yards of bast that had to be twisted would keep me fully occupied; I had to move my hand in the same way sixteen thousand times. If at the end of the month I delivered short measure again, the Governor, who could not actually punish me for insufficient work, would put me on to gumming paper bags, which was even more wearisome. The damp, smelly bast dyed my fingers. Confused sounds came to me from the passages and the rest of the prison; at intervals the bell rang, dividing up the day. I heard the warder unlock door after door down my passage, and got up from my stool, feeling tired and ill-humoured, and tied the scarf round my neck, preparatory to the daily walk. The warder appeared. I fell into line and followed on at the usual jogtrot, eight paces behind my neighbour. The chief warder was standing in a dignified attitude in the central hall. When he saw me, he leant over the bannister and said: 'Give me your work-book.'

Apart from the usual routine, the work-book was only required from prisoners who had been pardoned. I stood stock still, staring at the chief warder. He waited, drumming his fingers on the railing, impatiently it seemed to me. All hope leaving me, I turned about, went back to my cell and fetched my work-book. The chief warder took it, turned over the pages, and then disappeared.

I tramped along rapidly behind the others through the long passages. The narrow yard surrounded by its high wall opened

423

before me. The December sun had no warmth and the wind whistled round the corners. I stood for a moment at the top of the steps, looking at the small section of the world which was visible from this spot only: a strip of meadow, a country road, hills fading into the distance.

A warder took me by the arm: 'You're wanted in the office!' The Governor was standing in the central hall, with a stately expression on his face. I could hardly breathe. The Governor looked at me coldly and penetratingly. I stood before him, almost glad that I had obviously once more been mistaken. The Governor said: 'I have some good news for you . . . .

'When, when . . .?' My voice rose to a shout.

The Governor extended his hand to me laughing and said: 'You will be released at eleven o'clock.'

I pulled myself together, hesitated a moment, but finally shook hands with him. Then I turned, stumbled down the stairs, and ran to my cell with unseeing eyes. The chief warder was standing there; he unlocked the door, caught my wrist, and said: 'Pulse 250!'

I could not collect my thoughts. I threw all my things, books, papers, pictures, letters, into a box, and from that into another one; and I only realised dimly that this accumulation represented everything that I had valued during the past five years. The door was opened and shut continually. The whole cumbrous bureaucratic machinery of the prison was set in motion to eject me. I had to pack, bathe, settle my accounts, have myself shaved; I ran from my cell to the workroom, from there to the office; I rushed blindly past the warders and saw such prisoners as I met looking at me with the same expression of hostile envy as that with which I had year after year regarded those who had been discharged or pardoned. Suddenly I had grown strange to them, was excluded from their community. And I had just enough time for self-examination to be ashamed of myself for feeling all at once that they were despicable, outlaws, contemptible. I had just time to feel my heart beating against my brain, and my brain impatiently rejecting what the heart was trying to say, I was busy with little things which left me with only a dim veiled mental consciousness. At bottom I was afraid. Afraid of freedom? Afraid of the change, of release from the spell? Was the spell being loosed then? Yes, it was being loosed, but it was not turning to joy, it was changing to movement, to trembling, hasty, nervous movement, as though I had not a moment to lose, as though every second were of importance, and held the diversity of the world in it, as though it filled my whole being, leaving no room for simple feeling and willing. I remembered that there had been another time when I had been in just the same state of tremendous tension, when I had lived deeply and intensely and yet had not actually realised anything at all – when was it? Long ago, before my first battle?

And then I stood in the supervisor's room, stripped off the hated grey uniform, slipped into the starched, crackling white shirt, hurled the heavy nailed clogs at the wall, passed my finger tips, suddenly grown soft and sensitive, over fine linen and socks – the stiff, snow-white collar, the silk tie, the suit made of good, firm, blue material, how well it sat and fitted – I squared my bowed shoulders – suddenly felt self-respect rise within me again. I put on my hat, raised my feet which had grown so light, pulled on my gloves; my new suitcase with its shining locks was standing at the door, which opened before me to the gate . . . .

For five years I thought of the moment when the heavy prison gate would swing to behind me. Would not the sound go through me like an electric shock? Would not the world open out before me, larger and more glorious than I could bear? I would remember the first thought that came to me after I was free all my life till the last gate of all should open before me: that first thought would have in it all the sweetness of the world, or it would not be worth while achieving freedom. . . .

I stood in the dark gate. One of the prisoners, the yard attendant, clattered up to me in his clogs, grinned and raised a monitory finger: 'Right foot first, and don't look round on any account, or you'll come back!' – I smiled faintly. The warder opened the iron gate, a ray of pale sunshine lighted the passage. I picked up my heavy suitcase and walked out. The gate crashed behind me. I was free!

I thought: 'Shall I catch that train?' That was the first thought that came to me after I was free.

* * * *

I walked through the village street. The weight of my suitcase seemed to take all freshness from my sensations. I felt as if I had always known the low frame-houses with their big archways. There was nothing unusual about them. Some geese came round the corner gabbling and the village street was very muddy. Was not the sun shining? I believe it was. Did not the air smell fresh and sweet? I believe it did. Did not the peasant woman in her wide skirts smile at me? Perhaps – but it may also have been that she recognised me as a discharged prisoner and that her look was searching and suspicious. I did not know. 'Wake up, man, you're free!' my heart tried to tell my brain, but the brain answered testily: 'Yes, yes, all very fine, but hurry up, you've got to catch the train!'

In the booking office I opened the blue envelope which they had given me as I left the prison. This was the first time I was handling money again, a great deal of money, it seemed to me; the earnings of five years – nearly twenty Marks. The coinage had changed since I had last been free. I looked at the money awkwardly, turning over the silver and yellow coins. The booking clerk gave me my ticket; I counted out the fare slowly

and he said with twinkling eyes: 'I bet you haven't had any
money to count where you've come from!' – I blushed furiously
but almost enjoyed being teased. Nevertheless I chose an
empty compartment when the train came in.

I had come from restraint and inflexibility. For years I had
seen nothing but vertical lines and my gaze had been brought
up short by walls. I had seen the sky between the bars like a
piece of stage scenery or a wall, immobile and unfriendly.
The little bit of green in the yard was dusty, and the few,
usually bare, trees stood in the midst of a grey expanse. Thus
I had grown primitive, unreceptive, inelastic. Such desires
and dreams as would not be smothered, came during the long
sleepless nights, demanding space, air, variety, flowing hori-
zontal lines, bright shining lights. What were forests like? How
I longed to let my eyes roam over gently sloping meadows, to
breathe unrestricted fresh air. In one's dreams in the cell,
the countryside was open and vivid.

Now I was sitting in the train, and the countryside presented
its ever changing picture to me. I looked out of the window.
To the right were woods, with tall bare tree trunks. 'Rather
nice,' I thought and looked greedily out to the left. On that
side were empty fields. And I, who had for years longed to
experience the open country again, pulled out of my pocket a
newspaper, which the doctor had given me as I said goodbye,
and read it – until I realised. Then I screwed up the paper
and threw it into a corner and laid my head on the wooden seat.
I was in despair and yet my despair seemed to me like bad
play-acting. I simply could not feel anything. For five years
I had been outside the pale. For five years the dullest, most
trivial, chilliest apathy had been waiting to descend upon me
the very moment I was free and smother all perception. Apathy
was stronger than the greatest exaltation. I adjured myself
to be reasonable. But I did not want to be reasonable. Devil

take it, I would not be reasonable. I'd be damned if I would be reasonable. But could not the newspaper give me some idea of the forces that made up life in these days? I threw the paper out of the window; I was afraid of my own sensitiveness.

＊　　＊　　＊　　＊

I longed apprehensively for my first encounter with masses of people, for movement, hurry, for crowds in the streets and in the market places. The train arrived at the station. I pushed past the barrier numbly and stood in the square in front of the station. I was not particularly confused, but I had to eliminate all thought if I wanted to observe individual things, I had to avoid drawing comparisons, otherwise I should never have got my ideas in order. The numerous motor cars, the traffic, the bustle and hurry, the glaring posters, all this seemed at bottom familiar, though five years ago the mass of impressions could not have been so overpowering.

What shocked and chilled me were the people. They seemed to have no faces – or rather, all their faces were alike. All these people seemed to be inanimate, they seemed not to be conscious of space and action. They went about dully, joylessly and expressionlessly, almost like machines, like welltended, throbbing machines, pulsating with energy, but in no sense alive. They wore their trim, elegant clothes with a shattering matter-of-factness. They walked along confidently and incuriously – and I joined them. I joined the stream and automatically I lost all the pleasure I had felt in being welldressed, and realised that my face had suddenly taken on the same cold, efficient expression.

I was chiefly struck by the women. They had nothing in common with the women of my dreams in the cell. Their faces seemed colourless, naked, and were as monotonous as their invariable long legs. Only the little creases at the knees of their shining silk stockings were any reminder of the torments of the cell, for they alone seemed alive.

So far I had spoken to no one. I felt stubbornly antagonistic, I refused to recognise anything. I passed houses and streets which I knew and recognised but which yet were unfamiliar. I passed children playing and resented them. I bought a pipe, some tobacco and a box of matches, because I remembered that I had planned it for the day of my release, but I lacked all assurance when I got into the shop. I fumbled with the money and tried my level best not to let anyone notice how much I felt that everybody must know where I came from. I was lonely among the crowds and felt a sudden longing to be back in my cell, in the silence, in the uniform peace and security.

I thought: 'Now they're eating at home,' and 'at home' meant the prison to me. I stood before my mother's house and was afraid, horribly, pitifully afraid. I rang; nobody answered the bell and I drew a breath of relief. I went upstairs to my attic but it was locked. I wandered through the streets again, and finally went into a small quiet café, where I sat for a long time feeling cheerless and hostile.

When it got dark I went to HER house. I stood before the door like a beggar, experiencing the same breathless anxiety as if I were really one. She opened the door, started when she saw me, and drew me silently through the passage into the room. She laid the table for tea, while I sat in a deep armchair, well back among cushions, with every nerve on edge. Once when she looked over in my direction, I barked at her that I would not tolerate any sympathy. I spoke hastily and convulsively. The room seemed to get smaller and no sounds from outside penetrated. There were curtains over the windows, which gave me a sense of well-being. Then I realised that I was alien to the room, that I could not bear any comfort. I could not sit still any longer, having sat still for five years; I could not endure four walls, having lived in four walls for five years.

My brother came, surprised, eager, noisily pleased. I began to talk; told my tale confusedly, haltingly, searching for words, gesticulating furiously. I had lost all feeling for limits – limits of speech, of expression, of tact. I interrupted the others, I was inattentive to the point of rudeness, and every sentence I spoke began with 'I.' For years I had been my only interest; I had only had myself to talk to, and my own thoughts and questions as stimulation. I urged my brother to go out with me. When I stood at the door, I waited for it to be unlocked. Then I remembered and took hold of the handle. I had barely touched it before it opened. I opened and shut it three times. When my brother smiled, I raged at him.

*   *   *   *

That evening my brother took me to a café where he was meeting some friends. It was a party consisting of people of all ages, who filled assured positions in life and who behaved accordingly. I was very silent, listening to the talk and the music. The place was crowded; it had bare walls in some subdued colour and smooth, glittering metallic pillars. On a platform was a band playing curious black instruments with all kinds of silver stops.

I had crouched by the window of my cell on innumerable Sundays, listening to the confused sounds that floated over from somewhere in the little town – possibly from a concert on the promenade far away from the walls, and, as I pictured it, surrounded by cheerful crowds. The music in the café was loud and curiously squeaky. It consisted essentially of rhythm and was reminiscent of Grieg. I listened with interest, wondering whether it was naïve or extremely subtle. Then I told myself irritably that it was neither – it was simply obvious. But I was not so much engaged with the music as I imagined I should be, and I began to wonder whether I had any remnants of receptiveness left. Every now and then the conductor, an extremely elegant man in evening dress with great self-assurance, picked up a tin megaphone and with a beaming countenance roared something into the room, which apparently acted as a stimulant, for many of the women got a nervous, excited, eager look in their naked faces and twitched their legs and shoulder blades. Then a nigger sang and every head was turned towards him.

The multitude of impressions bewildered me. Yet I was sitting very comfortably in a soft chair, drinking a cup of coffee which tasted extraordinarily satisfying, and was trying to take in everything that presented itself. The men talked from behind their gleaming horn-rimmed spectacles about politics, motor cars and women. I heard things that were quite new to me and that dumbfounded me, but which I had to assume to be true, because they were said with such careless assurance. I felt how utterly lost I was among all these people. I should have liked to ask about a good many things, but I could not join in the conversation and that cramped me. The utter lack of eventfulness in my recent past so oppressed me, that I was afraid to say a word lest everyone should know where that past had been spent. At the same time I was longing to talk. I wanted to ask questions, I wanted to get at essentials in that wilderness of words and ideas – I wanted to assert myself, to storm the magic circle, but I seemed to be attacking a spongy yielding mass.

Nevertheless, these assured people were fettered in a way too – they never seemed to overstep their boundaries. Which of them had built his life as it can be built by one who is free, really free? At bottom they were all possessed by an emotional, self-satisfied discontent, while my discontent was burning and consuming.

THE OUTLAWS

When I made up my accounts for the last five years, there was a balance on the credit side. How could I have borne it otherwise? But I must not let myself succumb to the bourgeois point of view; for it is lethargic, flexible perhaps, but not alive. And I must live, live! I had been benumbed for too long to be able to wait for life any longer. Those clever, intelligent, adaptable men were under the domination of that same law of uniformity to which I had had to submit for five long years. But forces were latent in me which would not permit me simply to exchange one set of bonds for another. I must go from lethargy to energy, from gloom to joy, to straining action, to things that cannot be expressed in words.

We walked home through the old town. Bright lights flamed in the main streets, but here the moon shone above rows of pointed gables. Cats picked their way across the roofs with tails erect. What I saw was impalpable in its very reality, and I was comforted. I could not bear any more straight lines, and this hotch-potch, softened in the moonlight which flooded everything, and yet cast shadows, this multiplicity of shapes which gave life to the whole picture, all this calmed and strengthened me. I was free and five years were past and forgotten.

Other titles published by Arktos:

CPSIA information can be obtained
at www.ICGtesting.com
Printed in the USA
LVHW110414161118
597364LV00001B/2/P